WANDERING
STAR

WANDERING
STAR
A REUNIFICATION NOVEL

STEVEN J. ANDERSON

Published by Steven J. Anderson
© 2019 Steven J. Anderson

RuComm352@gmail.com
https://www.facebook.com/RuComm352

Cover by Fiona Jayde Media.
Interior Formatting & Design by The Deliberate Page.

Ebook ISBN: 978-0-9991788-0-5
Print ISBN: 978-0-9991788-1-2

CHAPTER 1
WANDERING STAR

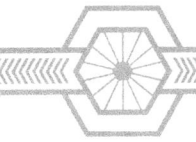

"Ted. Ted. Ted."

Having your name repeated endlessly while alarms are sounding and lights are strobing is a disorienting way to wake up. I couldn't do anything about the lights or alarms, but I could stop the voice saying my name. I reached up and put my hand over Jake's mouth.

"Again?"

Jake moved my hand away from his face and pulled me into a sitting position on my bunk. "Hull breach. Both aft engine rooms. Next time I'll leave you here to suffocate."

"That's what you promised last time."

He tossed a pressure suit at me. "Get tight. The sooner everyone's at the rally point the sooner we can get back to sleep."

I slid into the suit and checked valve settings and fittings. I made sure oxygen was flowing because I knew Captain von Muller would check and I did *not* want to fail inspection again.

Jake was waiting by the door with his helmet on, but visor still open. I snapped his visor down for him with unnecessary force. "Get tight."

His voice came to me through my helmet. "Get bent."

"Comm check good," I replied.

We hustled down the passageway to the central lab, our usual rally point unless the current disaster had already destroyed it. Von Muller and his Executive Officer, Lieutenant Velena Copeland, were waiting for us. We were not the last to arrive, which was good. Being the last to reach the rally point was always bad. It would delay my reunion with the comforts of my bed, and I'd have to listen to the Captain explaining to me *personally* why it was bad. He loved hearing himself speak almost as much as I loved my pillow.

Hannah Weldon was the last to report. As usual. This was her second hop and she liked to play the old hand, choosing what to take seriously and what to let slide. She cared about her work, but not the Captain and certainly not his random middle of the night safety drills.

We stood by waiting for our Captain's verdict.

"*Star*," he commanded, "report."

"Response time from similar scenarios has improved two points," *Wandering Star's* AI replied. "The odds of all hands surviving are now at eighty-five percent. Almost everyone ran this time."

Von Muller looked stricken, as he always did. His XO shook her head.

Our Captain was on his twelfth trip to the outer worlds, or maybe his sixteenth or twenty-fifth, depending on which version of his biography he was telling. Regardless of the number, every version had the same moral: be prepared if you want to survive.

He shook his head, morning our deaths. "A fifteen percent chance that one of you did not survive. That is unacceptable."

He reminded us that each of us had beat the odds to join the Reunification Commission, which selected only the top applicants. He told us how valuable we were, and then he detailed what death in space was like (gruesome) and what the odds of rescue were (zero).

The Captain was one of the best extemporaneous speakers I had ever heard. He told us that we were the unsung, unrecognized, unappreciated heroes of the Union. All he asked was that we please, please help him keep us alive long enough for us to accomplish the urgent work of reunification. Our jobs were hard and dangerous, and the people of Earth and the planets we worked to reunite might never know how we made their lives better, but we would know.

He rephrased and repeated every point until we couldn't help but feel more patriotic and filled with a sense of purpose and pride in our mission. It would have sounded better at 13:00 than 03:00, but damn, he was good.

Time passed.

Finally, the XO leaned over and whispered something in his ear. The Captain nodded and said, "All right, then. You may resume your duties."

Which to me was sleeping a couple of more hours.

Captain von Muller turned to Hannah. "Walk with me, Ms. Weldon."

Hannah, the XO, and von Muller headed forward. Jake and I headed aft.

Jake turned to me as we walked back to our quarters. "I don't know what the Captain will do to Hannah, but I don't think it will change anything." There was real concern in his voice.

"You care?" I looked at him. The warm lights of the passageway made him look more awake than I'm sure he felt. "You do care."

"I just don't want to see her get into trouble."

"Have you even talked to her?" I knew I hadn't.

We were two weeks out from Earth and Hannah still seemed an unapproachable mystery to me. Her appearance and behavior were both a little exotic. Short, dark-brown curly hair framed a face that always seemed to have a knowing smile and eyes with a perpetual wild look in them. She was always 'on' in our team meetings, always looking for a way to challenge what our team-lead was saying. Being next to her made me feel like something was about to happen. Something dangerous. Something bad.

"We've talked a bit. It's hard not to on a ship this small. She's all right. She's part of our team. I don't want any of us in trouble."

Jake was walking next to me staring at the gray deck under our feet. Was he trying to convince me or himself that his concern was just for a fellow teammate?

"OK, but don't you get into trouble. Don't forget what happened with Debra at the Academy, or Jenna in eighth grade. Or Libby in fifth grade."

"Libby? I never got in trouble with Libby in fifth grade." He finally looked up at me.

I smiled.

"Just shut up," he said.

"Now we're even for you waking me."

"Like I had a choice. I don't want you in trouble either."

We reached our cabin and I stripped off my pressure suit, dumped it in a pile on the floor, and collapsed onto my bunk. "Just don't wake me up anymore tonight."

Jake consulted his watch. "Not for forty-five minutes."

"Shit."

"Well said."

Jake developed a sudden interest in cross training in Hannah's mission specialty of linguistics. I'd seen him like this before, like a puppy chasing after rabbits. I tried to warn him that Hannah could probably eat him in one bite. He ignored me and followed her around the ship helping her do things she didn't need help doing. He sat next to her at meals, every meal, and made a nuisance of himself.

I expected it to end badly. Either she'd get tired of it and crush him, or worse, Angela, our technical team lead, would hear of it. I considered warning him again, but I'd known Jake since we were eight. He and Libby *did* get into trouble in fifth grade.

Jake was at least smart enough to be careful. He knew that if anyone suspected his new infatuation the consequences could include extra duty, loss of pay, or getting a trip home at his own expense.

Not that any of those fears diminished the longing in his eyes when he was with Hannah. I worried that the extra thrill from the danger of it might be making things worse.

Friendship on board was encouraged. Team building or anything to improve morale was great. The Reunification Commission contract we had signed prohibited anything beyond that as a 'romantic entanglement'. RuComm believed that a failed romance was bad for the efficiency of the team.

So it was up to me to keep him safe. As his shield to defray suspicion, I volunteered to cross train Hannah and Jake on geology, my mission specialty, while Jake and I learned linguistics. Jake was supposed to cross train us on biology, but he was always preoccupied when Hannah was there with us. I didn't need training on that kind of biology.

I think my real function was to help him to help her to do things she didn't need help doing. I also sat with them at meals, every meal, listening to him flirt with her and, occasionally, her flirting back with him. Her banter was sharper than his. She had a quick mind and the ability to find his weaknesses. It was hard to watch her toying with him, seeing my friend take the abuse. She made me laugh sometimes when she did it, and then I'd see that sly, knowing smile on her face as she looked at me.

We were four weeks out from Earth, two weeks into their covert relationship, and I was sitting with Hannah while Jake made his way through the chow line at breakfast. Jake looked exhausted, eyes half closed as if the lights were too much for him. Hannah was as alert as usual, working aggressively through a pile of scrambled eggs.

Jake sat heavily at the table. "I've got to get more sleep." He sipped his coffee, wincing at the heat on his tongue.

"Hannah doesn't seem tired," I noted. "Try to be more like Hannah."

"I never sleep." Hannah stabbed at her eggs. She maintained eye contact with Jake while she put them in her mouth and swallowed. "Sleep is for children and the dead. I have too much to do."

"Maybe you aren't doing anything exhausting enough," Jake challenged her.

"You seem to be. Perhaps you need to work on your stamina."

"OK, let's do that tonight. Maybe you could help me by–"

I kicked him under the table to shut him up while the XO walked by. This also had the unfortunate side effect of drawing Hannah's attention to me.

"What about you, Ted? Are you getting enough sleep?"

"No. Jake makes too much noise when he comes in late." I paused. "And he snores."

"Really?" Her eyes narrowed as though evaluating him for some future task she had in mind. She turned back to her eggs.

I pushed the potatoes around on my plate with my fork, added more salsa and shoved them around some more. Their romance was going to get out of control, if it wasn't already.

I gave up on the potatoes after another couple of bites and pushed away from the table. "I'm going back to our cabin to get my display pad. I'll see you both in the lab in a few minutes and we can look at geomorphology examples this morning."

"And after lunch, more on linguistic drift," Hannah added. "This time, Jake, pay closer attention to the way my mouth forms the vowels. Up here." She tapped her lips.

I sighed, dumped my tray in the recycler, and walked back to the cabin. I was still gathering some printouts when Jake came in, humming happily to himself.

"You need to be more careful. You and Hannah both."

"About what?"

"You know *Wandering Star* watches everything that happens, right?"

"Yes, but she can't report anything. It's in our contract."

"Not quite true, Mr. Barton." There was a little frustration in her normally calm, sweet voice. "I can't report anything to your team lead unless it endangers myself or our mission. You and Ms. Weldon haven't yet crossed that line. I would hate to see you leave the service even before your first planet fall, but it's happened before. Many times."

"How many?"

That's right, Jake, I thought to myself, *bait the damn ship that sees everything you do.*

The main display in our cabin illuminated with the flickering images of a dozen or more smiling young men and women whose actions had cut their RuComm careers cruelly short.

Star continued, pride now in her voice. "Captain von Muller and Lieutenant Copeland are the finest officers I have ever served. I will protect them and the RuComm mission. It's why I exist. Don't try me Mr. Barton."

I glanced at my watch. "We have places to be."

Jake joined me as we walked out into the passageway. "Later, *Star.*"

"I will always be with you. Have a good day, gentlemen."

I looked over at Jake as he walked along next to me. "That was stupid."

"You worry too much."

"That's because I'm worrying for two now. I'd say three, but I'm not sure Hannah knows how to worry."

"I like that about her."

"Jake, I'm going to miss you when you're gone."

"What is it with you, Ted?" He stopped and turned toward me. "We've always pushed the rules, all through school and everywhere else. Does *Star* actually have you scared?" He took a step toward me. "Or are you jealous?"

"Of you and Hannah? Yeah, no. More like you and Hannah are actually scaring me. We've had a lot of fun and pushed more boundaries than I can remember, with me usually saving your ass. But how am I supposed to protect you from..." I gestured at the ceiling where *Star* was certainly watching and listening. "Don't you get that this is different?" I wanted to grab him by the shoulders and shake him.

"I get that you're different."

"I'm not–" I stopped as Angela Dawkins came around the corner. She was an older woman, hair starting to go gray, with a perpetual look of disapproval on her face. She had spent her entire career in RuComm and was our tech team lead, lab manager, and acting senior engineer.

Angela stopped next to us and looked up at me from a fifteen centimeter disadvantage. "Mr. Holloman. Mr. Barton. Are you gentlemen planning on getting any work done today?"

"All day, every day," Jake replied. There was still some heat in his voice from our interrupted argument, enough to get a raised eyebrow from Angela.

"Yes, ma'am, we're right behind you," I added. She nodded, still suspicious, and preceded us toward the main lab. We followed at a distance.

"Suck up," Jake whispered to me.

I whispered back, "Yeah. That's how I plan to keep you from a zero expense paid trip back to Earth. You should be thanking me."

Jake snorted. "Not likely."

We entered the main lab. Dim lights, white noise from the ventilation system, and the gentle glow of the displays gave the space a serene, serious feel separate from the sterility of the rest of the ship. It felt like a refuge and always had a calming effect on me. I hoped it would have the same effect on Jake.

Hannah was already in the sim lab, of course. She was sitting on one of the tables next to a tray of core samples, legs swinging in the air, looking pleased with herself. My geomorphology simulation was already running, shimmering in the display tank. I had encrypted the geosim file, but apparently not well enough. Annoyed or impressed? I'm not sure which I felt. I decided it was some of both. It was only a geosim, but what else of mine had she gotten into?

I looked at her sitting there, daring me to say something, defiant amusement playing in her brown eyes and one lock of her dark hair falling across her face. I decided to let it go for now and spend the evening encrypting my whole damn file system. For all the good it would do.

"Since you two were running late I decided to set the sim up for you." She smiled an innocent smile.

"Thanks. I can't tell you how much I appreciate that." I smiled back at her. "Are you ready to get to work?"

"Born ready." She slid off the table and walked to the display tank, Jake following close behind her.

"We'll watch this several more times, but pay attention." Jake and Hannah leaned in, Jake taking the opportunity to press up against her. I placed the simulation in motion.

"This is the city of Palma Sola on Dulcinea."

Jake looked at the expanse of open ocean displayed in the tank. "This is where we'll be staying in a couple of weeks? *Star* told us there would be beaches. And dry land."

Hannah pushed him away to open up some space so she could whack him gently on the back of the head. "I think this might be a few years ago. Pay attention."

I added, "And it's the middle of winter in Palma Sola now, so don't get your hopes up for warm sand and bare skin."

"Damn."

"Maybe you were expecting this?" I switched to Palma Sola's current topography, showing a city built along a large bay, a long curve of beach, and tall white cliffs on the northern shore. "The goal is for you to be able to see this, as it is today, and be able to visualize the open ocean in the first view. I'll show you the processes that were occurring in deep time that would form white cliffs and sandy beaches millions of years later. What I want you to get out of this is to be able to see what's beneath the surface, both what you're standing on and how this moment in time is just part of the past and the future. "

"Do it." Hannah waved at the display. "Make it go again."

Jake's face wore an expression I'd seen many times sitting next to him in class. It meant, *OK, I'll watch, but I don't really care.* I reset the simulation and tried to cover a semester's worth of material in four hours. At least Jake might see Palma Sola as something other than Dulcinea's 'Beautiful City on the Bay'.

Hannah seemed to understand most of it, asking good questions and seeing the bigger picture.

We broke for lunch before moving to linguistics for the afternoon.

"Can we do that for each of the planets on this hop?" Hannah asked between bites of salad. "I want to see more than the surface; I want to see what's underneath and how it got that way."

"We can do it for Dulcinea and Malapert, but stop number two on Cleavus is a complete unknown. If there were ever any records of its geology, they were lost long ago. I'll take another look to see if there's anything to build on."

Jake asked Hannah, "So how does this help you understand the languages of the people that live there?"

She took another bite and tipped her head, thinking.

"I don't know yet. Language is used to describe the world around us, so maybe how the physical geography formed and evolves affects how language evolves?" Her statement ended with a question. "I don't know. I'll have to think about it." After a moment she said, "Maybe it's like with names."

"Names?" I asked.

"Sure. Names come and go in popularity. If someone becomes famous, their name will become popular and there will be a bunch of kids running around with that name for generations. Or someone will become infamous and the name will die with them. When was the last time you met anyone named Robert?" She shuddered, remembering the heinous crimes committed a century ago. "Knowing the history and meaning of names can help us understand who we are too, the same as the language we use."

"So, where does your name come from?"

"A statue of Hannah Duston near where I was born. She was famous eight hundred years ago, and here I am still carrying her name." She smiled, as if that confirmed her point.

Jake had finished eating and was scanning our plates for potential leftovers to poach.

I quickly finished the last of my food. "You know you could go back for more if you're still hungry," I told him.

"No, there's not really enough time." Jake examined what was left of Hannah's salad, which had included several non-Earth plants, some of which were purplish and full of little air pockets that released a salty flavor when they popped.

Hannah moved her bowl and put a protective arm around it. "Mine."

"And you can keep it."

"You need to be more adventurous." She took a last bite. "Just not from my bowl."

"I'm willing to learn."

"I bet you are. I need a student who is humble and enthusiastic–"

"That's me."

"–and obedient."

Jake and Hannah's noses were about a centimeter apart, Jake holding her gaze, but losing. He pulled back.

"Well, two out of three maybe." Jake smiled.

"Sixty-six percent is still a 'D'."

"I've had worse."

"Have you had better?" Hannah asked defiantly.

Jake looked around the mess hall before replying to see who might be able to hear him. "Maybe we should discuss performance issues privately."

"OK, my cabin, 19:00 hours." Hannah stood and picked up her tray. "Are you two ready? It's time."

We returned to the main lab where I discovered that language is a lot harder when you have to think about it. I don't speak with an accent, or at least that's what I always thought. To Hannah, all of us have an accent. She correctly placed Jake and me in the southern Rocky Mountains of North America based on different vowel sounds in *bite* and *boat*.

"Listen closely and I'll show you the differences. Bite, bite, bite. Which way do you say it?"

I looked at her blankly. "Um, they all sounded the same to me."

"The third one," Jake replied.

I thought Jake was guessing, but Hannah smiled at him as if her favorite dog had just learned a new trick.

"Let's try this one: metal, metal, metal."

"First one." Jake grinned at me, his idiot friend.

"All the same again." I sighed.

"Try watching my mouth while I say each word. Home, home, home."

I watched her lips. It didn't help. I felt like saying, *Maybe Jake is getting them right because he's spent so much time in close contact with your lips*, but it sounded petty even in my head. I usually catch on to new things quickly, but this was baffling to me. Watching the two of them batting words back and forth and giggling at incomprehensible subtleties was irritating. It was soon apparent that Jake had forgotten that I was even there and I'd about had enough.

"OK, I can see where this can be all kinds of fun, but tell me why I should care. How does this apply to anything we're supposed to be doing?"

There was a quick flash of anger in Hannah's eyes that I would question the value of her profession. It faded to cold before she answered, and I was reminded why Jake's infatuation with her worried me.

"All right, good question." She ran her fingers through her hair, pushing it back off her face. "Language drifts. Pronunciation changes, usage changes, sometimes spelling, but not as often. People create new words to describe new things and situations. In contiguous communities the change can be rapid. In isolated regions, not so much. For populations that stayed in close contact with Earth and speak English, the rate of drift has stayed almost constant over hundreds of years. Populations that became isolated as the Union fell apart three hundred years ago still speak like our ancestors did."

"And this helps us... how?"

"It's a window into the past. By studying them, we learn who we were before the breakup of the First Union. Knowing who we were then helps us know who we are now, and maybe who we are becoming. How you speak, the words you choose, how you say them, is a reflection of how your brain works, don't you think?"

"I guess I've never really thought about it." I waved my hands. "I just, you know, talk. Language exists to convey information, right? What else is there?"

Hannah's nose scrunched up as if she wanted to laugh, but was holding it in. Her eyes had lost the cold look from before and she seemed warm and playful again.

"Sometimes. I suppose. It's possible. But most of the time language is used to withhold information, distort the truth, convince and connive, to hide the knife hidden behind the back until the right time."

Jake seemed surprised. "I had no idea you were so cynical."

"It's not cynicism if it's true," she replied.

"Or are you just saying that to hide the truth of what you really believe?" I asked.

That got a genuine smile from her. "I like you. You can be taught."

Jake stood and put his arm around Hannah's waist and they looked down at me in my chair. "I've known Ted since we were kids. Trained, yes. Taught? No, probably not."

My irritation level was starting to rise again, looking at Jake there with his arm around Hannah and the smiles on their faces.

"So, Hannah, I have to ask. How is it that you're not worried about...?" I waved my hand at the ceiling.

"*Star*? She and I have an understanding."

"You have an understanding with the *ship*? How is that even possible?"

She stood there with her head tipped, not answering. "Sometimes silence can be language too."

I tapped my fingers on the desk. "OK, I'm done here. I have work of my own I need to finish." I stood and headed for the exit.

"I'm not sure he likes you much," Jake said as I left.

"I'm an acquired taste."

The hatch closed behind me, mercifully cutting off Jake's reply.

I went back to our quarters, not thinking about much of anything as I walked, just wallowing in a bad mood. I quickly changed into shorts and a t-shirt, left the cabin, and took the next passageway on the left, transiting to *Wandering Star's* outer ring.

"*Star*, Sonoran Desert, please."

Star replaced the six-meter wide corridor with what appeared to be a dirt trail flanked by creosote bush and cactus. Red rock mesas dotted the horizon. The illusion wasn't perfect, and the trail under my feet still felt like deck plate, but it was better than looking at gray painted metal for the next hour.

"Would you like a thunderstorm to cool you down after four laps, Mr. Holloman?" *Star* offered helpfully.

"I'll let you know." I started at a moderate pace, enjoying the desert smells and illusion of open skies.

The ship's designers had started with her four massive engines, added room for fuel, shielding, and everything else needed to push her from planet to planet. RuComm added modules for command and control, life support, crew and technical team quarters, science labs, raw material storage for food and water, and a pair of planetary shuttles. The hardware and seed software for *Wandering Star* herself was built-in from the start. Millions of sensors and connections all talking to each other made her intelligent and self-aware. From the outside, *Wandering Star* was not pretty, looking like a collection of geometric shapes that had melted into each other on a hot day. She had been born in space and, God willing, she would never touch a planet's atmosphere.

A fat corridor with regularly spaced airlocks ringed each of the central decks providing access to replenish stores while docked, and making a great alternative to the equipment in the gym for anyone needing a run. The ring on the technical team deck was a couple of kilometers in circumference and five laps might be enough for me to forget about Jake and Hannah long enough that I could sit with them for dinner.

I passed passageways leading back into the body of the ship that appeared as diverging dirt trails, helpfully marked with stone cairns and rough wooden signs. *Starboard Aft Engine Room* looked a little out of place for the Arizona desert, but at least *Star* tried for authenticity.

I ran, picking up the pace.

Jake and I had applied to share a dorm room when the Academy accepted our applications. Freshman admissions denied the request. We appealed and they rejected us again. My father told me to let it go and that I should be happy that there was an administrator there with more sense than either Jake or me. Dad knew how close Jake and I were having watched us grow up together. How could he think that sharing a room would be a bad thing?

The next sign read *Port Aft Engine Room*. During four years at the Academy, I think we spent more time in each other's rooms than our room-mates did. Sure, we had a few disagreements, but less severe than when we were kids. There were times when we were ten or twelve when I never wanted to see Jake again. We got over it.

I passed the next sign, *Science Lab*. At the Academy, I didn't have to be with him every minute of every day. I didn't have to know his every thought, every action, every biologic function, and every stupid emotion that seemed to drive him to do stupid things.

I ran faster.

The next sign, *Medical*. Jake had a serious girlfriend at the Academy, and at high school before that. So had I. Was Hannah any different? Dark clouds were forming on the simulated horizon lit by occasional flashes of lightning.

The trail to *Shuttle Bays* passed while I considered it and then the *Port Forward* and *Starboard Forward* engine rooms. Yes, Hannah was different. Our girlfriends in school had been like us; shared values, shared culture, shared goals, and shared passion for our futures. I smiled, remembering Kaelyn, the love of my life for two years. She was so serious in her studies and Jake loved to tease her for it. She had shipped out on the *Evening Star* two months before us. I wondered where she was now. Was she on some unknown planet doing the job she had dedicated her life to learn, or was she running laps? She was the one who had introduced me to the thera-peutic benefits of running.

The skull of a Texas Longhorn topped the next sign. *Bridge. Restricted.* "Nice touch, *Star*. It gets better every time." A cool breeze rose from the desert floor to blow across my face.

Hannah. What was her agenda? What were her goals and values, and what future did she want? Jake didn't seem to care. She had captured him and he seemed willing to let her destroy him.

The next sign, *Mess Hall*. Rusted tin cans lined the trail. I thought about asking *Star* about Hannah. Her full profile information was private, but I might be able to learn something about her. I just couldn't think of a way to ask that didn't put Jake at risk too. I'd really like to know what kind of understanding she and *Star* had.

Starboard Aft Engine Room came by again. One lap down and I wasn't feeling any better. I cleared my mind and looked at the distant clouds. A large thunderstorm was moving out across the valley floor, its top flattening out into an anvil and a narrow band of rain trailing out from its base. No more thinking about Hannah for now. No more thinking about Jake. I ran, watching for the wooden signs that marked my progress and waiting for the thunderstorm to finish its transit of the valley and cross my imaginary trail.

By lap four, I had decided that there was no answer. I could throw Jake to the wolves, but I would never do that. If I asked for separate cabins, it would raise too many questions and Jake would be just as finished. The only solution was to let it burn itself out and pretend to enjoy the ride.

I knew Jake. Infatuation led to obsession. Obsession led to disillusionment. Disillusionment led to heartbreak, and that led back to Jake being Jake. I could wait him out. In another month or two, he would understand why there were rules against forming this kind of relationship and the difficulty in continuing to work with an ex-lover for the rest of the mission.

The trail snaked through the engine core in a series of tight s-curves. I rounded the last one, and a flash of light blinded me followed by a boom loud enough make me miss a step. Cold rain and wind followed the lightning and thunder.

"Damn it, *Star*, I told you I'd let you know if I wanted a thunderstorm."

"Did you? I've been refining the effect. It's much more realistic now, don't you agree?"

I stopped and wiped rain and sweat from my eyes. I didn't want to admit it, but the rain did feel good. I looked at my watch. It was time to stop anyway and get cleaned up for dinner.

"Yes, very realistic. Thank you. Please close Sonoran Desert." The rain stopped, the sky cleared and faded away. "That was a lot of water, *Star*."

"It will all be recycled. Perhaps you'll be pouring it as milk on your cereal tomorrow morning."

I walked to the next connecting passageway, marked by a plain gray sign on the gray wall. A hot shower and dry clothes were my only thoughts now. And some shoes that didn't squish when I walked.

Jake was back in our cabin by the time I arrived, scrolling through something on his display pad.

"Assignments for Dulcinea are posted." He scanned down through several pages of text. "Way too much to get accomplished in the two months we'll be there."

"Well, like everything else, it's a test. Let me clean up a bit and we can go over it with Hannah during dinner."

I could feel him watching me as I entered our tiny bathroom.

"You need to run more," he called after me.

I paused to look back at him, waiting.

"You were pissed at Hannah and me when you left the lab. Now you seem like you're back to normal."

My mouth started to open in reply. No, let it go. Let it run its course. I closed my mouth before it could say anything. I smiled, shut the door, and got into the shower.

CHAPTER 2

BE CAREFUL

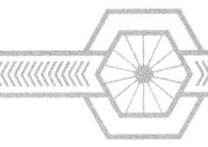

Hannah was sitting with Angela when Jake and I entered the mess hall. Her hair was tied back and she was taking what she was working on very seriously.

"You gentlemen have a plan yet?" Angela asked.

"Plan?" Jake and I said in unison.

"Well you better get something to eat. We have a lot of work ahead of us tonight. The task list always gets dropped on us at the last minute and RuComm wants our responses by the end of the day tomorrow."

I whispered to Jake. "Your meeting at 19:00 might be delayed."

"Try not to sound so happy about it."

"Did I sound happy? I didn't mean to." Yeah, I was happy about it.

Other members of the technical team drifted over to our table as they finished eating. Brian Jenkins, our astrophysicist sat down opposite Angela. "So boss, you have the schedule laid in yet?"

"I will once you and the others get me your 'shalls' and resource loadings. Hard to do much without that."

"What about the no-hoppers?" He gestured at Jake and me. "They have their S&Rs done yet?"

Angela looked at us, eyebrows raised. I looked at Jake. Jake looked at me. Hannah smirked.

Brian sighed. "I'll take that as a 'no.'"

He turned to the oldest member of our team, Omar Gizbar, chemist, and one of, if not the most senior active member of RuComm. It was rumored that he had been offered Angela's job as technical team lead a dozen times and had always turned it down. "Giz, are you up to teaching another class that the Academy can't be bothered to teach?"

Giz rubbed his eyes, which always seemed to be red and seeking a focus point he could no longer find. "Angela should be the one to help them, or really any of the rest of you is just as capable..." He turned from Angela to Brian to Charlotte Anaba, our anthropologist, and Mr. Mahajan, political science. "Horace, this is really a systems engineering task, perhaps you could do it?"

Horace Wicklow shook his head.

Charlotte placed her hand on Giz's shoulder. "We like the way you tell it, Giz. You include all the background and philosophy and you're always so gentle with them."

Giz sighed, accepting the inevitable. He ran his fingers across the top of his mostly bald head, gathering his thoughts. What was left of his hair was standing straight up, swaying in the slight breeze from the ventilators.

Giz's eyes locked on to mine, suddenly finding their focus point. "You, Theodore. You looked over your assignments?"

I blinked, surprised by the suddenness of the question and he continued before I could answer.

"Can you do everything on that list all on your own? Do you have time to do it all even if you were smart enough to know how?"

I started to open my mouth, but he answered for me. "No, you can't and you don't. What were you planning to do?"

I waited, expecting him to continue without me.

"Well?"

"Um, well, I guess I was going to start at the top and get as much done as I could?"

Giz looked over at Brian. "You're right about the Academy. Damn if it doesn't get worse every year. In my day, they'd load us up with so much work that we had to learn how to prioritize or die from sleep deprivation."

Giz settled back in his chair. "First you need to understand a bit about conditions on Dulcinea. Why do they want us there? Or really, who wants us there? Dulcinea's population was already a couple of hundred million when the old Union started to fall apart. Now it's over a billion. Their society is mature and prosperous, their technology as advanced as anything on Earth, more so in some areas.

"So why do they need us? Here's your first clue. Look at your task list. It was created by politicians on Dulcinea. More specifically, the University of Palma Sola and the Palma Federated States government working with the politicians on Earth that control the Reunification Commission. What do these politicians want? They want to keep on being politicians. After we leave, the assembly members on Dulcinea will tell their constituents how *they* got Earth to do good things for them. And the senators on Earth will tell *their* constituents what good works the Reunification Commission is doing bringing the Union back together again, boosting export markets and creating jobs."

Realizing that he was getting off track, Giz paused before continuing. "Let's look at this a little less cynically, and this is the real reason for us to spend time on a planet fall like Dulcinea. Their scientific community sees this as a two month long technical and scientific exchange meeting. We will be working one-on-one with some of the best scientists on an entire planet. They expect us to know something; more than can be learned from technical journals and virtual special interest groups. You'd better know what you're doing. And just maybe, you might learn something from them along the way too."

I sighed. No pressure.

Giz leaned back in his chair. "I'll try to help you get started since none of us will be ready until we all are. And you," he pointed a finger at Jake, "pay attention so we don't have to go through all this again. OK, Theodore, what are the main tasks on your assignment list?"

"Geologic survey of someplace called the Margo Islands. I haven't had a chance to look it up, so I'm not even sure where it is relative to Palma Sola. From the description it looks like they want information on its potential for agriculture, extraction of mineral resources, and the optimal location for a small port city."

As I talked, I noticed Giz exchanging glances with other members of the team. "Problem?" I asked.

"No, probably not. The Palma Federated States and the Oceanus Protectorate both claim the Margos. Twenty years ago they fought a nasty little war over them, but it was all settled by treaty."

"All wars are nasty and none of them are little," Charlotte added. "The death toll was over four thousand, most of them when an OP special operations team destroyed two PFS transport ships while they sat at anchor at Palma Sola. I was there on my first assignment when it happened. We were evacuated." She stood behind Giz with her arms crossed, reliving the moment. "I'd met a couple of the guys who were killed."

"Set the political situation aside for a moment. I doubt the PFS would send us anywhere dangerous or insert us into a potential combat zone." Giz's smile was unconvincing. Charlotte said nothing, but her eyes were closed and I felt certain that she was thinking it was *exactly* what the PFS was doing.

"Let's get back to your 'shalls' and resource loading. Your assignment document has several statements that start with 'Reunification personnel shall,' *shall* being the key word. You need to assign each statement a priority and decide how much of your time it will take to accomplish, whose help you need, and how much of their time it will take. Now, why do you think they want you for this job?"

"Well I don't know much about what makes good agricultural land or where to build cities, but I do know something about determining mineral distribution and extraction. I did my thesis on geomorphologic modeling as a technique to identify probable distribution of economically valuable mineral resources. It takes the existing landforms and then rolls time back to see how the landscape evolved and what's underneath it. I wrote the code for the simulation myself and tested it against known sites. It works pretty well."

Giz nodded. "That's probably what they're most interested in. Make it your number one priority and build the rest of your grid around it. For your time estimates make your best guess then double it before giving it to Angela."

"And I'll double everything again," Angela added. "That way it might be close."

Giz continued. "It'll be easier when we get to the next planet fall on Cleavus. It's uninhabited and unexplored, so we have a standard deck of tasks that we'll be working to." He looked at Jake and me. "Ask questions. Angela can do this in her sleep."

"And I have."

Giz focused on Hannah. "And just because you have one hop under your belt, young woman, doesn't make you an expert. Ask for help if you need it."

Hannah nodded, a touch of a smile hiding in the corner of her mouth. "Absolutely, sir."

Giz pushed back his chair, shaking his head. "Get to work."

Jake and I opened the template on our display pads and worked to come up with some sort of resource loading for each task on our lists. By midnight, we had gone through two pots of coffee and restarted a couple of times after Angela reviewed what we were doing. Hannah had finished her tasks and was helping us enough that I had some hope of seeing my pillow before *Star* started serving breakfast.

"Tell me again why we need to get this done by morning?" Jake had already asked that question a dozen times in the last six hours, so Hannah and I didn't even bother to look up from our displays.

Hannah's voice was a quite monotone. "Because Angela needs time to correlate, de-conflict and prepare her report. And because you and Ted appear to have no idea how long it takes you to do *anything* except maybe drink coffee."

Wandering Star must have heard him ask one too many times and decided to answer him in her own way. The mess hall lights flickered and came back red.

"Damn it, *Star*!" Angela yelled. "I swear I'm going to find every part of you and unplug it."

Star ignored her, of course, and we lost two hours standing around in pressure suits listening to Captain von Muller reminding us of the importance of our mission and his personal responsibility for our safety.

We were all finished at 05:00. Jake's and my inputs were judged to be 'adequate' and I assigned sleep a higher priority and longer duration than breakfast.

I slept for four hours before forcing myself out of bed. We were less than thirty-six hours out from Dulcinea, and for the past couple of weeks ship's time had been slowly synchronizing with the planet's twenty-two and a half hour rotation and Palma Sola's local time. Sleeping in now would just make adjusting worse. I found Jake already eating, or at least sitting at a table with his hand supported his head. Hannah was wide-awake and ready for the day.

"Are you excited, Ted?" Hannah looked excited, but that was her natural state.

"I am," I replied, and it was true.

She took a pickle from Jake's plate and crunched it between her teeth. "They have us booked into the Palma Sola Hilton, same as last time I was there." She passed me the room assignment sheet.

"Two months living in my own single room." I smiled. No Jake every minute of every day, no *Wandering Star* watching us or waking us up in the middle of the night. Not bad.

Jake looked up at me, his forehead wrinkled in concern. "Well, two months for us, but how long before you ship out to the Margo Islands? You'll probably be living in a tent. Try not to get shot while you're there."

"You sound like you'd miss me."

He considered that for a moment. "Being with you full time has been... interesting. But yeah, I'd miss you."

"You should be careful, Ted," Hannah added. "Jake would miss you."

I spent the next two days trying to learn as much as I could about the Margo Islands and the local political situation, but there wasn't much relevant to be found, other than Charlotte was right about the war being nasty. The Margo Islands treaty had established a joint Palma Federated States and Oceanus Protectorate foundation that required bilateral approval of all development on the islands. Years had passed without progress, but now maybe they had reached an agreement. Mr. Mahajan's professional political advice to me was not particularly helpful.

"You are a pawn," he told me. "Be careful."

Wandering Star achieved orbit on schedule and our team had a bumpy shuttle ride down to Palma Sola at 07:00 local time through a thick overcast. The surface temperature was -5 degrees C with light snow. As I walked through the terminal listening to Hannah and Jake's excited conversation, all I could hear in my head was everyone telling me, 'be careful, Ted, be careful'.

CHAPTER 3

PALMA SOLA

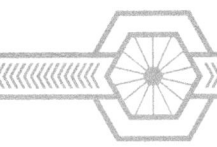

The Palma Sola terminal was built using the 'heroic renaissance' architecture that was popular at the start of reunification. I found it inspirational when I was growing up to see images of these buildings on so many other worlds, massive curved forms of concrete and steel reaching toward space, demonstrating a common bond for all humanity.

On Dulcinea, the terminal's architect had taken advantage of the eighty percent gravity to create shapes that looked like they might crash down on the tiny people below at any moment. Even the view through the four story tall windows of the city on the other side of the bay was of no comfort. Snow was falling, the low overcast seemed about to swallow everything, and wind was kicking up whitecaps on the bay. I found myself missing the snug enclosed passageways of *Wandering Star*, now docked three hundred kilometers above the clouds.

Jake was having none of my bad mood. "Why so glum? Fresh air and open skies, sort of." He gestured out the massive windows at the snow as the moving walkway carried us along. "We're off the ship and on another planet! This is what you dreamed of your whole life. Stop worrying about those damned islands for a few hours and enjoy the moment."

I took a deep breath. Jake was right. Why did I always start worrying about the next problem whenever I achieved a goal? I smiled at him as he and Hannah rode along too close to each other.

"OK," I said, trying to cheer myself up, "Angela has us scheduled all morning, but what are we going to do this afternoon? I want to spend at least a few hours being a tourist. Hannah, you were here a year and a half ago. What was your favorite thing to do?"

"It was mid-summer then. I spent part of every day with my bare feet in the sand and playing in the water." All three of us stared out the windows again. It was snowing harder and the city was no longer visible.

Hannah tipped her head to the side and looked at me. "There's a trail that climbs a short way up the cliff to a little restaurant overlooking the bay. They had a huge fireplace in the center, unlit when I was there. It might be fun to sit next to it tonight and watch the city filling up with snow while we drink hot chocolate. If the trail is open."

"I like it. And before that?"

"We'll explore the city, maybe walk to the University if it's not too far," Jake replied.

Hannah was still looking at the snow. "I'm glad I had *Star* print a warmer coat for me."

Walking out of the terminal to the waiting hotel shuttle was our first experience with real weather in a month. I climbed in and sat next to Charlotte with Jake and Hannah across the aisle. Charlotte's mood was the same as mine had been. She glanced at me and looked back out her window, shivering against the cold air blowing in through the open door.

She stared out across the bay, maybe looking for ghosts in the swirling snow. I felt I should say something to her, but no words came and I slipped back into my own worries.

Brian and Angela were sitting behind us. Brian reached over the seat and placed his hand on Charlotte's shoulder. "Cheer up, Anaba. Two months of a soft bed, good food, and pleasant work. This stop is a milk run. We could do it blindfolded."

Charlotte patted Brian's hand while she watched the snow. "Blindfolded." She smiled, but just barely.

The Palma Sola Hilton was built along the bay, the three story main building curving between the beach and the broad road that ran for several kilometers through the city. The hotel had added a more modern tower at some point to accommodate the increase in visitors after the start of reunification.

"Last time they had us up there." Hannah looked up as we unloaded from the bus. "The view is nice from the restaurant at the top, but the rooms are kind of bleh. The older rooms in the main building are nicer;

24

they all have a view of either the cliffs out the front, or the bay behind the hotel. And the rooms are bigger."

I swung my backpack over my shoulder as we entered the lobby, wondering how Hannah knew what the other rooms looked like, but decided not to ask. Angela confirmed our room assignments at the front desk where a sign displayed the hotel's pleasure in welcoming the members of the Reunification Commission to Palma Sola.

"We'll all be in the Morgan wing. Your display pad and watch should both now show what room you're in and either one will grant you access."

I tapped my watch, room 209.

"Please get settled quickly. I'd like to see you all for a quick meeting in thirty minutes. We have the use of the Colin Gray conference room for the duration. It's located in the center of this wing on the ground floor. Don't be late."

Jenkins looked at his watch and smiled. "Ocean view rooms. The advantage of being here during the off season."

Room 209 smelled as if no one had used it in a while, but it was twice the size of the cabin I'd shared with Jake and it was all mine. I dumped my backpack and bag in the corner and opened the blinds to look out at the snow covered beach and gray skies. I slid the balcony door open and let the cold air rush in.

Dulcinea. It had been only a name, its star a speck of light visible when the sky was very dark. Now I was feeling its cold wind on my face. I quickly closed the door and flopped down on the huge bed. "*Star?*" I said aloud. No answer. It made me smile.

A clock on the desk showed local time of 09:36. The early colonists had kept Earth standard minutes and seconds, days and weeks, so the clocks would look normal until they reached 22:38 when they would change to 00:00. It was going to take getting used to, even with *Wandering Star* having slowly shortening our days for the past couple of weeks. It was very easy to lie there on my back staring up at the ceiling. I felt as if I had run a very long race and had earned a rest. In the back of my head though, Angela's voice was whispering, *Now the real work begins*, and adding, *You are a pawn, Theodore. Be careful.*

I sighed, got up, and unpacked my bag, hanging up clothes and dumping my toiletries by the sink. I stepped out into the hall and closed the door.

Omar Gizbar and Mr. Mahajan were passing by on their way to the conference room.

"So, Ted," Giz asked, "how's your room?"

"It's wonderful," I answered.

Mahajan laughed. "I imagine it is after doubling up with your friend for two months. I think you were nuts for doing that."

I took a deep breath before replying. "It wasn't that bad."

Giz replied, "Easy to say when you have your own room for the next eight weeks."

"Until they ship me out to the Margo Islands."

"Yes, there is that." Giz was still smiling, but his eyes no longer reflected it.

I walked along with them to the conference room. We were early, so I poured myself a cup of coffee and walked around the room looking at the images of the city and surrounding countryside that decorated the walls.

Jake and Hannah came up beside me while I admired a picture of the Hilton taken from off shore. The water was a perfect turquoise blue, the beach wide and full of umbrellas and beach chairs. The white cliffs that enclosed the north end of the city glowed with warm afternoon light.

"We have *got* to come back here sometime when it's summer," Jake nodded at the image.

"It's crowded and I got a sunburn," Hannah said solemnly, looking at the beach.

"I bet you were just miserable," Jake taunted her, making her smile.

"I'll come back with you." She looked from Jake to me. "Anytime. It was wonderful."

Angela called the meeting to order and we spent the next hour reviewing assignments again, but more focused on who we would be working with and where. She stressed the importance of submitting progress reports on time, and on completing our impossible schedules and task lists. We would perform our work at the University, except for Hannah who was doing a study on street slang. Jake would get some outdoor time as well, doing a survey of the microscopic critters whose shells made up the White Cliffs, trying to document their variation and evolution across time.

"Good exercise, climbing up and down those cliffs several times a day," I whispered to him.

"Point eight gravity," he replied.

"In the snow."

"Theodore?" Angela called to get my attention. "The University has requested a presentation on your survey technology. Tomorrow morning. Do you have anything prepared?"

"*Star* has all of my notes and documents. I have presentations prepared for anything from a high-level, non-technical audience, to full details on the algorithms. Do you know who will be there?"

"They didn't provide an attendee list, but the briefing is set for one of the larger lecture halls in the geology building. You should be able to link to *Star* from there. Plan to start at a high level, but be ready to go as deep as they want. Dress nice."

"I always do."

"No, you usually dress like the only thing you need to do before going out into the field is to grab your rock hammer."

I looked down at myself. She may have a point. "I'll dress nice."

"The bus to the university will be here at 07:30. Please be in the lobby early. If there are no questions, we are done here. Enjoy your day off."

"Well, half a day anyway," Jake grumbled. "Hannah, I am once again at your mercy. What shall we do with our day off?"

Hannah looked at me, uncertain.

"Look, if you two want to..." I started.

Hannah linked her left arm through mine and put her right arm around Jake's waist. "No, you'd probably get lost in the snow."

Jake looked slightly disappointed.

"So you're going to keep me out of trouble?" I asked.

Jake laughed. "Your job is to keep *us* out of trouble, remember?"

Hannah pulled us out of the conference room into the hall before releasing us. "I'll meet you in the lobby in ten. Dress warm, we have some walking to do."

Most of the team had gathered in the hotel's pub, *Their Finest Hour*. Giz and Brian were absorbed in a game of chess next to a large central fireplace, the others were chatting over drinks. I walked in, my heavy coat and boots seeming out of place in the warm glow from the flames and the soft lighting.

"Going to walk about a bit?" Mahajan asked.

"Sure. You all are just staying here?"

Charlotte swirled her drink, the ice clinking against the sides of the glass. "It's snowing out there. This is about all the ice I care to see this afternoon."

I smiled. "I think one of us must be crazy."

Jake and Hannah came up beside me, bundled for the cold.

"Three," she said, pointing at us, "three of you are crazy."

"You ready, Ted? It's too hot in here with this coat on." Jake pulled on my arm.

I raised my hand in farewell to the room in general as Hannah and Jake tugged me away. "Be seeing you."

"Be careful out there," someone replied.

"Why does everyone keep telling me to be careful?" I asked Jake, but then we were out the door with the snow and the cold air washing over us. It felt wonderful, and I laughed out loud. Jake's silly grin said that he was feeling it too. We walked away from the hotel and I had no idea where we were going. Maybe it was the lower gravity, or the effect of the open air after over a month on board ship; I didn't really care.

I bumped Jake's shoulder. "Race you to the corner."

Hannah didn't say a word or even look up, but she was gone, running away from us. I took off after her with a shout of, "Hey!" Jake was laughing somewhere behind us, trying to keep up. We passed by several startled pedestrians, somehow avoiding any serious collisions. Hannah reached the corner first, grabbed the light post there and swung around it a couple of times to kill her momentum.

"You're quick," I panted. "Sometime we'll have to have a fair race."

"Never going to happen." She smiled, still swinging around the pole.

Jake caught up, bent over with his hands on his knees. "Can we maybe just walk the rest of the way?"

"No guarantees," I said, patting him on the back. "Sometimes it comes over me and I just have to run."

Hannah's eyes opened wide. "Like, now?"

She was gone again, me two paces behind her. We ran across the intersection and half way up the next block before she had to stop because she was laughing too hard.

Jake wasn't too far behind. He was fast when he wanted to be, as I had discovered many times in school.

Hannah looked at him when he caught up, eyebrows raised in a question.

"Hannah, no. Do you know how many people I had to apologize to because you ran them off the sidewalk into the slush?"

"Six."

"Seven."

She counted on her gloved fingers, shrugged. "OK. Seven, then."

We continued through town at a more pedestrian friendly pace, Hannah showing us points of interest along the way. They were mostly bars and sidewalk cafes.

"Did you do anything while you were here other than eating and drinking?" Jake asked.

"It's a college town, and in the summer at least, a resort town. Drinking, eating, and talking late into the evening are part of the culture." She ran her hand along the cast iron rail that separated snow covered tables from the sidewalk. "I did some great research sitting right here. People come to Palma Sola from everywhere. Places like this are where language is made and normalized. You should read the papers I published. Peer reviewed, even."

The snow had stopped for now and low clouds were moving quickly just above the rooftops. We crossed the street, walked a couple of blocks away from the coast and turned south again. I realized I still wasn't sure where we were going. "Is this the way to the University?"

"It's a nice walk and the campus is pretty. I knew you'd want to see the lecture hall before your presentation tomorrow."

She was right about that. "Thanks. I want to make sure I can connect to *Wandering Star* from the podium. I always like to know as much as I can about what I'm getting into before I jump."

"I get that about you." Hannah smiled and looked back at me. "Do you know why Angela always calls you Theodore instead of Ted?"

"Because it's more professional? She's like that with all of us."

"No, she's not. She calls you Theodore because it's more pompous."

That got a big laugh from Jake.

"I'm not pompous; I just take my job seriously."

"And yourself," Jake chuckled.

While my friends made fun of me, we arrived at the main campus of the University of Palma Sola.

"See?" Hannah pointed, "Pretty."

There were broad open spaces, buildings made of local stone and tall trees that appeared to have been there since the original colonization. It reminded me of the Academy, which reminded me of my friend Kaelyn, which made me a little homesick.

"Are those oak trees?" I asked, realizing that I hadn't seen anything on Dulcinea that wasn't from Earth. "Why aren't there any native plants?"

Jake answered. "The colonists pretty much brought Earth with them. They were worried about being able to eat what lived here and they wanted it to be as Earth-like as possible. Most of the native species are now limited to a few reserves."

I looked at him, eyebrows raised.

"What?" he said defensively, "I did my research. The job I take seriously, just not myself."

Hannah reached up and took Jake's collar, pulling him down for a quick kiss. "None of us do."

"Nice."

"Let's get moving," Hannah said. "There's a decent café on campus called *The Christie-Cleek*. I'm starving."

It was snowing hard again when we left the café after lunch. Hannah guided us across campus to the geology building, passing a few students along the way with their heads down against the storm. I stopped at the entrance.

"Wait a second, I want to see something." I brushed snow away from the sandstone blocks of the front wall. "Look at this. Fossils of some kind." I started to brush away more of the snow, but Jake grabbed my arm and pulled me into the building.

"I'm not standing in the snow while you look at fossils."

"I've never seen one like that before."

"Of course not. Not Earth."

I looked back toward the door longingly.

Hannah called to us from down the corridor. "Main lecture hall is this way."

"Sorry," Jake apologized. "Ted was about to take a take a rock hammer to the front of the building."

"Not true."

Hannah looked confused for a moment. "Whatever. Here's your venue for tomorrow, Ted. The schedule posted on the prompter says we have about twenty minutes before the next class, so go do whatever you need to do."

The hall looked like it could hold about three hundred or three hundred fifty people, with tiered seating and a stage and podium up front. The lights were set low except for the stage area. I walked down to the podium and called back to Jake, "They're using a Caster 300, same as at the Academy."

"Interstellar trade is a beautiful thing."

I entered my RuComm credentials and access codes for the ship. *Star's* reply printed across the screen saying how delighted she was to hear from me. More importantly, all my notes and presentations were available. At least that part of tomorrow should be easy. I opened my non-technical overview charts. It had lots of pictures, small words, and simplified graphics. A photograph of 19th century geologist Charles Lyell appeared on the screen behind me along with his famous quote, '*The Present is the Key to the Past*'.

Hannah had taken a seat in the front row next to Jake. She pointed up at the image. "That's funny."

"What? The quote?" I turned to make sure I was displaying the right slide.

"No, him. Lyell. You're standing in the Charles Lyell lecture hall. I noticed the name when I checked the prompter. Good omen."

"I hope so. I don't feel ready for this at all."

"Oh, you'll do fine." Jake comforted me. "You'll worry about it all evening, run through your slides a couple of hundred times staying up way too late over preparing, and you'll show up exhausted tomorrow. Then you'll ace it like you always do." He looked at Hannah. "Always. Every paper, every test, every final since I've known him."

"Nothing kills like overkill," Hannah replied.

I shut off the displays, logged out, and followed Jake and Hannah up the stairs. A movement caught my eye as I was about to walk through the doorway. There was a person sitting in the darkness of the back row. How long had he been there? I paused, looking at him. He waved almost as if he knew me, but didn't say anything. I continued out into the corridor.

"Did you see that guy sitting in the back row?"

"No," from Jake.

"Yes," Hannah replied.

"He waved to me. Do you know who he was?"

"Maybe a student arrived early?" Jake offered.

"No, he was older, wearing glasses."

Hannah shook her head. "No idea. But, Ted –"

"Don't say it."

"Be careful tomorrow."

"Where to next?" Jake asked as we adjusted our coats. The view out the glass of the front doors showed that another five centimeters of snow had accumulated just in the short time we had been inside the building.

Hannah sighed, looking sad. "Well, I'm starting to think that walking half way up the cliff for a cup of hot chocolate may not be my best idea. Let's just tour around campus a bit. Jake, I can show you where your building is, if you care. Then we could walk back into town, but I think we're going to run out of daylight pretty early."

I had been looking at the display panel by the door while Hannah was talking. As Jake reached to open the door I stopped him. "Wait a second. Look at this." I tapped the screen. "Did you know there's a geology museum on the second floor?"

Jake shoved the door open. "No, Ted. You'll have plenty of time for that later. Let's go see the building where I'm going to spend the next couple of months."

He opened the door and we went out into the snow.

We spent the afternoon wandering the entire campus. At times, the snow would almost stop. Then a new squall line would pass over the city and visibility would drop to zero. The students seemed divided in their attitudes to the storm. Some seemed intent on making it to their classes as quickly as possible. Others, the majority, seemed to have decided that God himself had declared a snow day and they intended to use it. By late afternoon, we had passed legions of snowmen rising from the fields and an epic snowball fight in progress that had twenty or more participants on each side. Jake and I were both ready to enlist, but Hannah had other ideas.

"I want to get back to *The Christie-Cleek* for some hot chocolate and to warm up."

So that's where we headed. The snow continued falling and the temperature was dropping along with the daylight. We made just one more stop along the way. Someone had made a row of snow angels lined up along the sidewalk for almost a hundred meters. Hannah agreed that it would not be right to pass by without adding three more to the row.

I was lying on my back next to her and Jake, looking up at the snow floating in the darkening gray of the sky with the black branches of the trees above me, and I thought, no matter what happens tomorrow, or even on the rest of the mission, this moment I will always have.

Jake's face entered my field of view. "If you keep lying there we're going to leave you to the crows. Or the things here that are like crows, but with extra wings and extra claws."

I reached up and he grabbed my arm to pull me up onto the sidewalk. "Onward?"

"Onward," he replied.

The café was crowded when we arrived, but Hannah got her hot chocolate and Jake and I sat with her by the window and watched her drink it.

"It seems to be a religious experience for her," I said, noting the careful process she used.

"Or maybe a sexual one," Jake added, looking at her smile and half-closed eyes.

"Do those have to be mutually exclusive?" Hannah asked. Then she ran her tongue around the inside of the cup to get the last vestiges of chocolate and whipped cream. She smiled, contented.

"Not if you practice the right religion, I suppose." Jake answered, his voice sounding far away.

Hannah put her cup down. "Dinner."

We didn't answer, the image of her finishing the hot chocolate still filling our minds. She waved her hand in our faces. "Hey! Dinner. What do you want for dinner?"

"Oh," I said, coming back to the moment, "something simple. Not exotic."

"Pizza it is then. I know the place. Comfort food for the home sick travelers."

The restaurant she selected was on the way back to the hotel. It was built out of rough bricks outside and in, and seemed the perfect place for a cold night. The service was slow and the menu options confusing, but the food was worth the wait. Hannah was right; a pizza and a cold beer made it feel almost like home.

Light snow was falling as we left the restaurant, the large snowflakes coming down slowly in Dulcinea's low gravity. It was still a couple of kilometers back to the hotel and it was cold, but no one suggested a taxi. Too many weeks in enclosed spaces had left us with a need for an open sky and free moving air, regardless of the temperature. I was walking a few steps behind Hannah and Jake, trying to ignore their banter and enjoy the magic of the snowfall.

Hannah gave up on convincing Jake that she was right about whatever it was they were arguing about and started a long commentary about the planet, the city, the university, and the restaurant we had just left using a mix of local dialects and idioms. It was funny enough that she had both of us laughing. As we moved past each streetlight, I watched the shadows move across her face as she talked. Her hair was full of snow and the corners of her eyes crinkled as she laughed at her own stories.

Amid the floating snow and laughter, I realized something. I was falling in love with Hannah. I glanced quickly at Jake, afraid he could hear my thoughts or that I had said it aloud, but he was still walking ahead of me, laughing at Hannah's imitation of the waiter pretending not to understand our pizza order. I think I hated Jake a little bit right then.

When we said goodnight at the hotel, Hannah gave us each a kiss on the cheek, which we reciprocated. I kissed her a fraction of a second longer than I intended. Jake didn't notice, but Hannah did. She tipped her head slightly to the right and those startling, intense, brown eyes focused into mine for a moment. "Pleasant dreams, Ted."

"You too." I stammered. "We'll see you in the morning."

She held my gaze, a smile on her lips. She turned, and walked down the hall toward her room.

I hate it when Jake is right about me. I ran through my presentations, added links to my notes in case the audience wanted to go deeper, and tried to anticipate what questions might come up. I also reviewed what was available about the geology of the Margo Islands, which wasn't much. There was one big island and a couple of smaller ones, granodiorite cores with some sedimentary deposits and a coral reef fringe growing offshore.

I only slept a couple of hours, but that had less to do with worrying about my presentation than I wanted to admit. Hannah's cheek had been very soft against my lips and there were small gold flecks in her eyes.

Jake, Hannah, and most of the team were already in the pub eating breakfast by the time I made it downstairs. Early morning sun was shining through the windows, yesterday's storm having moved on overnight. I joined them, and Jake slid a plate to me.

"Here, full English breakfast. The house specialty. You look like you could use fortifying."

Two poached eggs stared back at me alongside slices of tomato, ham, and two sausages resting on a bed of baked beans. I sighed. Coffee and a hard roll would have been better for the way I was feeling.

Hannah reached across the table and took one of my sausages, plopping it into a pool of syrup next to her half eaten pancakes. "Eat what you can. You'll feel better."

I ate, but I wasn't feeling any better by the time we all climbed into our bus for the short ride to the University. The city looked different without snow and mist filling its streets, less magical, more business-like. The men and women rushing along the sidewalks had more purpose about them.

As we stepped down from the bus, Hannah regarded the scene through green tinted sunglasses. She was dressed professionally, looking as if she could easily blend in with the working citizens of Palma Sola. She looked older. No, not older I decided, but more mature, with her hair tied back and a bag of the current style over her shoulder. Which was the real Hannah, I wondered; the one from last night with snow in her hair, or the one I was looking at now?

"The snow won't last long in this sun." She turned her attention to me. "You look good, by the way. Even your backpack works. No one would take you seriously as a geologist if your bag wasn't beat to hell."

"Thanks." I took a deep breath. "I think I'm starting to feel better."

Jake took my hand and shook it. "No worries, mate. We'll see you at *The Christie-Cleek* for lunch at 11:30."

"Thank you, Jake. No worries."

I turned in the direction of the geology building and found Angela blocking my way, looking at me with a critical eye. The corners of her mouth turned down and she brushed imaginary dust from my outer jacket.

"I'm coming with you." Her hand was still on my jacket. "The bastards still haven't given me a participant list for today or a schedule for your little field trip." She released me and we walked along the sidewalk together. "Some stupid bureaucratic foul up, I'm sure." We walked past the remains of a row of snow angels melting in the sun.

A man wearing a dark suit and a short haircut met us in the corridor outside the lecture hall. "You must be Angela Dawkins. It's so nice to meet you in person." He took Angela's right hand in both of his. "I didn't know you would be joining us this morning."

"Major Kilpatrick." Angela said, reading the badge hanging around his neck. "Since you and Professor Vandermeer didn't reply to my requests for a participants list, I thought I'd stop by to see for myself."

"Really? I'm sure I asked Lieutenant Conrad to send that to you. I'll have to speak to her." He smiling a convincingly genuine smile.

"Major, this is Theodore Holloman." Angela introduced me. He shook my hand in the normal way.

"Ted, please."

"Ted. Let's go in, I believe everyone else is already here."

I looked at my watch. We were almost twenty minutes early. So much for setting up ahead of time. A half dozen people were talking with a man seated in the front row of the lecture hall. Back a few rows, an older man was busy cleaning his glasses with his tie. I stopped next to him.

"Professor Vandermeer?"

He put his glasses on and looked at me through the tops of them and then the bottoms. "Ah, you must be Theodore Holloman." He stood and shook my hand while looking around me at Angela. "Ms. Dawkins, it's always so good to see you again."

"Professor," Angela greeted him. "Is this the limit of our audience? I don't see any other members of your department." All of the lights in the lecture hall were on full, leaving no place for anonymous spectators.

The Professor sighed and looked around at the empty seats. "Ah, yes. I'm afraid you will have to make do with me. And the members of the Foundation for Margo Islands Development." He lowered his voice. "Politicians, bureaucrats, and now the military has decided to take a lead role."

"And why is that, Peter?" Angela whispered.

"Under terms of the Margo Islands treaty, neither the Palma Federated States nor the Oceanus Protectorate can claim, develop, or even visit the islands without a joint agreement. Well, now we have one. Eight months ago, both nations sent science teams there. It didn't go well from the start. The OP team brought a security detachment along with them that was clearly military. So we sent a security team and they enlarged theirs. Now there're more people carrying guns than doing science. I've talked to my counterparts on the OP side and they are as frustrated and as powerless as we are."

Angela frowned. "You want to drag the Reunification Commission in on your side of this dispute? That's not going to happen. You know we can't take sides. Now I understand why you've kept this hidden so far."

"Please stop saying 'you'. This isn't my doing."

Angela didn't reply, but walked down the steps to where the others were gathered.

"Should I set up for the presentation?" I asked

"Wait there," she snapped back over her shoulder.

I couldn't hear everything they were saying, but it didn't sound good. After a few minutes, she gestured to me to come down.

"Theodore, please proceed with your charts." She accompanied me on to the stage and whispered, "Two of those suits are diplomats from the OP's Palma Sola embassy. I don't have grounds to cancel your participation since both parties are represented. I'm sorry. The one they're all gathered around is General Barrows, and he's the one calling the shots." She patted my chest and held on to the lapel. "Theodore?"

"I know. I'll be careful."

She nodded, gave my chest another pat and took a seat next to Professor Vandermeer. I connected to *Wandering Star* and pulled up my first chart.

"The Present is the Key to the Past," I started.

General Barrows interrupted me. "Your quote is backwards. Isn't the study of the past the key to understand the present and the future?"

"No, sir. The quote refers to the truth that the processes that we can observe today are the same as the processes that were active in the past. Erosion, deposition, volcanism, seismic activity, the drifting of the continents; all of them can be studied and measured today and their influence on the geology of the planet extrapolated to the distant past."

"And Charles Lyell? Who was he?"

Professor Vandermeer squirmed a bit in his seat.

"Charles Lyell was one of the founders of modern geology," I answered. "His promotion of the concept of uniformitarianism, meaning that the processes of today are the same as those that operated in the past, revolutionized science, not just geology. I imagine that's why the University of Palma Sola chose to name this lecture hall in his honor."

Angela gave me a scowl and her mouth soundlessly said, "Don't poke the bear."

"So your new tool is based on this old principle. What makes it better than anything else that's come along in the last five hundred years?"

"It takes advantage of improvements in data analysis and modeling of complex systems. The algorithms provide greater fidelity and are more efficient, so they provide better answers faster. And it's not used in isolation, but in conjunction with seismic and magnetotelluric imaging."

"And you're just giving this advancement away?"

"I work for the Reunification Commission. What I develop for them is theirs to do with as they please. They pay me." I smiled, but the General was busy talking quietly with the man next to him.

"So are we ready for the next chart?" I asked.

"How soon can you be ready to leave?"

I hadn't anticipated that question. "Leave? For the Margo Islands?"

"Yes. Are you ready to leave?"

I looked at Angela for help, but she just shrugged. "I have most of what I need in my bag or I can link to it on our ship, other than a few incidentals like clothes," I replied defensively. "And assuming that your lab there has adequate computing power and a simulation tank and your survey data is available. I had expected that most of the preliminary work, like loading baseline data into the model, could be done here at the University."

"There will be an aircraft waiting for you at noon. You won't need to bring any of your 'incidentals'. We'll provide everything you need. You can do your preliminaries on-site. Work with Professor Vandermeer for anything else technical that you need." He checked his watch. "Major, please make sure Mr. Holloman is on time."

General Barrows stood and walked up the stairs to exit the lecture hall, the rest of his entourage trailing behind.

Major Kilpatrick stopped next to Angela and Professor Vandermeer. "Please wait here. I'll be right back." He followed the others up the stairs and the door closed behind him.

I sighed and looked up at the black and white visage of Charles Lyell on the screen behind me. I'd never gotten off my first chart. I started to laugh.

"You think this is funny, Theodore?"

I stopped, the dark humor I'd been feeling when faced with the absurdity of the 'briefing' fading fast.

"I hope you appreciate the danger you're in. And you, Peter, you *knew* this was going to happen and you did *nothing* to warn us."

"What good would it have done?" He looked like he was near tears. "Would you have stayed on orbit, hid Ted away somewhere, bypassed Dulcinea altogether? You know that would have been impossible." He turned his attention to me. "Ted, my department and I will do everything we can to support you. We have a very good geophysicist already on the island as part of the survey crew, one of the best students I've ever had. She'll be expecting you."

"Peter, why are you doing this? Why didn't you tell them 'no.'"

"It would have been impossible. I'm sorry, Angela. I truly am."

Major Kilpatrick came back into the hall, the door banging closed behind him.

"Well, that was quick, wasn't it?" He smiled at us. No one answered him or smiled back. "I imagine you have some preparation work you can do before your flight. We'll need to leave campus by a bit after 10:30. Shall I meet you here?"

"Aren't there classes scheduled in here today?" I asked.

"Ah, no. General Barrows had us block out the entire day when we scheduled today's meeting so all the classes were moved or canceled." He smiled at us again. "Fine, then. I'll see you at 10:30."

After he was gone, Angela excused herself as well. "I need to have a private chat with RuComm."

The Professor stood when Angela did. He held his hand out to her, and for a second I thought she wasn't going to take it. "Angela, I'm very sorry this has happened this way." She took his hand, but didn't reply.

"Ted, you do prefer Ted, yes?"

I nodded.

"She always calls you Theodore, so I wanted to make sure."

I sighed. "That's just Angela."

"Ted, let's move to my office. I'd like to have you talk to a couple of our structural geologists and geomodelers and get your simulation loaded on our system. That way we can collaborate with you from a distance and help confirm your results. Will that be all right?"

"Sure." I shook my head. "This isn't how I expected today to go. Do things always move this quickly here?"

The Professor replied as we walked down the corridor. "Not at all. The RuComm visits have always been a pleasant exchange of information and new ideas. Times are troubled just now." He sighed. "But I'm sure it will all work out. I think you'll like working with our geophysist. Her name is Alice."

Professor Vandermeer's office was much like every geology professor's office that I'd visited. It contained various curiosities arranged in a chaotic, but somehow logical fashion, and it smelled of rock dust and old books. I worked with the Professor and other members of the department setting up simulations and loading data.

Once we had finished, I sent a note to Jake and Hannah to let them know I was going to miss our lunch date, and dinner, and that Angela would fill them in with the details. I paused for a moment looking at Hannah's name on the display, not sure what I was feeling. Maybe this was better, being thousands of kilometers away from her for the next two months. Easier anyway.

The Professor was sitting at his desk watching me. We had finished what preparations we could and it was just the two of us in his office. He picked up a rock from his desk. "Lava" he said tossing it to me. "If we study its mineral composition, the size of its individual grains, the rate of decay of radioactive material trapped in its matrix, it can tell us what it was like the day it came to be. What you hold in your hands is a solid bit of time, ready to tell you everything if you know how to ask it the right questions."

I sat the rock back on his desk and he continued. "All artifacts are like that. A dusty boot, the inside of my coffee cup, even the layers of paint on my office walls. Left undisturbed they capture and hold the moment they were created."

I smiled. "If these walls could talk."

"Who says they can't? Perhaps no one has asked them the right question." He looked around his office and smiled. "Perhaps that is for the best. My point, Ted, is keep your eyes open and make sure you are asking the right questions. Please be careful and remind the others there to be careful too."

It sounded like a warning, but I wasn't sure what he was warning me about. "I'll tell them."

There was a knock on the door. The Professor nodded and I reached around to open it.

"I thought I'd find you here. Are you ready to go?"

"Major Kilpatrick." I stood and grabbed my coat and backpack. "As ready as I can be. I'm not exactly dressed for this."

"We'll make sure everything is ready for you when you arrive. I've already spoken to the quartermaster at Margo." He looked at the heavy coat I was holding. "You do know where the Margo Islands are don't you?"

"About four thousand kilometers north and a bit west?"

"Yes, just north of the equator. You're in for a bit of a thermal shock, I'm afraid. The temperatures all this week will be very warm, upper-thirties mostly."

Professor Vandermeer pointed at the coat tree by his door. "It will be here waiting for you when you return. You won't need it for the short distances you'll be outside on your way to the airport."

"Thanks."

Major Kilpatrick led me outside to a vehicle conveniently parked on the sidewalk next to the building. "Nice service." I remarked, climbing in.

"Well, you're important to us, Ted."

I looked out the window toward where I'd planned to meet my friends for a nice lunch. I sighed.

"Something wrong?"

"No, nothing important. Lunch with friends."

"Sorry to have disrupted your plans, but think of it as an adventure."

"Just being here was supposed to be my adventure."

Major Kilpatrick laughed. "I grew up here. I suppose what one man calls an adventure, another just calls home."

We entered the main road and turned toward the airport. Bypassing the terminal, we crossed through a couple of layers of security gates and parked next to a long pier extending out into the bay. I'm not sure what I expected when the General had said he would have an aircraft waiting for me, but this wasn't it.

A small white seaplane was tied to the dock, a high wing design with two engines on top mounted in a tandem arrangement turning five-bladed propellers. The aircraft was unadorned except for small gray registration numbers on the tail and a seagull logo under the cockpit windows. It wasn't really a seagull, though. The 'bird' had small wings at the shoulder, bigger wings for flight midway back and a pair of clawed feet with too many toes hanging under its tail.

The aircraft's wings looked too short and the chord too narrow, a fact I mentioned as we walked along the dock.

"Yes, everyone from Earth, or from any other planet with greater gravity, makes the same comment. Don't worry; she'll fly just fine."

The Major shook hands and left me standing on the dock with my backpack, my nice clothes, and a bunch of worries. I ducked my head to clear the doorway and climbed into the aircraft. Warm air, soft music, and twelve empty seats greeted me.

The pilot up front was going through his checklist accompanied by the murmur of air traffic control on the speaker. Dumping my bag on a seat, I poked my head into the cockpit and introduced myself.

"Howard," he said reaching around to shake my hand. He was wearing a white shirt with the sleeves rolled up and tan shorts. "We're just about ready if you want to have a seat and strap in."

"No other passengers?"

"Nope. Nothing but cargo this run. And you, of course." He looked me over. "Nice suit. Just the one bag?"

"Well, this was all very sudden. They didn't give me time to change, or pack, or to have lunch for that matter."

He tapped a cooler behind his seat. "Got you covered for lunch. Sounds like you're either very important or somebody really doesn't like you."

"Yeah, something like that." I pulled a sandwich and a drink from the cooler and turned to go back to my seat.

"You can sit up here if you like. Just promise not to touch anything."

"Thanks. That would be great." He pushed the right seat back so I could stay clear of the rudder pedals and I made myself comfortable. "How long will it take us to get there?"

"Usually about six hours if the weather cooperates. You don't get motion sick do you?"

I looked at my sandwich. "I don't think so."

"Good." Howard tapped a few buttons on his display. "Here we go."

The dock detached itself and gave the aircraft a gentle shove before retracting. The engines came to life and Howard handed me a pair of headphones. "You might want these," he shouted over the harmonic thrum.

After a short run across the water, we were airborne and climbing steeply while Howard talked to the control tower. We circled back over the city. "Beautiful place, Palma Sola, even in the winter."

I looked down briefly, saying a silent goodbye to Jake and Hannah as we banked away to the north.

Howard leveled the wings and pushed back in his seat. "My job here is done. She can take us the rest of the way on her own, and I'm for a nap. I had a bit of a late night and then up early this morning. I do love a snowy night in a college town." He smiled.

"Autopilot the rest of the way?" I asked

"Truth is she could do the whole trip without me, but where's the fun in that?"

"My ship, *Wandering Star*, is the same way. She can do the job better than her crew ninety-nine point nine something percent of the time, but it's that small percent that matters. It's being there to do the job in person that keeps us human. That's supposed to be one of the big lesson from the fall of the old Union, isn't it? Too much letting the AIs do everything for us?"

"True. But still, it's nice to be able to lean back once in a while and let the machine take the stick." He closed his eyes and crossed his arms across his chest leaving me to look at the ocean below and the slowly scrolling map display.

I finished my sandwich, used the lavatory, and decided that a nap was definitely in order. My night had been short and the morning much too early. The seats in the cabin looked more comfortable than those in the cockpit and after some fiddling, I was able to get one to fold flat. Finding some blankets and a pillow, I stretched out and quickly fell asleep to the reassuring murmur of the engines.

I awoke hours later to moderate turbulence, my view out the windows a mass of dark clouds. Making my way forward required a good grip on the back of each seat. Howard was awake, but still letting the plane fly itself.

"How are we doing?" I asked.

"Typical weather for this time of year. We're about an hour out and working around a line of thunderstorms. We should be able to get ahead of them far enough to get safely down before they catch up with us." He grinned at me. "We're going to have a warm, wet, sloppy Margo Islands welcome for you. Hope you don't mind the mud."

"The desert is more home to me, but I'm flexible."

"That's good. Flexibility will make you popular here. Best strap in, this part could be bumpy."

Howard resumed manual control and the aircraft motions became noticeably more aggressive as he flew in and out of cumulus canyons, seemingly more for fun than a desire to avoid the worst of the storms. But he kept his word, and the sun was shining low in the sky when we touched the water and taxied up to the Margo Islands dock.

"Thanks, Howard, I enjoyed the flight. It helped make up for a very weird morning." I unstrapped while he worked through his checklist, shutting off systems. A couple of uniformed men were busy on the dock pulling the aircraft in and tying it down.

"You only say that because you slept most of the way. I'd offer to help you with your bags, but..."

"Yeah, I always travel light." I stopped on my way out to try to put the seats back upright, but Howard interrupted.

"Don't bother. I may be using it later if my luck holds."

The cabin door opened and hot, humid air poured in across us.

"Wow," I gasped.

Howard chuckled. "It does have that effect the first few times you experience it."

I stepped out onto the dock expecting some sort of welcome, but there were only the two men tying the aircraft down. We were in a small cove with a nice beach overshadowed by a peak shrouded in lush growth. *Granodiorite*, I said to myself, remembering the geologic survey. It was going to be impossible to see rock outcrops anywhere on the island with so much vegetation on top of it.

A vehicle approached, fat tired with canvas covering the roof. The driver got out, a sergeant if the stripes on his sleeve meant the same thing they did in the Union military.

He looked at me across the hood and shouted, "Are you Theodore Holloman?"

"I am."

"Let's get moving and we'll see if we can't get you indoors before we all get soaked."

I tossed my bag in the back and climbed in.

"Name's McKellar. Welcome to the Margo Islands," he said shaking my hand as he drove. "It's a hell of a place."

CHAPTER 4

MARGO ISLANDS

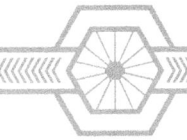

The trees blurring past the windshield were not really trees. The under-growth was green and leafy, but not like anything I recognized from home. For the first time since leaving Earth, I felt like I was no longer on Earth. It was early evening, but I couldn't tell if the growing darkness was from the late hour, the green wall of plant life crowding the narrow road climbing up from the cove, or the thick misty clouds rolling off the peak to the northwest.

"The original survey team built everything right there by the water. It must have been really convenient for them until the first big storm blew in and they had to scramble for higher ground in the middle of the night." The Sergeant laughed. "They had to rebuild from scratch up on Big Falls Terrace."

"Terrace?"

"That's what the surveyors named it. It's big and it's flat, and we built a camp on it on one side of the valley and the engineers are digging up the other side for gravel to build roads and make concrete for the new run-ways. 'Terrace' makes it sound grand, doesn't it? At least the mud isn't too bad across most of it."

The PFS had laid out the camp along several hundred meters of gravel road. The buildings had a typical prefabricated look about them, shiny tan composite showing the effects of harsh sun and too much rain. We stopped at the first structure. Sergeant McKellar and I got out and he squinted up at the clouds as we walked up onto the covered porch.

"We've just made it." As he spoke the rain started, heavy and warm coming straight down out of the clouds. I stood there a moment watching the lights coming on around the camp while the Sergeant pointed out its main features.

"This is Platoon Headquarters and infirmary, up the road there is the Post Exchange, chow hall, survey team quarters, the lab, and at the end of the road are the barracks for the enlisted."

"What are the lights by themselves up slope toward the mountain?" I asked.

"Armory and explosives storage."

"Explosives?"

"Your explosives, for doing seismic surveys."

"Ah."

"And clearing brush. Also fishing, when we can borrow a few to dump in the ocean. Beats standing around all day with a pole."

I laughed. The rain suddenly got heavier and the camp disappeared.

"Does it do this every day?"

"Sure. Sometimes it starts like this and just keeps going at it all week."

"Doesn't really cool things down, does it?"

"Does wonders for the humidity, though. We best get you in to see the Lieutenant. He'll want to be done and on his way to dinner soon."

Lieutenant Jeffers sat behind a desk that, like everything else in the room, matched the prefab worn look of the exterior. An air conditioner hummed loudly somewhere in the ceiling. Jeffers looked up as we entered.

"Holloman, glad you made it." He glanced up at a clock mounted above the door. "Chow hall closes in twenty minutes and I imagine you're as hungry as I am after your long trip." He passed a badge to me that had the same picture of me as my RuComm identity. "Keep this with you. It will grant access to the areas of the camp where you need to work and to your quarters. We gave you Parker's old unit right next to the lab. Major Kilpatrick said that you would need a full set of clothes, so you'll find them in your quarters. If they don't fit or you need anything else let McKellar know and we'll have the quartermaster print it for you."

He looked from me to McKellar and back to me again. "Questions?"

Realizing that I didn't know enough to have any questions, I replied, "None at this time." It was better than what I was thinking, which was, *what in the hell am I doing here?*

We stepped back out on to the porch and the Lieutenant selected an umbrella out of a tall bucket by the stairs. "See you at the chow hall."

McKellar shook his head. "He does hate being late for dinner."

We watched him for a moment and McKellar handed me an umbrella. It smelled moldy and wet when I opened it.

"Sergeant, can I ask you a question? What the hell am I doing here?"

McKellar laughed. "You seem like a bright boy. You'll figure it out."

We walked down the stairs into the rain and crunched along the gravel path following the distant figure of Lieutenant Jeffers.

The chow hall was crowded despite the Lieutenant's concerns. Most of the tables were full and the conversations loud and friendly. Whatever was on the menu smelled wonderful to me. I picked up a tray and followed McKellar through the line.

"Fish again?" He picked up a plate, looking disgusted.

"You're on an island, Sergeant, fish or synthetics, take your pick. Here, put some of these on it." The cook ladled a scoop of purplish tubes full of little air pockets on top of the fish.

"A friend of mine always eats those," I remarked. "I didn't know they were from Dulcinea."

As we exited the line with our trays, the Sergeant pointed at one of the tables with his elbow. "That's your survey team. I'll leave you to them."

"Thank you, Sergeant, you've been a big help."

He nodded and went to a table on the other side of the room where his friends greeted him with an obscene comment and laughter.

I approached the table where three members of the team were eating together, the others I assumed having finished and left.

"Hi, I'm Ted Holloman, mind if I join you?"

The man seated with his back to me didn't turn around, but said to his companions in mock horror, "It's the man from RuComm. I'll bet he's come to save us." He turned to look at me, dark eyes shining above a full beard touched with gray. "What if we don't want to be saved, RuComm man?"

I stood there stupidly holding my tray not sure how to respond. The woman on his right saved me.

"Have a seat Ted and feel free to ignore Marcus. I'm Lydie Debreaux, petroleum geology, stratigraphy, and bit of chemistry on the side. It's a small team so we all double up and more. That's Helen Weir," Helen raised her hand, "mineralogy and seismology. And Marcus Wright, biology, herpetology and cynicism."

"So the rest of the team has already finished dinner?" I asked. Helen and Lydie looked at each other while Marcus made a snorting sound.

"You're looking at it," he answered. "There were once twenty of us with a couple of guards. Now there're thirty guards, a military construction battalion, and just us three, I mean four," he corrected himself with an exaggerated bow of his head in my direction, "now that you're here to replace the dearly departed Parker." He placed his hand over his heart.

"He's dead?" I asked.

"No, just departed."

"What about your geophysicist? Professor Vandermeer said you had a good one."

"Huh." Marcus did not try to hide an expression of disgust. "Alice is *not* one of us." I must have looked confused so he continued. "The Professor didn't tell you that she's his daughter, did he. Typical."

"So if she's not here with the survey team..."

Marcus started to answer, but Helen cut him off. "Marcus' version would take until morning, so let me give you the short take. Alice has advanced degrees in geophysics, marine biology, and probably a couple of other things we're unaware of. I guess that comes from having two college professors as your parents.

"Anyway, a couple of years ago she had a bit of a personal crises and decided that her scientific studies were for naught. She went away and came back to Palma Sola a few months ago an ordained preacher with plans to leave for Bodens Gate as a missionary. Somehow, General Barrows found out about her and drafted her to come to the Margo Islands as a chaplain. Why her, I have no idea. She's a bit...different. But she's been helpful at times."

One piece of the puzzle suddenly clicked into place while Helen was talking. I looked at Marcus thinking that his cynicism might already be affecting me. "Of course," I said, "Alice is here so I would come."

"Oh? And how does that work?" Marcus wanted to know.

"Professor Vandermeer is the liaison for arranging RuComm support. Barrows knows that RuComm would never consent to being involved with a situation this volatile, so he had to make sure the Professor kept us in the dark until the last minute. Having Alice here gave him the leverage he needed. I found out I was coming to the Margo Islands at 08:00 this morning."

Marcus smiled. "Damn, I might have to start liking you, Mr. RuComm. That's just the sort of thing that bastard Barrows would do. So why does he want you here so badly?"

I took a bite of my fish before answering. Those purplish things really were pretty good with it. "I have no idea. I need to think about it some more. I've had enough unpleasant surprises for one day. I guess this one can wait."

"Would you like to get together at the lab tomorrow morning? We can try to bring you up to date on the survey results," Lydie offered.

I nodded.

"We're on tropical time here, so how about we meet at 09:00? It will give you a chance to adapt."

"Perfect."

We walked out onto the chow hall's porch after dinner. The rain had stopped and the sky was clear and full of stars. I looked at them briefly, wondering if my own sun was one of them. We walked down the stairs and Marcus turned off to the right while Lydie and Helen walked with me up the hill toward my quarters. "Marcus?" I asked, looking behind us.

"NCO club on the other side of the hill," Lydie answered. "They have better beer."

"The 'hill'?" I asked while we walked.

"The OP camp is just a kilometer away, up over the ridge. Marcus likes their beer better than ours."

"And Sergeant Jessica Villanueva is there," Helen added, smiling.

"I thought there was some... rivalry between you and the OP."

"Oh, there is in the capitals. Here mud is the common enemy. And boredom. We all get together for a binge, a big all night party, every week or so. Helen and I know some of their survey team from symposiums in years past. Now we get together, commiserate, and drink. And the military folk? Well, both the OP and PFS have men and women here, teenagers for the most part. Any excuse for a party is a good one. They're also finding out that they aren't as different as their officers in the capitals are telling them."

We stopped in front of my cabin. "Thanks," I said. "I guess I'll see you in the morning." Then, thinking of the daily report that I still had to write, I asked, "Oh, by the way, who's your team lead?"

Lydie and Helen exchanged a quick glance and I was silently praying, *please don't let it be Marcus.*

"You are," Helen said.

I started laughing and the two of them smiled at me.

"Sorry, Ted, I guess we still had one more surprise for you. When Parker left a week ago we were told that someone from RuComm would be leading the survey for the next two months."

I tipped my head back. "You know, the stars here are very beautiful."

Lydie and Helen followed my gaze. "Yes, they are. Have a good night, Ted."

"Goodnight."

I was still chuckling to myself when I opened the door and went inside. A bundle of clothes and fresh linens were sitting on the bed, the AC was humming, all of the lights worked and the toilet flushed. Surprising. If anything, the room was nicer than at the Hilton, really more of a decent sized apartment. Not bad, but I still didn't know why I was there or what I was supposed to be doing.

But first things first. I ripped open the package of clothing, found a comfortable looking t-shirt and pair of shorts and quickly changed. I left my dress clothes in a pile on the floor. Next, I sat at the kitchen table and pulled my display pad out of my bag. I connected to *Wandering Star*, and through her requested a secure connection to Jake.

Hannah answered.

"Well, look at you," she smiled. "How was your day?"

"You and Jake might have had a day. I had a week."

I brought them up to date. Jake was jealous of my time on the seaplane, and I wasn't surprised that Hannah thought she remembered meeting Howard once in Palma Sola. We talked about the heat and humidity and rain and mud and my newfound fondness for purplish plants with dinner. I wondered how it was possible to feel lonely while I was talking to the two people I was missing the most. Ultimately, the conversation turned to the more serious situation of me being trapped on the Margo Islands.

"Jake, how large a survey team would you expect there to be here?"

"A dozen at least, maybe more."

"Try three. Four now that I'm here. And not counting the geophysicist Professor Vandermeer promised me. It turns out she was recruited by General Barrows to be the camp chaplain instead. Oh, and she's also the Professor's daughter."

Hannah was just as quick to connect the dots as I had been. "Shit, Ted. Angela filled us in on what happened this morning. Have you told her about this yet?"

"Not yet. With all the chaos today I wanted some time seeing and talking to you, I mean to you and Jake, before getting a daily report created." I saw Hannah's eyes widen briefly at my verbal stumble.

"Ted, your biggest faults are that you are simple to read and you think everyone else is as honest as you are."

"Those are faults?"

"I love you for them, but yes, they are right now. Trust no one. And don't play poker while you're there."

"OK." We talked a while longer then I disconnected, wrote my report, and sent it off to Angela. I called her a few minutes later.

"Theodore," she said, "I've read it. I suppose now I'll have to forgive Professor Vandermeer given the circumstances. Do you have anything further to add?"

"No, I'm still trying to figure out why they want a RuComm person here so badly. I don't think there's much I can do here for the next few weeks that I couldn't have done at the University."

"Get some sleep and let me know if anything comes to you. I'll see what I can find out."

Sleep sounded like a great idea. It took only a few minutes to put a sheet on the bed and lie down with a blanket over me and a soft pillow beneath my head. But how was I supposed to fall asleep with everything that had happened and so many new problems? Sleep took me before I could remember what was supposed to be worrying me.

Several hours later, I was suddenly awake. The room was still dark except for a faint glow against the shades. I lay there a moment, listening. Nothing. My watch that I had set on the nightstand showed 02:38. Sighing, I got up and navigated in the dark to the kitchen looking for a drink of water.

The refrigerator was empty and the freezer held a single tray of ice cubes. Opening cupboards, I soon found a glass and better yet, a half bottle of something dark brown. I held it in the light from the fridge. The bottle was unfamiliar, but the *43% alcohol by volume* on the label looked promising. Putting a couple of ice cubes in the glass, I grabbed the bottle and stepped out onto the front porch. It was still warm, twenty-five degrees or more. I sat on the front step, poured some of whatever it was into my glass and tried a sip. It had a smoky, peaty flavor. I raised the glass in a silent toast, *God bless you, Parker, wherever you are.*

Somewhere out in the forest animals were calling to each other, whether insect-like or bird-like I had no idea, but from my front porch, it was a peaceful sound. Dulcinea's larger moon was low in the sky and the stars were as bright as any I had seen on a desert night at home.

The crunch of gravel interrupted my moment of peace as a figure approached down the middle of the road. She was incredibly slight, as many on Dulcinea are due to the lower gravity. She seemed to be mostly thin legs and thin arms; a woman composed of straight vertical lines and sharp angles, clad in t-shirt and shorts. She called to me while still in front of the lab building next-door in a soft voice as though she knew me, her voice carrying easily in the dense night air.

"Trouble sleeping, Ted? I'm usually the only one up at this hour."

"It seemed too beautiful a night to miss it sleeping," I lied. She came up the steps and sat down next to me. "Would you like a drink?" I offered. "I can get you a glass."

"No, don't bother, this is fine."

She picked up the bottle and drank. Her face was much like the rest of her; high cheekbones, angular features, and eyes that seemed to have been caught mid-laugh and sort of stayed that way. She put the bottle down and leaned back on her elbows, thin legs stretched out down the stairs. I could not help but smile at her.

"Do I look that odd to you?"

"No, not at all." I could feel myself blush.

"My dad is right about you."

"How so?"

"He said that you're a terrible liar."

"He doesn't know me that well. We only spent a couple of hours together."

"Sometimes that's enough." She paused, looking up at the stars. "And your boss told him the same thing." She grinned at me.

I refilled my glass. "I was hoping to get a couple more hours of sleep tonight."

"I thought you said the night was too beautiful."

"It is. What are you doing out this late?"

"I was on my way to pray. I have a favorite spot for the nights when I can't sleep. Come with me." She stood and reached her hand out to me.

"Why not?" I took her hand. "Can we drink while we pray?"

"Absolutely." She picked up the bottle and we crossed the street.

"Is it far?"

"No, just across the street and down the slope a few meters to where the terrace drops off toward the sea."

We passed beside Lydie and Helen's cabin opposite mine, and squished through mud for fifty meters before coming to a couple of wide chairs and a table. Looking behind me, I could still make out my cabin by moonlight. I sat in one of the chairs while Alice perched on the edge of the table. Below us was the cove where I'd arrived, the small seaplane shining white at anchor by the dock. I could just hear the sound of gentle surf on the beach.

I finished my drink and poured another, which I didn't really need. I could feel the effect of the first two rapidly spreading mist through my brain.

"Alice?" I tipped my head back to look at her and she looked down at me. "You are Alice, right?"

She grinned at me, eyes crinkling almost shut.

"Your dad said you're a geophysicist and the most brilliant student he's ever had. The team here mentioned marine biology and maybe more. Why did you give that up?"

She took another sip from the bottle. "How much of this have you already had?"

"Sorry. I don't mean to offend you, but I want to know."

"You want to know. That right there was the defining credo of my youth. I wanted to know... everything." She spread her arms wide, the bottle still in her left hand sloshing. "I grew up on campus with two professors for parents and I learned everything they threw at me. I'm really, really good at it."

She looked behind us, up toward the peak. "Listen. Do you hear them? I can tell you the names and habits of every creature that sings in the night. I'll take you to the tide pools tomorrow. I know all about the critters that live in them. And then there's geology. That's my dad's passion, so I made it mine. When I walk on the beach or up here on the terrace or climb the trails, I see..." She sighed. "I don't see the beauty, just the processes that create it. I can't *not* see the stratigraphy and the erosion and deposition and tectonic uplift and, well, that was my dilemma. I knew the creation so well that I could no longer hear the creator."

She drank from the bottle again and wiped her mouth on the back of her hand. "Do you know the passage in Luke where the leaders tell Jesus to rebuke his disciples for making too much noise and he says, 'if they remain silent, the very stones will cry out'? Well, the stones cried out."

"The stones cried out to you?"

"Not literally." She drank again. "I don't hear voices, and I don't think I'm crazy."

I nodded. "So now you're the chaplain for a bunch of soldiers far from home."

She sighed. "I was supposed to be on Bodens Gate doing missionary work. Do you know Bodens Gate? There's a lot of work to be done there." She suddenly sounded very sad.

"A little. It's the third stop for *Wandering Star*. A resupply stop. But what about here? General Barrows must believe you're needed."

"No, General Barrows needed leverage over my father."

"Do you know why?"

"No, but now you're here so I suppose he has leverage over the Reunification Commission as well."

I swallowed the rest of my third glass. "I don't think I'm that important to them. Not the way you are to your dad."

"Dizzy now." She laid back on the table and we spent the next few minutes in silence looking at the stars. I glanced over my shoulder at her and yes, Alice was a bit different, as Lydie had said. A sweet kind of different maybe, but definitely unique. I reached for the bottle, and thought better of it. I closed my eyes and slept in the fading moonlight with Alice stretched out on the table behind me sleeping, or maybe praying. I dozed for a couple of hours, my thoughts wandering.

There was a crunching of feet on gravel again, distant, getting closer. It woke me, and I turned around. Alice was still unmoving. Someone walked up my stairs, set a package down by the door, and then came back down the stairs. Crunch of gravel, and then he repeated the procedure at the lab building.

"Alice?" I whispered, "You awake?"

"Hmm."

"Do you get deliveries of anything in the mornings? Like milk or something?"

She rolled her head over and opened one eye to look at me. "No."

I pointed up toward the buildings. "Well, we are this morning."

"That's my cabin," she said as the figure came down her stairs.

A horrible realization hit me and shivers ran down my arms and legs.

"No." I rolled out of the chair and started running. I was chanting 'no' over and over again as if it would make the reality of what was happening go away. I rounded in front of Lydie and Helen's cabin just as the figure was coming down their stairs, a figure I could now see was short and wearing a uniform.

I was closing on him fast when the first explosion went off behind me. My cabin. I could feel the heat on my back. The second explosion hit the lab at the same time I collided with the soldier's back at full speed. I wrapped my arms around him and rode him into the mud where we slid for a couple of meters. I don't think he ever heard me coming. The third explosion went off, then the fourth, way too close, leaving my ears ringing as bits of building and dirt fell all around us.

Rolling off him, I grabbed the soldier's arm and flipped him over. No, not him, her. I was looking at the mud-covered face of a girl of not more than eighteen or nineteen. She was gasping for air, eyes not quite able to focus on me. She reached up toward me and managed a hoarse whisper.

"You're dead."

Alice had caught up by then and the girl looked at her.

"You're dead too," she said. She seemed to find it funny and started to laugh, but only a gurgle came out. She closed her eyes and tried to cough.

"I think I broke a couple of her ribs. She needs a medic."

Sergeant McKellar arrived along with what seemed to be everyone else on the island. He knelt down next to her and wiped some of the mud off her face. "Sweet Jesus, you've about crushed the life from her."

The remains of Lydie and Helen's cabin were behind him. An arm was dangling out of the front window, partially concealed by clouds of black smoke and flame. I closed my eyes, the effects of adrenaline, too much scotch, and little sleep starting to catch up with me.

The medical team arrived and McKellar helped lift the girl on to a stretcher where they started to work stabilizing her. I was still sitting on the ground absently picking at the layers of mud on my leg. One of the medics mentioned that the girl was wearing an OP uniform, although it was hard to see with all the mud on her.

That got a couple of the others excited and someone issued orders for guards and lights. I looked up at the stretcher. The bottoms of the girl's boots were a meter from my head. There were so many layers of mud on them that I couldn't even see the pattern of the tread.

"OK, let's get her indoors and cleaned up," McKellar ordered.

"No." I stood up. "Wait. I want her pants." All motion and talking ceased as everyone tuned to look at me.

"You want what?" McKellar asked, his tone hostile.

"And her boots," I continued. "The layers of mud on them might help us figure out who she is and where she got the explosives."

"She's wearing an OP uniform and she has a bag full of explosives just like the ones they use for doing surveys."

Alice stepped forward. She was shaking, quivers that seemed to start at her shoulders and move down her body in waves, but her voice was steady. "A crime has been committed, Sergeant. Don't destroy the evidence."

The medics looked from her to him, waiting for orders. "Fine, you can have the pants and boots. Do you mind if we try to save the girl's life first?"

"I'll go with you," Alice replied. "I'm a certified medical tech."

"Of course you are."

They loaded the stretcher into the truck and left down the hill, leaving me there to watch the crews working to extinguish the fires. My cabin, along with my display pad, watch, ID badge, and new clothes were in a molten pool of plastic composite. I had no idea where to go next.

"Mr. RuComm, you look like shit."

"Marcus." I gestured toward the burning cabin next to me, but no words would come. I could feel tears coming down my face. I hadn't cried since I was ten when Jake had hit me in the stomach.

"I know. Lydie. Helen. I think I was supposed to be next, but someone interrupted the assassin. I should thank you for that."

I nodded, and the slight motion was more than my head could stand. I found myself on all fours throwing up in the middle of the street. Scotch, fish, purple plants, everything came back out. Marcus waited for me to finish.

He reached his hand down to help me up. "Since your cabin seems to be having some issues, why don't you come with me? Have a shower, and I can loan you some clean clothes that won't fit. I'm sure the Lieutenant will want to talk with you whenever he makes it back from over the hill and gets himself organized. You might as well be presentable."

"Thanks, Marcus." The sun was just coming up as we walked.

"By the way, how is it that you're not dead?" he asked

"You know the table and chairs over by the edge of the terrace?" Marcus nodded. "I was down there with Alice drinking scotch and talking."

"I'd have paid money to see that."

We arrived at Marcus' cabin. I showered and changed, trying not to see the images that kept replaying in my mind of burning buildings, an arm hanging out a shattered window frame, and the muddy face of the girl that had tried to kill me.

"Why don't you have a seat? I'm going to go snoop around and see what's happening. Fix something to eat if you want. I know your stomach is empty."

"Thanks, I will." I drank a glass of water and sat on the couch with my feet up trying to gather the energy to find some food. I failed. As I collapsed into unconsciousness, Hannah's voice came to me, scolding, *why do you trust Marcus? He could kill you in your sleep.* Too late. I was asleep.

Around 10:00, the sound of the front door slamming woke me. I looked over the back of the couch at Marcus coming in.

"Finally awake I see. I brought you a present." He tossed a bundle of clothes to me. "There's a new ID badge in there too. And I brought you this." He held up a new backpack. "It's military standard issue, so it's probably crap, but it's better than what you have now. There's a new display pad and watch in it, also standard issue, so probably also crap. And a toothbrush. You may want to start with that, and then change into clothes that fit you. Lieutenant Jeffers and Lieutenant Recano of the OP are eager for your company. Alice and I have been holding them off all morning."

"Thanks, Marcus." I went in to the bedroom to change, calling back to him. "So what's going on out there?"

"Well, no one is shooting at anybody else yet, but that's probably a matter of time. The woman, Fiona Monroe is the name she gave, is still alive, but with six broken ribs, a punctured lung, and a concussion. Remind me not to make you mad. Lieutenant Recano is claiming not to know who she is and no one remembers ever seeing her before. Alice secured her uniform and boots for you."

Marcus chuckled. "I gotta tell you, that's a scene I'll remember forever, you standing in the middle of the street covered in mud yelling that you want her pants."

"I was yelling?"

"Yeah, I think your hearing was still messed up from the blast."

I paused. "Maybe I should have had someone check me out."

"Alice scanned you while you were sleeping. You're fine."

"Really? I don't remember that." I came out of the bedroom wearing a nicer shirt and shorts with lots of pockets. "Better?"

Marcus shrugged.

"Now I am starving," I said.

"Yeah, well now there's no time." He opened the fridge. "Take a pasty to eat while we walk." He handed me a cold doughy pocket full of something that smelled OK.

We stepped out onto the front porch. The three buildings across the street, mine and Alice's quarters, and the lab, were still smoldering. The soldiers had covered Lydie and Helen's cabin with tarps that hid everything from view, but did nothing to block out the images playing in my mind.

"You OK?"

I realized I was still standing on the porch. "Yeah, fine. Lead on." Marcus talked while I ate, but my appetite was not what it'd been five minutes earlier.

"The Foundation for Margo Islands Development wants me out of here as soon as possible. You might want to contact your boss soon. She's been calling about every ten minutes. I imagine they want you evacuated too."

"No."

"No? They're even pulling the construction battalion out."

"Does any of this make sense to you, Marcus? At dinner, everyone told me how well the two teams got along, that the only animosity was in the capitals, not on the island. Now the OP wants to kill your survey team?"

"If it's not the OP then who?" Marcus took another couple of steps then stopped. "Damn, Ted, you think this is a false flag? '*Innocent Scientists and Chaplain Killed in OP Surprise Attack*'." He sighed. "The church has a lot of pull in Palma Sola. We'll be at war inside a week. And killing you will drag the Reunification Commission in on our side, or at least keep them neutral." We started walking again.

"Alice told me last night that I was here because General Barrows wanted leverage over RuComm. Alive, I don't give him that, but dead I take on a whole lot more significance."

"So you want to stay here in a military encampment on the edge of war, to prove that our commanding General is a traitor and a terrorist?"

I shrugged.

"Get on the plane, Ted. Get on the plane and fly out of here. Let them burn."

A patrol of five soldiers in full kit passed us going the other direction, all of them younger than me, and all of them looking miserable in the tropical heat and humidity.

"I can't. We have to figure out what really happened."

We reached Platoon HQ where Alice was sitting on the steps, thin legs stretched out into the sun, her eyes closed. "Besides, what would I tell her father?" I held out my hand to help her up and we all went inside.

Marcus muttered, "I always suspected that stupidity was a requirement for joining RuComm."

The two Lieutenants were sitting together talking quietly, heads almost touching. When I entered, they both stood.

"Mr. Holloman, let me introduce you to Lieutenant Britt Recano with the OP Defense Force."

I took her hand and it felt cold in mine. Looking into her eyes, I saw that she was far more than tense or concerned. She was scared.

Jeffers didn't look any better. Only Sergeant McKellar seemed relaxed as he working at a desk in the corner.

"Mr. Holloman, I want to assure you that the person responsible for this attack is not part of my command and that we'll cooperate in a full investigation in any way possible," Lieutenant Recano told me.

"Does Lieutenant Recano's uniform look familiar, Holloman? It's the same as the girl's that you crushed into the mud this morning," Sergeant McKellar commented.

"That will be enough, McKellar." Lieutenant Jeffers ordered. His voice was a little higher than it should have been.

The Lieutenants were looking at me expectantly. As the personification of the Reunification Commission, they were assuming I was in charge, at least until senior officers said otherwise.

Deep breath, I told myself, prioritize. "Fiona Monroe is the key to this. We need to know who she is, how she got here, where she got the explosives, and whose orders she's following."

"Too bad she's unconscious or you could question her." McKellar again.

"There may be enough indirect evidence that we don't need to. You have her clothes and the charges she didn't have time to set off?" I asked, looking at Alice.

"Yes, but there are no instruments to do any forensic analysis." She gestured with her hands. "Boom."

"What exactly are you trying to prove, Mr. Holloman?" Lieutenant Recano asked.

Marcus answered for me. "If we can't prove that she acted without, what shall we call it, official sanction? Be prepared for the shooting to start. I plan to be off this island by then, but you two Lieutenants might care."

"We need weeks to do this right, collect soil samples from all over both camps and a full lab to do the work." I turned to Lieutenant Jeffers. "I don't suppose replacement instruments will be forthcoming."

He shook his head.

"It could be done at the University in Palma Sola or onboard *Wandering Star*, but it would take too long."

"What about my lab?" Lieutenant Recano asked.

"Holloman! I have your boss calling again. Are you going to take it this time?" McKellar detached his display and turned it so Angela's unhappy face was looking back at me. "She's got your boss with her too, Marcus."

I took the display from McKellar and muted it. "Is there someplace we can go that's a little more private?"

"Down the hall, last door on the right."

"Was he smirking?" I asked as Marcus followed me down the hall.

"Hard to tell with his face."

The office we entered had a large window looking into the infirmary. Fiona Monroe was restrained and unconscious with tubes and wires attached to her. A display showed her current condition and a close up image of her face. I found myself looking at her, momentarily frozen. She had brown hair and freckles on her nose, dark against pale skin.

"That McKellar is a thoroughgoing bastard," Marcus observed.

I put the display pad on the desk and unmuted.

"Theodore, you're looking better than I expected. We're working on getting you out of there, but you're about to be in the middle of a very big storm."

"It's tense here, but I don't think anything drastic will happen right away."

Angela gave me a small smile. "You think I'm being metaphorical. There's a major hurricane less than two hundred kilometers northwest of you. Inbound air and sea transportation is shut down until it passes sometime in the next two or three days. Theodore, why are you looking at me like that's good news?"

I told her what evidence we had gathered and what we hoped to be able to prove.

Angela was not impressed. "I've been involved in forensic investigations. You need weeks, not two days in the middle of a hurricane."

"Marcus," his boss added, "tell me that you're not thinking about just handing over all of our evidence to the OP."

"Yes, Trevor, that's exactly what I'm going to do."

I was looking at Monroe's face on the monitor while they argued. I could hear her voice in my head saying *you're dead* over and over again. After Marcus had threatened to quit for the third time his boss acquiesced, I think mostly because he expected Marcus to be dead soon anyway.

"Angela," I asked, "what's the mood there in Palma Sola?"

"Confused, scared, and angry. Trending more toward angry as time passes."

"Can RuComm do anything to slow that down? We need time."

Angela shook her head. "I don't know. I can talk to General Barrows."

"Um, Angela, he may not be the one you want to talk to if I'm right about this."

Angela closed her eyes. "I'll see what I can do. Maybe. Anything else?"

"I think I need Hannah. I just realized something. Marcus, the way Lieutenant Recano talks, it sounds sort of like southern Louisiana, Gulf Coast to me, if we were on Earth. Is her accent typical OP?"

"I suppose."

"When Monroe talked to me she sounded like everyone I've met in Palma Sola."

"How much did she say?" Angela asked.

"Just two words, but she said them twice."

"Very, very, thin."

"I know, but it fits. I need Hannah to talk to her when she wakes up. It might help us figure this out."

Angela sighed. "No travel, remote only."

"Thanks." We disconnected and I turned to look at Monroe again. She was so young.

"You act like you're feeling sorry for what you did," Marcus said.

"I've never hurt anyone like that before. I don't know what I'm feeling."

"Why? Because she's a young, pretty girl? You need to get over it, or next time you might hesitate and get yourself or one of your friends killed. Someone like me. Her life is over anyway."

"I imagine she'll be behind bars for a very long time." I sighed.

He chuckled without humor. "No, a very short time. She'll have a very quick trial and a quicker execution. It won't matter which side she was working for. The real kindness would have been for you to have killed her there in the mud."

I was feeling very far from home as we left the office to rejoin the others.

CHAPTER 5

MARGO ISLANDS MUD

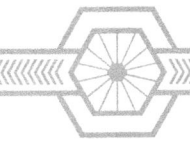

When we came back into the office only the Lieutenants were still there.

"Where's Alice?"

"She and McKellar are at the chow hall," Lieutenant Jeffers answered. "I ordered her to make herself available for any personnel that want to talk to her. It's her duty as our chaplain."

"Have you reached an agreement on using Lieutenant Recano's lab? I'd like to get started on the analysis of Monroe's boots and clothing while we have others collecting soil samples. I hear there's a storm coming and I want to collect as much as we can before the weather shuts us down."

Jeffers looked away from me toward Lieutenant Recano while he answered. "I'm waiting for approval to turn the uniform over to you for analysis."

"OK, we can start on soil samples then. Lieutenant Recano, did your survey team do any analysis around the camp areas or will we be doing this from scratch?"

Recano looked at Jeffers while she answered. "I am not at liberty to share survey data with personnel outside the Oceanus Protectorate until authorized by the proper authorities."

Her stress level seemed to be even higher now. Her accent was more noticeable as she stretched out her vowels and clipped the end of her words. I wished Hannah was there with me to hear it.

"And your survey team?" I asked, already knowing the answer.

"All OP personnel are required to stay on our side of the hill until further notice."

"Lieutenant Jeffers?"

"Lieutenant Recano and I received similar orders ten minutes ago."

"Do your orders mention RuComm personnel?"

"Not explicitly, but I would encourage you to stay close."

I looked at Marcus. "So, no access to the uniform, no access to the instruments we need to analyze the uniform, no one to collect new soil samples, no access to OP's existing samples and all of the PFS samples destroyed. Who would have backups of the PFS data?"

He smiled sardonically. "Professor Vandermeer at the University. Do you have a game on Earth called dominoes? Little tiles that you set up and then one falls and hits the next one that hits the next one, until they all fall down?"

"All it takes to break the chain is to remove one of the tiles before it falls," I answered.

"Very optimistic when the last tile is on the way down."

"I need to talk to Alice." Marcus opened the front door for me and we stepped out onto the porch.

Marcus paused, still holding the door. "Oh, Lieutenant Recano, are you headed back over the hill now?"

"Not just yet," she answered, still looking at Jeffers. Marcus let the door slam behind us.

"That wasn't very nice."

Marcus shook his head, smiling. "Star crossed lovers. Let me have some fun in the few hours of life I have left."

"I thought there was someone over the hill that you were friends with too."

"There is," he answered as his smile disappeared. "Several."

Alice was sitting at a table off to one side of the chow hall eating lunch with four soldiers. Another three stood by listening to her talk.

"Huh. Looks like Alice has doubled her congregation since last Sunday," Marcus commented.

"She's not popular with the soldiers?"

"Um, no. We have a hundred young men and women on this island who do what you would expect young men and women to do. When they see our chaplain, they feel guilty about what they've been doing. So they avoid her and keep doing what they've been doing. Then they don't feel quite so guilty about it. That and, well, it's Alice."

We walked over to her table. "Chaplain, may Marcus and I speak with you privately for a few minutes?"

"Of course, Mr. Holloman." She squeezed the hand of the young man sitting next to her. "If you will all please excuse me for a moment."

We stepped out onto the porch. The air was hot, heavy and still.

"Hurricane weather," Alice commented. "It's always like this before the big storms move in, so I've heard. It should buy you a couple of extra days at least. Almost an answer to prayer, wouldn't you say?"

"You're taking credit for the weather now?" Marcus challenged.

"I only ask. God provides."

I interrupted before Marcus could reply, and told Alice how we had been outmaneuvered. "Alice, can you get the soil data from your father, assuming they exist?"

Alice looked out across the camp for several long seconds before answering. "You made a plan, Ted, and General Barrows has destroyed it. Stop focusing on the plan. Trying to put the pieces back together is a waste of time. Go back to what you were trying to prove in the first place and come up with a new plan using the resources still left to you."

"Well, that's helpful," Marcus replied. "So with no resources, I predict we'll have no results."

I ignored him. "Our goal is to convince enough people that Monroe's attack was a false flag, an inside job by rogue elements inside the Palma Federated States. We might be able to do that by showing she was supplied by the PFS and not the OP."

"Or we can get her to confess." There was a hard look in Marcus' eyes as he said it.

"What lines of evidence do we control?" Alice asked.

"Control? None. Those we might have access to?" I ticked them off on my fingers. "One, soil on her uniform. It should all be from the PFS camp, not anything from over the hill. Two, the chemical composition of the survey charges should *not* match the existing stock of OP charges. Three, if the PFS printed her uniform, it won't match OP standard issue. And four, I think she's faking her OP accent. I have a friend who might be able to verify that if Monroe wakes up and if we can get her to talk."

"OK, so what is your new plan?"

I shook my head. "Without a mass spectrometer, about all I can do is try to prove her accent is fake and that won't convince anyone."

"Or we can get her to confess," Marcus added again.

Alice closed her eyes. "There's a polarizing microscope in the infirmary. It might give us good enough data to at least make everyone pause."

"Maybe. If Lieutenant Jeffers will let us use it."

"I suspect that the Lieutenant will be otherwise occupied, so don't ask, just go back there and take it."

"OK," I said doubtfully, thinking *and if he tries to stop us?*

"Marcus," she continued, leaning in close to him, "please don't open the door to Lieutenant Jeffers' private office, no matter what you hear."

Marcus laughed. "All right. That's not something I want to see anyway."

"Go, and be quick about it. Sergeant McKellar is still at lunch. I'll keep him here as long as possible."

"McKellar?" I asked.

Alice looked at me with the same look of sympathy my friend Kaelyn used when I was being especially dense. "Ted, who do you think has been relaying your every move to General Barrows?" She put her hand on my shoulder, looking into my eyes. "Who do you think was on duty last night in the armory where the survey charges are stored?"

"Oh."

"Take the samples you need, but leave the uniform and bag of explosives in the Platoon HQ or they'll be missed. I doubt anyone will miss the microscope with everything else going on. I'll meet you at Marcus' cabin when my duties here are completed."

"We could use your help," I pleaded. Alice already had her hand on the door to the chow hall.

"What good will it do for you to save their souls if they lose their lives?" Marcus called after her.

"Backwards, as usual, Marcus," she answered as the door closed behind her.

We stepped back down into the street. "Why do I feel like we should be running?" I asked.

"Because we should be if it wouldn't attract too much attention. Walk fast." Marcus looked over his shoulder at the chow hall. "You know, I get why we need Alice right now, but I will never like working with that woman. She is just–"

"Unique?" I offered.

"–weird," Marcus finished.

We walked softly onto the porch and slowly opened the door. No one was in sight, but there were definite sounds of life coming from the small private office. Marcus walked over, seemingly about to put his ear to the door.

"Marcus!" I whispered tapping my watch.

He shrugged and followed me down the hall. "On the edge of war, hurricane approaching, and this is how they spend their time."

We opened closets and lockers until we found what we were looking for. Marcus pulled out a pocketknife and cut three samples from the pants leg of Monroe's uniform and placed them in a small bag. He was about to scrape mud from the boot when I stopped him.

"Wait. Did you see any tape, the heavy duty kind, like fifty millimeters wide?" I asked.

"Yeah." He reached back into the closet and tossed the roll to me. "What for?"

I pulled a meter or more off the roll and stretched it across the floor, sticky side up. "Scrape the mud off slowly as you move the boot over the tape in one direction. We should be doing a core sample to get the individual layers, but this might work." Marcus scraped and the particles stuck to the tape I was holding. "Now put another piece of tape over the top, sticky side down to hold it all in place." I rolled the tape up and put it in my pack along with the uniform samples.

"Won't the glue on the tape contaminate your sample? Marcus asked.

"Probably. I'm making this up as we go."

We looked at the bag of survey charges with its warning label showing a stick figure engulfed in flames.

"I'm not too keen about opening one of those up to get a sample," Marcus remarked.

"The tampering would be obvious anyway." I reached in, took one of the three remaining tubes, and added it to my pack. "Let's just hope no one notices it's gone."

"Or the holes in the uniform."

"Right." I walked to the end of the hall and reached to open the door into the infirmary. Marcus placed his hand on the door, keeping it closed.

"Wait. Let's check first." He opened the door into the office we had used before with the window looking into the infirmary.

Fiona Monroe was awake, but looking groggy as she talked to the medical AI.

"That complicates things a little," I said.

"Listen, she's complaining about the restraints." We listened for a moment. "Normal OP accent, it sounds like to me." Marcus looked at me, eyebrow raised. "You better be right about this, Mr. RuComm."

"I need to record this." I fumbled in my pack, pulled out the display pad, and set it up. Marcus tapped on his watch to remind me of the time passing by.

After a couple of minutes, I shut it down and stuffed it back into my pack. "OK, that will have to do."

Marcus pointed at a row of desks along the far wall. "There's your microscope. It's small, thank God. I'll distract her while you shove it in your pack with everything else."

Marcus opened the door to the infirmary and walked to the foot of her bed while I circled around to the far side of the room.

"How much do you remember, Fiona?" Marcus asked, sitting on the end of the bed. The sympathy in his voice sounded genuine.

"Nothing, nothing at all," she answered weakly. "I had only just arrived on the Island and was out for a walk when, when... I don't know. Was I attacked?"

I tried to close my pack over the top of the microscope while I watched Marcus' sympathetic expression change into a cold smile.

He patted her leg tenderly. "You just try to get well. I wouldn't want you feeling poorly for your execution."

"You have to help me. Tell this machine to let go of me. Please."

"That won't be happening. And in your condition you would die without what it's doing for you." He tipped his head and leaned closer to her, pressing his hand down on her chest. "Of course you're going to die soon anyway. Maybe there's something you'd like to tell us that could change that?"

She didn't answer.

Marcus pushed down a little harder and she closed her eyes after a moment. Tears rolled silently down her cheeks.

I came over next to them. "We should leave."

"Nothing to say, Fiona?" He pulled his hand back and she gasped, trying to catch her breath. "Lieutenant Jeffers will be around should you change your mind."

Before we left, she whispered to me, "You're the one who hit me, aren't you?"

"Yes," I answered.

"Then my death is on your hands."

The door closed behind us while I struggled with my pack. "You didn't have to hurt her," I whispered.

"You best wake up, Mr. RuComm, or neither of us will live to see the sunrise. Let's go. We are way out of time."

Jeffers' door was still closed.

"The man has greater stamina than I gave him credit for," Marcus remarked. "One last thing." Marcus calmly walked over to Jeffers' desk where Lieutenant Recano's uniform jacket lay crumpled on the floor while I waited with my hand on the front door imagining the sound of footsteps coming up the stairs outside. He pulled out his pocketknife and carefully cut off a piece of fabric. He smiled and dropped the jacket back onto the floor. "Got to have something to compare."

"Can we leave now?" I whispered. "We should go around behind the buildings. We'd be less visible."

"No, it would look like we were up to something. Slow and steady, straight up the middle of the street." He glanced over at me. "And stop looking guilty. Smile. Laugh. Talk to me about the geology of the Margo Islands or something."

"OK." I thought a moment. "I don't know anything about the geology of the Margo Islands. I was supposed to take the data you collected and set up simulations and geomodels. Why don't you tell me what the survey team found? I never did get that briefing."

Marcus shook his head. "It was all pretty routine and quiet until you got here. A little bit of work during the day, and then a cold beer and warm company in the evening." He looked up at the mountain and out toward the seemingly endless ocean to our right. The seaplane that had brought me had just taken off and was circling the camp, getting out ahead of the storm.

"It *is* beautiful here." Marcus sighed as though he was seeing it for the first time or maybe for the last. "What we found was one of the last places on Dulcinea that isn't covered over by Earth biology. This is a place that should be preserved as it is. Not developed, not reclaimed, not corrupted."

"So why the rush to develop it? It must have something valuable to risk going to war."

"Not so much. The gravel we're walking on is the most valuable thing on the island. Great for making concrete runways. There might be some strategic value in the Margo's location, but I think it's mostly a case of 'we want it so you can't have it.'"

"People die for that?"

"It won't be the first time. We went through all this twenty years ago when over four thousand died."

"How did you manage to avoid total war that time?"

"The OP had sent a small assault team to blow up two transport ships in Palma Sola harbor, although the OP denied doing it. There was a young Marine Major on board a destroyer next to the ships and he saw the assault team trying to escape. He managed to intercept them and kill them all. Quite the hero. With over four-thousand dead and the OP denying everything, the statesmen on both sides were able to reach an agreement to avoid any more bloodshed, despite the urging of the heroic Major to launch a full attack on the OP."

"Must have made his career," I commented.

"Oh, it did. He went on to... to." Marcus stopped dead in the street and smiled. "He went on to become General Barrows. He was only a Major then."

"You think he's still looking for revenge?"

"That would be the charitable opinion."

"You think he was part of a plot that killed four thousand of his own soldiers?"

Marcus was silent as we continued past the burned out remains of the cabins.

"I don't like our odds," Marcus said as we climbed up his front steps.

"Of proving that this wasn't an OP attack?"

"Of surviving at all. You, me, and Alice, we should all have been on that plane that just left."

We watched as a patrol passed by, rifles slung and helmets on. Marcus raised his hand in greeting and called out, "You all are looking a bit warm with all that kit."

A couple of them waved back. "Just keep the beer cold for us, Marcus."

"I'll do that," he called back, then turning to me, "Well, they don't seem intent on hunting us down just yet, but it's still early."

I looked up and down the street at other groups patrolling. A pair of wheeled vehicles sat in front of the barracks at the end of the road with heavier weapons mounted on their backs.

I shifted my pack uncomfortably. "Can we dump this stuff inside? That tube of high explosives we stole is digging a hole in my spine."

"Sure." We went inside and emptied the contents of my pack on the kitchen table.

"I want to make sure the microscope survived the trip." I inserted the analyzer and polarizer and turned on the light source. "We'll need a bunch of small re-sealable bags and something to dig with for doing the soil samples. Do you have anything?"

"I've got bags that I use for collecting biological samples, but I'll need to print a couple of trowels. They'll be ready in ten minutes or so."

"That should give me time to make sure this thing is working." I pulled my display pad out and noticed two missed calls from Angela and three from Jake. I ignored them for the moment, synced the pad with the microscope, and placed one of the uniform samples on the stage. The image looked good.

"Which sample is that?" Marcus asked over my shoulder.

"Um, that's Lieutenant Recano's," I answered, checking the tag

"That's a textile, not printed."

"You're right. Is that true for all OP uniforms?"

Marcus pulled the sample off the stage and replaced it with one from Monroe's uniform.

"Printed." Marcus said, pointing at the synthetic matrix on the screen. "You can see it even through the dirt."

"One good data point. We still need to collect soil samples before the storm hits, as much as I want to pursue this right now."

I disconnected, looked at my missed messages and requested a secure connection to *Wandering Star*.

"Mr. Holloman," *Star* answered, "Angela Dawkins is very eager to speak with you."

"Before connecting her I have a couple of questions for you. I need to do some fieldwork. Can you tell me how much time I have before the weather closes in?"

"You should have about three and half hours. After that I recommend that you be indoors and on high ground."

"Thanks. Also, can you find out if all military uniforms used by the Oceanus Protectorate are fabric based or if they're printed?"

There was a barely perceptible pause. "The McLaren & Birch Textile Company has an exclusive contract to provide uniforms to the OP. They use a blend of wool and synthetic fibers and claim superior all weather performance and durability over printed garments."

"Thanks. I guess I'm ready for Angela."

"She is already on." *Star* replied.

Angela's image appeared on the screen. "It sounds like you've been busy, Theodore."

"Yes, ma'am. We've taken samples of both Monroe's uniform and a standard issue OP uniform, and we have soil samples from her boots and pants. And we have access to a polarizing microscope to do some basic analysis. All I need are local soil samples and we should be able to cast some doubt on this being an OP attack."

"Should I ask how you were able to get all of that?"

"Probably not. Please don't mention it outside the team, either."

"Evidence without provenance isn't worth much," she said frowning. "Theodore, is that a tube of survey explosives on the table next to you?"

"We didn't want to open it to take a sample so we took the whole thing," I explained. Angela had her eyes closed and was rubbing her temple with one hand.

I asked her, "Have you found anyone willing to listen to us about what we find?"

"I have a couple of members of the legislature and one reporter who are willing to listen. The political situation here isn't good, so you better be fast."

"Angela, I'd like to keep a link open to *Star* and as many members of the team as can stay on with us for the next couple of days. That way you can see the results as we get them and you'll know as much as possible in case we get interrupted."

Her eyes narrowed. "Interrupted? How safe are you?"

I thought a moment before answering. "I don't know, Angela. I think we're safe, but I really don't know."

"If there's someplace else you can go that *is* safe, do it. Forget the damn samples, Ted, and get out."

"Is that what you would do?"

She sighed. "We'll keep the link open. Go get your samples."

"Thanks. I haven't had time to contact Jake and he's been leaving a lot of messages. Can you please let him know I'm fine, just busy? Also, I have a recording of Monroe's voice that I just sent to *Star*. Can you have Hannah listen to it?"

"I will. Go do your digging and I'll see you in a couple of hours." She moved out of view, but the link remained active.

"Marcus, do you have a map of the camp area? We need to plot out where to take samples."

"Sure." He moved to a large display on the wall and tapped a few keys. The screen turned blue with the word 'RESTRICTED' in the center. "Well, I used to." He cleared the screen and detached a pen from the side of it. "This is the cove and dock area," he sketched black lines on the white background, "and the road up to the Patrol HQ and then past my cabin to the barracks. On the other side are the quarry and the trail over to the OP camp. Don't hold me accountable for this being to scale." He continued drawing in buildings and added a north arrow.

"It would take a week or more to sample the whole area. What route would you use if you were trying to sneak in unobserved, pick up some explosives and come down along the road?"

Marcus tapped the pen to change colors and added a green line. "Here, along the coast south of the quarry where the runways are being built. The crews don't work after dark. Then along the quarry access road to the main road by the Patrol HQ, then to the armory, and back down along the road past the chow hall." He looked up at me. "To your cabin."

"It would be more efficient collecting samples for you to start at one end and me at the other, but..."

"Feeling spooked?"

"Yeah, a bit."

"Fine. We'll start at the point where you planted Fiona's face in the mud and work backwards from there."

Did he have to say it that way? "We'll sample about every ten meters since that's all we have time for. Nothing fancy. Take a scoop of soil off the top, dump it into a bag and I'll seal and number it. Try to wipe off the trowel as much as possible between samples." We grabbed water bottles, towels and hats.

"Your people will be watching and listening the whole time?" Marcus was looking at all of our equipment set up on the table. "I'm not sure I like the idea of being monitored like that."

"Really? I guess on Earth we're just used to it. There's always an AI watching and listening. We just ignore it." We stepped out onto the porch.

"Another beautiful forty degree day in the Margo Islands," Marcus commented.

I looked at wispy clouds streaming around the peak. "Pray that it holds."

It didn't take long for us to attract the attention of passing patrols as we knelt digging in the middle of the road.

"Marcus! They finally found a job you're good at. Marcus! Are you keeping the streets clean for us now? Marcus! You missed a spot over here."

As we turned up the road to the armory, Marcus put his trowel down and said, "You owe me for this Mr. RuComm. Your turn to dig while I bag."

"I promise to buy you a beer if we live through this," I joked.

He squinted up at me from under his hat, not smiling. "You know, that would be a lot funnier if I expected to be alive tomorrow."

I took the trowel from him and wiped it on a towel. "Don't worry so much, these guys all seem to like you."

"Yeah, well, they liked the folks on the other side of the hill yesterday too."

We took turns digging and bagging, working up past the armory, down behind the chow hall to the Patrol HQ, and down the access road past the idled machinery at the quarry. The clouds became thicker and darker as we went. By the time we stood on the jetty looking at the runway the PFS was building along the south shore, the waves were banging hard against the rip-rap barrier protecting it.

"They're really serious about this, aren't they?"

"Yes. That they are," Marcus replied. "There used to be a nice beach here, the water full of little fish. This storm will be the first test for that rip-rap," he said pointing at the huge boulders. "My money is on the hurricane."

"We need to be headed back. I think my backpack is a good forty kilos heavier than when we started."

"What was the final count?"

"Um, one hundred sixty-two."

The rain caught us as we passed the chow hall, a fine mist driven hard enough by the wind to sting where it hit bare skin. We increased our speed to a trot, mud splashing our legs and the samples feeling heaver with each step. We ran up onto Marcus' porch and Alice was there waiting for us, curled into a ball trying to stay out of the rain.

"Why didn't you go inside?" Marcus shouted.

She held up her ID badge. "Doesn't work on your door."

Marcus pushed the door open and we tumbled in, the rain and wind following us until he was able to slam it shut again. "I'll grab some more towels."

"And a blanket," Alice added, still shaking.

"Do you own anything other than the clothes on your back?" I asked her.

"No."

I pointed toward the room I was borrowing. "There're some clean clothes scattered on the bed in there. At least put on a dry shirt."

Marcus returned and tossed a towel to me. "All our stuff is still here." He sounded surprised.

"You expected otherwise?"

"Yeah, I thought about trying to hide it before we left, but what would have been the use?"

Alice came back with her hair towel dried and wearing an oversized sweatshirt. She took a blanket from Marcus, wrapped it around herself, and sat in one of the kitchen chairs.

"You're still shaking. Do you want something hot to drink?" Marcus offered.

"No, thank you. It's not the cold. It's that I'm scared. I get scared easily. It takes me a while to get over it. I've always been this way."

Marcus looked at me and rolled his eyes. The lights in the cabin flicked once and came back on steady. Alice closed her eyes and a larger shiver passed through her.

I sat down in a chair next to her. "Tell me what happened."

"Oh, nothing new, nothing specific. It's just the three of us here now, all together, the three they tried to kill last night and missed. My mind," she paused, pushing damp blonde hair back behind her ears, "it keeps creating scenarios of what might happen, and I can see them so clearly. They keep replaying again and again."

She smiled weakly. "I think, maybe they'll try a second time, and I imagine I hear the footsteps coming up on the porch and the sound of a heavy bag landing against the door and the flash and heat of the explosion. Or maybe they'll just smash the door down and shoot us all. But mostly I think I'm running, trying to get away and someone, someone like McKellar, catches me and pushes my face down into the mud and I can't breathe and I there's the pressure on my back, my ribs breaking and blood running from my mouth."

Marcus was standing in the kitchen sipping a cup of tea. "The problem is that nothing she just said is at all crazy." He looked into his cup, considering the problem. "There is a place not far up the mountain where there's a network of small caves. We could get there even in this storm and it would be safer than staying here."

"I know the area," Alice said, brightening. "We could take the samples with us. We could do the analysis after the storm passes when we aren't so isolated. When we aren't so vulnerable." She looked at me, her eyes pleading.

"No," I replied. "Well, OK, there's no reason you two can't go, but I have to stay. If we don't get at least some of the analysis done in the next few hours it won't matter if we ever do. No one will care what started it once the shooting starts."

Marcus looked at Alice as if he was visualizing spending the next two days alone with her in the back of a cave. "Fine, we'll all stay then."

"Yes, of course. That's the right thing to do. Marcus, may I have a cup of tea now?" Alice had stopped shaking, which I hoped was a good sign.

I moved my display pad closer. "*Star*, have you been following all this?"

"I have, although I should mention that the link is slightly degraded due to the jamming coming from your end."

"Really? Can you isolate the location?"

"Somewhere near the quarry southwest of you I should think. It is not a serious concern. Their systems are not as sophisticated as I am."

I smiled at the sound of pride in her voice. "*Star*, I'm going to connect the microscope into the display pad so you'll see what we see. Please track everything for us. Keep me updated on who else is online too, please."

"I have notified everyone that you are back and ready to begin."

"Let's get the textile analysis out of the way first," Marcus suggested. "The soils are going to take forever."

"OK. I think we've already shown that Monroe's uniform is not OP standard issue. Let's see what it does match. Marcus, do you have anything the same weight as the PFS uniforms?"

"Even better. They issued one to me when I first got here. I think it's somewhere in my closet. I never wore it, of course."

He returned and held it up for us to admire.

Alice giggled. "Definitely not you."

"What? You don't think it goes well with the beard?" He pulled out his knife and cut a section off one cuff. "At least I finally found a use for it."

I placed the samples on the microscope stage one at a time, adjusting light settings and rotating the analyzer for each as *Star* looked on. "The birefringence looks the same to me," I commented. I slowly adjusted focus to move from the top to bottom of each sample, looking at the halo line move next to each fiber in the matrix showing the refractive index. "And the Becke line on the matrix looks close. What are you seeing, *Star*?"

"Based on what you have so far, I would conclude that the materials used for each sample are the same chemical composition. Slight variations in fiber diameter and form factor indicate that they were produced on different machines, but using similar techniques. Also, Angela Dawkins, Hannah Weldon, Jake Barton and Mr. Mahajan are now on line."

The lights flickered out again for several seconds as the cabin was shaken by a strong gust, the structure creaking as it adjusted to the wind load. I looked at Marcus in the glow from the display pad.

He shrugged. "It's survived worse."

"Hannah? Have you had a chance to listen to the recording I sent you?"

She moved closer to the screen and I could see she was dressed for work. Her current research project meant clubbing every evening somewhere in the city listening to the language around her. I couldn't help thinking that the shoulder that her dress left bare was at risk of getting cold in the Palma Sola winter.

"I have, but I'd like to have time to do a proper interview. I *think* she is not a native of the OP, but I can't tell how much of the way she sounds is due to her injuries. I would say maybe a seventy-five percent chance she's faking the accent? Maybe?"

"Thanks, Hannah. I'll let you know when we get an opportunity to talk to her again. Angela, do you want us to continue work to quantify the fiber analysis and determine actual values or is this good enough for now?"

Wandering Star interrupted before she could answer. "You should be aware that the nature of the jamming signal has changed and has increased in strength. You should assume that the unknown actors creating the jamming are aware that your signal is still getting through and that they cannot stop it or break my encryption."

I looked at Marcus who was silently mouthing the word *caves* and at Alice who was slowly curling into a ball again. "Angela, can you do anything with the limited data we have provided so far, the fiber analysis and voice recording?"

She turned to Mahajan. "What are you hearing in the legislature?"

Mahajan shook his head. "It's volatile right now. It could go either way."

"What do you want to do, Theodore?"

I looked at the sample bags lined up along the floor waiting for analysis, the irreplaceable uniform and mud samples, and the microscope we had stolen. And the survey charge. How could we just walk away from it?

Star made up my mind for me.

"Good news," she reported, "the jamming has stopped."

Alice whimpered from somewhere inside her blanket.

"We're leaving." I detached the display pad and propped it up on the kitchen counter, partially hidden behind cans and containers. "Angela, I'm leaving the pad running and muted from your end. You'll be able to hear and see anything that happens here and they won't be able to see or hear you."

Angela and Jake both replied. "Be careful, Ted."

I turned to Marcus. "The caves, is that really our best option?"

"They are unless you want to walk up the street to the barracks and turn ourselves in."

"Yes, that's exactly what we should do," Alice said. She stood and folded the blanket over the back of the chair. She seemed to have conquered her fears, at least for the moment. "I should be with the soldiers anyway and it's the safest place for the two of you as well."

"How's that?" Marcus asked.

"We won't be able to run fast enough or far enough if everyone is in on this conspiracy. They will chase us down in the mud." She paused, took a couple of deep breaths as that scenario replayed itself in her mind again, and then continued. "Instead, we'll go to where all the soldiers are, just like we belong there. Which we do. We'll ride out the storm with them."

Marcus had been stuffing cans of food into his bag. He dumped them out and put in a bottle of scotch, thought about it a moment and added a second bottle. "It's going to be a long night and those boys and girls get thirsty."

He turned to me. "Ted, go fetch some ponchos from my closet. What do you want to do about all this?" he gestured at the kitchen table.

"Leave it. We've done all that we could do."

We were ready a minute later. Ponchos on, we stepped off the porch and were pushed by the storm toward the lights of the barracks.

Marcus leaned close to Alice and me as we staggered up the street, his face very serious. "You had better be right about this, Alice. If you're not, I will have wasted two bottles of scotch."

I started laughing and that got the other two laughing as well. Marcus pushed his hood back, laughing at the rainwater streaming down his face and beard. "First round's on me, then. But you, Mr. RuComm, you still owe me a beer."

For the first time since arriving on Dulcinea, I wasn't worried about anything. We had made our final play, and now we would wait and see if the last domino would fall.

CHAPTER 6

REDEMPTION

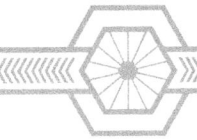

We stumbled up the stairs of the barracks, the wind almost strong enough to lift Alice off her feet. A guard was waiting for us at the top, arms crossed and resting on the buttstock of his slung rifle.

Marcus greeted him. "Corporal Bantoo, whose ass did you forget to kiss to pull this duty?"

Bantoo nodded, a smile just barely touching his lips. "Marcus." He nodded to Alice, who had pushed her hood back and was staring at him eye to eye. "Chaplain." His glance slid past me and back to Marcus. "A little wet out for an evening stroll isn't it?"

"Well, the truth is," he rummaged in his bag and pulled out one of the bottles, "I needed someone who could keep up with me and these two were unequal to the task."

Bantoo grinned. "Well, I'm off duty in about half an hour and we'll see if I can't match you."

"Excellent. Anyone playing poker tonight?"

"Always."

Marcus reached around the Corporal and opened the door. "I'll be waiting for you inside."

Bantoo moved back a step and touched his cap as Alice walked by, "Ma'am."

We hung our ponchos in the foyer. To the left and right, long hallways led to the dorm rooms. In front of us was a large common area where several of the soldiers were sitting talking, eating, playing games, or looking at display pads. Lieutenant Jeffers was sitting by himself, intent on whatever his pad was displaying.

"Lieutenant," Marcus said, sitting down opposite him. "How are things?"

Jeffers put the pad on the table face down before answering. "Better now that comms are mostly working again. We have several patrols deployed and I don't like being out of touch with them for so long. What about you? You look about drowned. What brings you up here?"

"Lonely. Bored." He glanced over at where Alice and I were standing, tipping his head in our direction as if our presence was answer enough. "Who's running things with you here at the barracks?"

"McKellar, Pruitt, and Meyrick volunteered for the first shift. I'll be back down there at 02:00 to relieve them."

"And Monroe?"

"Better, I guess. She was chatty all afternoon, complaining about being in restraints, claiming someone attacked her, that she's the victim, blah, blah, blah. I had the medical AI increase her pain meds and she went back to sleep."

Jeffers eyes kept drifting back to his pad. "I have a few things to finish up before I go down there and I'd like to try and get a couple of hours of sleep..."

"Of course." Marcus stood, grabbed several plastic cups from the food counter and walked over to where three soldiers were playing cards. He sat down without waiting for an invitation and passed out the cups. Alice had settled into a comfy chair next to the food and was busy doing chaplain things. I followed Marcus.

"Mr. RuComm, come join us!" he called, waving me over.

"I can't. I promised a friend I wouldn't play poker while I was here."

Marcus pulled a chair over and shoved it at me. I sat.

"Really? Who? Your girlfriend on the display pad this afternoon? She's cute."

"Hannah? She's just a friend. My best friend's girlfriend, actually."

"That's not good. He's going to kill you when he finds out."

I replied, speaking slowly. "Finds out what?"

"That you're in love with her."

"What makes you think that?"

"Your voice changes when you talk to her, the look in your eyes, the speed of your breathing, and about three other things." Marcus smiled.

Everyone around the table was smirking at me, apparently having seen Marcus do this trick before.

"Now, how about playing poker with me?"

The Corporal sitting to my left placed the cards in front of me to cut. "Don't let it bother you. Marcus reads all of us. As long as he's buying the booze," she tapped her still empty cup, "it's still a worthwhile game."

Marcus filled the cups while she dealt, and over the next hour my brain grew fuzzier and my weekly salary drained away to the other players. Corporal Bantoo joined us at some point and did his best to keep up with Marcus. It really was a pleasant way to spend the evening even with the barracks shaking from time to time as the hurricane moved across the island.

"How is it that they let you drink like this?" I asked, noticing that my cup had been magically refilled again. "What if you have to go on duty?"

The Corporal next to me, Carotti was her name, placed a small red bottle on the table, about the size of a shot glass. "Nox. One sip of this and your body will forget about every drop of alcohol floating around in your bloodstream. You don't have that were you come from?"

"I don't think so."

"Probably not," Marcus said. "Don't ask what it does to the rest of your body. Knowing Earth, it's probably illegal there."

A couple of hands later, the barracks shuddered. The lights flickered, and everyone looked up to make sure the roof was still there.

"I don't think that was–" The alarm wailed, cutting Bantoo off.

"Well, shit. Crazy OP bastards. They make their move in the middle of a hurricane?"

Carotti took a sip from the Nox bottle. "Waste of a perfectly good buzz."

She handed it to me and I let a drop touch my tongue. The effect was immediate and wonderful. I was awake and alert, the scotch I'd been drinking not even a memory.

Marcus and I ran to the foyer. Alice came up behind us, pressing herself against my back to stay out of the way of the soldiers gathering weapons and foul weather gear.

Marcus yanked the blinds on the front window open. The flames engulfing his cabin reflected off the sheets of rain and muddy road.

"Oh, god damn it," he swore.

I reached around him to grab my poncho so I could join the soldiers running down the road. Marcus blocked me. He shoved me back hard and I squished Alice against the wall as I stumbled. She grunted as the air came out of her.

Marcus glared at me. "Ted, will you ever *not* try to run toward the point of greatest danger? Go call your RuComm buddies. Ask them what the hell happened to my home."

"Yeah." I looked back out the window. "Is that a body in front of your cabin?"

"I think so."

"I'll see what I can find out."

I found one of the communal display pads and sat down in an over-stuffed chair, Alice perched on the arm next to me, rubbing her ribs. *Wandering Star* put me through to Angela, who seemed to have most of the team with her in the hotel conference room as well as several people I didn't recognize.

"Angela, Marcus' cabin just exploded into flames. Did you see what happened?"

She nodded. "About half an hour ago–"

"Here, let me brief him." Major Kilpatrick interrupted, sliding in next to her. "I was keeping notes as it transpired. I see you have Ms. Vandermeer with you too. That's excellent."

He referred to a small pad on the desk in front of him while Angela leaned back looking unhappy. "At 20:42 local, Sergeant McKellar, Corporal Pruitt, and Private Meyrick entered Marcus Wright's cabin. We could see and hear everything that was said in the kitchen and living areas through Theodore Holloman's display pad."

He looked up from his notes and gave me a fleeting smile. "Very clever to have concealed it there, by the way." He looked back to his notes, skimming through a couple of pages. "Sergeant McKellar was very agitated and repeatedly expressed the urgency of 'destroying all the evidence'. He was particularly upset by the presence of the microscope and uniform samples in the cabin, knocking the instrument to the floor and kicking it."

"I liked that microscope," I whispered to Alice. A smile touched her lips for a second.

"He was also upset that Marcus, Theodore, and Alice were not present. He mentioned that Fiona Monroe's sacrifice would not be forgotten. Pruitt and Meyrick searched the cabin while Sergeant McKellar remained in the kitchen area. He took the survey charge from the table plus two others he had brought with him, removed the safeties and adjusted the timers. He showed the timers to Pruitt and Meyrick saying they had fifteen minutes to finish up and get out. McKellar then stepped out of the cabin onto the front porch, remaining visible through the front window. Five minutes later, while the others were still completing a final sweep, the charges went off," Kilpatrick looked up from his notes, "and the transmission was lost."

Angela leaned forward reaching for the display pad, but the field of view suddenly rotated before she could touch it. Alice and I found ourselves looking at General Barrows.

"Ms. Vandermeer, Mr. Holloman, so good to see you. Mr. Wright and Lieutenant Jeffers are not there with you?"

I shook my head, not trusting my voice.

"That's OK. I'll catch up with them later. Let me just tell the two of you how we appreciate what you've done to investigate this terrible attack on the Palma Federated States. While we will never know who was responsible, knowing that the OP government was not involved, at least not directly, will prevent a lot of bloodshed, a lot of bloodshed. The four of you are true heroes in my book, and I'll make sure the whole world recognizes your achievement. Ted, what an example you are of our legacy of mutual respect and cooperation between the Reunification Commission and the PFS. Your superiors should be very proud of you, very proud indeed. I want you to know that I have personally arranged for transportation for all of you once the weather clears."

The sound of Alice's breathing changed abruptly as she wrapped her arms around herself, probably already running mental scenarios of an aircraft gone missing somewhere over the vast open ocean.

"Angela," I asked, "Alice and I have some other things to tend to if the rest of this can wait. I'd like to catch up with Marcus and go down to the Patrol HQ to check on Monroe."

"Oh, haven't you heard?" General Barrows interrupted. "I was just told that Fiona Monroe is dead. Medical overdose. Enough medication to kill her ten times over."

Alice whispered to me, "She was just one more piece of evidence that had to be destroyed."

"What was that?"

"Nothing, sir," I answered. "We need to go." I disconnected, knowing Angela would understand and that was all that mattered to me right then.

"You don't suppose Lieutenant Jeffers...?" I asked Alice.

"No, it's not in him. McKellar must have killed her before he went to Marcus' cabin."

I nodded and we walked back to the front of the barracks. "Are you ready to go do some more hero work?" We slipped ponchos over our heads and looked out the window at the last of the flames dying, no match for the heavy rainsqualls.

She sighed as she adjusted her hood. "You be the hero, I'll be the chaplain. Why do I feel like crying?"

I opened the door for her. "That's OK. It's dark and it's raining and no one will notice if you do." She gave me a quick smile and we stepped outside.

Marcus was by his cabin, poking around the ruins. Sergeant McKellar's body was still in the street, a lone Private standing by waiting for a truck to take it away.

Alice looked at the body calmly, rain running down her face. "He should have realized there was something wrong with the timers after what happened to Fiona. The charges wouldn't have gone off while she was still so close unless they wanted her to get caught."

I turned to look at McKellar. I had never seen a dead body before yesterday and now, looking at him, someone I had known and talked to, I just felt tired.

"He knew," I replied.

Marcus came up to us. "Couldn't stay away, could you?"

"General Barrows says to say 'hi,'" Alice answered.

"Does he now?"

"Don't you know? We're all heroes. You, Ted, me, even Lieutenant Jeffers, all heroes. Barrows is taking credit for stopping the war before it started and will be telling the world about how light our losses were. Only Lydie. Only Helen." Alice surprised me then by kneeling in the mud next to McKellar and placing a hand on his shoulder, her head bowed in prayer.

"Monroe is dead too," I told Marcus.

"Yes, Jeffers told me." He had his hood back and his face was wet. "We all should to go back to the barracks now. We need something to eat and a dry place to sleep."

"Barrows is sending transportation for us once the weather clears. Do you want to get on that plane?"

Marcus smiled sardonically, which was the only way I ever saw him smile. "I think we're more valuable to him alive now than dead. I won't lose any sleep over it."

I looked down at Alice.

"I'm ready," she said.

We each took an elbow and helped her back to her feet. She felt very light, the thinness of her arms lost in the loose bulk of the poncho. The rain was already washing the mud off her thin, bare legs back onto the street and none of us looked back as we walked up the hill to the barracks.

The hurricane blew itself out overnight, tracking south toward the equator and leaving the Margo Islands with clear skies and the seas running high. There would be no ships or seaplanes for at least a couple of more days.

I found Alice sitting on the front porch writing on a display pad, her feet up on the railing.

"Found some new clothes I see," I sat in the chair next to her.

"The quartermaster here is really efficient. There was a bundle outside my door this morning along with this." She held up the pad, and then whispered to me, "I think I intimidate him."

"I can understand that. Have you seen Marcus this morning?"

"He's working, believe or not. Up there somewhere," she pointed at the peak, "trying to finish a population survey on the big blue lizards with six legs that live here. *Lacerti hyacinthi*."

"What are you working on?"

"Comments for this evening's memorial service for Lydie and Helen. I wanted to include some words for McKellar, Pruitt, Meyrick, and Monroe, but Lieutenant Jeffers won't have it."

"I don't blame him."

She nodded. "You're still angry. Come and talk to me about them when you aren't any more; when you're ready to forgive."

"That may be awhile."

She nodded again, still typing on her pad. "What are your plans for the day, Ted?"

"I thought I might do some exploring, see if I can figure out what makes this place worth dying for. And killing for."

"I don't think the answer to those questions can be found here, but give me a half hour and I'll go exploring with you, if you don't mind my company."

"I'd like that. You can keep me from getting lost."

She smiled, still typing.

After she had finished, we walked up toward the peak past the caves.

"There's a thin lens of limestone here," Alice explained, "no one has really figured out why. Maybe a drop in sea level or maybe tectonic uplift." She shrugged. "It recurs at the same elevation intermittently all around the peak. It's fossiliferous near the top of the unit and the index fossils are the same at each exposure."

"There *is* a geologist inside you somewhere," I said, examining the traces of shell embedded in the rock.

"I still let it out sometimes."

We continued up, following Alice's plan to do all our climbing before it got too hot and then work our way back down to the OP camp for lunch. The trail we were following stopped about a third of the way up the peak, high enough to afford a view of the north side of the island, but still a thousand meters short of the summit.

"Has anyone made it to the top?" I asked

"Marcus says he did, but with the thickness of the vegetation I think he may be exaggerating."

The north side of the island was undeveloped and the lumpy green canopy was solid all the way to the ocean. "I grew up in the desert where the landscape is naked and you can see the Earth's bones," I commented. "It was perfect for a geologist, but I can see why a biologist would love this place."

"He's been here so long that this is home for him. It'll be hard for him to leave."

The temperature had already reached the low thirties by the time we started back. We came across one of Marcus' blue lizards sunning itself in the middle of the trail half way down. It was almost a meter long nose to tail, and it was watching us warily with one eye.

Alice stopped and whispered to me, "Watch this."

"Hello, there," she called out to it.

"Hello," the lizard answered before racing into the undergrowth.

Alice looked at me, smiling. "Bet you don't have those on Earth."

"No, we don't. Just an automatic response?" I asked hopefully.

"Probably. They repeat back the first part of whatever you say to them."

"We have birds that will learn a few words, but it takes a while to teach them. Some of them even understand what they're saying."

"Really? That's weird, sharing the planet with another species that has some level of intelligence. Even at the height of the old Union, I don't think anything was ever found smarter than that lizard."

"It's strange, isn't it?"

The chow hall at the OP camp looked like it had been manufactured by the same company that had built its counterpart on the other side of the hill. Our presence there didn't excite any interest; there were several uniformed members of the PFS already sitting with OP soldiers.

"My two Lieutenants may not be the most effective officers to ever serve in their respective militaries, but this," she gestured at the tables of mixed uniforms, "deserves more credit for keeping the peace than it will ever receive."

I nodded toward where Jeffers and Recano were sitting eating lunch together. "Maybe what you would expect from leaving the two lovers in charge."

"Exactly. I worked hard to push them together, and they created a cadre of men and women who don't look at the other side as enemies."

"With a few notable exceptions."

Alice frowned and handed me a tray. We looked at the meal selections of synthetics, fish and strips of some sort of meat that smelled like teriyaki beef.

"What is that?" I asked the cook, my mouth already watering.

"Lizard."

"The big blue ones?"

"That's them."

"I think I'll have the fish. The fish, they don't, um, talk do they?"

He looked at me as if I was crazy as he put a plate on my tray. "Of course not, they're fish."

We sat and I ate while Alice talked. "The memorial service will be just before sunset on the beach down by the dock. The Lieutenants are planning a binge party right afterwards. Lydie and Helen would like that. I suppose it will be the last one here." She chewed thoughtfully for a moment. "I won't stay for the party, of course."

"Why not?"

She smiled, making her eyes crinkle. "I don't think you realize how unpopular I am here. The last couple of days have been the exception. Things are back to normal now and a chaplain is just in the way."

"Stay for a while at least."

"Maybe. If you want me to."

We finished eating and then walked slowly back over the hill to the barracks. The heat was climbing past thirty-five and the clouds were trying to form up for an afternoon thunderstorm. Alice stopped on the porch, moved a chair into the shade and sat, tucking her legs under her.

I stood undecided, listening to the beckoning hum of the air conditioner. "A little warm out here, isn't it?"

"I like the heat," she answered. "I must be part lizard."

"Hello, there."

"Hello," she replied, her eyes crinkling.

"I have reports I need to write for Angela this afternoon. I think I'll sit out here with you while I do it and soak up some heat. It's snowing again in Palma Sola today."

Connecting the display pad to *Wandering Star* brought up two messages, one from Jake and one from Hannah. I paused, my finger hovering, undecided for a moment before sending Hannah a greeting. I opened my report template and alternated for the next couple of hours between working on my delinquent status charts and chatting back and forth with Hannah.

Her comments on the mood in the capital were funny and insightful, as I expected them to be. Barrows was a hero for stopping the war, no one trusted the OP, and everyone expected them to try another sneak attack sometime in the future. There was no mention of anyone named Alice, Marcus or Ted. Lieutenant Jeffers, on the other hand, was the big hero of the Margo Islands. He was going to have an opportunity to enhance his career significantly, but I wondered how Lieutenant Recano was going to fit into that future. The two of them were going to have some decisions to make.

I sent my reports off to Angela, told Hannah that I was looking forward to seeing her, and disconnected.

I stood and stretched. Alice had curled herself into the chair, eyes closed, and sound asleep. I left her and walked down past the Patrol HQ to the beach. Several soldiers were there chopping and stacking wood and getting things ready for the evening party. The Corporal that I had played cards with was there so I walked over to her.

"Corporal...," she moved her hair out of the way so I could read the name printed on the edge of her t-shirt, "Carotti. Anything I can do to help?"

"Sure," She handed me the axe she was holding. "You know how to use this?"

"Yeah, it turns big sticks into little sticks."

She pointed to where a large pile of tree trunks had been stacked. "That guy is using the chainsaw to cut the logs down to two meter lengths, but someone needs to lop off all the smaller branches so everything will stack the way it should for the bonfire. The wood is pretty soft and," she looked me up and down, "you look pretty strong, so I don't think you'll have too much trouble."

I spent the afternoon not thinking about Marcus or Alice or Jake or Hannah or Fiona. I chopped wood and dripped sweat and by the time the sun was drifting lower, I felt much better about life. I bathed and played in the surf with the soldiers when we were done and then we stood on the sand and let the last of the sun and gentle wind dry us.

Alice found me when she arrived, dressed in her PFS chaplain uniform. She placed her hand on my chest and said, "You look like a whole new Ted, all sunburned and smelling of the ocean."

I suddenly felt underdressed. "I'm not exactly presentable for a memorial service, I should change."

"You didn't know Lydie and Helen very well. Trust me; they'd love the way you look."

I found a place to sit on one of the logs and Marcus soon joined me. "How are your lizards?" I asked as he made himself comfortable.

"Not as numerous as they should be. The damn cook over at the OP camp keeps serving them for lunch and dinner."

Alice stepped up onto a low platform once everyone had gathered. She spoke about the love Lydie and Helen shared for the Islands and for the mission, and how much we would miss them. She didn't mention those who had killed them, but spoke of the need for forgiveness and then she stepped down. Each of the Lieutenants spoke briefly about how proud they were of everyone and how the Margo Islands garrison was an example of what was possible between the OP and PFS. They stepped down, the Lieutenants lit the bonfire, and I found myself with a cold beer in one hand and a stick with something to eat on it in the other.

Marcus put his mouth next to my ear so I could hear him over the music that was now throbbing over the beach. "That was good of you to help Corporal Carotti this afternoon."

"It was good for me. I needed it."

He nodded to where Carotti was dancing by herself near the flames. "You should go over there. I think she'd like to thank you in person."

I looked up and she made eye contact, smiling.

I shook my head. "No, I better not."

"Why? Still hung up on Hannah, who belongs to your best friend?"

"I don't think Hannah belongs to anyone but Hannah."

"What makes her so special?"

"She's smart, smarter than me, and she's easy to talk to."

"I don't think it's talking that Carotti has in mind." He pushed me with his shoulder. "Did it escape your attention that you almost died yesterday, like twice? Go. Do something life affirming."

I looked at Carotti, watching the swaying of her body in the firelight, the soft smile on her lips as she looked back at me. I was remembering what she had looked like when we played in the water that afternoon.

Alice sat down on the sand in front of me blocking my view. She had changed from her chaplain uniform back into a t-shirt and shorts and looked much more comfortable. "Ted, I'm glad I was able to find you. Do you have time to talk, assuming you're not otherwise occupied?"

"Damn it, Alice, leave the boy alone," Marcus growled.

"Um," I swallowed hard, trying to get my voice back, "sure, Alice." I stood, ignored Marcus, and helped her up. She took my hand and led me toward the dock. I looked back over my shoulder once. Carotti was talking to someone else and started to dance. I sighed.

We walked to the end of the dock and sat with our legs dangling down, listening to the soft slap of the water on the pilings and the distant music from the party.

"I'm sorry that I had to rescue you. It's things like that that make me unpopular here, I'm afraid."

"Who were you rescuing me from, Carotti or Marcus?"

"Silly. From yourself, of course."

"So did you really need to talk to me or was that just a ruse?"

"No, I do. Well, it could have kept until morning, but I'm excited. I talked to my father this afternoon. The OP and PFS delegates to the Foundation for Margo Islands Development have agreed to abandon the Islands. He was able to get it approved before General Barrows could interfere. By the end of the week there won't be anyone left here."

"How did your father do that?"

"You don't get to be the head of a department at a major university, *or* the liaison to the Reunification Commission without being shrewd and ruthless. The kindly, slightly befuddled professor act is just an act. He's been angry about the way Barrows manipulated RuComm since the beginning. He thinks that only he should be allowed to do that. Now that Barrows is on the defensive, my dad is looking for revenge."

"Where does that leave you?"

"That is the question." She leaned back on her elbows, looking up at the stars.

"Can he keep you safe?"

"No, probably not, but the church can. I'll be leaving for Bodens Gate."

"How soon?"

She looked at me and giggled with excitement. "When you do. Dad negotiated with Angela and Captain von Muller for passage for me aboard *Wandering Star*."

I laid down next to her, looking at the beauty of the night sky.

"I suppose your dad already knows when we're leaving."

"Three weeks, max. RuComm is pulling your team out early, but there are things they want to finish first. And Mr. Mahajan will be staying behind in Palma Sola as an adviser to the legislature."

We laid on the dock together looking at the stars and listening to the music. Around midnight the smaller moon rose over the peak and shimmered on the water.

"Ted?"

"Hum?" I answered.

"Do you think Carotti is pretty? Were you attracted to her? I'll know if you lie to me."

"Yes, she's very pretty."

"If I hadn't taken you, would you have gone to her? Would you be with her right now?"

"Are you shrewd and ruthless like your father?"

She chuckled quietly and didn't ask me any more questions. We dozed and watched the sky together until the sun came up and washed the stars from the morning sky.

Howard came back the next afternoon, the white seaplane circling the island in a tight turn before settling on the waters of the cove. I watched it from almost half way up the peak where I was searching for outcrops under the thick vegetation while Marcus chased lizards up and down trails that were invisible to my unpracticed eyes.

"Have you ever been to the top?" I asked him.

He looked up at it. "You'd have to be crazy to do that."

"Yeah. Have you?"

Marcus laughed, "Just once."

By the time we returned to the camp for dinner, two large flying boats lay anchored near each other farther off shore. The gray paint of one was adorned with the emblems of the Palma Federated States, the other for the Oceanus Protectorate.

At the chow hall, Alice was eating with Jeffers and Recano and I noted a few other OP uniforms, friends having dinner together one last time. I sat with Marcus.

"What will happen to all the buildings and equipment?" I asked.

"Most of it's probably not worth moving, so it'll stay here waiting for the political situation to be resolved. If that doesn't happen, in a few years Dulcinea will have reclaimed it and you won't be able to tell humans were ever here. I'd like to come back, but I'd be just as happy if it was left the way it is."

"What will you do while you're waiting?"

"I'll teach Dulcinean biology next term. I have tenure at the university."

I nodded, watching Alice approach him from behind.

"Are you ready to go home?" she asked, placing her hands on his shoulders.

Marcus winced. "Yes, Alice, I am. I find that I have very little to pack."

Alice swung into a chair opposite me, ignoring Marcus' sarcasm.

"While you two were having fun today, I was helping the Lieutenants get everyone else ready. They'll be flying out tomorrow evening, but the three of us will be going with Howard in the morning. Lieutenant Jeffers was supposed to go with us, but he requested to go with the rest of his soldiers and Major Kilpatrick approved it."

"And what about the lovely Lieutenant Britt Recano?" Marcus asked.

Alice sighed. "I don't know. I haven't found a way to fix that yet. I feel responsible, having brought them together in the first place."

We finished dinner and walked through the evening twilight back toward the barracks.

"I'm going to go sit and look at the cove one last time. Would you like to join me?" Alice asked as we passed the burned out cabins.

Marcus closed his eyes and shook his head.

"Ted?" she asked. "We can talk about, um, about," she stammered to a stop looking at her hands as I took them in mine.

"Alice? I'm going back to the barracks and sleep in a bed tonight. If I walk down to the overlook with you I know that's where I'll be come morning." I let go of her hands.

"OK," she answered softly, still looking down.

Marcus was silent while he and I walked the rest of the way to the barracks. As we climbed the stairs to the porch, he turned to me and said, "Mr. RuComm, I think you're going to have an interesting time on your way to Bodens Gate."

"Why is that?"

"Alice believes that no one is as smart as Alice. Or as right or righteous. She always gets what she wants, whether by her own talents or with the help of her father."

I looked at him, blinked. "So?"

Marcus shook his head. "Never mind. Just know that she'll manipulate you to do what she wants, and in the end, you'll think it was your idea all along. I'm sure Jeffers and Recano think their relationship is their own doing."

Marcus reached for the door then thought better of it. "Sergeant Villanueva," he said softly to himself with a smile, then to me, "We're going over the hill for a beer."

So we walked over the hill to the OP camp, I bought Marcus the beer I owed him, and I did finally get to sleep in a warm bed my last night in the Margo Islands. Just not for as long or as restfully as I had planned.

CHAPTER 7

HANNAH

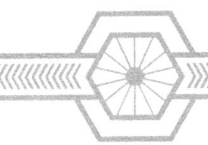

We left mid-morning, the small seaplane making a short run across the water away from the island and climbing quickly. All of us slept most of the way back to Palma Sola, our pilot included. With the loss of time zones, it was nearly dark when we taxied to the dock and Howard shut down the engines. A single figure bundled in a long coat was waiting for us on the dock, standing beside an unmarked gray bus.

Marcus turned to me as the aircraft tied itself down to the dock. "If General Barrows has come to greet us, I'm not sure I can bring myself to shake his hand."

"I'll help you push him into the bay if you like."

Alice looked up at us from her display pad. "He's not here. I don't imagine he wants to see any of us either, other than for publicity purposes. That's Major Kilpatrick out there."

"I was hoping it was your father bringing me the coat that I left in his office."

Alice smiled. "Stop by tomorrow morning around 10:00. I know he wants to talk to you."

Marcus gave me an '*I warned you*' look, but said nothing.

A sharp wind was blowing across the bay into the city making the short walk to the bus unpleasant, especially when the Major insisted on shaking each of our hands and welcoming us 'home' before we entered.

Finally seated in the relative warmth of the bus, I asked Marcus, "So how are you feeling about our odds of survival now?"

"Ask me that when I'm back in my own apartment. No, ask me that a year from now."

"Always the optimist."

The bus dropped me off first. I grabbed my backpack and Kilpatrick said, "We'll have a debriefing tomorrow in the hotel conference room at 15:00. Please make yourself available."

I nodded and looked at Marcus and Alice. "Until tomorrow, then." I shook Marcus' hand and Alice got off the bus with me so she could wrap her arms around my shoulders.

"Tomorrow," she said in my ear.

The bus left, I stepped over a pile of slush, and entered the lobby. Jake was standing next to the hotel pub watching me with a pint of beer in his hand.

"I remember a time when we were in eighth grade and you wore shorts to school because it was April and you said April is spring and spring is warm. It snowed that afternoon. I see you have no more sense now than you did then." He put his arms around me, threatening to spill beer down my back. "Damn, I'm glad to see you back in one piece."

When he released me, I saw that Angela and several other members of the team were there. We ate dinner and drank, and I answered their questions as best I could, making the story seem more confusing and more heroic than it actually was.

Hannah was not there.

"Still at work," Jake explained. "She's been in a panic since the schedule was cut short. I haven't seen much of her the last couple of days."

After dinner, I walked with Angela and Jake back toward our rooms. We dropped Jake at his door and Angela continued on with me.

"Theodore?" I looked at her and sighed. She smiled. "Ted. You've changed in the past few days. Your time there seems to have knocked some of the Academy freshness off you. You seem more confident. I *might* be seeing the Reunification Commission scientist you *might* someday become."

We stopped in front of my room. "Um, thank you, Angela. That sounds like a good thing."

She patted my arm and walked away from me down the corridor. "If you live long enough," she said without turning around.

I stood there for a moment thinking about what she had said, then tried to open my door, the door that was keyed to the watch and display pad that were both now part of a melted mass of composite four thousand kilometers away.

"Damn." I turned and walked back to the front desk hoping my Margo Islands ID would be sufficient to convince them to resync access to my new watch and display pad.

It was, and I was turning to go back to my room when Hannah arrived. She came up to me without speaking and gave me a tight hug, the dusting of snow in her hair cold on my cheek.

"Welcome back, prodigal." She stepped back and looked at me with her head tipped. "If I didn't know the truth of it, I'd say you were just back from vacation, what with that sunburn. Come buy me a hot chocolate."

We found a table near the fire and ordered. I looked at her for a long time, not saying anything.

"Nothing to say, Ted?" she finally asked.

I laughed. "One of the guys I met on the Island saw you on my display pad and asked me what made you so special. I told him it was because you were easy to talk to. Now that I have you in front of me I can't think of anything to say."

"So, you were talking about me while you were there." She reached across the table and touched her fingertips to mine. "Tell me what happened to you on that island."

I went through it from the beginning and she listened, asking few questions, and offering only the look in her eyes for reassurance.

"Hannah, those people died there," I said at the end, "and I don't know what it was for." I swallowed the last of my drink. "We were all pawns in somebody else's game. I survived, they didn't, and there's no reason for that. It wasn't superior skill or intelligence. I was supposed to die, and instead I'm here with you."

"It's changed you."

"Don't say that."

"It's true. You're still Ted, but you'll never look at the world around you in the same way. It's a good change; it was just a painful way to do it."

I sighed. "Tell me something normal."

"Well, I've been working twelve or more hours every day trying to finish my project, which leaves me no time for anything else. Jake has been pissed at me every day because I have no time for him either. He's a bit of a pain that way, isn't he? But I've learned a lot. Did you know that there's an entirely new slang subculture developing on the city's north end? It didn't exist last year when I surveyed the clubs there. I'm working on a theory with Mr. Mahajan relating factors of political and economic uncertainty to the speed of subculture speciation."

I listened to her talk and tried to ask questions in the right places while she explained the nuances of lingual drift and the influences of youth rebellion. Mostly I was listening to the cadence of her voice and watching her face as she spoke, the way her hair was starting to come down across her left eye and how she kept pushing it out of the way.

The next thing I knew she asked me, "Ted, are you falling asleep?"

"I'm sorry, I shouldn't be tired. I slept most of the way here."

"That's OK. I should be getting to my room anyway. I have a couple of hours of writing to do before bed."

I walked Hannah to her room and she opened her door. We looked at each other, uncertain.

"I think I should not kiss you goodnight," I said.

"Why not? You have before."

"I know. That was when it was only a kiss between friends."

"And what is it now?" she asked, lowering her voice.

"I don't know."

She took a step closer to me and kissed me gently on the lips, no other part of us touching.

She pulled back after a moment and licked her lips. "I really do have a couple of hours more work to do."

"I know. I'll be here tomorrow."

She smiled. "I'm glad you made it back."

"Me too."

Her door closed and I went to my room, got ready for bed and didn't sleep. The clock rolled from 22:38 to 00:00 and then 01:00.

Sometime before dawn, I dreamed I was one of Marcus' blue lizards running for my life down the narrow trails on the Margo Islands. The OP cook was chasing me, knife in hand. The cook looked like Jake. As he was cutting off my legs, I heard Marcus saying sadly, '*I told you he would kill you when he found out*' and Alice reassuring me, '*It's OK, I'm a certified medical tech.*'

Still groggy, I rolled out of bed, took a quick shower, and got dressed. Everyone had left an hour earlier by the time I got down to the lobby. Everyone but Hannah. Her schedule was six hours out of sync with the rest of the team. I looked down the corridor that led to her room and shook my head. No. I might already be standing on the edge of that cliff, but I wasn't quite ready to jump.

The walk to the University wasn't too bad as long as I stayed on the sunny side of the street. I stopped for a cup of coffee at *The Christie-Cleek* and then spent an hour in the geology department museum. Even on Earth, scientists are constantly making new discoveries as they try to understand our natural history, but it still surprised me how much of Dulcinea remained unknown. I was sitting at one of the hands-on exhibits looking at the fossils of tiny-shelled creatures through a 10x loupe when Professor Vandermeer found me.

"What do you think of those little guys?" he asked.

"Weird. Same basic morphology as a bivalve, but with three segments of shell." I put the sample down. "It's like you've only just started reconstructing this planet's evolutionary history. It's exciting."

"It is at that."

We walked back to his office where I gratefully retrieved my coat.

"Did you walk the whole way here? I'd have frozen to death."

"I think I stored up enough heat on the island to last me a few months."

He stood looking out his window at the campus for a few moments. I expected him to apologize for the danger he'd put me in, but he didn't.

"Alice has told me about what happened, of course. She was very impressed with your ability to improvise. I think it's fair to say that the people behind the incident had not anticipated how effective your intervention would be."

"Six people died. All of the evidence I collected was destroyed, most of it unexamined."

"Yes." The Professor turned from the window and sat behind his desk, motioning me to sit as well. "But you were only one step behind them the whole way. They knew what the evidence would show and they couldn't risk that, so the operation had to be called off."

"Supposition. I can't prove anything."

"No, and you never will." He smiled slightly. "It's funny, if I had thought anyone would have had a chance to disrupt the plan it would have been Marcus Wright, given his background."

"Oh?"

"He was in the PFS Internal Security Group before joining the faculty. I was part of the panel that interviewed him when he joined the University."

"He was a spy?"

"Nothing so glamorous. He specialized in human intelligence, more of an analyst really. His travels led him to become interested in Dulcinean biology and how little of the original ecology still exists. He left the ISG and went back to school here to become a biologist. A damn good one too. I was sorry to see him to join the Foundation for Margo Islands Development, but I suppose it was inevitable. He wanted to see original Dulcinean life so badly he didn't really care who was paying for it."

"He seems to be happy that development is on hold, probably forever."

The Professor nodded. "It's a better result than I could have hoped for."

I felt cold suddenly and shivered.

He smiled at me, his eyes sharp behind his glasses. I shivered again.

"I see you understand. On to happier topics. Alice."

"I did everything I could to keep her safe."

"No, you didn't. If that were true, she would have been on the plane that left ahead of the storm. You did something better. You made her work through her fears and do her duty. My biggest failing as a father has been my desire to keep her safe. She's leaving with you in less than three weeks, Mr. Holloman. Is she in good hands?"

"Yes, sir. I would trust my life to any member of this team."

He stood. "I will let you get back to them, then."

I put my coat on and the Professor turned back to the window with its view of students hurrying to class.

As I put my hand on the door he said quietly, "Don't hurt her, Ted."

"She's stronger than you think, Professor."

"She is, isn't she?" He turned and smiled at me again as I slipped out into the hallway.

I sent a message to Jake to see if he was available for an early lunch. He replied that he and Hannah were planning on meeting at *The Christie-Cleek* in half an hour. I walked around campus until then not sure how to interpret my conversation with Alice's father.

"So," I asked between bites of sandwich, "how do I know where I am on the spectrum that goes from naïve to healthy skepticism to cynicism to paranoia?"

"Why?" Jake asked.

"What would you say if I told you that Professor Vandermeer just implied that he was complicit with the attack in the Margo Islands, told me how important his daughter is to him, and then threatened me if I allowed her to get hurt?"

"Paranoid." Jake ruled.

"Maybe cynicism," Hannah said thoughtfully. "This planet is all wheels within wheels. After listening to people talking every night, nothing would surprise me."

I sighed and took another bite. "I'll be so happy when we make our next planet fall on Cleavus. No inhabitants, no problems."

Hannah took her foot and ran it up the back of my leg then slowly down again. "Only those we bring with us."

I stared at her and hoped that Jake hadn't noticed that I had closed my eyes for two seconds. Hannah's eyes were soft looking back at me.

"Yeah," I replied, "just those."

Jake looked at his watch. "I need to be getting back to my work on the cliffs. Do you want to come with me, Ted? I could use your help in classifying the little shells. They all have three parts here."

"No," I answered. "I have a debriefing with General Barrows at 15:00 at the hotel. I think I'll just hang out there until then."

"OK, I'll see you tonight for dinner."

Jake left and Hannah hailed a cab to take us back to the hotel. We didn't talk as the vehicle carried us the short distance.

"My room," Hannah said as we entered the lobby.

"Why?"

"Because it's closer." She took my hand as we walked down the hall.

She shoved her door open and pulled me in. I was just able to give it enough of a kick with my foot for it to close behind us. She led me into her bedroom and then turned and kissed me with surprising tenderness given how urgently she had been pulling me along. I put my hands on her cheeks as we kissed, letting my fingers get tangled in her hair, caressing her ears. She tipped her head back, sighing, and I kissed my way down her neck to her collarbone. I slowly unbuttoned her blouse, never letting my mouth leave her skin as I followed downwards until the last of the buttons were undone and her blouse fell open.

I felt her heart beating rapidly under my lips, matching the sound of mine pounding in my ears. She sat down on the edge of her bed and I slid her blouse down over her shoulders and kissed her right breast and then her left, circling the nipple with my tongue, holding it gently between my teeth. She pulled her shoulders back, arched her back, and pushed up against my mouth, moaning softly. Her hands moved down my sides and lifted my shirt up over my head. I came back down on her after the interruption, and let my mouth travel gradually down her side, across her belly below her navel, pulling the waist of her skirt up to kiss under it.

"Don't stop there," she begged, "it opens in the back."

I flipped her over roughly and she giggled. I pulled her skirt down and noticed that she wasn't wearing anything under it.

"Must have been kind of drafty," I commented as the skirt joined my shirt and pants on the floor.

"Oh, it was." She giggled again as I flipped her onto her back. "You should check for frostbite."

I started at her knees and worked my way up along the insides of her thighs until I was sure that every part of her was warm and happy. It took a long time, but I wanted to be thorough.

When I had finished, Hannah was lying with her hands over her head with her eyes closed. Her mouth was open in an almost smile, almost snarl. I kissed her softly in the hollow between her breasts, tasting the sweat on her skin.

She opened her eyes and smiled. "I'm getting cold. Will you please cover me up?"

I laid down on top of her, spreading her knees apart. She wrapped her legs around me.

"Yes." She sighed, then panted. "Yes, that's exactly what I needed."

Sometime later, Hannah woke me, her head comfortable on my shoulder.

"Ted, I need to get ready for work and you need to get ready for General Barrows."

I opened my eyes, looked at her, and closed them again.

"Ted, if you don't get up I'll miss work, you'll miss your meeting, Angela will come pounding on my door, and we'll both be fired. It will be a terrible scandal."

"So?"

"I think I may have compromised your ability to weigh risk and benefit." She sighed, getting up. "I'm going to take a shower."

I got up and followed her, but she put her hands on my chest and pushed me back out of the bathroom. She gave me a lingering kiss, her tongue lightly touched mine, and then she closed and locked the door.

"Ted?" she called out to me. "I'll come to your room when I get back tonight. Be ready."

"OK," I answered, not exactly sure what being ready might entail.

I dressed, returned to my room, and tried to focus on being ready to answer questions from General Barrows.

I need not have bothered. Major Kilpatrick had reconfigured our conference room with a podium up front and a few chairs on each side. A row of cameras and media personnel faced the podium. I sat between Alice and Marcus while the General read a prepared speech and then we posed with him for still pictures. Afterward, Marcus, Alice and I slipped away from everyone and went to the hotel pub.

"So, how do you two like being nothing but props for the General's little theater?" Marcus asked.

"Fifteen days, six hours and 22 minutes," Alice said, raising her glass to me. I touched my glass to hers, smiling.

Marcus looked confused. "Fifteen days...?"

"Until we're on board *Wandering Star* and breaking orbit," I answered.

"I almost wish I was going with you. *Almost*," he emphasized as I started to invite him to enlist. "I'll just have to settle for Alice's prayers." He said it sarcastically, but Alice's answer was serious.

"I've told you before that I pray for you every day, Marcus."

"And with that I think it's time for me to go." He stood and shook my hand. "Ted, I don't know when I'll see you again, but next time you're on Dulcinea call me. I'll buy the first round."

I got up and hugged him. "You can count on it."

I sat back down, still smiling.

"Did you notice that Lieutenant Jeffers wasn't in attendance?" Alice asked.

"Yes, I did. I thought it was odd that the General never even mentioned him."

"It seems he's gone missing, Absent Without Leave."

"You know where he is."

She frowned at me. "I never know these things, I only suspect or conjecture."

I raised my glass to her again. "Then here's wishing the Lieutenants Jeffers and Recano a long happy life together. They earned it."

"Yes," she said, but her eyes had turned sad and I feared that Jeffers' life would be neither long nor happy.

She studied the ice in her glass for a minute, then said, "I like this pub, *Their Finest Hour*, it's very cozy. It's been years since I was last here. The hotel has a lot of history. Did you know part of this structure was built shortly after initial colonization as the original Hilton?"

"Really?"

"I've never stayed here, of course, but I hear the rooms are nice."

"I suppose so. Mine is kind of old fashioned and musty."

"Nice view?" she asked, staring into her drink.

I paused before answering, feeling as though the temperature in the room had just gone up five degrees.

"It's OK. I imagine it's better in the summer." Alice glanced up at me briefly then went back to slowly stirring her drink with her straw, waiting for me to continue.

"You, um, you'll have to see it sometime before we leave." I liked Alice. People had tried to kill us on that island and we had helped each other survive. She was an amazing person and my friend, but after having spent part of the afternoon in Hannah's arms and in Hannah's bed, inviting Alice to my room seemed like a very bad idea.

Alice looked up at me with a shy smile, but then her expression changed to one of frustration, almost anger. I quickly realized she wasn't directing it at me when Angela and Professor Vandermeer came over to our table.

"Dad, I had thought you must have left by now."

"Not at all. I was just talking to General Barrows about one of your pet projects. I thought we could share a cab and I'll tell you all about it."

I glanced at Angela, who looked as lost as I was. I wondered if either Alice or her father ever approached a conversation other than obliquely.

"Fine," Alice replied, pushing her chair back from the table. "Ted, perhaps we can get together sometime for a quiet lunch?"

"Yes, I'd like that." I stood and she held her hand out. I helped her up, which seemed to please her.

After they left, Angela and I sat back down.

"Any idea what that was about?" I asked.

"Which? What the Professor and Barrows were talking about or the back and forth just now between you and Alice?"

"The Professor."

"No idea. I overheard them talking about why Lieutenant Jeffers wasn't able to attend, but I wasn't really paying attention."

"That would be Alice's pet project. I told you about Jeffers and the OP Lieutenant, Recano? Alice arranged that particular match."

Angela nodded. "And you and Alice?"

"I don't know for sure, but I think she has an interest in spending more time with me. Considerably more time."

Angela frowned, looking at me with her eyes narrowed. "Remember the terms of your contract, Theodore."

"Would that apply?" I asked, feigning innocence. "She's just a passenger on her way to Bodens Gate, not a member of RuComm."

Angela's eyes narrowed further as she prepared an angry reply, but I held up my hands to stop her. "Don't worry. I'm not interested in that kind of relationship with her. She's just my friend."

"Keep it that way, and do it without hurting her. I don't want to lose you to some stupid romance."

"Yes, ma'am." I hoped she would assume the flush in my cheeks was because of Alice.

"I want you to work with Jake for the next week. With the schedule cut short he'll need all the help he can get."

"I'd like that."

I got a message from Jake as I walked back to my room asking me to meet him for dinner at the *Paloma Cantina* near campus.

He was sitting in the bar when I arrived, talking to a waitress with short shorts and long blonde hair. Her body was not as radically adapted to the lower gravity as Alice's, but she seemed very slight by Earth standards. Jake introduced us.

"Ted, this is Erin Cardiff. She's a graduate student in the biology department helping with the cliff study."

She smiled and shook my hand. "And Jake has been supporting my tuition payments by coming here every night and over tipping. What can I get you, Ted?"

"A beer would be fine." She hurried away and Jake watched her, a smile on his face.

"So, Jake, Erin seems very....nice."

"Brilliant, actually. She's considering joining RuComm after she graduates next spring."

My beer arrived, Jake and Erin exchanged smiles, and she went to wait on other customers, almost tripping over a bar stool as she looked back at him.

"Where does this leave you and Hannah?"

"Hannah seems to have moved on to a new love."

I choked slightly on my beer. "Oh?"

"Her work. It seems that's all she cares about. Certainly not me. Lunch today is the most I've seen or talked to her all week."

I smiled. "So not your true love after all?"

"Well, Hannah never was the sort of girl for loving, really. More just a girl for fucking, if you know–"

I slammed my glass down on the table, cutting him off.

He looked at me, shocked. "What's with you?"

"Hannah is our teammate and our friend. Show her respect."

"Sure. I will. I just thought you'd be thrilled that we were done with each other."

"I am. More than you know."

"You've changed."

"So people keep telling me." I sighed and took a long drink from my glass, nearly draining it.

"Jake, tell me about the little tri-valve mollusk things you're studying."

"Sure." He took out a stylus and started sketching on his display pad, explaining the ages and distribution of the dozens of different types of shelled creatures making up the white cliffs north of the city. Erin brought us food and joined us when she could, adding detail to Jake's drawings and greater depth to his explanations. He was right about her; she was brilliant.

After dinner, Jake and I walked back to the hotel together.

Jake asked me, "Do you want to meet at the pub later for a drink? I have a report to write up first. Or are you planning on spending the evening in bed reading?"

"I plan to go to bed early and stay there."

"Boring."

"That's me. I'll see you in the morning, Jake."

I went back to my room and slept for a couple of hours, my dreams troubled and incoherent. The gentle tap on my door at 22:30 was so soft that I almost missed it.

"Are you ready?" Hannah asked when I opened the door. "There's not much time, we need to hurry. Get your coat."

"Where are we going?" I asked as she hurried me along the hall and silently down the stairs. Or at least she was silent. I felt like I was stomping the whole way in comparison.

"Shush," she warned, "try to be quiet."

"Sorry, I have big feet."

"I noticed."

She pushed the door open on the beach side of the hotel and we walked across the cold sand down to the water.

"We probably could have done this from your balcony, but this is better," she explained. She looked at her watch and pointed at the eastern horizon. *"'Behold, a marvel in the darkness'."*

The larger moon was just rising in its final quarter, its light reflecting off the waters of the bay. As we watched, the smaller moon joined it, rising faster and slowly crossing in front of her larger sister following her own orbit across the night sky.

"I was talking to an astronomer last night and he mentioned that this conjunction was happening at moonrise. I had to see it. Have you ever seen anything so beautiful?"

I looked at her, the pale light reflecting in her eyes. "Yes."

She laughed. "You know we can all tell when you're lying, Ted."

She looked at me closely, tipping her head. "Damn." She stepped closer and slid her hands into my coat pockets wrapping her fingers around mine. "You know that just because you think something is true doesn't make it true."

"It does tonight." I kissed her and we turned our backs on the beauty of Dulcinea's moons.

When we reached my room, I asked her, "Hannah, have you finished your reports for tonight?"

"No, but that's OK. I can do it later. It should only take an hour or so."

"Do it now. I'm all right just being here with you, and I don't want you to be thinking about anything else later."

She slipped her coat off, smiling at me. She was wearing her dress that left one shoulder bare and I regretted my offer.

"Do you know the difference between you and Jake?"

"I'm not sure I want to have that conversation. Ever."

"Jake is simple," she continued anyway. "I always know what he's thinking and what he is going to do. Jake is mostly all about Jake. For example, I knew that if I ignored him for a few days that he would drift away. There are so many distractions for him at the University." She sat on my bed, adjusting pillows to make herself comfortable and logging onto her display pad.

"You, Ted, sometimes surprise me. I think it's because you over-analyze everything. It takes you forever to reach a decision, and it's always logical in some way, I just can't always predict in what way. On the plus side, your ability to take your time and pay attention to the details can be very... satisfying."

"If you keep talking like that I'm not going to let you finish your report."

She smiled and wiggled her toes at me.

I sat at the table and pulled up the status reports Jake had sent me, trying to understand the project he was working. Hannah and I talked quietly back and forth for the next hour until she finally set her pad aside and walked over to the window, pulling the blinds open.

"Can you please turn off all the lights? I want to look at the moons again."

Once it was dark, I came up behind her and placed my hands on her hips. She leaned back against me and I kissed her neck and bare shoulder. She put her hands on mine and guided them down to where she wanted them to be.

"Ted?"

"Yes?"

"Undress me please. Right here."

I undid the clasp on her dress and she let it fall around her ankles.

She turned sideways to the window and I embraced her, looking down at the blue moonlight shadows highlighting her breasts.

"When did you first know that you wanted me?" she asked, her breathing becoming more ragged as I lightly traced descending circles down her back with my fingernails.

"I fell in love with you our first night here, walking back to the hotel after dinner."

"Yes, I know that. But when did you first *want* me?"

I went to my knees in front of her, my mouth traveling slowly from left hip to right.

"Answer," she gasped. "Want to know."

I looked up at her, my cheek resting on her belly, feeling her hips still swaying. "When you stole my geosim program, and then sat there on the table with your legs swinging back and forth, defying me to challenge you."

"Yes. Thought so." She put her hands on my shoulders pushing me lower and made a sound somewhere deep in her throat.

We made love there on the floor in front of the open window, moonlight glistening on her skin, the urgency of our desire too great to make it to the bed. When I could breathe again, I picked her up and placed her under the covers. I laid down next to her, curling up against her back. She pulled my arm around her, kissed each of my fingers and went to sleep, a slight smile just touching the corners of her mouth.

For the rest of our time on Dulcinea, I spent every day with Jake and Erin working to understand the creatures that had lived in the oceans thirty million years ago. In the evenings, I attempted to get a couple of hours of sleep. My nights were like a second life, filled with Hannah. We would work on reports, talk, and then make love and lie in bed together talking and snuggling. Then we would make love again until it was almost time for me to go to the University.

"I came to visit you this afternoon on my way to work," Hannah told me one night as she was taking off her coat.

"I didn't see you."

"You know the little garden area by your building? With the native plants and benches?"

"Sure."

"I could see you through the windows from there. I sat on a bench and watched you working with Jake and Erin for almost an hour."

"Why didn't you come in?"

"I don't know. I, ah, I don't understand it. I was sitting there, feeling very happy just looking at you, and then my whole chest started hurting and I felt all gooey inside. I'm worried about me."

I smiled at her. "How old are you, Hannah?"

"A year older than you, and *much* wiser."

"So twenty-six. How many times have you been in love?"

"Do you really want to know how many lovers I've had?"

"No, I'm asking how many times you've been in love."

She looked at me, not understanding the question.

"I love you, Hannah. What you described? That's how I feel every time I'm with you or look at you or even think about you. When you love someone you give them so much power over you, power to make you happy or sad, to feel pain or ecstasy."

I put my hand under her shirt and placed it on the bare skin above her heart. "This heart is wild and fierce, but have you ever risked letting it be free?"

She put her hands on me, pushing back, trying to look defiant. "I tell my heart what to do," she said. "It obeys me. It always has."

"I think you may have a rebellion going on."

Her eyes softened after a moment, the defiance fading. She started undoing my shirt. "Yeah, I think that's true."

"Have you chosen which side you're on?"

She started kissing my chest, her teeth gently nipping at my skin. "The rebels are too strong for me, I'm afraid. I have no choice but to join them."

When we were two days and one night away from departure, Jake seemed depressed and Erin despondent. I kept finding them in some corner of the lab, holding hands, whispering. I was feeling a sense of dread myself. Hannah would be on board with me, but once again under the careful scrutiny of *Wandering Star*.

"How do they do it?" I asked Hannah when she arrived in my room that night. "Charlotte and Brian and Horace and Angela. Well, maybe not Angela, but how does the team not form 'romantic entanglements'?"

"They cheat," she answered. "And don't count Angela out. Have you seen the way Professor Vandermeer looks at her? There's history there, I'm sure of it. Two months on a planet is plenty of time for things to develop." She kissed me on the ear. "Remember too, *Star* and I have an understanding."

"I look forward to seeing a demonstration."

"Tomorrow is a free day since we'll be headed to the airport at 20:00. What would you like to do?"

"Jake and Erin are going to the zoo in the afternoon. There's a concert of local folk music there at 15:00."

"I'd like that." She sat on my lap facing me, her knees by my hips, rocking gently. "What shall we do in the morning?"

I kissed her and she braced her hands on the back of the chair behind me continuing her gently rocking.

"Hah. I have you trapped now," she said.

She leaned back briefly and I kissed her breast where her nipple was pushing against the fabric of her shirt.

"Ah."

I pulled her shirt up and she raised her arms so I could pull it over her head, but I stopped with her hands still entangled. I kissed her there again, holding her arms above her.

"Hey! No fair. I had you trapped." I continued kissing her chest. "No fair," she said more quietly. I let go of her arms, but she kept them crossed over her head, whispering *no fair* as I lifted her off my lap and carried her to the bed.

Hannah left early the next morning to go back to her room. She kissed me before she left and then patted her side of the bed.

"Goodbye comfy bed," she whispered. "I did my best to wear you out."

"I'll meet you in the lobby at 09:00," I told her. "I love you."

She smiled, came back and kissed me again. "I do love you." The admission seemed to surprise her, so she kissed me one more time as though to be sure. Then she left, closing the door gently behind her.

Hannah and I spent the morning exploring the local shops, buying small souvenirs we didn't really need, and enjoying the late winter sunshine. The zoo was a confusing mixture of Dulcinean life and animals imported from Earth and a dozen other worlds.

The afternoon concert was beautiful, the music unlike any I remember hearing on Earth. It left me in such a happy mood that I didn't realize that Hannah and I were holding hands until I noticed Jake was staring at us. I smiled at him, not really caring what he was thinking.

He and Erin headed back toward the University to say their goodbyes, and Hannah and I walked back to the Hotel, the last daylight of our last day on Dulcinea fading quickly around us.

"You'll need to let go of my hand now," Hannah reminded me.

"I know." I gave her hand a final kiss before releasing it. "I don't want to."

"We have to play the game or leave the service."

"If all our planet falls are like this I won't live long enough to resign."

"Poor Ted. He suffered so much on this planet."

"There were times last night that I thought *you* were trying to kill me."

She smiled at me, eyes bright. "You're welcome."

We entered the lobby and Hannah was once again just my friend and teammate.

It is traditional for the RuComm team to share their last meal on planet together. The menu is designed to suggest a hasty departure, consisting of the sort of simple food that you might take camping or on a road trip. Everyone's bags were packed and lined up along one wall of the conference room reminding us that time was short.

When Jake arrived, he pulled me out into the hall away from the others.

"Are you *insane*?"

"Not that I know of, Jake."

"Hannah? Really? Do I need to have *Star* replay everything you said while I was..."

"Insane?"

"Yes, insane. There's like this bubble of crazy around her. Pull yourself out of it before it's too late."

"It's too late."

"You're an idiot."

"This is different."

"Different how? Different from me? Oh, sure it is. Because you've thought it through. Your motives are noble and pure, unlike mine. This is why the contract says what it says, *Theodore*." He took a step closer to me. "You probably think she loves you."

I pulled my fist back to hit him and he stood there waiting for it.

"Is that what you want to do?" he asked me.

I put my hand down and walked back into the conference room to find Angela. She was talking to Charlotte, but I interrupted her anyway.

"Angela, is it too late to request separate quarters? Separate from Jake?"

Her eyes narrowed as she looked up at me. "Interesting. Jake asked me the same thing ten minutes ago." She paused, trying to read my face. "Of course. I'll have your new assignments once we're on board."

CHAPTER 8

BETWEEN WORLDS

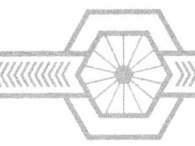

We left on schedule. A short walk to the bus, a few minutes to the port, and we were on board one of *Wandering Star's* shuttles being pushed into our seats as we accelerated out of Dulcinea's gravity well. There were no windows to look out of and I don't think I would have looked anyway.

Hannah was in the seat next to me and the thought of her there filled me. Twice I had to pull my hand back when it started to drift into her lap. Three times, she had to do the same. Finally, she crossed her arms and extended her fingers to brush my sleeve. I crossed my arms as well so that our fingers could reach each other. Just being able to touch her was a relief. I adjusted myself in the seat and looked over at her. Hannah had her eyes closed, the corner of her mouth holding a secret smile as her fingers rubbed gently against mine hidden from view behind the folds of our coats.

We passed through the area of fluctuating gravitational fields around the ship and docked. Ship gravity was still at eighty percent, but *Star* would be increasing it gradually to eight-five over the next week to match our next planet fall on Cleavus. We were also getting back our twenty-four hour days, plus an extra fifty-two minutes.

Charlotte touched my shoulder as I followed Hannah toward the front of the shuttle. She and Brian had been sitting behind us.

"Ted," she whispered, "I thought you should know that there is quite a large gap between the seats when viewed from behind. You need to be careful."

"Oh, um, thank you?"

"Don't mention it."

So much for being discreet. At least she seemed to be OK with keeping our secret.

Angela had us gather at the front of the shuttle bay for welcoming comments from Captain von Muller. It gave me a few minutes to speak to Alice and introduce myself to Sipa Patel who was joining us for the rest of the mission. He was an economist from Bodens Gate who had been working for RuComm in Palma Sola for the past year. Mid-thirties and happy to be leaving Dulcinea, he seemed pleasant.

Alice was trying to look as complacent as the rest of the team, but I could tell she was excited. She was shaking.

"Everything is so different," she told me. "It even smells different and does the floor always vibrate like that?"

I smiled at her. "Yes, all the time."

"And the *Wandering Star* AI, she's always watching everything we do?"

My smile faded a little. "And always listening. All you have to do to get her attention is to say her name and ask her a question. She can access any information known, help you find your way around the ship, or locate someone. She talks to us through our comm pins." I touched the top of Alice's ear. "*Star*? Where are we?"

"You and Ms. Vandermeer are in the port shuttle bay. Welcome back, Mr. Holloman. I've been working on the Sonoran Desert simulation while you were away. Let me know when you're ready to try it."

"Thank you, *Star*, I'll do that."

"She's like a person."

"Yes, think of her as a very nosy neighbor."

Von Muller's welcoming comments were mercifully brief, reminding us that his obligation was to keep us safe and our obligation was to follow his orders including mandatory safety drills.

Angela spoke to us next, thanking us for our work on Dulcinea and asking us to get our final reports in quickly so she could consolidate and format them for submission to RuComm. She also welcomed Sipa Patel to the team and introduced Alice Vandermeer as our temporary chaplain until we reached Bodens Gate.

I picked up my new cabin assignment and walked with Hannah into the body of the ship. She had been talking to Sipa while I was with Alice, planning the next section of her paper.

"Between Sipa's insights into the Palma Federated States' economic stagnation, and Mr. Mahajan knowing what's happening in the legislature, I think we can really show causality for the rapid changes in language happening in the capital."

We stopped at my new quarters. "I'd love to see what you have so far. Can I stop by in an hour or so after we get settled?"

Hannah's cheeks flushed slightly. "Sounds good. I think you'll find it exciting."

My new cabin was smaller than the one I had shared with Jake, but seemed less crowded without him in it. I dumped clothes and the rest of my stuff where they belonged and adjusted the display panels to show images of my favorite geologic locations.

I then searched for an image Angela had used in a presentation at the start of the mission that showed pictures of all of the team members with their names and a three-line biography. I found it and moved it to the largest screen. The small picture of Hannah in the corner perfectly captured the confident, aggressive smile that had been on her lips when she had stolen my geosim program. I smiled back at her picture.

"Are you feeling all right, Mr. Holloman?" *Star* asked.

"Sure, why do you ask?"

"Your heart rate has jumped fifty percent above your normal resting rate."

"It must be the excitement from being back on board."

"Of course. I'll disregard it for now."

I passed Alice in the corridor while I was walking toward Hannah's cabin.

"Lost or exploring?" I asked her.

"Is there a difference?"

"It's exploring as long as you don't miss a meal."

"*Wandering Star* has promised to guide me if I get lost."

"Yes, she enjoys doing that."

"Want to join me?"

"I'm sorry. I promised Hannah that I would review a paper she's working on with Mr. Mahajan."

Her smile slipped away. "I understand."

"I really am sorry."

"I know you are." A touch of her smile returned and she patted my arm. "Go."

Hannah answered her door at the first tap and invited me in.

"Let me show you what we have so far, Ted." She opened her pad and tapped an icon labeled *Sleeping Star*. The screen changed to a timer counting down from one hour. She tipped her head and looked at me. "Impressed?"

"Uh, not yet."

"*Star*, where am I?" she asked.

There was no answer

"*Star*, where is Ted?"

There was still no answer, so I tried it. "*Star*?" I smiled at the silence.

Hannah wrapped her arms around me and kissed me, sliding her hands down inside my back pockets. She let go after a long moment, nuzzled my neck, and glanced at the ceiling.

"Now I'm impressed. How do you do it?" I asked.

"All of the *Star* series ships use an older language system for their AIs. I'm good at languages. I found a way to hide myself within her matrix without tripping any of her safety monitors, or leaving a trace in the security logs. I think of it as like putting a pile of sand in a shallow stream. For a time the water diverges around it, but it soon washes away and you can't tell it was ever there. I worry that she'll feel it if I go over an hour or do it too often, but for now she is blind and deaf to what happens in this cabin."

"How often is too often?"

Hannah shrugged. "I don't really know. I've never used it more than once a day and never more than two or three times a week. I'm afraid that she'll notice that I'm punching holes through her brain. We also need to make sure we're close to the same location where she last saw us, or she might notice the jump."

"Have I told you that you're brilliant?"

"Yeah, but you can tell me again."

I kissed her and held her tight against me. "You're brilliant," I whispered.

"You really should look at the paper we're working on. Mr. Mahajan sent me updates while we were on the shuttle. I want you to see them and it will only take a few minutes."

"OK." I released her, she pulled up the new pages, and we talked about the way she was interpreting the data. I made a few suggestions for changing chart types to better show the correlation between her variables and constants. We looked at the results and tweaked a few more things.

After a while she said, "Now, my love, where were we?" She settled herself on my lap.

I looked at the timer on her pad. "Ten minutes from the end."

She swung her head around to the display and her body went limp as she buried her head on my shoulder.

"Why did you let me talk so long?"

"I love listening to you talk and working with you."

"But we could have done that it the lab tomorrow."

"Not like we did. Did you notice that our bodies were in contact the entire time we were talking?"

"Yes, I noticed, believe me I noticed. But that was supposed to be just the prelude for much greater touching. Enhanced touching. Brilliant touching." She looked at the timer again, watching the seconds streaming by. "Just hold me, please. Anything else would make it worse at this point."

"Try again tomorrow?" I asked, nuzzling her ear.

"Yes. And no talking. None."

"Just grunts?"

"Groans would be OK too. Maybe moaning."

I went back to my cabin and slept fitfully. It was strange to be alone, no one's hand to hold in the middle of the night, no one sleeping on my shoulder.

Alice was eating breakfast when I arrived in the mess hall the next morning. I picked up a couple of rolls and a cup of coffee and sat down next to her.

"How did your explorations go last night?"

"I only got lost twice," she said, proud of herself. "*Star* showed me the gym and the running trail you've been using. I'm going to have to exercise more as the gravity builds up. I feel heavier today."

"We'll be at Cleavus in three weeks. Gravity there is only a little over point eight five so you should be OK. Bodens Gate will be harder for you. They're ten percent over standard."

She sighed. "My body wasn't designed for that."

Hannah joined us, sitting down directly across from Alice. "Hannah Weldon," she introduced herself. "What wasn't your body designed for?"

"Alice Vandermeer." Alice held her hand out which Hannah held briefly. "Oh, we were just talking about how I was going to need strenuous, aerobic exercise to cope with the increasing gravity. I was hoping Ted could help get my heart rate up."

Was that what we had been talking about?

Hannah started eating, slicing up her sausages and stabbing at them with her fork. "I'd be happy to help too. We can run together if you think you can keep up."

"I think you may have an advantage. Being from Earth, I mean. It makes you larger."

"I'm happy being a little larger." Her eyes darted downward. "And stronger and faster."

"But you always have that extra force pulling all of your parts downward. It must be distressing."

"Alice," I interrupted, "have you had a chance to talk to Jake since we came on board? He's been staring at his display pad and looking unhappy since I got here."

Alice and Hannah turned; ready to shift their attacks away from each other and onto me.

Alice sighed, unwilling to give up the fight with Hannah, but doing so for the sake of a new target. "Yes, I talked to him when I got here this morning. He's sad about leaving Erin and upset with you for some reason. He said he and Erin are sending a lot of messages back and forth now, but I suspect that will resolve itself with time and distance. By the time we reach Cleavus, she'll have drifted away. Anyway, Ted, you should go talk to him. What was it that he said your argument was about?"

"Insanity?" I suggested.

"Yes, that was it. One of you is insane and one of you is not, I don't recall which is which. He said that you came this close," she held her fingers a millimeter apart, "to hitting him in the face."

She turned back to Hannah. "Are all of you who are 'stronger and faster' also so violent?"

Hannah pushed her chair back and stood up.

"Hannah, I think it's time for us to get to the lab." I pushed her toward the exit.

"Yes we are, when there's a need for it," Hannah called to Alice over her shoulder as we left.

Once out in the passageway I started laughing.

"You think that was funny, Ted?"

"Amazing, really. I haven't seen two people escalate a conversation from zero to an almost brawl that fast since I left home. My sisters did that sometimes at the dinner table when I was a kid, except they usually ended up rolling around on the floor with my dad yelling at them to break it up."

Hannah smiled ruefully. "That's what I was going to do next."

"I'm sorry. I was hoping that you and Alice would become friends. She's not a bad person."

"She wants you, Ted, in case you hadn't noticed. If you're too nice to shove her big nose out of your cabin, I will." Hannah took another couple of steps and said under her breath, "I should have told her that. She *does* have a big nose."

I was still chuckling when we entered the main lab.

Sipa Patel was there as well as Charlotte, Brian, and Giz. Others came and went, working on reports or getting ready for Cleavus. Hannah and Sipa sat at one of the worktables with its larger screen area and started going over the input from Mr. Mahajan. I found a cubicle where I could glance up at her from time to time and worked with *Star* to dig into the old archives, trying again to find the original three hundred year old Cleavus survey.

Not long after lunch, I found a cache of misfiled seismic and mineralogy reports that gave me enough data to try a simple simulation. I stopped by to see how Hannah and Sipa were coming along and to let her know I'd be in the sim lab. She nodded and barely looked up, intent on following the evolution of some obscure verb usage over the past twenty years.

The anonymous, long-dead geologist who had performed the survey, or at least consolidated the data, had mapped the instability of Cleavus' orbit and used it to explain the alternating layers of limestone and evaporates that covered much of its surface. He had postulated that even though there was no surface water on the planet when he had conducted the survey, that there were thousands of layers showing that Cleavus had just as often been entirely covered in water. I played with the sim all afternoon trying to create a model that produced results consistent with the survey. I was getting close by the time Hannah came to fetch me for dinner.

"I need a couple more hours," I complained.

"Nope. I'm hungry now."

We ate dinner with Charlotte and Brian, which was good because I needed Brian's expertise in astrophysics to help refine my orbit model. Hannah was quiet through most of dinner, moving the food around on her plate, but not eating very much of it.

Hannah and I excused ourselves after dinner and I went back to the lab for an hour before happening to walk past her door at about 19:00.

She let me in and said, "Let me show you the progress Sipa and I made on the charts you helped with yesterday." She brought up *Sleeping Star* and started the timer.

"I know you said 'no talking', but are you OK?" I asked. "You seemed distracted at dinner."

"That's fine, I need to talk." She sat on the edge of her bed, looking troubled. "I didn't get anything done after you left to work on your sim. Sipa did, but I just sat there unable to concentrate. I'd look up and you weren't there and then all that I could think about was that you weren't there. I knew you were just across the lab, but I couldn't see you." She scooted back on the bed putting her head on the pillows. "There's something wrong with me."

"There's nothing wrong with you. Do you think I'm thinking straight when you aren't around? This is part of being in love with each other and knowing we can't show it." I took her shoes off and started rubbing her feet. "We're on board the ship together. I can't be more than a few hundred meters away without Captain von Muller having to give a two hour speech about how 'horrible is death in the vacuum of space'."

I got her to smile.

"I don't want to be like Charlotte and Brian," she said. "They go through their lives and no one knows they're in love. No one *can* know. I want people to be able to see it in my eyes. When I walk down the street, I want them to point me out to their friends and say, '*That girl there, she's in love. What a lucky guy he must be*'."

I moved from her feet to massaging her legs. "I do see it in your eyes, and I am lucky." I undid her pants, pulled them off and kissed each of her knees. "Our problem is that I think everyone else on board can see it in your eyes too. And in mine."

"Less talking, more grunting." She pulled me up on top of her.

Ten minutes later *Wandering Star* initiated our first safety drill.

"I hate you, *Star*," Hannah whispered as tears slipped from her eyes.

"Do you have an extra pressure suit?" I asked.

"In the closet. It should fit you, it fit–" She stopped.

"It's OK. It fit Jake?"

"Yes. I didn't want to hurt you."

"It doesn't. I know it's me you love."

She gave me a quick kiss, her eyes sparkling.

Hannah shut down *Sleeping Star* and we waited a second to make sure *Star* was tracking us again. We suited up and ran down the passageway together to spend the rest of the evening listening to our Captain's words of inspiration.

The next day, I stayed in the main lab while Hannah and Sipa worked. She looked tired, but otherwise OK and seemed happy with the day's results when we talked during dinner. I was at her door at 19:30 as we had arranged. After I entered, Hannah hesitated a moment before engaging her *Sleeping Star* program, wincing as she tapped the icon.

"I've never done this three days in a row," she explained. "We can't keep this up."

"You never did this with…"

"No." She shook her head. "I didn't need to be with any of them like I need to be with you."

"We can skip a day if you want."

She shook her head again and sat down in the middle of her bed, legs crossed. "Ted, how would you describe me? *Just* my personality," she added when she saw my smile.

"OK. Confident, aggressive, intelligent, creative, playful, independent, determined, innovative… Brilliant. What else should I add?"

She nodded. "That's how I saw myself. I was in control, I set the agenda and I didn't need or care about anyone else's opinion. Independent? Not anymore. Now I can't work unless I have you within my line of sight." She flopped back on the bed. "Damn it, Ted, what have you *done* to me? I feel like I'm drowning and can't catch my breath. If I could have you here for one full night, I think I could go two or three without you. Or if I could hold your hand during the day, give you a quick kiss or a hug when I wanted to, I think I'd be able to sleep at night." She put her arms behind her, holding onto the headboard. "The waters are closing over me. I'm not sleeping at night which makes me ineffective during the day which makes me worry all night instead of sleeping."

I laid down next to her and she climbed on top of me, trying to press as much of her to as much of me as possible. She nuzzled her head into my shoulder and I shivered as sharp teeth nipped at my ear.

Then it stopped.

I gently lifted her hair away from my eyes and looked at Hannah asleep on my shoulder. I pulled the covers over us and listened to her breathing, letting it tickle my neck, feeling her body press against me occasionally as she dreamed. With five minutes left on the timer, I slid out from under her and kissed her forehead.

"I need to leave you now."

She didn't open her eyes, but said, "It's OK, my love. Dreaming about you."

I returned to my quarters hoping that Hannah would sleep through the night. I know I didn't. Hannah and I had only slept together for a bit over two weeks on Dulcinea, yet somehow my body and mind had accepted it as not just normal, but required.

Things did not improve as the days went by. I only slept for a few hours a night; I think Hannah only slept for the hour we were together. And we were continuing to punch holes through *Wandering Star's* brain every night, something she was bound to notice sooner or later.

Ten days after leaving Dulcinea, Alice stopped me in the corridor when I was returning from Hannah's quarters.

"Can you meet me for an early breakfast tomorrow? Just you?"

"Sure, Alice, what time?"

"Is five too early?"

"No, I'll be awake anyway."

I was there before her, drinking a cup of coffee and rereading survey reports from Cleavus. Alice poured herself a cup and joined me.

"You look terrible, Ted."

"Thanks. Good morning to you too."

"I'm serious. You and Hannah both." She looked around the empty mess hall. "There's no place to speak privately, is there?"

I shook my head. "Thereby hangs a tale."

"I'll just talk then. There is a saying on Dulcinea that your destiny is determined by who you invite into your bed." She smiled. "It's usually phrased more crudely. When I first heard it, I thought it was just a witticism. I've come to believe there is much truth in it."

"Your point?"

"Watching the two of you together is like looking at two magnets forced apart, that now so desperately want to go *clack* back together."

"We're just friends."

"Let me try it this way." She held up a small pitcher that was on the table. "You, milk. Hannah, coffee." She poured some of the milk into her coffee, stirring it until it was a uniform light brown. "See? Can the two be separated?" Her eyes held mine. "Don't deny what is obvious to every single one of your teammates."

"On board this ship we are just friends."

Alice looked at the ceiling again, frowning, struggling to stay within the limits.

"I have heard that sometimes people who are in love suffer when they are forced apart. If they accept that being in love means being out of control, they can survive. They'll be in pain, sure, but they'll be OK in the end. But if they have never experienced love before, for example if their previous lovers were all like, let's say Jake, and she was always in control from the beginning, and she released them when she was done with them, then she has a decision to make. Does she want to have control or does she want to be in love? No one can have both."

"An interesting theory."

"Yes it is, although I don't want to collect the empirical evidence to prove it."

"Thank you, but I don't think any of this helps me." I looked at her and put my head on my hand because I was too tired to hold it up. "Anything else?"

"Did you know I was married before?"

I lifted my head back up. "No, I didn't."

"I was very young, only..." Her eyes squinted as she did the conversion between Earth and Dulcinean years in her head. "Barely nineteen. We were married for seven years."

"What happened?"

"There was an aircraft accident. They're rare, but they happen. Two years ago he got out of my bed, kissed me," she touched her cheek as though she could still feel it, "and he was gone."

"I'm sorry."

"It kind of proves the wisdom of the saying, doesn't it? No longer having him in my bed forced me to face several truths about myself. It's why I am the way I am."

"Alice, I suspect you've always been the way you are. You are one of the few constants in my life."

She smiled. "I like you, Ted. You always tell me the truth once you're tired enough or I get you drunk enough, but you didn't know me back then. One last thing. My father asked me to offer both you and Hannah a position at the University should you have an interest in returning there some day."

"Thank you, Alice. It's a generous offer." I looked at my watch and stood up. "I'm going to go work in the sim lab for a while."

"You don't want Hannah to see you talking to me."

I nodded. "That's truth."

That night in Hannah's cabin, I talked to her about our options before I let her sleep.

"We can't go on like this, Hannah. We will both literally die."

She blinked at me, saying nothing.

"We're only a few days from Cleavus. Assuming the full sixty days there then eight days to Bodens Gate, that would mean that we could break our contracts in less than three months."

"And be stranded on Bodens Gate? Do you know what it's like there? They use every language ever used on Earth and they've been inventing new ones constantly for the past three hundred years. It's total chaos. People die on Bodens Gate. They die a lot."

"I talked to Sipa. He's from there and he could help us find work. We could save enough for passage to Earth, or back to Dulcinea, which would be cheaper. We could probably save enough for that within eight or ten months, get there, work at the University. The point is we would be together, not rich, but with no one watching, no timers running. We could just... live. Or a few more weeks past Bodens Gate to Malapert, or we're six months away from Earth if we can hold on that long."

"So this is what you have done to me. I can have three months of misery, and then give up everything I've worked for to live in poverty on the most dangerous planet in the Union, or I can become Charlotte and live a lie every day pretending I don't love you. Or I can just die like I'm doing now."

"During your time on Dulcinea did you ever hear the saying that your destiny is determined by who you invite into your bed?"

She smiled weakly. "What a polite way of saying it."

"I have been in your bed and I don't want to leave. Now we have to choose our destiny."

"Will you carry me to my bed, please?"

I picked her up out of the chair, set her on the bed, and laid down next to her. She curled up on top of me.

"It's been a beautiful dream, Ted. All of it. From the very beginning, it's been a beautiful dream."

I held her and she slept until it was time for me to leave.

The next evening, Alice came and sat with us while we finished dinner. Hannah glanced up at her and sighed, too tired to fight. She went back to cutting up the last of her food.

"Brian and Charlotte did something this afternoon. I don't know what the consequences will be, but you need to know about it." Alice was shaking, as she had on the Margo Islands when her fears were overcoming her.

"Were you involved?" Hannah asked.

"Yes, I was there. But Hannah, I didn't do this. I would have advised against it."

"Just tell us."

Alice looked troubled, unsure how to begin. "Brian and Charlotte created a petition to exempt the two of you from the Romantic Entanglements clause in your contract for the duration of the mission. Everyone signed it, including Jake, including me." She trailed off into a whisper. "Even Captain von Muller signed it. Charlotte asked me to come with her and Brian when they presented it to Angela. They gave it to her and she frowned as she read it and she must have read it three or four times. It looked like she was studying the names at the bottom. Then she looked up and said, 'No. Will there be anything else?'

"Brian started to argue with her, but she cut him off saying that it was against the contract everyone had signed and would set a bad precedent. Then Charlotte started to argue and Angela said, 'So if I approve this, how long will it be before you ask for one for you and Brian?' That pretty much ended the conversation.

"I'm so sorry," Alice continued, "I know what this would have meant to you, to end the pain you're in."

Hannah didn't say anything, but she had a look of determination in her eyes. She picked the napkin off of her lap and carefully placed it beside her plate. She stood and said, "*Star*, where is Angela?"

"Ms. Dawkins is in her office in the main science lab."

Alice closed her eyes and tears started to run down her cheeks as she bowed her head. I turned and ran after Hannah, catching up with her in the passageway.

"Hannah, you don't want to do this. You haven't slept. You're not thinking it through."

"I'm pretty sure this is exactly what I want to do. I've been in constant agony for twelve days, every hour of every day. It has filled me until there is nothing else inside. It's time to share it."

I took her arm and led her toward the outer ring corridor. "Walk with me first. *Star*, Sonoran desert, night, twenty-three degrees C."

We entered the ring and a quite desert night surrounded us. There was the sound of crickets and a sky full of stars.

"This is where you grew up?"

"Close by."

"It's pretty."

We walked in silence for a minute and then Hannah stopped.

"This doesn't help me." She looked around. "This is just one more beautiful thing that I can see, but not touch." She waved her hand through one of the cholla plants beside the trail. "It's not real."

"I'm real." I put my arm around her waist and she put hers around mine.

"Mr. Holloman, Ms. Weldon, I am concerned by your conversation and close proximity. Please step away from each other."

"*Star*, Hannah has injured her foot and I am helping her walk back to her quarters."

There was a pause of almost a second before *Star* replied. "So noted."

"She took too long," I said quietly to Hannah. "She did something."

"You lie so easily now, Ted. I suppose that's my doing. My gift to you for loving me."

Hannah started to cry, softly at first and then sobbing so hard she could no longer walk. I picked her up and left the trail, carrying her back along the passageways to her cabin. She kept her face buried in my shoulder, her body convulsing as she wept. We passed other members of the team on the way and I kept my eyes straight ahead, not looking at them as they stepped out of my way, ignoring their whispering behind me.

I laid Hannah on her bed and kissed her for a long moment, trying to brush the tears from her cheeks, tasting their salt.

"Mr. Holloman, Angela would like you to come to her office immediately."

Hannah put her hand on my cheek and tried a brave smile. "Go now. You'll be OK."

I entered Angela's office and sat down, feeling angry and defiant, but knowing that I had no ground on which to stand.

"You're aware of this?" she turned her display around so I could see the petition, the dozen signatures at the bottom. "You requested it?"

"No."

"Hannah requested it?"

"No."

"Then that just shows how deeply you have disrupted this team. Brian and Charlotte are on their twelfth hop together, did you know that? Now because of you they are acting like foolish children, jeopardizing their careers. And look at you and Jake. You haven't spoken in almost two weeks. Is that how a team is supposed to function?

"The rules of your contract are written in blood, Theodore, the blood of those that came before us. RuComm created every one of them to prevent a recurrence of something bad that happened in the past. This one, that you have violated and now want to ignore completely, is there because three people died when a love affair went out of control. You and Hannah, you act like you're the first people to ever be in love. Believe me, you're not."

I opened my mouth to answer, but she held up her hand to stop me.

"Don't. Just don't. Omar Gizbar was in my office this afternoon. The Grand Old Man of the Reunification Commission spent an hour in here quoting Shakespeare at me as if the two of you are some tragic heroes. Damn it, Theodore, what does 'Love is blind, and lovers cannot see, the pretty follies that themselves commit' even mean? I wish I had left you and Hannah on Dulcinea. There was enough evidence to terminate both of you right then and there, but I need a geologist for Cleavus and there wasn't time to replace you."

She sighed. "Here's what's going to happen next. I know I'm going to regret it, no, I already regret it. Giz convinced me to keep this incident out of the official record, so this is a verbal warning. Any hint of a recurrence, though, and you're finished.

"You and Hannah are both confined to quarters for the next seventy-two hours. No sending messages to anyone and no coming out for meals, they will be printed in your quarters."

"And if we refuse?"

"Damn, I knew I'd regret this. Then you're done right now. You will forfeit your pay, have to reimburse RuComm for all expenses, including your education at the Academy, and you will be confined to quarters forcibly until we arrive at the next inhabited planet. In this case, God help you, that means Bodens Gate."

I sat there holding her gaze until she looked back at her screen. "Your seventy-two hours starts right now, Mr. Holloman."

When I got back out into the main corridor Hannah was coming the other direction, Angela having summoned her. Her face was down, but I saw the tears still on her cheeks and her hair was disheveled from when I'd carried her.

"Hannah, are you OK?"

She shook her head, but said nothing. She never looked up as she passed me and never looked back as I stood there watching her walk away.

I reached my quarters and the door sealed behind me. The first thing I noticed was that my largest display panel was now blank, the image of the team with Hannah in the corner gone.

"You are very thorough, *Star*."

"Thank you, Mr. Holloman."

"Not a compliment this time."

"You should rest. I have been authorized to offer you something to help you sleep if you desire, and something to help you regain control over your emotions."

"No. I want to spend the next seventy-two hours learning everything I can about Bodens Gate. I'll need your help since I can't talk to Sipa."

"Very well."

What I found was worse than the rumors I'd heard. The Union had established Bodens Gate as a logistics depot for traffic traveling between Earth and the outer worlds to refit and refuel. Every ship that passed through had at least a few crewmembers that wanted to stay and try their hand at colonizing a new world. For those with money and skills, that worked pretty well. The Central Government in the larger cities was elected by the citizens, made and enforced laws, and encouraged economic development.

But the majority of the people on Bodens Gate were non-citizens as far as the Central Government were concerned. Unrepresented and unprotected, their only hope of survival lay with the clans that ruled in the Warrens, an ungoverned area in the shadow of Bodens Gate's capital, Eindhoven. There were clans based on language and ethnicity, geographic location, religion, corporate allegiance, ideology, family ties, and who knew what else. Most had only a few hundred adherents, but there were thousands of them and they fought for control and dominance, more than willing to use extortion, kidnap, rape, and murder to expand their reach.

The Central Government ignored the clans as long as they left the citizens alone. If they didn't, retribution was swift and brutal. Two years before, one clan that was targeting citizens for kidnap and ransom simply disappeared. Somewhere between three and four hundred people vanished overnight and no trace of them was ever found. After that, it was said that a citizen could walk through the worst parts of the city and remain unmolested. For a time.

My dream of living there with Hannah while we tried to save for passage to Dulcinea vanished. We'd never survive without sponsorship to become citizens, and even if Sipa helped us find a sponsor, that would commit us to staying there for at least five years.

When I managed to sleep during those three days, concern for Hannah haunted my dreams. I didn't know what I would find on the other side of my door when our confinement ended.

On the fourth day *Star* woke me and said that my door was unsealed. I showered, dressed, and went to the mess hall. Hannah was there eating breakfast and talking to Sipa. She had tied her hair back and she looked rested and alert, better than I had seen her since leaving Dulcinea. She was gesturing with her fork while she and Sipa talked.

I sat down across from her. Sipa nodded to me, took a last drink of his coffee, and excused himself.

"You look good," I told her.

"I've been sleeping. You should try it. *Star* gave me something and I slept for like fourteen hours. I almost feel like me again." She looked up, but at the wall behind me, over at other people, anywhere but at me.

"What else did she give you?"

"Something for anxiety, something to help me concentrate, maybe a couple of other things. It's weird. I can still feel like an aching here," she put her hand on her chest, "but it doesn't quite reach here." She tapped her head. "The pain is gone and I can work again. I feel like I'm back in control."

She took a bite of her food and pointed her fork at me. "You should try this stuff. You won't hurt anymore. *Star* mixed it in with my pancakes. I can't even taste it."

"I think I prefer the pain."

She smiled her old aggressive smile, tipping her head slightly. "Really? I wish I had known that about you back when we were on Dulcinea. We could have–" She cut herself off looking confused, took a couple of deep breaths and swallowed hard.

"I think I'm going to have to not see you for a few more days. The way you look, the way you smell, it's too much for me right now."

"You smell me?"

"Yes, damn it, I smell you, OK? Now go away until I can sit by you and not need to touch you."

Alice entered the mess hall while we were talking. She rested her hand on my shoulder briefly in greeting as she walked by us.

"And please don't spend time with Alice. Please. I'm begging you, not right now. You should go sit with Jake; he's the one that needs you. He told me when I got here that Erin has stopped replying to his messages. He needs his friend back, and you need him."

CHAPTER 9

CLEAVUS

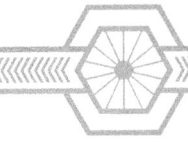

Jake looked up at me when I sat down across from him.

"Ted," he looked back at his plate, "about you and Hannah–"

I cut him off. "Please, I don't want to hear 'I told you so' about Hannah from you right now."

"OK, but let me say one thing, please. Remember the night we left Dulcinea?"

"The night I wanted to hit you?"

He smiled. "Yeah, that night. I was wrong about you and Hannah. She does love you. It *was* different. And I'm sorry."

I looked back at her. She was working on her display pad and finishing her pancakes.

"She did love me. I don't know now."

"She still does, I was watching her while you talked to her. The meds they gave her are suppressing it pretty well, but that spark she gets in her eyes is still there."

Sipa sat down next to me, a fresh cup of coffee in his hand. I nodded a greeting and turned back to Jake. "Do you know what they're giving her?"

"No, but I can guess. The stuff to help her sleep is benign and it wouldn't hurt you to try it. The rest of it is suppressing all of her emotions. She'll feel sort of a pleasant glow, but nothing else will reach her. No joy, no anger, and no love. It will give her a feeling of well-being and control, but not much else."

Sipa looked at me sympathetically. "I don't know Hannah as well as you do, but watching her fall apart over the past two weeks was distressing. I think this is worse."

"Maybe they can get her off of them quickly."

"Not with you around, my friend," Sipa said. "I was watching the two of you just now. Without the meds she would have wrapped herself around you the moment you walked in."

"Yeah, I know that feeling."

Jake frowned. "We're only two days away from Cleavus. You'll be on the surface for two months doing geology, but there's not much work for a linguist on an uninhabited planet. She should be able to wean herself off while you're gone."

"I hope so," Sipa added. "I've seen this before. You don't want to stay on that stuff too long, or you're never coming back."

Hannah approached our table, looked at Jake, then at Sipa.

"Are you ready to get some work done?" she asked.

Sipa stood, resting his hand on my shoulder. "Most certainly."

I turned back to Jake after watching her leave. "When are we having our planning meeting for Cleavus?"

"Um, we had that last night. Angela assigned you all of your tasks."

"Great."

"It should be OK, there's a standard deck for uninhabited planets being visited for the first time. We'll do an on-orbit survey and then select a couple of areas for surface exploration."

"No one bothered to mention the simulation I built last week?"

"Alice did, but Angela dismissed it. She didn't see any reason to deviate."

"There should be massive cave complexes covering large areas of the surface. The standard on-orbit survey will miss most of them." I sighed. "I suppose I need to go talk to Angela."

"Want me to go with you? I could hold your hand."

"Shut up, Jake." I smiled at him.

"You never could stay mad at me. Admit it."

"I suppose." I examined the bottom of my empty coffee cup. "So, how's your friend, Erin?"

"You had to go there?" he sighed. "Just one more victim of our service to the Reunification Commission. I haven't heard from her in a couple of days."

"I'm sorry."

"You go talk to Angela. I'll stay here drinking coffee and being miserable."

I stood and patted him on the back. "Thanks, you do that."

Angela didn't look happy to see me. "What can I do for you, Mr. Holloman?"

"I'd like to talk to you about my tasking for Cleavus, specifically about the on-orbit survey and selection of surface sites."

"Have you reviewed your tasking?"

"No, not completely." I hadn't looked at any of it.

"Perhaps you should before you come in here to complain." She turned back at her display, dismissing me.

"Are you planning to do a Synthetic Aperture Radar search?"

She looked back up, irritated that I was still there. "No. It would require a lower orbit and take additional time. In the long-range images Cleavus looks the way Mars used to. It's mostly a waterless red ball. I don't want to waste the resources."

"You should do it anyway. Getting a radar signal to bounce around inside the cave openings my simulation shows are there is the only way you will ever find all of them. If you want this survey to be definitive, we need to do it."

She tapped her fingers on her desk. "I'll consider it. Anything else?"

"Not at this time. I'll review the rest of my tasks first and let you know."

She gave me a very slight touch of a smile. "Thank you, Theodore."

Jake was waiting for me when I left her office.

"That was quick. Are you going back to your quarters now for the next three days?"

"Real funny. I'm going to go review my tasks and work on the geosim model the rest of the day."

We entered the main lab. Hannah was sitting at one of the work areas, her back to us. I realized I had stopped walking when Jake ran into me.

"You've got to stop doing that," he whispered. "You have to let her go."

"I don't see that happening, Jake. I don't see any way to make it happen."

"Meds like hers would do it, but I know you. You'd rather be miserable for the next six months than admit you're in pain. I remember the summer you broke your foot and still finished a twenty kilometer trek before you told anyone."

I stopped at the door into the sim lab and looked back at her. "Yeah, that's just what it feels like."

Jake left, and I went in to work on my simulation. Alice was there with the sim already running. "Does *everyone* have access to my stuff? I keep locking it down and I keep finding it open."

Alice looked up, hurt. "I'm sorry. You left it running when you went to dinner four days ago. I suppose you had planned to come right back. I saved what you had before I made all my modifications."

"No, I'm sorry, Alice. Unlike others on board, my emotions are a little raw right now, but I've no cause to yell at you."

She nodded. "It's OK. I'd rather have you like this than to be like what they did to her. Please, let me help."

I looked at the red landscape shimmering in the display tank. "Show me what you've done."

Jake and I met for dinner that evening without Alice. I felt guilty about spending the day with her working after Hannah had asked me not to. Then I felt guilty again for asking Alice not to join us for dinner.

"Hannah needs to heal before either of you can move on." She had smiled a patient smile when I asked her. She left to sit with Charlotte and Sipa Patel.

"Jake," I said sitting down with my tray, "I think we can expect there to be water in the caves, I just don't know how far down. There could be something for a biologist to do after all."

"You don't even know for sure that there are caves, now you're postulating water and life?"

"More than postulating. Angela is adding tasking for you right now."

"My friend. Do you remember the last time we were underground at Kartchner? I still have nightmares."

"Yeah, you got stuck exploring the lower section. I had forgotten about that."

He shook his head. "I'll stay on the surface and you can bring the critters out for me."

"Fine," I answered. "Coward."

Jake nodded and kept eating.

Wandering Star maneuvered into a polar orbit around Cleavus that night. By the time we met for breakfast, she was already providing preliminary results for the areas that had passed under us as we slept. The main display in the mess hall was showing real-time results as *Star* processed them.

"Here," I said setting my roll down on the table and tapping the screen. "And here and here. Those are caves. Really good reflections coming back. Do you see them?"

Angela's voice answered directly behind me. "That's good, Theodore. If they hadn't been there, I was going to deduct the cost of this survey from your pay."

I smiled, thinking she was joking, but she didn't smile back.

"What about these features?" Brian asked, tapping a grouping of bright rectangles. Two sides of each shape reflected brightly in the radar image. "It doesn't look natural."

"It's not. Those are definitely buildings." I turned back to Angela. "Do we have optical for this yet? I'd like to see a fused image to be sure."

Angela was staring at the screen. "Cleavus was never colonized. We *know* that. I reviewed every record and there was nothing. *Star* has been scanning a full range of frequencies as we approached and no signals are coming from the surface. Whatever is there must have been temporary and abandoned long ago."

"*Star*? Do you have optical imaging for this region?" I drew a circle around the structures with my finger and the image changed to a medium resolution picture of the area taken in late afternoon sunlight.

"This is the same resolution as the radar image. I have a better image at twenty centimeter resolution if you'd like to see it."

"Show me, *Star*."

The new image showed shadows from the buildings stretching far to the northeast of each structure doing a good job of revealing relative sizes and rooftop details.

"Is this true color?" I asked.

"Yes," *Star* replied, "I compensated for the angle of the sun and dust in the atmosphere."

"Look here." Sipa was now crowding the screen. "Green cultivated fields south of the buildings."

"And here." Charlotte tapped three long shadows. "Are those people?"

"We need to let the survey complete," Angela said. "There are only a few structures there and some fields. If this planet was colonized and then forgotten, there could be more elsewhere." She turned to Giz. "Please load the first contact survey deck and let's go through the tasking again. *Star*, how long until you have imagery for the entire surface?"

"I will be finished in under two hours. Would you like me to reprocess the data to identify other potential structures on the surface at the same time?"

"Yes." Angela looked at the rest of us. "We'll meet in the main lab in two hours. This is a rare opportunity. I want to hear innovative ideas in addition to what's in the first contact deck."

Giz was standing next to me still studying the image of a couple of dozen low buildings in the afternoon sun.

"Giz," I asked, "how many first contacts have you been on?"

"Just one."

"How did it turn out?"

He smiled at me, deep wrinkles around his eyes. "I'll let you know."

I looked at the long shadows of people near the buildings, a few others by the green fields.

"They have no idea how their world is about to change."

"Are you speaking of the people on Cleavus, or to those of us in this room? This is what everyone that joins RuComm dreams of."

"I was just looking forward to spending my time exploring some caves, maybe finding some weird little creatures living in the subterranean waters there."

He slapped me on the back. "You're having quite the first hop, Mr. Holloman. I hope you don't expect all of your missions to be this exciting."

I found it hard to smile back at him.

"Don't despair, Ted," he said, lowering his voice, "who knows what the future holds, other than surprises?"

Our meeting opened with a review of the two other groups of structures *Star* had identified south and west of the colony we had already seen. Both were larger, but obviously long abandoned, their streets full of drifted sand and many walls showing signs of collapse. We would explore them, time permitting, but the surviving colony would be our first priority. Members of the team without anything planned for Cleavus had already started to prepare for our planet fall on Malapert, three months out. Now they were scrambling to complete their plans for first contact. My tasking remained unchanged. There was a complex of cave openings ten kilometers north of the colony and Angela expected me to explore that area and the associated karst features surrounding them.

Hannah was struggling. Whatever else the meds were doing to her, they were also preventing her from being able to change her focus rapidly and come up with meaningful answers. She looked flustered and frustrated as her mind was unable to solve what she knew should be simple problems. In the end, Angela sat with her and did most of her work.

I was not surprised when Jake told me over a late lunch that he had overheard Angela ordering *Star* to stop the meds other than something to help her sleep.

"Good," I replied.

"Ted?" Jake whispered back to me. "Stay away from her while she's coming out of this. She's going to be emotionally... volatile. Go explore your caves. Maybe camp there for a week or two, OK?"

All I could think about was Sipa telling me that morning how Hannah would have wrapped herself around me if it weren't for the meds. I looked at her sitting two tables away, wanting to wrap myself around her.

"She's hurting, Jake, and I'm forbidden from doing anything to help her."

"Stay away for now. That *will* help her."

I sighed. "I know. I will, but it's hard."

Angela entered the mess hall along with Captain von Muller and his XO, Lieutenant Copeland.

"We're going down initially with a small party. Hannah, for helping us understand their language, Charlotte for anthropology, Ted, myself, and our XO for security," she told us.

"Why geology?" Alice asked.

Angela gestured to Charlotte.

"There have been a couple of first contacts where the colony had devolved into a patriarchy. Having four women show up without any men might be taken poorly."

I smiled slightly. "So I'm a figurehead."

Charlotte looked at me fondly. "Exactly. Angela also wants you to supplement Velena for security if needed."

I looked at our XO. I think she spent all of her off duty time exercising or practicing combatives. I had no doubt she could take me in under five seconds. She smiled as though she found the idea of me being of any use amusing.

"Don't worry." Angela continued. "The rest of you will have your turn down there. For the initial team, please be in the port shuttle bay by 15:30. The colony site is about four hours out of sync so it will be almost noon there when we arrive. *Star* will be correcting our time over the next couple of days. It's about twenty degrees C on the surface now, but that will be dropping quickly by late afternoon. We'll only be staying for four hours max so you don't need to pack for a long exploration. Above all else, follow my lead. Questions?"

There were none. Velena approached me as the meeting was breaking up.

"So, Ted, you ever done security?"

"No, but I imagine that's obvious."

"I read the reports on your Margo Islands adventure. It sounded like you took care of yourself OK there."

"That had more to do with luck than anything else."

"Well, I don't believe in luck." She handed me a shoulder holster and a mean looking sidearm. "You ever use one of these before?"

"I've used a pistol, various rifles and shotguns." I turned the weapon over in my hand. It was heavy. "Never anything quite like this."

"What's the biggest thing you ever killed?"

"A coyote. I was out for a run in the desert and he was following me, keeping thirty to fifty meters back. I didn't think anything of it at first; coyotes do that some times. Three or four of his friends joined him and they started closing the distance. I stopped and fired a round over their heads and they all scattered except for one. He kept coming so I had to shoot him."

Velena nodded. "If you have to use this," she caressed the barrel, "don't waste ammo on a warning shot. Understood?"

"Yes, ma'am."

She took the gun back and released the magazine. "First three rounds are regular slugs. The next fifteen are plasma rounds. You ever use those?"

"No, but I've seen them. They explode on impact and do a lot of damage to soft tissue."

"That's right." She inserted the magazine and handed the gun back to me. "Use the holster and wear a loose fitting coat. Don't pull it out unless I do."

I went back to my quarters and changed. I reached for my pack, thought better of it, and walked to the shuttle bay. Angela was standing on the boarding ramp.

"About time."

I glanced at my watch. "I'm early."

"Not as early as the rest of us. Strap in."

Hannah looked up as I got on board, made eye contact, and smiled very slightly before looking away. I sat next to Charlotte at the back of the shuttle.

"Scared?" I asked.

"Terrified. All I can think is, please God, don't let me screw this up."

The shuttle shuddered as it detached from *Wandering Star* and then again as we passed through the gravitational flux outside the hull. We started our fall toward Cleavus.

"We should have brought Alice to pray over us."

Charlotte nodded. "I thought about having her along to help smooth the way with the colonists, but I'd rather look around first before she starts evangelizing everyone."

"Yeah, she'd do it too."

Charlotte continued talking, trying to distract herself and calm down. "You and Hannah, you came back on board burning hot enough to cut through deck plates. Then there's Alice, cold as space, with an obvious interest, but just watching, making a comment here, a nudge there, assessing the situation and biding her time. She's an interesting one. I've talked to her quite a bit over the past week and I trust and admire her as our chaplain. As a woman... Watch out, Ted. She's patient and her mind is always tipped about ten degrees from where you think it is."

Star interrupted her to let us know that the shuttle had just released twenty-five freshly printed autonomous sensors that would provide real-time situational awareness for us, and that we were ten minutes out. Angela came around handing each of us a small pin to clip to our ears that would provide an additional audio link back to *Star* and with each other. Then we were on the ground and the only sounds were the engines spooling down and the hiss of compressors equalizing internal pressure.

Velena and I were the first ones down the ramp. There was no one there so we walked all the way around the shuttle in opposite directions looking for anything odd.

"What did you see?" Velena asked me when we were back at the ramp.

"The landing pad is in great condition considering they've had no use for it for two or three hundred years. And there's an elderly woman approaching us from town moving very slowly."

"Why send her?"

"Maybe no one told her to run and hide from the scary spaceship."

"Huh. More likely, they see her as the least valuable member of their society. If the scary spaceship kills her it's no big loss."

We stood together on the edge of the pad watching her.

"Should we go down and meet her? This is going to take forever."

Velena paused, listening to *Star's* voice whispering in her ear. "Go get the others. Tell Angela it looks safe for now."

The five of us walked down from the landing pad, Velena leading, me trailing and watching over my shoulder from time to time. The old woman stopped and waited for us. She looked at us without any great curiosity.

"What have you brought us?" She asked. Hannah's head tipped to the side as she listened to the accent, trying to match it to something known. Watching her made my chest hurt.

I noticed that Velena was no longer paying any attention to the old woman and was keeping her eyes moving from building to building looking for threats. I did the same.

"We bring you news from the Union," Angela answered. "Where can we meet with your leaders?"

The woman was disappointed. "News? Not worth my time." She turned and started walking slowly away.

"Velena," I called. "This side." A group of seven men and two women had emerged from a structure behind us. The man leading the procession walked with an arrogant stride, not looking at the others, assuming that they were keeping pace. He looked to be in his early forties, strongly built and muscular, but coasting on past physical glory. Four of the men with him were younger with a hard, mean look about them. He may have thought of them as bodyguards, but I felt sure he should be watching his own back. The two older men looked like they had gained weight and prestige by telling their leader whatever he wanted to hear. The women stayed back, glancing at us occasionally, but mostly looking at the ground or at the leader. They seemed kind of twitchy, as if they were used to someone yelling at them or hitting them.

"This looks more promising," Angela muttered as she turned to face the new group.

"And who might you lot be?" the leader asked. He looked sharply at each of us in turn for a couple of seconds, his eyes assessing who we might be.

"Angela Dawkins." Angela held out her hand. "Reunification Commission. We are here to help your colony reintegrate into the Union."

"Hetman Christof Skorzeny," he replied taking her hand. He looked around at his companions, smiling. "We are right pleased to be meeting you."

"Mr. Skorzeny–"

"Hetman. It is my title. It means I am in charge here."

"Hetman Skorzeny," Angela continued, Skorzeny nodding. "Is there someplace we can go to talk? There is much we need to discuss."

"My courthouse chambers. I will keep my advisers with me." He gestured toward one of the larger structures down the street fronting a square that may have once had a small park at its center. The building looked like it was made of adobe and, like all of the others, was the same color as the surrounding hills and in a poor state of repair.

Angela walked along with him, followed by the two older men and the women. The rest of our party followed a few meters back. The four bodyguards had stayed behind talking together in the street, but then followed us fifty meters back.

"What are you hearing, Hannah?" I asked, keeping my voice as natural as possible.

She answered without looking at me. "Can't tell yet. It's not like any example of old English that I've ever heard. The vowel shifts are unusual." She shrugged.

"Charlotte?"

"I'm glad you and Velena are with us. He acts more like a gang leader than a politician. You can tell a lot about a society by how they treat their women. I'm not liking this so far."

Velena added, "The technology looks primitive enough for a lost colony other than being able to still manufacture clothing. I would have expected homespun. At least we're not seeing any weapons." She nodded to where Angela was walking with the Hetman. "Dawkins is all in on this 'lost colony' theory. What about you, Ted?"

"Me? I'm just here to shoot the coyotes following us if they get too close."

That earned me a smile.

We reached the courthouse and I hesitated at the entrance. "Should one of us wait out here?"

"No." She watched the guards finding spots of shade around the square, getting comfortable. "The sensors *Star* deployed will warn us if anything happens."

The Hetman's chambers were primitive. An old wooden desk and a dozen chairs were pushed to the front of the dirty room. The lighting panels glowed a dull yellow from low current coming from the rooftop solar system that we had seen in the on orbit survey images, their light supplemented by lanterns hanging from the open trusses in the ceiling.

"Sit." Hetman Skorzeny indicated the mismatched chairs. "Angela Dawkins, you sit here." He patted the chair in front of his desk.

Angela introduced her team, and then Skorzeny introduced his two advisers, Symon Hevsky and Byron Namenko. Angela waited for a moment, and then turned with a questioning look toward the two women. They were sitting together on a bench along the side of the room.

"Of course," Skorzeny continued. "My wife Lana." He pointed at the woman who was about his own age. "And my wife Buna." The other woman was about thirty years old, wearing a faded yellow dress and a defeated expression.

"You have two wives?" Angela asked.

"Three, actually. I am also newlywed of just one month. Tirana could not join us, being too pregnant." I noticed Buna turn her head at this, looking toward the back of the room away from her husband.

"It is the duty of Hetman," one of his advisers explained. "He has demonstrated superior qualities of strength, intelligence, and wisdom in order to become leader. These attributes must be passed on to future generations."

Skorzeny nodded. "Just so, well said Symon."

Angela took a deep breath and I realized how hard she was trying to make this go well. First contact, something so rare that even Giz had not been on one, was going to succeed or fail based on what she did. I should have felt sympathy for her, but I still hated her for what she had done to Hannah.

"Hetman Skorzeny, how many citizens do you have here?"

"Citizens? We have no citizens here," he replied defensively. Symon leaned over and whispered in his ear. "Oh, you mean how many of my people are joined with me? Three-hundred fifty-two. Fifty-three in two months when Tirana comes to her term, and should no one else die or be born between now and that time."

The conversation went back and forth between Angela and Hetman Skorzeny. She gained permission for us to occupy a couple of empty buildings near the landing pad for the survey team, and permission to talk with other members of the colony that he would make available to us. She agreed to provide food and new printers to supplement the ancient ones that they had managed to keep running. They would have their discussions on evacuating the colony to another planet over the next several days or weeks. The Hetman had no desire to stay on Cleavus, but his list of demands sounded like it would be lengthy.

I was relieved when we were finally on the shuttle and feeling the engines pushing us back up to *Wandering Star*. By the time we were safely back in the port shuttle bay, it was nearly 20:00 ship's time.

"I know it's late and the day has been stressful, but we need to get together with everyone while it's all still fresh in our minds. We'll meet in the mess hall in fifteen and we can eat while we talk."

I sat with Giz and Jake during the meeting. Alice joined us, taking an empty chair when she arrived. Hannah glanced at me, sighed, and turned away. Angela had each of us give our perspective of the colony, and then answer questions and make recommendations.

Hannah was back to her sharp and insightful self, but seemed easily angered, snapping at Angela when pressed to make her analysis fit the narrative of a long lost colony that Angela wanted Cleavus to be.

"Angela, don't ask me to know what no one can know. This will take time."

Charlotte's initial thoughts were more definitive. Her opinion was that the Cleavus colony had devolved to a state where RuComm couldn't integrate it into the Union, nor relocated to any other civilized planet. Her recommendation was to have RuComm send a team of social engineers to reform the society *in situ*, not allowing any outside contact until that task was completed.

Giz whispered to us, "She's right, of course, but such a path would not lead to much glory for Angela Dawkins."

Alice nodded. "So we stay."

"So we stay."

CHAPTER 10
THE TARAKANA

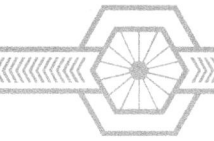

Angela led half the team back to the surface the next morning, Velena providing security. They planned to meet with Hetman Skorzeny and work on reintegrating the colony into the Union. Hannah, Charlotte, Sipa and I followed in the afternoon. My task was to collect samples and examine the local geology while Hannah and Charlotte met with the Hetman's three wives and Sipa looked at the colony's agriculture.

Hannah and I had a chance to talk in the shuttle bay while we waited for Charlotte and Sipa, who were uncharacteristically late.

"Jake wasn't too happy about being left behind. He and Alice will be the only ones on board except for crew," I commented, trying for innocent small talk.

"Maybe you should have invited her. You two seem to work very well together."

"I'm sorry. I wasn't trying to make you mad. It's a small team. It's hard to avoid working with any one person."

The anger drained away from her face as she fought against it, the cold look in her eyes softening. "It's the meds. I know it's the meds, but I still feel angry. It's like the only emotion that's really back." She sighed, frustrated.

"Let me help if I can."

She nodded. "Just be around, but not too close."

"I can do that."

"And not so much time with…" She couldn't bring herself to say Alice's name. "Big nose."

"Humor is coming back."

"That was sarcasm." She grinned.

"Close enough for now."

Hannah and I were standing about three meters apart smiling at each other when Charlotte arrived.

Collecting soil samples around the colony site made me uneasy. Kneeling in the street scooping dirt into sample bags felt too much like the Margo Islands. More than once, I thought I heard a voice behind me that sounded like Sergeant McKellar, or the sound of feet on gravel. After a couple of hours, I went back to the vacant structure that we were building out as a lab and dormitory. Charlotte was there having completed the interviews.

"Done already, Ted?"

"Needed a break. Hannah and Sipa?" I asked.

"I think Sipa is still walking through the fields south of town and Hannah went to listen in on the negotiations. I was headed there myself once I finish this report. Why don't you come along and sit with us for a while?"

"OK. How were the interviews?"

"Read over my shoulder. I want to finish this and get over to the Hetman's chambers."

"So," I asked as we walked through town to the courthouse, "you talked to all three women for almost two hours and then concluded that everything they told you was a lie."

"Let's just say that I don't take them at face value. Except maybe Buna. She's the only one that thinks that this isn't the most perfect, supportive, serene society ever created."

"It would make sense that she's bitter. She was the Hetman's favorite for several years. Now he has a new toy to play with."

"You say that like it's acceptable to treat another person like a toy and discard them when they grow tiresome."

"I'm not saying that. It's hateful. But I thought you were supposed to be objective and non-judgmental as an anthropologist."

"Not in this case. I need to judge whether these people can become part of the Union."

We reached the courthouse and Charlotte shoved the heavy door open forcefully.

"Careful there! Don't let it escape." The Hetman's four guards were looking under the chairs and behind furniture in the antechamber. Each man had armed himself with a large water bottle.

I looked around, not seeing anything. "What are you hunting?"

"Tarakana. There was one right under the couch, but it vanished when you two came in."

I looked around again. "How big are they?"

"About this big." He spread his arms far apart. "Forty kilos or so."

"How can something that size hide in a room this small?"

"Ho! Here it is!" One of his companions called. He sprayed water into the corner. The wall and floor seemed to shimmer and detach themselves as the creature hiding there writhed and changed colors.

"Hit it again!" They sprayed more water and the Tarakana rolled on its side, six stubby legs flailing. I couldn't tell if the legs had multiple articulations or were more like tentacles. It was in obvious distress.

"Stop! Why are you doing that?" I grabbed his arm.

"Because it's fun." He shook his arm free. "See the colors change? The more water you spray on it the faster it tries to change and the legs go flying around and those two tentacles on its head start to waving. Sometimes they even make a little squealing sound. If we can get it wet enough all at once it will die, but you don't want to do that right away." He sprayed it again while the others laughed.

"Whoa, there he goes again!" The Tarakana rolled to its feet and started to run. I opened the door and it disappeared outside, moving with surprising speed.

"Hey! Why did you do that?"

"Because it was fun," I answered.

The two of us were glaring at each other when the Hetman and Angela arrived, responding to the noise of the Tarakana hunt.

"What is all this?" he demanded.

"We had a Tarakana trapped until this *citizen*," he indicated me, "let it escape."

"There are more important worries today. Go outside. The lot of you, outside." He turned to me as his guards left. "You like our little pets, huh? Great fun, aren't they?"

"They're amazing," I answered. "How much do you know about them?"

"They live in the hills." He waved his hands dismissively. "Sometimes they wander into town and we have some sport with them. I have a couple in the cold storage if you would like to cut them up and see what is inside. Don't eat them though, the taste is disagreeable and their flesh causes nightmares."

I looked at Angela. "We need Jake."

She nodded. "We'll have everyone down here tomorrow. I want to finish fitting out the dorms so we're not wasting fuel running back and forth to *Star* every day. Charlotte, you help too and I'll send a couple of the others. Find Sipa and draft him as well."

"Yes, ma'am," Charlotte replied and we stepped back out on to the street. The guards were still wandering around the square watching us as we walked back toward the landing pad.

"I don't think you made any friends there," she told me.

"They are vicious and cruel, and they had to be stopped."

"I think I'll add that line to my report." She glanced over her shoulder and at the crumbling buildings around us. "They certainly picked an appropriate name for this place, didn't they?"

"How's that?"

"Cleavus. He was a historical figure although he probably never actually existed. Now it refers to anyone who blames their criminal behavior on a lifetime that's 'dogged by poverty and hard luck.'"

"Yeah, that seems appropriate."

Sipa was waiting for us when we arrived, and Horace and Brian showed up a few minutes later. We built bunks, assembled portable wall sections and tried to get the three hundred year old toilets to work.

"I suppose we can just walk up to the shuttle whenever someone needs to go." We all looked at the remains of what had once been a bathroom.

"*Star*?" Charlotte said. "Next shuttle that comes down have them throw in three portable toilets please."

"Consider it done."

We were finished by the time Angela, Velena, Giz, and Hannah arrived.

Angela looked around at what we'd done. "I'd like to have dinner here before we go back to the ship for the night. Are we set up to produce synthetics?"

"We are." Horace answered. "I tested it myself."

"When we return tomorrow morning, be prepared for a two week stay."

Angela briefed us on the negotiations while we ate under the glare of portable light panels. "Hetman Skorzeny is acting like we owe him every perk and luxury imaginable. I don't see us reaching an agreement anytime soon."

Giz was unconvinced. "But what's his leverage? Will he refuse to leave? He's counting on your concern for the people here, your desire to bring them back. We don't have to, you know."

"I think you misjudge him. What I heard was genuine concern to make a better life for his people. We can't leave over three-hundred people in these conditions."

"I don't believe there are that many here," Sipa commented. "The acreage they have cultivated wouldn't support half that number."

"They have the printer as well. The Hetman claims to be using agricultural waste to feed it."

"Even so, it's not enough unless they have another source of food they're not telling us about. Otherwise, if there are more than a hundred here I'd be surprised."

We ate in silence for a minute.

"We should leave them here," Charlotte said.

"Your opinion has already been noted," Angela reminded her.

"Ted, tell us about the Tarakana, about how they treated it," Charlotte asked me.

I related the story, their cruelty, and the anger when I let it escape. "We'll know more about them once Jake gets down and examines the two they tortured to death this week."

Hannah looked at me, head tipped. "I've seen you kill a spider, Ted, and be happy about it. How is this different?"

"I didn't pull its legs off one at a time to take pleasure from its suffering."

"You're holding the Hetman and his people to an impossible standard. The factors you see as cruelty are what let them survive here on their own. Look around you. I don't think *you* could survive here." She was angry again, her eyes scrunched almost closed.

"Thank you, Hannah," Angela took Hannah's hand and pulled her back down into her seat. "Good point."

Charlotte touched my leg and whispered to me, "It's still the meds, Ted. You know how she loves to be contrary in every meeting. Now she's going to disagree with whatever you say, no matter how bizarre. Give it a few more weeks."

I sighed and finished my dinner.

The next morning it felt good to be walking away from the town, dressed for fieldwork. *Star* had located an area about three kilometers outside town where there should be good outcrops showing layers of evaporates and limestone. It looked promising in the remote sensor images, but I wanted to see it myself and collect samples to determine the age of each layer to plug into my simulation.

The first Tarakana joined me about a kilometer out of town. Two kilometers out and there were eight or ten of them walking along with me. I was able to see what they looked like more clearly now. The main body was about a meter long with a thick bump of a 'head' at the front with no visible eyes. They didn't have a tail. A pair of meter long tentacles ending in flattened elliptical tips were attached at the base of the head. They held these aloft, the tips constantly rotating back and forth. They easily kept pace with me.

Having them there made me happy. There was nothing threatening about it. It was like being out for a walk with a group of friends.

"Hello, there," I called, half expecting them to answer *hello* back. They turned the tips of their tentacles toward me for a second and we walked on.

I reached my survey site after an hour cutting cross-country and looked down into the ravine. It was too steep to climb down so I sat on a rock to take a break before scouting for an easier way to the bottom. From there I could try to work my way back high enough to examine the layers.

The Tarakana gathered around me to see what I was doing. They scurried back a bit when I pulled out my canteen, seeming to know how the colonists had treated their comrades.

"It's OK," I reassured them, "this is for me."

They came closer, watching me drink. By the time I put the canteen away, a couple of them had sat down next to me, legs tucked in under them somewhere.

"I'm really sorry about the way they treat you," I told them. "I'm not like that. Most of us aren't like that." I smiled at them, watching the tentacles waving and tips rotating.

Then one of them touched my hand. It felt warm and it magnified the general happy, friendly feeling that I had while walking with them tenfold.

"Oh, I wish you hadn't done that." I looked at my hand, expecting it to be turning black or purple or something before it fell off. There were more of them coming now.

"Jake?" I called, "Can you hear me?"

Jake's voice answered in my ear. "Sure. What's up?"

"One of the Tarakana touched me."

"Oh?"

"Yeah, there are a bunch of them here and we were having a pretty good time, just walking along together, me talking to them. I really like them, they're friendly, but when one touched me this weird feeling came over me, like they really like me too, almost like they know me."

"Are you on your way back?" Jake sounded concerned. "There could be a chemical in their skin that's doing that to you."

"No, I'm OK here. I think if they were hostile they could just overwhelm me, there're so many of them."

"How many?"

"I don't know, twenty maybe. I'll show you."

I pulled my display pad out of the pack and panned it around. "See them all?"

"That's more than twenty, Ted. There must be at least fifty.

"Yeah, they keep coming. We're all best friends now. Oh. Another one touched me." I laughed.

"I'm coming to help you. Do you still have the gun Velena gave you? You might need it to get out of there."

"No, stay there. I have it, but I don't need it. I'm OK, really. I just wanted someone to know what was going on."

"So I know where to come and collect your body?"

"Something like that. I'll call for you if anything bad happens."

"Ted, I'm working on dissecting one of them right now. I'm finding a lot of weird structures. These aren't just animals."

"I'm not surprised. There're a couple of them touching me right now. It's strange. I'm going to go walk with them now."

"Damn it, Ted, if you die out there Angela's going to blame me for letting it happen."

"No worries. I'll be in touch."

I got up and walked with the Tarakana along the edge of the ravine going south. We came to an area where the bank dropped low, providing an easy trail to the bottom. I turned to walk back north toward the cliff face Star had identified, but they had other ideas. They touched my hands and leaned against my legs until I understood. We walked south less than a kilometer to where erosion had carved the side of the ravine into a series of stair steps. Limestone capped each step, preserving the layer of evaporates underneath.

"You guys are the best," I told them. I reached out, touched the tip of one of their tentacles, and held it for a second. It made them very happy. I could feel it.

I worked the rest of the day, taking measurements, recording strike and dip angles, and taking samples of each layer. Most of the Tarakana had drifted away by the time I was done, leaving just six that had spent the day with me, sometimes keeping their tips pointed at me, sometimes seeming to sleep, the tentacles lying flat along their sides.

"OK, friends," I told them. "I need to go back to town for dinner."

They followed along with me until we were about a kilometer from town. I walked on a short distance, then turned and waved to them rotating my palm the way they did their tips. "See you tomorrow."

It seemed to amuse them. One of them hooted, a low sound from somewhere underneath him, and they scurried back to the south.

Jake met me just outside of town where he was keeping vigil.

"I'm glad you made it. I was watching the feed from one of *Star's* sensors, but I didn't trust the Tarakana to let you leave until the last of them turned back. I haven't told anyone about your experience with them because I knew Angela would have wanted to kill you and me both. Assuming you made it back alive."

"Jake, it was amazing. It was as if they knew what I was looking for and led me straight to it. Best local guides I've ever worked with."

"I'm not surprised. After completing the dissections I'd be surprised if they aren't smarter than you and with more sense."

I looked at him. "You're serious."

He stopped while we were still a hundred meters away from the building. "It scares me a little. They have a distributed nervous system, but what must be the brain is huge and there are parts in them," he shook his head, "I have no idea what they are."

"Maybe they control the color changes?" I suggested.

"There's much more to them than that. They breathe through their skin, at least in their current form. The cellular structure makes me think they might be able to change shape as well. Although if they could, why would all of them look the way they do?"

"Because they think they are so beautiful," I answered without thinking, knowing it was true.

"Sure. What are you going to put in your report to Angela?"

"I don't know. I'm afraid she won't let me go back out if I put in everything I felt. Or she'll think I'm crazy and have *Star* start mixing meds in with my breakfast. I'll mention the Tarakana going along with me, but I want something a little more empirical before I report everything."

Jake nodded. "You go ahead. I'm going to finish the dissection on the second Tarakana and then I'll join you."

I looked around our makeshift mess hall. "Where is our chaplain this evening?"

"She's having dinner with her new flock," Charlotte answered. "The Hetman gave her permission to use an old church on the square next to the courthouse. She was talking to a good sized crowd when I left town."

"Is she safe?"

"I'm sure she is for now. The colonists seemed eager to hear what she had to say. I think it's been awhile since there was any authority here other than the Hetman. If we stay long he may regret letting her talk."

Charlotte nodded toward the table where Brian and Hannah were sitting. "Why don't you get something to eat and join us?"

"Are you sure?"

"It would be good for both of you. Controlled environment, plenty of interesting things to talk about. If you say anything offensive I'll tell you to leave."

I filled my tray and sat down opposite her. "Hannah."

Her eyes locked onto mine and my heart skipped a beat. She turned back to her food, but not before I saw the flush in her cheeks.

"How did your field trip go today, Ted?"

I told her about what I had found, but left out the stranger parts of my experience with the Tarakana. Still, it was hard not to sound excited by the geology I was exploring.

"How are the negotiations going? Is Angela making any progress?" I asked.

She tipped her head and looked at me before answering. "You don't like the Hetman and his inner circle, do you?"

"I don't know them well enough to dislike them."

She smiled. "Still not a good liar, Ted. It's OK if you hate them. They have no place in the Union. We prefer our brutality sheathed in layers of civility like the conflicts on Dulcinea. When this colony is relocated, more civilized men, *and women*, will replace the Hetman and his group."

Charlotte gave me a warning look, which I ignored.

"He doesn't seem like the kind of man who will graciously step aside when that time comes."

She leaned across the table toward me, her eyes intense, and hit the table with her knuckles. "Exactly. You see it too. There are others here who are ready to step in during the transition, but Angela refuses to even talk to them. They could be the leaders these people need. They have a vision of what their future could be." She pulled back, realizing she had said too much. "I'm sorry. My emotions still get the better of me."

"That doesn't mean you're wrong. More like brilliant." Her excitement swept me along with her, as it always did.

She looked at me, longing in her eyes, her face flushed, and then she turned away. "I need to excuse myself, get some air." She got up and walked toward the exit.

"You shouldn't encourage her outbursts, Ted," Brian warned. "She needs to relearn the ability to express herself calmly. Whether she's right or wrong, brilliant or stupid is irrelevant."

"I'm sorry. It's the first time I've seen anything in her eyes other than anger in a while. That wild look she gets is why I–" I stopped and looked at them. "How much damage did I do?"

Charlotte took my hand. "Not much. It's going to be a few more weeks before she has full control. Until then, stay back and be there when she needs you, not the other way around." She looked at Brian, then back at me. "Ted, you do know that your emotions are just as messed up right now as hers, right? You keep acting like you want things to be the way they were on Dulcinea, but you know that can't happen, not for many months and not unless you both choose that path when the mission is over."

"I know that. I know I have to wait and that we might not ever be together, not like we were." I turned so she couldn't see my eyes. "Then I see her or talk to her and nothing else matters. I *need* her. I want the impossible, even knowing it's impossible."

"Not impossible, just not here, just not now."

I woke the next morning at 02:38. The walls we had used to build out the dorm were thin and I heard Hannah crying in the dark, Charlotte's low voice comforting her, knowing that it was my fault.

After she stopped, I was only able to sleep for a few more hours. I was up drinking a cup of coffee by the time the sun was rising over the red hills east of town.

Alice sat down next to me, looking bulky in layers of sweaters and coats against the morning chill. I was not surprised to see her.

"I hear you did good work yesterday," I told her.

"I did. *The harvest is plentiful, but the workers are few.*"

"I was going to ask you to help analyze what I collected yesterday, but it sounds like you plan to be a chaplain today, not a geologist."

She looked at me closely. "Yes, a chaplain today because that's where I'm most needed. Someday, maybe, something else."

"I want to start *Star* chewing on my samples to get dates for each layer. She should have them done by the time I get back and maybe you'll have time to help load them into the simulation."

"That will take her days. Where are you going?"

"The caves ten kilometers north of here. I'll leave this afternoon and be gone four or five days at least. I'll take food and water for a week, but my time in the field is limited by how much I can carry back. Have you ever been spelunking?"

She shook her head.

"I'll probably be taking several trips there. You should come with me some time. Jake refuses. He got stuck in a narrow passageway about three hundred meters down once. His lights failed, and his radio died, and..." I looked at the expression on her face. "I'm not doing a very good job of talking you into this, am I?"

She shook her head again and smiled at me. "I'll be here waiting for you. Let me know when you're back and ready to work on the sim."

I spent all morning preparing the samples and making sure *Star* understood what to look for to start building a geochronology for Cleavus. I finished before lunch and Jake promised to make sure the auto-loader was working, and to let me know when it had completed its analysis. I was busy stuffing packages of food into my pack when Angela found me.

"I read your report from yesterday. It looks like a promising start and I'm looking forward to what the radiometric dates tell us. Seeing Cleavus the way it is now, it's hard to imagine it covered by a planetary ocean."

"It's funny," I told her. "As a geologist, I look at the layers in the hills and it's all that I can see. Ocean, then desert, then ocean again over and over." I smiled at her and stuffed more food into the pack. "The ocean is coming again. Give me a week and I'll tell you when."

"Have a good trip, Theodore, and let me know what the Tarakana do. Our focus is on reintegrating this colony, but I don't want to ignore the native animal life." She tapped her ear. "Stay in touch."

I finished with the provisions and picked up my freshly printed camping equipment. I was ready to leave when I saw Hannah sitting at our long dining table eating lunch by herself and working on something on her display pad. I closed my eyes, willing myself to open the door and leave.

I sat down opposite her, and leaned my pack against the table. I had a brief glimpse of what she was working on before she blanked the display. It had looked like the *Sleeping Star* algorithm.

"I'll be gone for the next few days exploring the caves north of here," I told her, not looking directly at her. "If you need to talk to me, just say my name and I'll hear you."

She nodded, touching her ear. "Thank you."

I wasn't sure if she was thanking me for the offer to talk or for leaving.

"Will you have your friends with you, do you think?" she asked.

"My friends?" I looked at her then. She had a mischievous tilt to her smile.

"The Tarakana. I read your full report from yesterday. And Jake's."

"The *full* reports? I thought only Angela could... Never mind. Yes, I imagine they'll be walking along with me."

"How smart do you think they are?"

"Jake thinks smarter than me. A low bar, I know, but I think it's possible after being with them yesterday. There are things I didn't put in the report or tell you about at dinner last night."

"I thought so. Did you talk to them? Do they have a language?"

"I don't know. It was like we understood each other." I looked into her eyes and the wild look was there carrying me along with her. "Maybe... No. I'm sure they do, but it's so different that I'm not hearing it yet."

"A non-human language." Her eyes sparkled as she considered it.

I started to open my mouth, about to invite her to come with me, to leave with me right then to study the Tarakana for a week or more. To share my tent with me.

I stood, shattering the dream. "I need to leave. I want to find a good place to camp before it gets dark. I'll let you know if I start to understand them. So far it's all been kind of subliminal."

"Of course. If there *is* a language, maybe you can co-author my next paper with me."

"I'd like that." I gave her a last smile and made it through the door without looking back.

The first Tarakana met me just outside of town as if it had been waiting for me. Others soon joined us. Although not as numerous as the day before, these were more bold, walking close to me, touching my hands, nudging up against my legs. They were soon encouraging me to deviate from the path *Star* had mapped to the caves and I followed along willingly, ignoring her whispered *not recommended* in my ear. We reached a deep valley about an hour later. *Star* had planned for me to cross well to the east, down and back up a complicated series of switchbacks. The Tarakana led me to the valley's narrowest, steepest section where a five-meter wide bridge spanned a gap of little less than a hundred meters.

"*Star*," I asked, "how did you miss this? Do you have one of your sensors over me?"

"I see it, Mr. Holloman. It does not show up in my survey imagery. Could it be recent construction?"

"I don't think so." I walked across the bridge, tapping my fingers on the railings. "It's made of some kind of metal."

"I'll have the sensor drop down for a closer look after you and the creatures near you have passed."

"Thanks."

It was late afternoon when I reached the first cave entrance, having crossed a terrain of basins and sinkholes for the past hour. The opening was at the bottom of a wide depression and cold air was welling out of it as the cave breathed.

I dropped by backpack and stretched, rolling my head back and forth. The two Tarakana still with me seemed to find the display interesting. "I don't suppose you guys know of a good hotel nearby. Soft beds and maybe a pool?"

They stood facing me, rotating their tips back and forth.

"Or a nice place to set up my tent would be fine too."

I followed them a short distance to an ideal spot. Drifted sand made a flat, firm floor and it was protected from wind on three sides by outcrops, but with a clear view of the sky.

"So," I said as I laid out a ground cloth and started erecting my tent, "there are some things that are bothering me about you. Like how is it that you know what I want? How do you make me feel like I kind of understand you?" I gestured at one with a tent stake. "And how the hell did you hide that bridge from our optical and radar scans?" They didn't answer.

I finished the tent and built a fire ring a couple of meters away while the Tarakana continued to watch. There was no wood, but I had a dozen self-igniters that would each burn for several hours. I sat down in front of the fire when I was finished and the Tarakana came close, turning one side, then the other to the flame seeming to enjoy the warmth as much as I was.

I shook my head at them. "Or are you just curious about me like I am about you?"

I logged onto my pad and wrote my daily report while the two Tarakana occupied themselves with the fire, passing the tips of their tentacles quickly through the flame and then gently butting their heads together. I had a feeling of amusement from them, as if they were playing.

I continued typing while I scolded them. "If you burn your tentacles off don't come crying to me."

A minute later one of them hooted and I looked up. The colors on their tips now pulsed the same colors as the flame, making it look like the ends of the tentacles were on fire.

I laughed. "Great. Surrounded by super intelligent aliens and they send the two class clowns to keep me company."

I submitted my report, including my concerns about how *Star* had missed seeing the bridge, and the three of us sat around the fire while I ate dinner. I talked to them late into the evening. I told them my life story, about what Earth was like, what I enjoyed about my friends, and how the Union was being reunified. At the end, I told them about Hannah.

The Tarakana sat by the fire listening. I don't know how much they understood, but they let me talk until it was all out of me. I watched the sky for a while after that, seeing an occasional meteor flash briefly in the dark. Sometime later, I noticed that their tentacles were lying flat against their sides and I climbed into my tent and slept peacefully through the night.

CHAPTER 11

MONSTERS

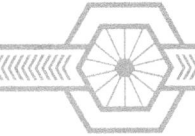

Something was splashing in the water, but I was having trouble finding it. The beam from the light strapped around my helmet swung across the surface finding only ripples. I was a couple of hundred meters below ground and an hour away from the cave entrance. I had sent one of *Star's* sensors off exploring the cavern my first morning and it had created the map that I was using, keeping me from wasting time on blind passageways and guiding me to more interesting features.

Another splash somewhere to the left. I turned quickly. Nothing but ripples, too large to be from water dripping from the ceiling. I knelt, filled a couple of vials from the pool, and made a notation on their labels.

"Next time," I said aloud, "I'm bringing a boat with me. See if you can hide then."

Five days of exploring had yielded a good thirty kilos of material for me to carry out, and hundreds of images of cave formations and of the karst features on the surface. The Tarakana had accompanied me most of the time, but I was alone now as I started back to the surface. They had led me south and east of the camp, both on the surface and below it. Looking at the map, I realized I had no idea what lay north or west. Next time.

It was late afternoon when I reached the cave entrance. The low angle sun warming the red rocks reminded me of home. I looked at my display pad as it resynced with *Wandering Star*. There were lots of messages from Angela, Jake, and Sipa. I sat down and took my helmet off while *Star* connected me.

Angela answered, Sipa on a split screen next to her. "What's up?" I asked.

"How quickly can you get back to the landing pad?"

"A couple of hours at least. My pack is heavy and it's getting dark."

"Leave everything and start back now while we talk."

There were Tarakana gathering around me and for the first time since being with them, I felt an emotion from them other than friendly good-will. I felt fear.

I detached the light from my helmet, grabbed the spare from my pack, and started walking. "I'm on my way. What happened? Sipa, why are you back on the ship?"

Sipa leaned forward. "Do you recall that I had misgivings about the colony's ability to supply as much food as they claimed? Well, I found the answer today hidden in one of the buildings." He held up a brown wrapped package. "Synthetics, packaged on Bodens Gate."

"How did those get here?"

"How indeed. None of this really made sense from the beginning. The farms were too small, the number of colonists insufficient to be genetically stable, yet Jake's tests showed nothing abnormal. Their language is nothing like what we expected and the power they can generate with their solar system at the courthouse is not enough to run their printers more than an hour or two a day. After I found the synthetics, I contacted friends I have in the Bodens Gate Central Government. I took a while, but I finally got them to admit to something they didn't want to reveal. A couple of years ago there was a clan called the Bovita that was attacking citizens and holding them for ransom."

I interrupted. "I know this story. They all disappeared, hundreds of them."

"Yes. No one knew where they went. Until now."

"Is everyone else back on *Wandering Star*?"

"No," Angela answered. "I'm still here and Jake refused to leave without you. I didn't have time to argue with him. And Alice. I can't find her. She's been spending all of her time with the colonists. I mean clan members," she corrected herself. "She's not answering."

"I'll be there as quickly as I can. Is Velena there with you?"

"No, I want as few people on the surface as possible. The Bovita don't know we suspect anything yet, but I don't know how long that will last. *Star* was not able to identify any place a shuttle could land near you. Did you see anything she may have missed?"

"No, it's too rough here. I'll let you know when I'm getting close."

I consulted the route *Star* had laid out for me and veered west. The Tarakana blocked me, wrapping tentacles around my legs.

"You're crazy," I told them, "this way will cut a half a kilometer off the trail between here and the bridge."

I pushed past them to the top of the rise and understood.

"Go east you told me. Stay south." I looked down into a slot canyon that broadened out across the desert floor. There were too many openings in the rock walls to count, structures built on the canyon floor and green fields stretching out into the valley. Artificial light filled the windows and there were Tarakana everywhere.

"You did a good job hiding this from us. I'd like to know how." I came back down from the rise, letting them lead me along their path to the bridge, my mind numb. We reached the ridge above the bridge about an hour later. The town was a couple of kilometers away, the lights from our lab glowing bright. One of *Star's* shuttles circled the landing pad settling with a swirl of dust. About the same time, a thick plume of black smoke rose over the town square followed six seconds later by the distant sound of the explosion. The sound of gunfire followed. The flashes of plasma rounds were visible in the streets.

"Jake?" I called. No answer. "*Star*?" Nothing.

I started to run, the Tarakana easily keeping up. I was half way across the bridge when six of them blocked the far side, more crowding in behind them. I could feel that they were determined not to let me pass, and I knew there was no way for me to force my way through them.

"My friends are down there, you have to let me go to them."

The tentacles waved and the tips rotated and they did not move.

I turned to go back the way *Star* had originally mapped, far to the east. Three Tarakana entered the bridge on that side, advancing toward me with more behind them. I backed up, knowing that they were driving me into the others, but unable to stop myself. Emotions washed over me and I couldn't tell which were mine and which came from the Tarakana. Fear, anger, frustration, compassion, friendship, love all mixed together.

"Please let me go," I whispered. I felt tentacles wrap around me from behind. They were around my head and around my chest making it hard to breathe. I collapsed to my knees. They were inside me now, poking gently at my thoughts. I wanted to scream, but couldn't.

The three Tarakana in front of me changed as they came closer. Their shape shifted in an instant and they transformed. I was looking at three women, beautiful and naked. Their thoughts filled my head, forming into words.

"You don't have to be afraid. We will protect you. You are safe here."

I forced the words out, like trying to speak in a nightmare. "No. You can't hide what you really are. You can't fool me. I've seen you. You're monsters."

"Monsters? We are not the monsters. Our shapes are fluid, but no matter what shape we take it must always reflect the beauty within us. It is you that use your hard shapes to hide the monsters inside you."

"Why won't you let me go?"

One of the women knelt and put her hand on my cheek. The illusion was perfect, the feel of her fingers and the look of compassion in her eyes. But the voice when she spoke was in my head and her mouth did not move.

"There are pieces of you dying, several are already dead. We can keep you safe here."

"Pieces?"

I felt the Tarakana thinking together.

"We are one, with many pieces. It is more difficult with you. You are both one and a piece which makes no sense."

The other two woman put their hands on me and I closed my eyes. "Why did you take this shape?"

"In your mind this is beauty. We thought it would calm you. A mistake."

When I opened my eyes, the women were gone. "Please let me go. If you see my thoughts, you know I have to."

The Tarakana backed away from the bridge and I felt sadness from them, and regret.

I ran, calling for Jake and Angela and *Star*. No answers. The shuttle that was on the pad took off and our other one replaced it. It stayed only a few minutes before leaving. I was still a kilometer away when the two shuttles returned and then quickly left again.

I ran into the town, not knowing if it was safe, not knowing what I would find. There were bodies in the street in front of the courthouse. Hetman Skorzeny was lying in the dirt with his first wife Lana and pregnant third wife Tirana. Plasma blasts had torn their bodies apart. The four guards lay nearby, shredded into pieces. There may have been more inside the courthouse, but what was left of it was burning.

I ran to our lab. Jake was sitting leaned up against the wall by the front door. I knelt down next to him.

"How you doing, Jake?" It looked like he had been hit in the shoulder and blood was soaking his shirt and left sleeve.

"About damn time you got here. Been waiting."

"I see that. You're an idiot. You should be on *Wandering Star* right now."

"Yeah, well, I didn't want you to have an adventure without me again."

"Let me look at your shoulder." I reached for him, but he shook his head. He was breathing hard, as if he'd be running.

"Don't bother. My back is worse."

I sat down next to him. "What happened here?"

"We lost the ship. There was a firefight. Different factions of the clan. Killing each other. Don't know how they got weapons. We lost the ship."

"Angela and Alice?" I asked.

"Don't know about Alice. Angela is dead. She was by the ramp, by the landing pad when the first shuttle came in. Hit in the chest. I saw go down. They hit her over and over. Eight, ten times. I ran toward the sound of the gunfire."

"Because you're an idiot."

He smiled, "Yeah. I came around the corner. Someone yelled '*not him, we need him*'. They killed me anyway."

"You're not dead yet."

"Don't pretend it's going to be OK."

I sat with him for a while, listening to him breathe. It seemed to be getting harder for him.

"Ted, you know how. How they were able to take the ship. You know."

I didn't answer and he gathered what strength he had left.

"Only one person could defeat the safeguards that are built into *Star*. You *know* that."

"It could have been something else. It must have been something else."

"Now who's the idiot?" He paused, his eyes looking at the sky as the first stars appeared. "Keep thinking about my folks. They worked so hard. To get me through the Academy. To reach this dream you and I shared. When you tell them–" He paused again, finding it hard to finish.

"I'll tell them how much it all meant to you."

He shook his head. "Don't tell them that. This is going to be hard for them. Tell them that I love them. That'll be enough."

I held his hand for a long time and then, sometime after it was fully dark, I reached over and closed his eyes for him.

I was still sitting next to him when Alice found me. The beam of her light moved down the street, shining into the buildings as she searched, but I didn't call out to her.

"Ted, are you all right?"

I nodded and stood up. "Are you OK?"

"I'm fine. Jake? I saw him get hit, but I hoped it was minor."

"He's gone. Where were you when all this was happening?"

"I was in the lab when it started. I saw Angela get hit. There's not much left. And then Jake was hit and I ran."

"Away from the gunfire."

"Yes," she whispered. "I let this happen. I let my friends die and our *Wandering Star* get stolen while I hid and did nothing to stop it." There was disgust in her voice, a cold, pitiless self-hatred. "I'm a coward. They're dead because I'm a coward."

I held her against me, feeling how thin she was under her coat, her forehead cold when I kissed it. "If you had fought against them, it would have been just one more grave for me to dig, one less friend for me to hold."

I held her for a long time, not wanting to do anything else, not wanting to face what I knew had to come next. In the end, Alice said it.

"We need to move Jake and Angela. I'll get a couple of blankets. There's nothing more we can do tonight."

I helped her wrap the bodies and we carried them to the base of the ramp by the landing pad. She prayed over them and we returned to the lab.

The rooms were dark and cold. *Wandering Star* had been powering all of our lights and other systems remotely. We had the batteries in our lights and display pads, and no way to recharge them.

"We should eat," Alice said.

"I'm not really hungry."

"That's your heart talking. Your stomach knows better." She handed me a plate with synthetics of some kind on it and we sat at the long table in the middle of the room and ate by the light of the stars coming in through the shattered windows.

Alice talked while we ate. "This stuff won't last more than a day without refrigeration, but we have some packaged food that will. I imagine the batteries will last a month or more if we're careful. The solar power system on top of the courthouse is smashed. It will be awfully dark at night. And cold. Cold all the time."

It suddenly overwhelmed her. "Ted, what will any of it matter? It could be years before anyone comes here again."

"Have I told you about the Tarakana?"

"Those big chameleon things with the tentacles on their heads?" She waved her hands by her head. "The folks here told me that we can't eat them. They're poisonous."

I smiled. "I'm not talking about eating them." I told her everything I knew about them, how they trapped me on the bridge to protect me and the massive city built into the cliffs that *Star* had been unable to see from orbit or with her local sensors.

"Are they safe?"

"Safe? I don't think so. When I looked down into their city, I was terrified. They are intelligent, but not like us. We overlap in some areas. In others, we'll probably never understand each other. They seem to have perfect communication between all of them all the time, so they're kind of like one big mind, maybe one big distributed organism. What we would call an individual is just a 'piece' of that whole to them."

"They seemed to understand what you think is beautiful."

I blushed, thankful she couldn't see it in the dark. "Yes and no. Beautiful, and unbelievable in how perfect they looked. But they thought having three women in front of me like that, in that situation, would be calming. Not so much. I think it was more terrifying than seeing the city that they had kept hidden from us."

"Will they help us?"

"I think so. They viewed the Bovita clan as monsters and I can't disagree with their assessment. They seem to like me."

I helped Alice clear our plates and set them by the non-functional recycler.

"Thank you for making me eat," I told her. "I feel a little better."

"Sure." She looked up at me, shivering.

"Are you cold?" I looked at my watch. "I hadn't realized how late it is. We should try to get some rest, although I don't expect I'll sleep much."

We walked into the dorms and I helped her find extra blankets for her bunk. She dumped her coat on the floor and slid between the covers still fully clothed. I sat down next to her.

"Ted?"

"Yes?"

"Please take this at face value, I mean nothing else by it. I don't want to be alone here tonight. Will you please lie down next to me?"

"Of course. I don't want to be alone either." I took off my coat and slid in next to her. She pushed up against me and put her head on my shoulder.

"Tell me about Jake."

"Jake?" I was surprised how hard it was to say his name. "What do you want to know?"

"I want to hear stories of the two of you growing up. Funny stories."

"OK. There're a lot of them. I hope you don't need to be anywhere else for a while."

She smiled. "Not for a while."

I tried to tell them in order, but one story would remind me of something that happened years later and that one would bring me back again to when we were little. After an hour I noticed that Alice had stopped responding. I put my arms around her, closed my eyes and we slept together that way on the first night.

I felt Alice stir and looked at her. Pale, pre-dawn light was visible in the windows.

She frowned at me and said, "I don't like God very much sometimes."

"Oh?"

"I love the Lord and always will. I respect him. I fear him. But this morning, I don't like him."

"I understand."

"No, it's not what you think. I don't blame God for the horrors that we create for ourselves. You and I will be burying friends today, but that's not God's doing.

"I had a teacher at seminary," she continued, "who always told us that we should be careful about continuing to pray for something after God had told us 'no'. He said that we risked God becoming tired of us asking, that he would relent and give it to us and that we may not like it. 'Here, Alice, here's what you prayed for. Is this really what you wanted?' Sometimes the way prayers are answered seems so cruel."

I held her a little tighter. "What did you pray for, Alice?"

"You know what I prayed for," she whispered.

"Tell me anyway."

She sighed, a ragged sound, and said very softly, "To have you in my bed and to wake up in the morning with your arms around me."

"That's an interesting thing for my chaplain to be praying for."

"Hush. It was a long term goal. I've been married and had my husband taken from me. I want that intimacy again that comes from sharing your life with another person, not just the physical ecstasy that comes with sharing your body with someone you love."

"Alice..."

"You don't need to say anything." She pressed on my chest with her hand. "I have no claim on this heart. I know who owns it. There isn't a situation I can imagine that would lead you to forsake her. I would still like to be your friend. When I die, I want you to have as many good stories with me in them as you do with Jake. That's my new prayer. It's probably just as dangerous as the last one."

"There're already a few I could tell."

She smiled. "I need to get up."

"Yeah, me too."

We got ready for the day, ate a cold breakfast and stepped out onto the street. The smell of smoke from the courthouse still lingered.

"There are tools in a shed by the farms," Alice said. "There should be shovels."

We walked there together, the depth of the catastrophe making the morning sunlight seem unreal.

"We're the only ones here."

"Yes," Alice replied. "The Hetman's inner circle are all dead and the rest are on board *Wandering Star* with our team. I pray for their safety."

I looked at the hills around us, the abandoned fields, and decaying building. "On the whole planet, just us."

Alice stopped. "Don't do that. You're about the only thing holding me together right now. If you start to slide you're going to take me right along with you."

"I'm sorry." I looked around at the horizon again.

"What are you looking for?"

"The Tarakana. I thought they would be here this morning."

Alice looked at me as if she was starting to doubt what I had told her the night before. "I'm sure they'll be along, Ted."

We dug two graves near the bottom of the ramp leading up to the landing pad. It seemed appropriate to lay them to rest there. Alice and I prayed together when we were done and I captured an image of it with my display pad to show to Jake's family whenever I might see them again.

"Are you close to Jake's family?" Alice asked while we were walking into town, shovels over our shoulders.

"My mom died when I was eight, about the same time I met Jake. His Mom became my mom, his Dad a second father to me."

"Your father never remarried?"

"No, my sisters and I would have been OK with it, we even encouraged him. But he was busy with work, busy raising three kids. My mom left a particular shaped hole in his heart and he could never find anyone else that could quite fill it."

"Not a family trait, I hope."

"What do you mean?"

"Look," Alice pointed. "Your friends the Tarakana."

There were a dozen or more of them in the square, touching the bodies gently and exploring the remains of the courthouse.

"You may want to go slow with them," I advised. "Let them get close and bump up against you before letting them touch you."

Alice sat down in the street in front of the nearest one. When it approached, she put her arms around it and nuzzled her face up against its head. The two tentacles wrapped around her and the tips caressed her back.

"Or you could just do that." I sat down next to her and she looked at me, a faraway look in her eyes.

"They'll help us with the graves and with food and water and power to keep us warm in the night. The seasons are changing and it should be warmer here in a few weeks. They understand what we want to do with the bodies, although I don't think they understand why. After that, we—" More of the Tarakana were touching her and her eyes lost focus completely. After a few seconds she closed them and started humming to herself.

"OK, I think that might be enough for a first time." I lifted her up, breaking physical contact.

She looked at me, refocusing. "How could you have spent a week with them and not lost yourself, become part of their group mind?"

"We're too different. They don't think the way we do."

She nodded. "They know you. They say your thoughts are... what is it? Like the horizon? No. Straight lines?" She smiled. "Like when the sun is just over the horizon and the desert air is so clear that it sparkles like looking through the purest glass and distant things look like you could touch them."

"You got all that from a few minutes of contact? Not that it makes any sense."

"It does make sense. They just don't think like that. The Tarakana's thoughts are all cross currents and tangled passageways. There are thousands of paths to get to any conclusion and they travel all of them all the time."

"You could get lost in that?"

"Oh, yes. It's beautiful. It's the way I think, but so much bigger."

"I'm not sure introducing you to them was a good idea."

She smiled. "I'm OK. I'm still me, still human. They wouldn't want me in there for very long either. I may be a closer match, but there are still things about them that we will never be able to understand. I think you're right about them being a single organism. It's like one soul shared across thousands of pieces, one body connected by thought instead of muscle and bone."

The Tarakana were moving the remains of the Hetman and his wives from the street.

"Where are they taking them?"

"There's a cemetery behind the old church. They'll bury all of them there and let us know when they're done. I'd like to pray for them."

We found a bench on the sunny side of the town square and sat for a moment just listening to the silence.

"I want to go back to my campsite sometime soon. It's too late today, maybe tomorrow. I'd like to get the samples I collected and some of the supplies."

"Lost without your backpack and rock hammer, aren't you?"

I smiled at her. "You're getting to know me."

"We should get something to eat when the Tarakana are done." Alice suggested. "I'm hungry."

"I think I'll go help them. I can't sit here thinking about how long we might be..."

"Marooned." Alice finished for me.

"I wasn't going to use that word."

"Stay here. Did you see the bodies when you came into town last night?"

"Not really. I was in a hurry and it was almost dark."

"Having the Tarakana here to bury them is a blessing. Let's explore the other buildings for a while. We might find something useful."

I nodded. "I'd like to find the cache of packaged synthetics that Sipa located. We might need them and I want to know if any of them are more recent than two years ago. If the Bodens Gate government is dropping food off here on a regular basis we might be able to hitch a ride."

"I'm sure they are."

"Why would they do that? If this clan was challenging the government why not just kill them all?"

She smiled. "Governments don't think in straight lines. Making them disappear was much more effective in keeping the other clans in line. Dumping them out the airlock into empty space would've worked just as well, but I imagine that wasn't viable politically. No one wants to say they killed three-hundred fifty men, women and children in cold blood. So they made Cleavus into a prison using an abandoned old Union colony, and they never mentioned it to the new Union or anyone else." She looked back at me before we entered the first building. "It's what I would have done."

"You scare me sometimes."

"Good."

We searched the buildings around the square, but didn't find much of value. There were clothes, furniture, a couple of packages of food, and one small stuffed animal in the shape of a Tarakana that someone had made for their child.

Alice looked around the square when we came back out. "We need to search the courthouse. The Hetman kept anything of value close to him."

"I know. Look at it, though. The second story has mostly collapsed into the first floor, and part of that is now in the basement. It's not safe."

We walked up to where the front door used to be and looked down into the rubble leading into the basement.

"I'm smaller and lighter than you. I should be fine. Just help me down onto that big block there and I'll take a look around."

"Alice, no."

She looked back at me and smiled, about to say something clever, then stopped. "It must be from being so near the Tarakana. For a second I didn't just hear the concern in your voice, I felt it. I felt how you're afraid for me." She gave me a quick hug. "I'm going to be fine. Really. Now help me down. I need to know what's there."

"You need to know."

"Exactly."

I helped her down and she disappeared from view as she explored. I looked at what was left of the walls and prayed that they would go on being walls and not tons of rock and adobe covering the only other human within millions of kilometers.

One of the Tarakana joined me, leaned against my knee, and extended its tentacles out over the drop into the basement.

"Yeah, I'm worried too," I told it.

Alice's voice drifted up to me. "Found them. There's a lot of debris on top, but I think I can get a few." She reemerged, her arms full. "Here, I'll toss them up to you."

There was a rumble from where she had been as the building settled and dust floated up around her. She looked behind her. "It might be hard to get any more."

"Damn it, Alice. That wasn't being careful."

I helped her back up after she had tossed me the last of the packages.

"Why weren't you afraid?"

"I don't know." She sounded surprised. "I should have been. For some reason I'm feeling very brave today." She looked at the Tarakana next to me. "I see the graves are done."

"Yes." I examined the packages. "I don't know what these dates mean. Do you know the Bodens Gate calendar?"

Alice reached down and gently held the tip of the Tarakana's tentacle. "There was a ship here about two months ago, but they don't keep a regular schedule." She closed her eyes in concentration. "If they follow the same pattern the next one will come somewhere between twenty-three and fifty-six days from now." She smiled at me. "I really love these guys."

I touched the tip of the other tentacle and immediately let go, jerking my arm away. Alice took a step back, dropped the tentacle she had been holding, and stared at her fingers.

"I'm sorry, Alice. I let go as quickly as I could."

She looked at me and then at her hand. "That was you in there. I saw you, just for an instant. When you touched the other tip, I could *see* you."

CHAPTER 12

INTERLUDE

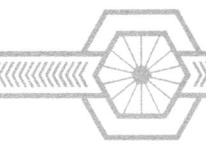

"OK, now I *am* scared." Alice was still breathing hard while we walked to the cemetery.

"These guys will do that to you. Everything seems all warm and friendly and then something happens and you realize the magnitude of how different, intelligent, and powerful they really are."

"And how vulnerable we are right now."

"So, what did I look like in there?" I asked.

"Kind of glowy."

"If I had reached out, I think I would have heard every thought in your head and felt every emotion."

"Please don't ever do that."

"I won't. I have my own secrets to keep."

"Not like mine." Alice kept her head down.

I smiled at her, but she wouldn't look up. "You're not as dark as you think you are, Alice Vandermeer. You glow. I've seen it."

She smiled at me, a little lopsided, with a sweet look in her eyes. "Thank you." She took my hand while we walked. "I'm not as scared now."

Alice prayed for the dead, asking forgiveness for them. When she was done, she and I stood together looking at the mounded dirt.

"I wish I had a flower to put on Tirana's grave for her and the child she was carrying. I think she was only fifteen. Maybe sixteen." She sighed. "There's nothing here but red dirt and rocks."

"Do you know which is hers?"

Alice shook her head.

I pulled the little stuffed Tarakana I had taken from one of the buildings out of my pocket and placed it on the nearest grave. "It's not much."

Alice kissed my cheek. "It's good."

There were Tarakana at the lab when we got back; working on installing a power source and making the lights work again. They were using a variety of shapes, some taller, some longer, some shifting while we watched. Alice was chewing on her lower lip.

She gasped and turned away with her hand up to her mouth.

"Well, that would be convenient," I said, surprised. "If you need a couple of extra arms, just grow them out of your–"

She walked away from me, out the door, and didn't stop until I caught up to her in the middle of the street.

"Are you all right?"

"It's too much."

I held her. "We should be out of here in a few weeks. Just hold on." I smiled at her, moving her hair away from her eyes. "After this, think how normal your work on Bodens Gate will seem."

"No. I just want to go home. I've never been homesick in my life, but I think I understand the feeling now."

She was starting to shake, so I told her, "I'm going to go talk to them. You can stay here in the street if you want."

She looked up at me and the fire came back into her eyes. "Are you taunting me?"

"I want to make sure that the woman who climbed into a collapsing building earlier today because she had to know what was down there isn't getting lost."

She pushed away from me. "*I'll* go talk to the damn Tarakana."

I smiled and watched her walk away from me and back into the lab.

When I entered the lab, she had her face nuzzled into one and actually kissed it when she let go.

"I thanked them for what they're doing and asked them not to come with us when we hike to your camp tomorrow. They seem to understand." She stepped around them and started making lunch. "I also asked them why they're helping us."

"What did they say?"

"It's because of you."

"Because of the one I saved from the Bovita clan?"

"No. They appreciate that, but it's more that they just like you. They like being inside your head."

"Wonderful. Do they like me as a friend or like a pet?"

She smirked at me. "I didn't ask, but I can guess."

By nightfall, we had lights, heat, and a small flow of water from the pump. We could recharge the portable lights and the display pads, and if we shut everything else down we could power one printer, but slowly.

I covered the two shattered front windows with blankets and the lab and dormitory felt surprisingly snug and warm. It was warm enough that Alice was back down to a t-shirt and shorts when she went to bed that night. I sat on the end of her bunk talking to her before we shut down the lights.

"We did well today," I told her. "We buried our dead without too many tears, we have light and food, and we know that rescue will come. That's a lot to be thankful for."

"I am," she answered. "We also have allies here that scare the crap out of me."

I turned the lights out and laid down in a bunk next to hers.

"I'll be right here if you need anything."

"Brave Ted. Who will *you* call for if you need something?"

"You, of course."

I woke in the morning with her nestled against my back. She told me that I was calling for Jake in the middle of the night and I don't doubt that I was. My dreams were troubled.

We gathered food and water for our hike, including extra blankets if we decided to stay the night. And soap. The flow of water from the small pump was insufficient for the showers, but there was a good-sized lake at the bottom of one of the basins by my old camp.

When we opened the front door, there was a large German Shepherd dog lying on the sidewalk. He raised his head off his front paws and looked at us.

"Did the Bovita have dogs?" I asked.

"No."

"So not a dog then." I knelt down and scratched him behind the ears. He closed his eyes and his tongue lolled out.

"Tarakana dog. I can feel it, but it's muffled. It's not like touching the ones yesterday. Try it."

Alice lightly touched his fur. "Soft. You're right, there's not a direct connection, but I feel it in there."

I continued scratching his ears. "Have you ever owned a dog?"

"Cat."

"Makes sense."

"What do you mean?"

"Most cats I've met think the way you do."

"So, are we going hiking today or are you going to play with your new not-a-dog? And no, he's not coming with us."

"But look at those eyes."

"Tarakana don't have eyes."

"I think they can have whatever they want." I stood. "Ok, I'm coming." I resisted the urge to tell him to 'stay'.

"I'm going to name him Merrimac," I told Alice while we walked out of town. "I had a dog that looked just like him named that when I was little. We always called him Mac."

"These things don't scare you at all, do they?"

"I accept them. We'd be dead by now if they meant us harm." I looked at her walking next to me, her head down. "Giz told me that no one knows what the future holds, other than surprises. I guess I just try to enjoy the ride since I know I'm not the one in charge. You should know that too, Madam Chaplain."

We walked in silence for almost ten minutes before Alice looked up at me. "Merrimac is a good name. If he's still a dog when we get back."

I nodded. "I've been thinking. Even without all the sensors and other electronics we normally use, we should be able to do a reasonable survey of this area. Do you feel like being a field geologist for a few weeks?"

"Sure. Beats staying home all day with the dog." She grinned at me.

"We're going to be OK, Alice. The time will go quickly."

A half hour later, we reached the spot where the valley narrowed to a steep walled canyon, the spot where the Tarakana had hidden a bridge from us. There was no bridge. There was no sign there had ever been a bridge.

"It was here." I tossed a rock at where the bridge used to be, half expecting it to bounce off a hidden structure. It took over two seconds for the rock to reach the bottom of the canyon.

"You said *Star* had plotted a different path for you?"

"About half a kilometer east."

Alice started walking.

I caught up to her. "You're not going to say anything?"

"Nope. Just enjoying the ride."

"I deserve that."

"You do, but you're also right."

We dropped into the valley and climbed back up the other side, arriving covered in sweat and with our skin scratched from climbing up along a scree slope.

"I see why the Tarakana put in a bridge. Why do you think they removed it?" Alice asked while we rested at the top.

"I'm not sure yet. I want to go by the overlook above their city. It's not too far out of the way, maybe twenty minutes from here."

"What do you expect to see?"

"Nothing."

"Nothing?"

"Let's just go look."

The walls of the slot canyon where the city had been were covered in small openings that looked like the result of natural erosion. The canyon floor was empty and the valley beyond was a red sand wasteland.

"It would be really easy for me to think that I had imagined the whole thing, the bridge, the city, even the Tarakana." I sat down on a rock and looked out across the valley lit by the late morning sun. "Alice, tell me you remember the Tarakana."

"The who?"

I looked at her and she couldn't keep from smiling. "If your camp isn't there and all the caves are gone, then you and I are going to have a conversation."

"I thought they might do something like this, go back into hiding before the next ship arrives. They seem to prefer that no one knows that they exist."

"So Mac the dog may not be there when we get back."

I shrugged.

We finished our hike and I was relieved to find everything where I had left it.

"I guess you're not crazy yet, Ted."

"Not yet. What do you think? Swim first then lunch, or the other way around?"

"You set up for lunch. I want to go see your lake. Is the water warm?"

"Go see. It's just over that rise." I pointed.

I got out some of the packaged food and spread a blanket next to my fire ring. Alice climbed up the slope and disappeared down the other side. I stared after her, listening to the wind moving the fabric of the tent. Sudden panic swept over me. I ran up the slope and skidded to a stop looking down at the lake.

Alice was kneeling down with her hand in the water checking the temperature. She looked up when she heard me come over the top.

"It's warm," she called. "Geothermal?" She looked at me watching her. "What's wrong?"

I walked down the slope. "Nothing. Lunch is ready."

She looked at me closely and her eyes crinkled. "You were afraid you'd come over the top of that hill and I wouldn't be here."

"Something like that. It crossed my mind."

"Food first, then swim."

We ate, we swam, we explored the caves, and in the evening, we sat around the fire and watched the stars.

"Where do you suppose the Tarakana come from?" I asked her.

"I don't know. Certainly not from Cleavus. There's nothing else here other than some moss by the lake and probably microbes in the soil. You have a theory?"

"Maybe. They hide, not just individually, but they hide their entire civilization. They could be on the same planets we are and we'd never know it. If there had been a dozen on board *Wandering Star* would we have known about it?"

"*Star* would have known."

"Would she? I'm not so sure. They hid a bridge and a city from her."

"Our *Wandering Star*. I miss her." Alice sighed, staring into the flame. "Doesn't she have safeguards that should have prevented the Bovita clan from taking the shuttles and stealing the ship? How was that possible? Could the Tarakana have helped them just to get the clan off Cleavus?"

"I don't know how they did it," I lied. "I suppose that's possible." Alice looked at me. I looked at the fire.

"They should be almost half way to Bodens Gate now. I pray for them all the time, they're always in my thoughts." She smiled at me. "I don't imagine Velena is taking to captivity very well."

"If she gets free you should be praying for the clan."

Alice laughed.

We spent the evening there talking about our friends, those on Earth and Dulcinea, and those on the ship. We planned what we needed to do to create a geologic map of the area and then we watched the stars some more. Late in the night, we climbed into the tent and I slept holding her hand to make sure she didn't disappear.

"No, Ted, no, no. no. That does not make sense. Look at the thickness of this layer compared to what you measured south of town. And it's at a different elevation. You can't correlate them that way." She reached in front of me and moved the formation with her finger, sliding it down the screen. "Now it matches better."

"OK, those six layers match now, but nothing else does. And you know you can't trust the elevation data. This thing," I gestured at the display pad, "is using air pressure to determine height. Who knows what truth is?"

Alice leaned back. "I suppose there could be discontinuities. Some of the layers might pinch out. We need an intermediate point."

"Like the canyon where the bridge used to be."

"Yes. We can enter the valley where the trail to your camp cuts across and then follow it back to where it narrows. There're good exposures there."

"OK. It's been almost a week since we were last at the lake and I'm getting tired of sponge baths. We can leave in the morning, work on the survey, and have a late afternoon swim."

Alice nodded. "We've been working on this map for six weeks. It needs to be right."

"It will be. We work well together. You piss me off most of the time, but it's hard to argue with the results we're getting."

She smiled at me. "I want to get up now and your dog is sleeping on my feet again."

"Were you thinking about your feet being cold?"

"Maybe."

I looked at him under the desk. "Mac, I think her feet are warm enough now. Go sleep somewhere else." Mac shuffled a couple of meters away, flopped on his side and went back to sleep.

"He does that really well, considering that everything he knows about being a dog he's pulling out of your brain."

"Maybe that's why I can't help but love him."

Alice shook her head. "Hopeless."

"I'm going to shut all of the lights down and try to print some rope for tomorrow. I'll be lucky to get two meters an hour out of it, so I'm going to look around town and see if I can find more while it's running."

"OK. I want to stay here and work on these correlations." She glanced up at me. "Don't get lost." She looked back at the screen.

I set up the printer and then stood in the doorway watching her work. She had one leg tucked under her and was leaned forward with her nose almost touching the screen.

"Alice?"

She looked at me questioningly.

"Never mind. Back soon." She turned to the screen and didn't notice me watching her for another five minutes before I left.

The next morning I coiled up twenty-five meters of rope while Alice set up our signs and beacons against the possibility that a ship might come while we were away. We walked out of town, leaving Mac behind to guard the lab.

"That rope doesn't look strong enough to climb."

"It's not for climbing. See the marks on it? They're ten centimeters apart. I'm going to attach this at the top of the cliff and throw it over the edge with a big rock tied to the other end. We can get a couple of pictures of it from the other side and the application on the pad will tell us how thick each layer is. It won't give us strike and dip, but we may not need them."

She smiled at me. "Smart and lazy is a great combination."

We set up the rope then climbed down into the valley and back up the scree to the other side. I took Alice's hand and helped her over the last boulder to the top. She was sweaty and breathing hard.

"Ted?" She looked up from the rock where she was resting with her head leaned against my side.

"Yes?"

She stared at me for a moment. "Never mind. Let's go see how your rope looks."

"I'm hoping we have enough sun on it. We might have to move the rope to the north side and do this over again."

I took the pictures and waited while the application tried to interpret the data and compensate for the angle looking into the canyon. Alice leaned over my shoulder and watched the numbers fill in for each layer.

"Look at that," Alice said. "Survey all done." She kissed my cheek.

"More time for swimming. We can plug the new numbers into the model this evening and see if the correlations work any better."

We stopped by the camp and dropped off our packs.

"Give me a ten minute head start to get clean and then you can join me." Alice took the soap and left me in the camp.

I waited the allotted time and followed her. I took off my boots and shirt and waded out to where she was floating on her back.

"My turn for the soap. I'm smelly." She rolled over, dove gracefully and came back to the surface next to me.

"I like the way you smell."

"Uh huh. Soap please." She handed me the bottle and I washed what I could with her there.

We spent the afternoon in the water swimming, playing, laughing, and talking until I noticed it was starting to get dark.

I swam to the edge of the lake and called back to her. "It's getting cold out here. Come up onto the beach and I'll bring you a towel."

I dried off and came back to the shore. Alice walked out of the lake in the fading light, water sparkling in her hair and dripping from shirt and shorts.

"It's freezing out here." She took the towel from me and started drying her hair.

"You start at the top, I'll start at the bottom and we'll try to get you dry before it's too late."

She spread her legs apart a little and I knelt, took my towel, and dried her. When I finished she was looking down at me with a strange smile on her lips.

"Ted, I don't think those shorts are hiding your feelings quite as well as you think they are."

I glanced down and then back up at her. "Says the woman wearing the wet t-shirt." She parted her lips in a crooked smile and rested her hand on my shoulder.

I stood and she moved close to me.

"Alice, I don't want you to do something you'll regret later."

She put her arms around my neck and pulled me down to her, her lips touching mine while she talked. "Like walking away right now? I know I would regret *that* later."

I held her close to me. "That t-shirt is cold."

She stepped back and pulled it up and over her head with one hand, dumping it on the sand. "Problem solved."

She took another step back and held my eyes with hers, glowing pale blue defiance in the twilight. "I need to ask you something before this goes any further."

I looked back into her eyes, trying to ignore the beauty of her body as she stood there in her shorts, the surface of the lake shimmering behind her.

"If you're just a boy looking for a pleasant interlude between now and when we're rescued then we should stop now, that's not what I need. A month ago, your heart was not yours to give. Have you reclaimed it? Can you offer it to me now without reservation?"

I knelt in front of her, my eyes still on hers. "I can."

"I'm a jealous lover, Ted. Jealous of who receives my love and whose love I take."

"Alice, I have spent every minute of my life with you for over six weeks. On most nights, we've slept in each other's arms and given comfort to each other against the loneliness and to keep the nightmares at bay. I've never known anyone so deeply and so well. We've worked together to survive." I smiled at her. "Not a day has gone by that we didn't argue, loudly, about something, and not an argument has passed that I didn't love you more at the end."

She smiled back at me. "That's because I won all those arguments."

"Really? Is that how you remember it?" I reached up, took her hands, and pulled her roughly down on to the sand, both of us kneeling, so close together that I felt her breath on my face.

"Alice, there is a part of my heart that I will never reclaim and there is nothing I can do to get it back. Also, you should know that looking at you now," I finally let my eyes look away from hers and travel down, "I *am* that boy who wants the pleasure that comes from being with a girl. But I am also a man who loves you and I know what that means." I looked back into her eyes. "I will work at it hard the rest of my life, trying to be worthy of the woman I love." I took her hand and pressed it against my chest. "Do you feel it? The heart that you own?"

She was breathing hard and her eyes glistened bright. She took my hand, kissed the palm and placed it on her chest. "It's been yours for a long time. You had only to claim it."

I kissed her lips. A long, gentle kiss.

"Take me someplace warmer, Ted."

We held hands and walked back over the hill to camp.

She sat on the blanket in front of the tent and leaned back on her elbows while I started one of the self-igniters. I pulled two more from my pack, put one on each side of the blanket, and started them too.

"How many of those do we have left?"

"There was a box of a hundred in the lab. We won't run out."

"I like the effect. I can feel the warmth on my sides and feet and the cold air coming down on top of me. Hot and cold at the same time."

She smiled at me as I sat down next to her.

"You're staring at me, Ted. Do I still look so strange to you? Like I did the night we first met?"

"No, not strange. Enchanting. Beautiful." I put my hand on her hip and ran my fingers under the waist of her shorts. I looked into her eyes, feeling rational thought rapidly fading away. I straddled her on all fours and kissed her mouth and then her neck as she leaned back, one arm behind her head, her other hand on my chest caressing its way down.

I could feel her tongue on my ear as she whispered, "Why don't you show me what it was that your shorts were failing to hide?"

We made love under the stars, the flames around us keeping us warm. Sometime after midnight we went into the tent and slept in each other's arms late into the morning.

I woke to the sound of Alice unwrapping some of our packaged food. She was sitting on the blanket in front of the tent wearing a heavy sweatshirt, but nothing else. Mac was lying next to her, his head in her lap and she was absently scratching his ears while she ate.

"Thanks for waiting for me." I called out to her.

"I tried to wake you. You said bad things to me so I left."

I climbed out of the tent and stretched. "When did Mac get here? Doesn't he know that he's supposed to be on guard duty?"

"He was here when I got up. I think he decided that you were more in need of protection than the lab. I've been telling him that he's too late."

I kissed the top of Alice's head. "I'll be right back." I went to where we had established a latrine, and then put on a sweatshirt and shorts. I sat down in front of her.

"Oh," she sounded disappointed. "You got dressed."

"Not planning on getting any work done today?"

"Not the kind that requires getting dressed."

I put my hand on her foot, rubbing her bare toes. "I think we've earned a couple of vacation days."

I reached over to scratch Mac's other ear. It was normally easy to forget that he was a Tarakana and not a dog because he kept the mental and emotional connections so muted. Normally, but not this time.

Alice gasped and then I was looking at her, bright and glowing in my mind. I felt a momentary resistance as she hesitated, tried to hide, and then whispered *yes, this too*. I don't know how long it lasted, having her in my mind and me in hers, but my hand was still on her foot when it ended. Mac was sitting a meter away, looking just as startled as Alice and me.

"Damn it, Mac." There was despair in Alice's voice. "How could he still want me after seeing that? How could anyone want me?"

I pulled her toward me until she was on my lap. "You didn't see all my darkness?" I asked.

She shook her head. "There was no darkness."

"Blind girl. What was it you didn't want me to see? That you plot and manipulate to get what you want? I've been your willing victim. That you're afraid all the time? Let me be always there to comfort you and help you be brave." She had her face buried in my shoulder, not crying, just holding on tight. "Or is it that after two years, that you still love your husband and miss him every day? I love you all the more for that. It doesn't decrease your love for me."

"You and Hannah." She tipped her head back to look at me. "I didn't know. I tried to drive a wedge between you. That was foolish. How can passion burn that bright? Both of you, near insanity whenever you were together. It's still burning in your soul, burning low, but still burning. Can there be fire like that for me?" She sighed, her cheek against my chest. "I saw it. I saw inside you and felt it. I just don't know why."

I kissed her, my hands moving up under her sweatshirt, lifting it up over her head. She leaned back and I kissed her neck, down across her shoulder to her breasts.

"You don't want breakfast first?" Alice asked, looking down at me.

"I'll find something to eat in a few minutes."

She sighed, a sound that ended in a soft moan. "Don't let me interrupt you then."

We stayed in camp for another two days enjoying our vacation. Alice explored more of the caves with me, we swam in the lake, and we tromped around the desert. We climbed hills just to hold hands at the top and admire the beauty of the view, trying not to think about the geologic processes that created them.

The weather stayed warm and our clothes stayed in our backpacks most of the time. Alice was adorable walking across the sand wearing nothing but hiking boots and a big hat to shield her eyes. Helping her put on sunscreen each morning was one of the best parts of my day. Mac was with us most of the time. I don't know how much his presence was amplifying our feelings, but I didn't care. Alice had been inside my head and she loved me.

Two days later the morning sunlight shining through the fabric of the tent gave everything an orange glow. Alice was lying completely on top of me, a tangle of arms and legs wrapped around my body, her hair covering her face. I watched her sleep, afraid to move. When she finally woke, she stretched. It was a slow process that started with her feet, moved up her legs to her hips and ended with her wiggling up higher across my body until her lips were on mine for a good morning kiss.

"If you wake up every morning like that I will be happy for the rest of my life." I told her.

"OK. I can do that."

"Are you ready to go back to town today?"

She considered it for a moment. "Yes and no. The last couple of days I have felt more at peace than I have for a very long time and I don't want it to end."

"It won't."

She gave me a quick kiss, thought about it and then gave me a longer one.

"I'm kind of looking forward to being back in the lab," she continued. "I want to correlate the information from the canyon that we got on the way here. I'm excited to see what it shows."

"I know you are. I can still feel you a little bit in here," I tapped my head, "even though it's been two days since we connected. I can't read your mind, but I feel your emotions."

"I know. You're still in my head too, although it's pretty easy to know what you're feeling."

"Love for you."

"That's in there. Mostly something else right now that starts with the same letter."

"Lust? I think that feeling might be rolling around in your head right now too."

She scowled at me. "I'm not sure I like you knowing what I'm feeling."

I kissed behind her ear and along her neck.

"No, I was wrong. I do like it."

We broke camp a couple of hours later and made our way back to town.

On the morning of the fifty-sixth day, Alice came and sat on the desk in front of me. I tipped my head back and she kissed me.

"You know what today is, Ted." She didn't say it as a question.

I nodded. "This is the longest that Bodens Gate has gone without resupplying Cleavus."

"And you know what it means."

"Yes. I know you do too, although we haven't talked about it because we both hoped this day wouldn't come."

Alice said the words calmly. "Their Central Government knows that the Bovita clan is back on Bodens Gate, or maybe they captured them all. Regardless, there's no longer any reason for them to come here. RuComm thinks the clan killed us along with Jake and Angela. No one is coming for us. Not ever."

"Someone will come eventually."

"Ted, how long ago was the last survey here?"

"Two-hundred seventy-three years."

"I'll be an old woman by then."

I laughed and reached out to take her hands. "Rescue may still come. We'll live day by day until a ship comes or death overtakes us. We have food and water enough to last a lifetime and more. We have a planet to explore and we'll leave a record of what we do. Our lives won't be wasted."

"And someone might come tomorrow," she added.

"Exactly."

But they didn't. Or on the next day.

On the ninety-first day, our geologic report was completed. We had a geochronology of relative dates for a sequence of over twelve-hundred cycles of a saltwater sea inundating Cleavus, and then the land emerging and becoming arid again. Alice sat on my lap with her head leaned against mine as we scrolled through the finished product of geologic maps, cross-sections and descriptions.

"Do you want your name first on this paper or should we do it the logical way and make it alphabetical?" I asked her.

"You always seem willing to let me come first in other things, so you can have your name at the top on this one. I pray that you are able to present it sometime. It's a brilliant piece of work."

"Brilliant because of you."

Mac came into the lab and pushed up against Alice's legs, excited. "See?" I said. "Mac agrees with me."

He tried to climb up into Alice's lap, which was hard for him because Alice was still in my lap.

She put her hand on him to push him off and her eyes lost focus when she touched him. "Don't touch him, Ted. He's in pure Tarakana mode again."

"What's he telling you?"

After a moment, Mac jumped off and curled up on top of my feet.

Alice had a silly, crooked smile on her face. "Don't ask me how he knows, but he says a ship just cleared the Deep Space Hole between here and Ratatoskr. They should be on orbit in three days."

"Does he know what ship?"

"No, but it's a ship. Coming to Cleavus." She rotated on my lap until she was facing me, her knees wedged in beside my hips. She kissed me hard then leaned back smiling. "Are you feeling my emotions, Ted? Do you know what I want?"

"Right now?"

"Oh, yes. Right now."

CHAPTER 13

BACK IN THE UNIVERSE

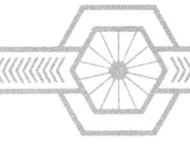

Alice and I celebrated the rest of the day and into the night. She was busy early the next morning organizing the samples we had collected, updating her journal, packing things she wanted to keep, and radiating so much happiness that it filled the lab and spilled out into the street. I finished my packing, and then Merrimac and I sat together watching her.

"Do you have everything you want to take with you packed already?" she asked accusingly.

"You're planning on coming with me?"

"Of course."

"All done, then."

"Ted, you are very simple."

"Do you mean uncomplicated or not all that bright?"

"Take your pick."

I got up and gave her a quick hug. "What can I do to help?"

She looked around the lab. "I think I'm done for now. We should go back to the camp one last time just to make sure we haven't left anything there."

"I was thinking the same thing. I plan to abandon the tent and blankets and other camping stuff, but we should do a last look. I don't want to spend the night though, unless you really want to."

She shook her head emphatically. "Definitely not. I know the ship is still a couple of days out, but I keep finding myself listening for the sound of a shuttle and I've already checked my display pad four or five times this morning to scan for new connections."

"What are we going to do with Mac?" He was lying under the desk, his tail thumping the floor at the mention of his name.

"He's a Tarakana. We leave him here and he goes back to having a couple of tentacles growing out of his head."

"You need to talk to him. I don't think he wants to stay. You've always been better at seeing his thoughts and I don't seem to be able to read him at all right now."

"So you need me because my thoughts are just as twisted as the scary alien that you keep pretending is a dog?"

"Yeah. And I know you like him despite that. I've seen you petting him and playing with him."

She sighed and sat down on the floor and Mac trotted up to her. She put her hands on his face and closed her eyes. Mac pulled away after a few minutes and went back under the desk.

"What did he say?"

Alice frowned, seeming confused. "He's going with us." She paused, thinking. "There's a lot there and I don't understand it all. He can't go back to the others because he's no longer a piece of that group. There was also a feeling that we owe him something for the help the Tarakana have given us."

"I can't argue with that."

"There's something else, something hidden in the tangled passageways that I'm not seeing. When he said he was going with us it wasn't a request."

"Is there a danger in taking him?"

"No, I'm sure of that, but I don't know why I'm sure." She looked back at him. "Please don't ask me to talk to him again."

"I won't."

Her eyes were scrunched up and full of worry.

"Alice? Did you know there's a ship on its way here?"

She smiled and the happiness flooded back into her.

That evening we took a couple of chairs up onto the landing pad after dinner and sat holding hands while the sun went down.

"We always seem to find ourselves sitting together watching the stars come out, Ted. Why do you suppose that is?"

She had her head tipped back gazing into the darkness, and I watched her for a moment before answering. "I do it because I like looking at beautiful things."

She smiled at the compliment, but didn't turn toward me. "I do it to reset my thoughts and try to gather the courage to be able to sleep through the night. The universe is so big and we are so small, but we're brave enough to toss ourselves out into it, to cross between the points of light." Her eyes crinkled in a smile. "I think God is proud of us."

"Alice, are you planning on staying on Bodens Gate for your missionary work?"

Her smile faded. "I don't think so. My father has believed me dead for the past three months. I think I should go home, but I'll go wherever you want to go. What about you? Are you going back to the Reunification Commission?"

"I don't see how I can. The thought of not having you in my bed for even a single night is hateful. I've tried pretending not to love someone. Never again. I should go back to Earth and see my dad. I need to talk to Jake's folks. But I'll go wherever you want to go."

"Let's wait a few days and see where God leads us next."

We hiked to the camp the next morning, had lunch, and went for a swim before checking for any items we wanted to take back with us. I didn't find anything worth keeping, but Alice found a blue t-shirt left half buried in the sand by the lake. She rinsed it out and held it up for me to see.

"Do you remember this?"

"I do."

"I'm keeping it."

"I didn't know you were sentimental."

"This is special."

I waded out to join her in the water and kissed her. "I'm looking forward to seeing you wear it again."

She changed right there, putting the shirt on even though it was still wet or maybe because it was.

"Stay there a moment," I told her. I unfolded my display pad. "I need one more image of this basin with the lake at the bottom. You standing there is perfect for providing scale."

"If you ever show that to anyone else..."

"I'm going to send it to your father. Proof that you're still alive and well."

She came up out of the lake and chased me back over the hill to our camp. We kissed when I let her catch me.

"Let's go home."

We walked back to town holding hands most of the way.

Alice kept fidgeting after dinner, looking in boxes, reviewing files and checking her pad every few minutes. I grabbed her around the waist when she walked past me for the tenth time.

"Alice, you know that the pad will notify you when there's a connection available."

"I know. But what if I miss it? I might not be paying attention. Or it might not work. Or I might have gone deaf." She sat down next to me. "How can you just sit there? I can feel that you're just as excited as I am."

"I am. I just don't show it the same way." I looked into her eyes. "Alice, this is probably our last night here, the last night that we can say we are the only people on an entire planet. What would you like to do with it?"

She didn't hesitate. "I want to make love to you under an open sky one last time, a ring of the self-igniters around us. I want to scream as loud as I can and know that there is no one else to hear me. I want to have you in my bed and wake up in the morning with your arms around me."

I stood and walked toward the dorms.

"Where are you going?"

"It's almost dark. I think we should get started right away, don't you?"

We pulled mattresses off the bunks and put them in the middle of the street. Alice reclined on her elbows and watched me start the fires. Then I laid down next to her under the stars and surrounded by the crumbling remains of the town lit by the firelight.

"I really am planning on screaming later," she told me.

I leaned over her and she kissed me. "I'll do what I can to give you a good reason."

She chuckled, a deep throaty sound. She kissed my cheek and her teeth tugged gentle on my ear as she moved under me.

Much later, while we talked quietly in the dark under the blankets, I heard the soft chime of the display pad establishing a connection to the ship.

"02:38," I said, looking at my watch. "I suppose it can keep until morning."

"You just try and keep me here."

"OK." I put my arms around her.

"I *will* bite you, Theodore."

"Race you back to the lab?" She was gone, but I think she would have beat me even if I had been trying.

Alice was perched on the edge of the chair in front of the desk, one leg under her and the other knee up by her chin. She had wrapped herself in a blanket taken from our makeshift bed.

"You are very beautiful this morning, Alice Vandermeer."

She glanced at me. "Stay focused, Ted." She smiled. "You may want to put something on." Alice looked back at the screen. "She's the *Falling Star*, out of Ratatoskr bound for Bodens Gate for resupply and then on to Dulcinea. They were stopping here to recover our bodies. Even her AI sounded excited when I connected. She's notified the Captain and the RuComm tech team lead. It's about 23:30 ship's time right now, so they were asleep."

Captain Adriensoon was the first to appear, dressed sharply in uniform and looking wide-awake.

"Vandermeer and Holloman?" she asked without preamble.

"Yes, ma'am." Alice answered. "Angela Dawkins and Jake Barton were both killed when the clan stole our ship."

"I'm sorry to hear that, although needing to recover only two bodies instead of four is still a blessing. You are both looking well. Is there anything you will need right away?"

"We could use a ride out of here," Alice replied, getting the Captain to smile. "And can you please let our families know that we're alive?"

"*Star* has already sent notifications. The one to Dulcinea should arrive in about thirty hours and about ten hours after that for the relay to Earth."

The tech team lead sat down next to the Captain, the viewing angle automatically changing to include her.

"Sara O'Dell," she introduced herself. She still seemed half asleep.

"Sara, can you tell us what's happened to the *Wandering Star* team?" I asked.

"Oh, the Bovita clan." She yawned. "Our XO is the expert. He's from Bodens Gate and has been following this from the beginning. RuComm ransomed all the members of the tech team and they're back on Earth now awaiting reassignment, I think. Except for Hannah Weldon, of course."

"Hannah?" There was something wrong with my voice when I said her name, as if the air wouldn't come out of my lungs.

The Captain motioned to someone off screen and Lieutenant Kelang, Falling Star's XO, joined us.

"Hannah was a friend?"

"Yes," I answered. "My friend."

"Ms. Weldon was ransomed with the rest of your team and was staying with them at the Union embassy in the capital, Eindhoven. She convinced the staff there to allow her to go out in the evening to one of the local clubs, saying it was for research."

"She was our linguist." I explained.

He nodded. "Yes. I've studied her file. She never returned. The club was close to the border with the Warrens, the areas controlled by the clans. The local police told us that one of the clans most likely robbed and killed her. If that's true, the people who did it will never be found."

"You sound like you don't believe it's true."

Lieutenant Kelang looked away before answering. "No, she probably was taken. No ransom demand was received and it's possible she was killed if she put up a fight." He hesitated again.

"Or?"

"I'm sorry. The clans took her and sold her. That's what always happens in cases like this. She was young and pretty, and in the Warrens everything has a price. She would have been more valuable on the market block than any ransom would bring and at less risk for whichever clan took her. The Central Government won't acknowledge the facts, but that's the truth of it."

Alice took my hand under the desk. "What's being done to get her back?" I asked.

"You don't understand the Warrens. Citizens don't go there; not the police, not even the military, other than in force. Do yourself a favor and accept the CG's version of the truth. That was over three months ago. Even if she could be found, you wouldn't want her back. She wouldn't be the friend you remember. Do you understand? Not after three months being sold in the Warrens."

"We understand, thank you." Alice answered for me because she knew I couldn't.

I stepped away from the screen and let Alice talk to them about arrival times, uploading our files, and arranging to load our collection of geologic samples. When she was done, she came and sat beside me on the floor where I was wiping my face on Merrimac's fur.

"I'm sorry, Alice. This should be the best, happiest day of our lives and I'm sitting on the floor mourning an old lover while I wipe my tears on the dog."

She looked at me, not saying anything.

I touched the blue t-shirt she had on. "I don't want you to question my love for you. I remember the commitment we made to each other that night at the lake, the night you wore this. Nothing has changed."

She smiled gently. "You love deep, Ted. It's one of your best features. I'm not jealous. You lost a good friend just now. Never let friends or family or a lover leave you without tears. It's what tears are for."

She sat with me for a time, her hand gentle on my back.

After a while, she stood and offered her hand to me. "*Falling Star* won't be close enough to launch a shuttle for another twelve hours, and it's still an hour before dawn. If we hurry, there's time enough for me to fall asleep so I can wake up in your arms."

We walked back out into the street. The last of the flames were guttering low, but the stars were bright enough to see by. I laid down and Alice snuggled close to me under the blankets.

I turned my head to the side to make room for her and saw that the blue t-shirt that she had been wearing was back lying in the sand again.

"Huh." I grunted.

"What is it?"

"You look very nice in that blue t-shirt, especially when it's wet." I spoke softly, caressing her bare shoulder.

"Thank you."

"You didn't need to hide it."

"What do you mean?"

"At the lake. You left it there so that you could find it and wear it again when our rescue was near. You wanted to wear it to remind me of what we said to each other that night. You were worried about what would happen when I could be with Hannah again." I kissed her forehead. "You didn't need to be."

"You really think I'm that devious?"

"Of course you are. My point is that you're wasting it on me. My love for you is unconditional."

She kissed my chest. "Why do you love me?"

"I fell in love with you right there, working with you every day in the lab, you arguing with me about every conclusion, pointing out every error in my analyses, making me better than I could ever be without you."

"So you want me to argue more with you?" She continued working her way down my chest, kissing and nipping at the skin.

"Yes, but gently, always gently." She came back up and nuzzled her head into my neck humming softly to herself.

"Alice, one thing is still bothering me. The blue t-shirt was so obvious that I can't help thinking that you knew I'd figure it out. What are you really up to?"

"You have no idea the plans I have for you. Now, hush, and let me sleep."

The shuttle arrived late in the afternoon and we watched it from when it was a small bright speck until its engines cleaned all of the red dust from the landing pad, obscuring everything. Alice and I didn't wait for the dust to settle before coming out of the lab and starting the climb onto the landing pad. Lieutenant Kelang, Sara O'Dell, and their team geologist, George Hallett came down the shuttle ramp. Alice hugged each of them in turn, welcoming them to Cleavus.

I knew George from the Academy where he had been a year ahead of me. Not a close friend, but still a familiar face from several classes and study groups. We always shortened his first name and called him 'Geo'. He shook my hand, a big smile on his face as he looked past me at the hills north of the town.

"Look at the strata exposed on those hills. I had to see it for myself after reading through your survey this morning. Nice job, Ted. Brilliant actually, considering the tools you had available."

I smiled back at him and pointed at Alice who was introducing Sara and the Lieutenant to Mac. "She's the brilliant one. I'm just adequate. Isn't that what you always called me in our mineralogy lab?"

"I did. You never could remember chemical compositions longer than it took to pass the next test."

"It's good to see you, Geo."

He laughed. "After being stuck here for over three months I imagine you'd be happy to see anyone. It must have been lonely."

I looked back at Alice and Geo looked with me. "I'm happy to be leaving, but it wasn't lonely. Not lonely at all."

"Professor Vandermeer's daughter?"

"You know the Professor?"

"I worked for him for two months last year. Her I know only by reputation. If half the stories they tell about her are true she's not someone you want to hook up with. She's crazy and not in a good way."

"Quite a bit more than hooked up, Geo."

He turned back to me. "I'm sorry for what I said, then. All that time together here, not knowing when rescue would come, or if it would ever come." He shook his head and looked back at me as if I might be a little crazy now too. "It's going to make it hard for you to reintegrate into RuComm."

"I know. Impossible."

"Maybe not impossible. There's more to RuComm than drifting between planets doing surveys, but you haven't even finished your first hop yet. I guess it depends on what you want to do next."

"I'm not sure." I looked back at Alice. The three of them were kneeled down now petting Merrimac, Alice laughing. I could feel how happy she was from fifty meters away. "As long as we're together I'm sure it will work out."

"The Professor's daughter. You must really enjoy the rush that comes from being in constant danger."

"Something like that." We walked back to the group, Geo shaking his head.

The XO stood up as we approached. "I had forgotten how nice it is having a dog around," he said. "It must have made your time here more bearable, he's such a big happy fellow. Hard to believe the Bovita clan just left him here."

He helped Sara stand and she held his hand a moment longer than needed, smiling at him. Now that they were no longer touching Merrimac, Sara took a step away from the Lieutenant, looking slightly confused. I glanced at Alice who was chewing her lower lip.

"Sara, can you and the Lieutenant help us with a few things?" Alice asked.

"Of course. I'm sure you're anxious to be off this planet." She looked at the abandoned buildings and lengthening shadows. "It's desolate. Did you find anything that would have justified the original colony?"

"No," I answered. "There was nothing here of value that we didn't bring with us."

We paused at the two graves at the bottom of the ramp and the XO removed his cap.

"I'll stay behind for the next shuttle," he told us. "Our medical officer and a couple of volunteers will help me recover your friends. They will be treated with respect and we'll get them home for you."

"Thank you, sir." Alice responded.

I sat next to Alice on the shuttle after our samples and bags were stowed. I took her hand, kissed it, and she raised her eyebrows at me.

"Pretty bold for a RuComm guy. Not worried about being caught?"

I closed my eyes and leaned back in my seat enjoying the feel of the thrusters carrying us off the planet. "Past worrying. Past caring." I turned my head to look into her eyes. "We're part of the universe again. You're not having second thoughts about *me* are you, now that there are tens of thousands of other men eager to be in love with you?"

"How little you know me and the life I've led."

"I know all I need to know. I've seen you glowing when my mind was in yours, and I've seen you glowing when you are breathless and sweaty in my arms. Your past is as far as the east is from the west for me. You can whisper it to me some night after we've exhausted ourselves in other activities if you want. I'll still love you."

"Thank you." She leaned back in her seat, closed her eyes and squeezed my hand. "Don't let go."

Sara O'Dell was not happy with me when I refused her offer of separate quarters for Alice and me.

"Ms. O'Dell," I told her, "I would like to remain with RuComm if it's at all possible, but Alice and I are in love and will continue to be in love. I will not deny it, hide it, or sleep in separate quarters. If this ship cannot accommodate us then please put us back on Cleavus and we'll wait for a ship that can."

Sara didn't seem to know how to respond, but the Captain did.

"Sara, give them one of the vacant double cabins. If you really are afraid that their story will erode team discipline, I'll make room for them in the crew quarters. They've been through hell together and it's a miracle that they're still alive. And Mr. Holloman still managed to complete his RuComm assignment. You should cut them some slack."

"Fine. You can have cabin twenty-one. Ask *Star* if you have trouble finding it. Please avoid displays of affection in the public areas of the ship. Will that be acceptable to you?"

"Yes, ma'am. I appreciate you working with us."

I nodded my thanks to the Captain and she smiled back, her fingers buried in Mac's fur scratching his neck.

"Nice bluff," Alice whispered to me while we walked to our cabin.

"What? Asking her to drop us back on Cleavus?" I smiled at her. "Not a bluff."

"Oh."

"But I knew the Captain would back us up because..." I gestured at Merrimac walking along next to us.

Alice nodded. "Yeah. Your dog worries me. Everyone that touched him today had their emotions messed with. It's worked to our advantage, but I'm scared; scared of what we've done bringing him on board."

We entered our cabin and I glanced at the ceiling so Alice would know that *Star* was listening. Mac crawled under one of the bunks and watched us, looking contented.

"Dogs are emotional amplifiers. The dog I grew up with, the original Merrimac was sad when I was sad and always comforted me. He was happy when I was happy, excited when I was excited, but he never amplified negative feelings like anger. When I was mad, it just made him anxious. I think this Merrimac is like that. The Captain sympathized with us. Mac just made the feeling stronger in her, like any good dog."

"What a comforting theory. Tell me what that means for our feelings for each other."

"It might have accelerated how quickly I fell in love with you, but that was going to happen one way or another. What about you?"

She came close to me, speaking softly. "I fell in love with you on the Margo Islands. No dogs there. Just people trying to kill us and you chasing after Corporal whatever her name was dancing in the firelight."

"Oh, I had forgotten about her. She was pretty."

Alice put her arms around me. "I saved you that night, do you remember that part?"

"Uh huh."

"What are you feeling now, Ted?"

"That I love you." I kissed her and held her close, losing myself to the touch of her lips on mine and the feeling of her body pressed against me. After a couple of minutes, I looked up at the ceiling.

"*Star*?"

"Yes, Mr. Holloman?"

"Thank you for your understanding."

"Of course, Mr. Holloman, Ms. Vandermeer."

Alice looked at me, eyes narrowed. "What else are you feeling, Ted? It's dark. Vengeance? Is that what I'm feeling from you?"

"You refuse to see the darkness in me. I keep telling you it's there."

"*Wandering Star* kept you apart and it almost destroyed you both. I understand the need for a little revenge for you and Hannah." She glanced at Mac. His eyes were open watching us from under the bunk. "Just don't let it get amplified."

"Would you like to get out of this cabin for a while? It's almost 17:30 ship's time. We can see what's available for dinner that's not packaged synthetics."

She smiled at me, looking beautiful. "Absolutely."

Alice was walking slower than usual on our way to the mess hall. "It's the gravity," she complained. "I gained almost six kilos coming up from Cleavus. Don't you feel it too?"

I nodded. "It's like having a backpack I can't put down. Give it a week and you'll be used to it."

"Just in time to gain another five kilos on Bodens Gate."

"I could carry you if that would be easier."

"Would you? I'd enjoy that." She smiled at me.

"Have I told you that I love you?"

"You may have mentioned it."

We entered the mess hall, which looked just like the one on *Wandering Star*.

After we picked up our food, I told Alice, "I'd like to sit with Lieutenant Kelang and find out more about what happened after *Wandering Star* was taken if it's OK with you."

Alice shook her head. "Not during dinner. I want to sit with the team lead and thank her again for our quarters. Why don't you set up a time with the Lieutenant for tomorrow and then come and join us?"

I set up the meeting with the XO for 09:30 the next morning and sat down beside Alice and across from Sara O'Dell. Neither of them did more than glance at me because they were so deeply engrossed in a conversation about which restaurants in Palma Sola were the best and why. I noticed that Alice had the same food selections on her plate as Sara. Not an accident, I was sure.

I ate in silence, not listening to them, but instead took out my pad and started a letter to my father. It was hard writing about Jake, especially since

I knew that his parents would see the letter too. Sitting in a ship's mess hall just like the one where Jake and I had shared so many meals made it even harder. After many false starts, I decided it would be best to tell him about all we had done together since leaving Earth and to say how much I missed him.

"Ted, have you been listening?"

I looked up. "No, Alice, I'm sorry. I was writing a letter to my dad."

"Sara and I have been talking about some of the planetary survey projects that RuComm is trying to staff. There's a couple on Dulcinea that that could use a geologist and they're starting soon. It's a twelve month commitment, but fraternization with the native population is permitted." She was happy, as if she had just presented me with the best gift imaginable.

"That sounds great, but I'd like to look them over before committing."

I could feel frustration sharp in her mind. "They both sound perfect, Ted. You don't have to leave RuComm and we'd be on Dulcinea."

"I'll send you the project and position descriptions," Sara promised. "We'd need to know in the next day or two if you're interested.

I nodded. "Not a problem. I'll let you know by noon tomorrow."

Alice didn't say anything to me while we cleared our plates or as we walked back to our cabin. I could feel she was hurt and her growing anger.

She turned on me as soon as the door closed, cold pale blue eyes looking back into mine. "So, Ted, you won't know until noon tomorrow?"

"I want to review the projects first, make sure I'd be a good fit."

"That's a lie. Noon tomorrow would be right after we meet with the XO so you can find out more about conditions in the Warrens. But even that doesn't really matter, does it?" She thumped me hard on my chest. "Your heart has already decided what you're going to do. I don't know which is worse, that you're lying to me or lying to yourself.

"Have you even thought this through?" she continued. "You'd have to leave RuComm if you want to search for her. You know that you'd probably be killed in your first few days in the Warrens, don't you? Even if you survived, she's probably already dead and then you would be stuck on Bodens Gate with no job and no way to live. Or maybe you'll find her and she's been broken, everything that made Hannah, Hannah crushed out of her. Are you willing to spend the rest of your life trying to put those pieces back together? Because that's what it would take. Maybe you're thinking that she's somewhere just waiting for you to ride in and rescue her. What happens then, Ted? What happens to us?"

"Alice…"

"Three weeks, Ted. In *less* than three weeks we could be back on Dulcinea where I don't weigh as much as a damn cow and you could be doing work that you love and that you're truly great at. Let it go, Ted. Let *her* go." She pressed her face against my chest and tears soaked through my shirt. "Please, Ted, just let her go."

She leaned back and I wiped her tears away with my fingers.

"Ted, you promised that you would go where I want to go. Please take me home and be there with me."

"I will, but not yet. You made a promise too."

"I hate you." She put her head back against my chest.

"I know you do."

"I didn't promise to help you destroy yourself. I didn't promise to help you find *her*."

"Hannah is probably dead." It hurt to say it, more than I expected. "I have to know for sure. Or know that she's beyond my reach."

"Why you? The government didn't look for her. RuComm left her. Brian and Charlotte and Velena and everyone else that knew her got on the next ship to Earth. Damn it, Ted, why you? What would Jake be telling you right now?"

"That I'm an idiot, and he would be right. Let me meet with Lieutenant Kelang tomorrow. He'll probably talk me out of it."

"Lying again."

"And I'll send a message to our embassy in Eindhoven. They probably have more information and that will be the end of it."

"Still lying."

I pushed her backwards until we came to the bunk. She sat down on it and I knelt in front of her, looking up into her eyes.

"Alice, let me be at peace about this. It will haunt me if I just walk away. I need to know that she's not trapped there, scared, hurt, wondering why no one's come for her. I'd do this for any of my friends."

"More lies."

"I would have done it for Jake. I would do it for you."

She looked at me, tears starting again, shaking her head slowly. "Why can't I hate you?"

I pushed her the rest of the way onto the bunk and sat down next to her. "Because that would be too simple. You like complexity in your life. There's more opportunity for you to influence the outcome."

She hit my shoulder softly. "That was a rhetorical question. Please don't try to analyze me right now. I don't know what I'm feeling."

She closed her eyes and I kissed them gently, then each cheek and the tip of her nose. "Would you like me to tell you what you're feeling?"

"Don't tell me. Show me."

I started by taking off her shoes. I rubbed her feet and then worked up along her legs, massaging through her pants until I reached her waist. I undid the pants, pulled them off, then massaged my way back down ending at her toes. Alice kept her eyes closed and didn't speak to me, but her breathing had slowed and I felt her relaxing.

"Take off your shirt and roll over," I told her.

She did as instructed, moving the pillow out of the way and folding her hands under her head as she lay on her stomach. When I first met Alice, her body had seemed extreme in its adaptation to Dulcinea's lower gravity. Now, with her naked on the bed, the long lines of her body looked graceful and elegant. Any additional curve or softening of angles would have ruined the purity of her appearance.

I forced my hands to move more slowly, trying to feel what she wanted. When I reached her lower back, I kissed it, causing her to giggle.

"Not yet," she warned. "Finish the massage first. I'll want your mouth on me soon." She sighed. "Very soon."

When I was done with her back, she rolled over and put her arms around my neck.

"You know this doesn't make me less mad at you?"

"But it's a start?" I asked.

She closed her eyes as I continued the massage. "Yes, it's a start. A damn good start."

CHAPTER 14

FALLING STAR

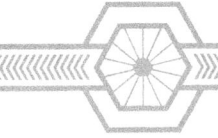

I woke the next morning to the smell of coffee, Alice sitting at the desk typing.

"What time is it? I asked.

She started to open her mouth, but *Star* answered for her. "Ship's time is 06:23 hours."

"I was going to say it's time for you to get up and take a shower," Alice added.

I put my head back on the pillow. "I'm not sure I can. After last night I think I need additional recovery time."

She smiled at me. "Yeah, there are parts of me that are a little tender this morning too. Stay in bed a while longer. At least that way you won't be going out trying to get yourself killed."

There was a desperate yearning in her voice despite her smile.

"So this isn't about Hannah at all, is it? It's about you having lost your husband and now being afraid you're going to lose me." I got out of bed and sat in the chair next to her, turning her to face me. "I am not going to die."

"That's what he told me too."

I took both of her hands in mine and looked at what she had been writing. "Sending a letter to your dad?"

She nodded. "I already sent one to the church on Bodens Gate this morning."

"Telling them you're not coming?"

"No, telling them that I'll be there in a few days, but that I seem to have picked up a husband along the way. I should have an answer back in a few hours. They'll find work for you there. It won't be much and you'll hate it, but you can do your search. Until you get yourself killed."

"What about you?"

"I'll mostly stay in the church compound where it's relatively safe." She saw the confusion on my face. "Where did you think my assignment was, in the nicer parts of Eindhoven ministering to the citizens? We'll be living in the Warrens working with people that need our help." She sighed. "Until you get yourself killed."

"Stop saying that."

"I watched you on the Margo Islands. You would have died at least twice if Marcus hadn't stopped you from doing something stupid and noble. You and Jake were alike that way. And now you're going to go do something stupid and noble and I can't stop you."

I looked for a way to change the subject from my imminent death. "You said husband?"

"Yes. I think we'll need to formalize our relationship, if you have no objections. The church probably won't recognize the verbal commitment made by two half naked people kneeling on the sands of an abandoned world."

"They should. It was a beautiful ceremony."

She squeezed my hands, a flicker of joy moving in her thoughts. "It was, wasn't it? Even if God was our only witness."

"If you want me to be your husband, you should tell me something of the man that had that position before me."

"Philip. I suppose I should. I'll need to tell you things about myself that I don't want to, but you deserve to know." She let go of my hands and tucked one leg underneath her. "I have never been very attractive. I'm too thin and angular even by Dulcinean standards. When Philip looked at me I felt as though I might possibly be the prettiest girl God ever created."

"I like him already."

She scowled at me. "Hush. I'm telling a story."

She thought about it for a moment before continuing. "I need to go back further. I was fourteen when my dad became Department Chair. One evening in late summer, I came into his office in our home and he was working on matching graduate advisers to the grad students starting the new term. He explained it to me as he always did no matter what he was doing. He was struggling with one boy. The geophysics program had accepted him, but the adviser already had too many students. I looked at the boy's transcript and saw that his physics grades were marginal, but that he'd excelled in biology. I told my dad, 'put him with Professor Bolton.' My dad said, 'But Bolton's a paleontologist.' I replied, 'So is this boy. He just doesn't know it yet.'

"My dad and I reworked the entire roster that night and I stayed up way past my bedtime. Mom was so mad at him." She smiled, remembering it.

"You were an evil child."

"It gets worse. I started interfering with the undergraduate classes too. Some students would find that the classes they wanted were already closed and they had to accept alternatives that I had chosen for them. I like to think that they went on to happier, more productive careers as a result, but the truth is that I did it because it was fun. It was like moving pieces around on a game board.

"When I was sixteen, I realized that studying transcripts wasn't enough so I started going to some of the parties on campus in the evenings, listening to the students talk, sometimes meeting them before I either denied or allowed them the academic careers they wanted."

I realized, listening to her, that she wasn't embarrassed telling me this. There was pride in her voice.

"It didn't take them long to figure out who the skinny blonde girl was and to start warning each other whenever I showed up. Some tried to be nice to me, others avoided me entirely, but that was just one more data point in deciding what I'd do with them."

"Did your dad know you were doing this?"

"Of course. The students I selected during those four years performed brilliantly. It wasn't personal. It was good for the department and the University." She sighed. "And then there was Philip."

"How did you meet?"

"He wanted to be a petroleum geologist, but he was terrible at chemistry so I shut him out. He found me at some party and introduced himself. He wasn't angry or threatening. He accepted that I was the one doing this and he sat with me and presented his case. To him, I wasn't the Professor's daughter or the 'little scheming bitch' the others called me when they thought I couldn't hear them. I was the woman that could help him achieve his goals and he treated me with respect. And his eyes never left mine while he talked. They were deep brown, soft, expressive, welcoming..."

"Alice?"

"Sorry. Philip got the classes he wanted and he became one of the best petroleum geologists the University ever produced."

"Did you stop trying to manipulate him?"

She laughed. "No, of course not. But whenever he caught me at it, he just thought it was cute. He asked me to marry him the day he graduated with his bachelor's degree." She smiled at me. "Just like I had planned for him to do. I was eighteen."

"You loved him very much."

"I did. I do." She looked back at the letter she had been writing. "I think that's all I can tell you about him right now. Go take a shower and we can get some breakfast and then take your dog for a walk before the meeting."

After breakfast, we picked up Merrimac and went to *Falling Star's* outer ring corridor.

"*Star*," I asked, "what trails can you simulate?"

"I have the standard selection including sections of the Camino de Santiago, Pacific Crest Trail and Dulcinean Heritage Trail."

Alice's eyes were shining. "Show us the DHT, please."

The corridor faded to an illusion of a rocky trail crossing subalpine meadows. Deep glacial valleys dropped off on each side and a cool breeze had risen.

"My mom and dad took me here every summer." She took a couple of steps and stopped. "*Star*, can you set gravity to Dulcinea standard?"

My inner ears wobbled as they adjusted to the change. "That's not going to help you get ready for Bodens Gate, you know."

"I know. Indulge me. My back hurts this morning."

"It's hard for me to say no to you."

"Let's keep it that way." She took my hand and kissed it.

We walked for a couple of kilometers, Mac running ahead and circling back, playing the good dog.

"Ted, have you noticed that there are a couple of things that Mac doesn't do that all dogs should do?"

"You mean nothing goes in and nothing comes out?"

"Exactly. What does he live on? Air and light? Someone," she glanced up, "is bound to notice."

"I don't think anyone will. I don't think Mac will let them."

"Can we please get rid of him as soon as we're on Bodens Gate? Sell him, give him away, turn him loose, something?"

"Oh, yeah. As soon as we're out of the terminal. Maybe sooner." Mac looked up at us and I could feel that he was happy. "I think he's looking forward to being rid of us too."

"We should go back into the ship. It's almost time for your meeting. *Star*, close the DHT please."

"*My* meeting? You're not coming with me?"

"No. I want to see if I have a response back from the church and then I think I'll have a nap. I was up too early this morning."

Lieutenant Kelang arrived at his office door at the same time I did. He ushered me in, offered me a cup of coffee and we talked for a few minutes about life on board *Star*-class ships before coming around to the Bovita clan.

"You can review the reports your teammates filed for specific details about what happened on the way from Cleavus to Bodens Gate. RuComm is still trying to understand how the Bovita were able to get control of the ship, and *Wandering Star* is still on orbit at Bodens Gate. The last I heard they had yet to commit to repairing her instead of parting her out. Captain von Muller has refused to leave her and has been leading efforts to restore the AI, but she's a mess. It's as if someone punched thousands of holes through her brain. She doesn't have direct control of any of her critical systems from the shuttles to the door locks. Half the time she still thinks she's at Cleavus. Von Muller and his team are trying to manually erase all of her sensor information, basically wipe her memory of everything that happened from then until now. Having it in there just confuses her and it's unreadable to us." He sighed. "It might work, but she's an old ship and RuComm may still decide she's more valuable as scrap."

"How did the Bovita get everyone off the ship when they reached Bodens Gate?"

"She assumed orbit and made routine contact with the port, but when she launched her shuttles they landed in the Warrens instead of at the terminal. By the time the Central Government could respond, the Bovita had melted away along with the hostages."

"How did they get almost three-hundred fifty people on board two shuttles designed for fifty apiece?"

"It must have been a tight fit, but they were down to about two-hundred eighty by the time they reached Bodens Gate."

"What happened? There were only eight bodies on Cleavus. I know because we watched, I mean, Alice and I buried them."

"Lieutenant Velena Copeland," he said with a sharp gleam in his eyes. "The Bovita had confined the tech team to the mess hall and the crew were locked in their quarters. Velena overrode the lock on her door and made it to the bridge. She was able to get *Star* to identify a group of about seventy Bovita in the port aft engine room. She opened the entire compartment to space."

"They caught her afterwards?"

"They did. They took her to the mess hall with the intention of making an example of her in front of the tech team. They were going to torture her to death. Your friend Hannah pleaded for her life and was able to convince the leader that Velena was still more valuable to them alive. Courageous women, both of them."

"Do you know Velena?"

"No, but I plan to introduce myself at the earliest opportunity." He smiled, a look of love on his face. He squinted at me. "I know what you're planning to do, Mr. Holloman."

"What do you mean?"

"I've been working closely with Captain von Muller as he tries to save *Wandering Star*. We're using my ship as a template for restoring some of her functions. After Hannah went missing, he told me things that he probably wouldn't have if he thought either of you were still alive, things that aren't part of the official record. You and Ms. Vandermeer seem to be pretty tight right now coming off three months alone together on Cleavus, but you're still planning on trying to find Hannah, aren't you?"

"I feel like I have to. If she's still alive, I need to know if she can be saved. And if she's dead, well, I need to know that too. Hannah is my friend. The thought of her trapped in the Warrens haunts me."

He nodded. "As a citizen of Bodens Gate and a Union officer I will tell you that what you're planning is a fool's errand and that you'll end up getting yourself killed. That said, what are you planning, Ted? There may not be much I can do, but I'd like to help if I can."

"Alice has agreed to continue with her mission commitment to the church. I'll be joining her in the Warrens doing some sort of support job while I try to find out what happened to Hannah. Anything you can tell me about conditions there would be helpful."

"I'm surprised Alice would agree to letting you search, knowing why you're doing it."

"She knows I need closure. She doesn't like it, but she understands that the thought of Hannah somewhere, in distress, wondering why no one's come for her will never give me peace."

"Alice must be very brave."

I smiled. "I'll tell her you said that."

"What are you giving her in exchange?"

I looked at him, not understanding.

"She must have asked something from you."

"Maybe she did, now that you mention it. She tells me that the church will want us to be married before we arrive."

Kelang laughed. "She'll let you hunt, but she shortened your leash. Alice is both brave and cunning." He took a sip of his coffee. "OK, I'll tell you what I know, but the situation in the Warrens is changing rapidly. The Bovita are arguably the wealthiest clan now thanks to the RuComm ransom payments. In the past, the clans always squandered any windfall, but not this time. They've been working to form alliances with other clans by direct payment, intimidation and targeted killings. The last intel I had showed they had absorbed six clans outright and had formed alliances with another fourteen."

"What's their goal?"

"If you asked my brother in the CGIS, Central Government Internal Security, the Bovita are trying to expand their reach to have greater sway over local graft and crime. He thinks it will all soon fall apart into fractious infighting."

"And your opinion?"

"I think they're after something bigger. They killed their hereditary leaders back on Cleavus. To me it looks like they're trying to build a coalition to challenge the Central Government itself. The CG controls about a third of the population and ninety percent of the wealth. Keeping the clans fighting each other provides stability and a cheap source of labor for the citizens in the short term, but it's not stable. If the Bovita succeed, the CG is going to have a problem in a year or two. Maybe less."

"So my search will need to start with the Bovita."

He nodded thoughtfully. "It's possible they took her again to avenge what Velena did. Being in the church's mission will provide you with a small amount of protection. The clans respect the church. They don't play in the clan struggles and they provide services the clans can't. But you'll need to be very careful. There are no maps and the growth of the Warrens has been organic. No one knows what might be down a particular alley other than those that live there."

"I wish you could stay on orbit and provide imagery for me."

"I can't, but I suspect Captain von Muller will be needing to test *Wandering Star's* survey systems from time to time over the next few months. I'll send him a note to expect you contacting him."

"Thank you."

Lieutenant Kelang stood and we shook hands. "RuComm was wrong to leave Hannah there without at least trying to find her. I wish you luck and safe travels in the Warrens. When you're done and if you want to come back to RuComm let me know. I'll put in a good word for you."

"Thank you. One last thing, Lieutenant. Do you think Captain Adriensoon would have time for a wedding ceremony before we reach Bodens Gate?"

"It's been a while since we had one of those on a RuComm ship, but I'll see what we can set up." He shook his head. "You lead a complicated life, Mr. Holloman."

Alice was asleep when I got back to our quarters, Mac's nose peeking out from under the bunk. I sat down next to her and gently moved her hair away from her eyes.

"Hey, sleepy head, it's almost time for lunch."

She yawned and stretched. "Not just head. Whole body is sleepy."

"How would you like to get married in the next day or two?"

She opened her eyes. "Is that a proposal?"

"I think you've been my wife since the night of the blue t-shirt." She smiled, her eyes crinkling. "But yes, it's a proposal."

"Does that mean that we'll share our love with each other?"

"Yes."

"And we'll share our bed with each other?"

"Yes."

"You'll care for me and help me be brave, and you'll let me care for you and try to keep you from–" She stopped and bit her lip, unable to finish.

"Yes, that too. And I'll expect you to argue with me every day to make me better than I could ever be without you."

"OK. I just wanted to make sure nothing was changing. Your proposal is accepted." She wrapped her arms around me and pulled me down on top of her.

When she was done kissing me, I asked her, "I know you planned for me to propose to you. Was I on schedule?"

She giggled. "Close enough. You don't mind? It doesn't bother you?"

"I find it endearing and attractive. But I'd like to read the letter you wrote to your father. It might tell me what comes next."

"Never. I want you to feel that you have some control over your life. Now get off me so we can get some lunch. I have a wedding to plan."

She sighed as we walked to the mess hall. "There should be family with us, and friends. But I have you and that will be enough." She looked up at me. "We may want to do this again someday. I'd like to meet your dad and sisters, see where you and Jake grew up."

"I'd enjoy that. I'll marry you as often as you like." She smiled, holding hands with me as we walked.

Two days later we were married on the Dulcinean Heritage Trail, a warm simulated sun catching red highlights in Alice's hair and making her eyes sparkle. Captain Adriensoon's words were simple and brief and the assembled personnel of *Falling Star* applauded our first kiss as husband and wife.

When Geo shook my hand afterward he told me how happy he was for me, but the expression on his face seemed to be one of wonder, the wonder one would have watching someone jump off a cliff. But then I looked at Alice where she was sitting with the XO and Sara O'Dell, both hands gesturing as she told them a story, and I had no doubt that I was in the right place, or at least the place Alice planned for me to be, which at that moment were the same thing.

Captain Adriensoon pulled Alice and me aside as the celebration started to break up.

"Ted, this is a signed hardcopy of your certificate of marriage," she handed me a large envelope, "and a small wedding present from Captain von Muller and myself. When we reach Bodens Gate tomorrow afternoon you'll find that RuComm has deposited your full pay for this hop into your account. Also in this envelope are copies of your twelve-month leave of absence papers from RuComm and letters of recommendation. You are free to apply to any position you wish for the next year, consistent with your new marital status. I hope that you'll choose to come back to us. Your RuComm access will still work for the next year and you can keep your display pad and watch."

Alice kissed the Captain's cheek. I settled for a handshake.

"Alice, would you excuse us for a few minutes?" the Captain asked. Alice nodded and went to talk to Sara. Captain Adriensoon leaned forward and spoke softly to me, "Bring Hannah back if you can, Ted, but don't lose your life trying the impossible. You have other responsibilities now." She frowned, struggling with how much to tell me. "I've known Professor Vandermeer for ten years working with him for our RuComm visits. The way Alice is now, confident, happy, and almost beautiful."

"Almost?"

The Captain smiled. "She's glowing. This is how I remember Alice from most of my time on Dulcinea. But not the year after her husband was killed. You need her to tell you about that time if she hasn't already. I think she's healed, partly from her time with the church, but mostly from your love for her. You hold her life in your hands. Don't hurt her, Ted. I know what Hannah meant to you not that long ago. You chose a different destiny on Cleavus. Are you strong enough to see this through?"

"Would you believe me if I told you that I'd seen inside Alice's soul while we were on Cleavus and that she'd been inside mine? You don't need to answer; I know how crazy it sounds. There's a lot I don't know about her, but there isn't anything that can separate us. I still love Hannah, but the feelings we had for each other were too close to insanity to last, even if Angela hadn't forced us apart. What I feel for Alice is deeper and more stable." I smiled. "Every day we're together we love each other more."

I looked at where Alice was moving her head back and forth, kneeling down then standing on her tiptoes trying to resolve the illusion of a cliff face *Falling Star* was using to hide a bulkhead in the ring corridor. She waved at us when she noticed us watching.

"How could anyone not love her?"

The Captain smiled at me. "Just keep believing in her, Ted. You'll be fine."

The Bodens Gate terminal was not as grand as the one in Palma Sola. The concrete support beams around the windows were short and stout to support the weight of the roof against the extra gravity. The windows looked out onto a wall of trees that hid the view of Eindhoven twenty kilometers distant and the view of the Warrens that crowded much closer.

The trees might have obscured the Warrens, but they did nothing to block the smell. I looked at Alice and wrinkled my nose.

"Burning trash," she said, "and open sewers. They warned me about the smell." She was bent forward slightly under the weight of her backpack. It held everything she had printed before we had left *Falling Star* and RuComm behind.

I glanced at where the clean white metal of *Falling Star's* shuttle was still visible through the window by the gate.

"Second thoughts already, Ted? It's springtime in Palma Sola now, the flowers are blooming and the air is warm and sweet."

I remembered Hannah telling me about sitting in the sidewalk cafes near the University on long summer evenings, wearing a light sundress, taking notes about the words and conversations flowing around her as she worked on her next paper.

"No," I told Alice, "no second thoughts."

"Wow. The emotions that just flowed through you... You scare me sometimes."

"Good." I smiled at her.

We reached the main concourse and Alice approached an elderly man dressed in stained work overalls. She embraced him and kissed both of his cheeks.

He put his hands on each side of her face, his smile making the lines around his eyes deeper than they already were. "Alice, you've traveled a long, weary road to be here with us. I pray that the yoke ahead for you is easy and the burden light."

"Seeing you makes it so. Father Ryczek, let me introduce you to Ted Holloman, my husband."

He took both of my hands in his, squeezing with surprising strength. Penetrating gray eyes looking into mine. "You are looking for something here. For you I pray that you find even more than you hope for."

"Thank you, sir. Or should I call you 'Father'?"

"As you wish." He smiled. "The people here have called me many things, but I'm still me." He looked around us. "I was told you had a dog with you."

Alice let out a happy little sigh.

"I thought this might happen," I told him. "Merrimac was abandoned by the Bovita on Cleavus."

"So perhaps he is on his way home now?" Father Ryczek asked.

"I suspect he is, although I thought he'd at least say good-bye."

"We must be on our way as well if we're to reach the Mission by nightfall. Here, girl," he helped Alice remove her backpack and put it on himself, "let me carry this for you. You look like a twig bending under too much snow."

"Thank you, Father."

We loaded our belongings into a boxy vehicle of a type unfamiliar to me. It looked to be heavily worn and weathered, but durable, and it ran smoothly once started.

"Do you see that city north of us?" We looked out the window at the towers reflecting the afternoon sun. "Eindhoven. Take a good look because this is as close as you'll get." We came around a curve, descending from the high ground of the terminal and Father Ryczek pulled over and stopped on the shoulder. "That's the Warrens." There was an endless chaos of low buildings built without any obvious plan, all shrouded in hazy smoke rising from countless small fires. "Eight or ten miles on a side and still growing. You know miles?"

I nodded. "I just convert it to kilometers in my head."

Ryczek nodded. "That's the Mission, right there." He pointed. "It kind of stands out, don't you think?"

I looked, not seeing anything that stood out. "I'll take your word for it."

He nodded as if I had passed some sort of initial test. "I think you're the first person from Earth to ever volunteer here. You all seem a little too civilized to me to be able to survive in the Warrens." He looked into my eyes and I held his gaze. "But then you aren't here to serve God, are you?"

"No, sir," I admitted.

"That's OK. I think God can use you anyway." He turned to Alice who was sitting between us in the front seat. "And you, young woman. I know why you're here too. Don't worry, I'm sure God will use you just as you are."

Alice opened her mouth to reply, and then closed it, looking troubled.

We continued down from the terminal, passing through security checkpoints and an impressively high wall. We went from wide paved roads to narrow dirt ones and then we were in the Warrens, houses and shops pressing in on us, people walking on the streets and talking with friends, the smell of food cooking. Some of the people we passed lifted a hand in greeting to Father Ryczek as we drove past them.

After a few minutes, Alice asked him, "Father, we were told what a dangerous place this is, but these people don't seem afraid. They're just going about their lives, laughing, shopping, sitting and talking. It looks so normal and safe."

He laughed. "That's your first lesson. The people that live in the Warrens are people. They're generous and cruel, they laugh and love and fight sometimes, not so different from you. A surprising number of them are seeking after God. Now your second lesson. There is a tight social order in the Warrens. That woman there." He pointed at a girl who looked fifteen. "She's perfectly safe on this street, but take her a mile or two away and she'll never make it home. If you want to survive, remember Matthew 10:16, '*I am sending you out like sheep among wolves. Therefore be as shrewd as snakes and as innocent as doves.*' You will hear gunfire tonight, little Alice. It's the sound of people killing and people dying."

Her fingers intertwined with mine as she took my hand.

When we reached the Mission, the front gate wouldn't open. Father Ryczek got out, pulled a hammer from under his seat, and banged on the gate until it started to move. Then he pushed it the rest of the way. After we passed through, he pushed the remote to close it and a couple of pass-ersby helped shove it until it latched.

"It's working pretty well today. Wait a month until the cold weather starts to settle in and it will take four or five of us to move it."

After we parked, Alice got out and opened the back of the vehicle to get her pack and bag. She let out a little chirp of a scream and I glimpsed her falling backwards onto the ground. I ran to her and found Mac next to her looking concerned.

"Well, your dog seems to have made it after all, although how such a big creature could have smuggled himself on board is a mystery." Father Ryczek scratched Mac's head and looked into his eyes. "Merrimac, you should know that we have a few cats around here to keep the rats and mice under control. I trust you will be able to behave yourself around them?"

Mac's eyes closed and his tongue lolled out, enjoying the head scratch. "I will take that as your promise, then." Father Ryczek looked at Alice and me. "He's a good boy. There's something gentle and peaceful about him. I can understand why you couldn't bear to leave him on Cleavus."

I looked at Alice who was still sitting on the ground, a pleading look in her eyes. I helped her back to her feet.

"Yes, sir," I answered, "he does seem to enjoy our company for some reason."

"Leave your bags here for now, they'll be safe enough. I need to get in and bless tonight's meal so everyone can start."

The dining hall was set up with a cafeteria line. Several long tables were already filling with a cross section of the neediest of the area's residents. Father Ryczek hurried to the front of the room and raised his arms to bless the evening meal. Alice and I made our way through the line, each getting a tray with a large bowl of soup, a generous piece of bread and as much salad as we could possibly want. Dented metal pitchers on the tables held cold water for us to drink.

We sat between a woman who hadn't bathed for some time and a small child of six or seven who was fascinated by the fine texture of Alice's hair. But the food was good and after the woman next to me introduced herself, I found her to be intelligent and thoughtful, interested in who we were and what had prompted us to come to the Warrens. When I told her that I was looking for a friend who had gone missing, she said she was sad for me.

She told us her own story, how the cruel Bovita clan had killed her husband six weeks ago and kidnapped her two children and the children of other leaders to hold as hostages to ensure her clan's allegiance. The Bovita, she claimed, would brainwash her babies and if she ever got them back, they would be Bovita and not hers anymore. She claimed that she once had held status, but now the Bovita had reduced her to the charity of the church, for which she was nonetheless thankful. She kissed my hand.

After dinner, Father Ryczek helped us get our bags and carry them to our room. He showed us how to use the key in the ancient lock. "Turn the key then lift up hard on the knob to get it to turn. The building has settled over the years and nothing lines up quite right anymore."

He turned on the lights and one of the panels winked on, then off, then on, then off until he tapped in gently with his finger.

"It seems like you need a lot of small repairs," I commented.

"Indeed we do. I expect it'll keep you very busy."

I must have looked surprised, because he turned toward Alice who was sitting on the edge of the bed looking at the floor.

"Alice, you didn't tell him?"

"No, Father. I was going to wait until morning."

He sighed. "Very well, I'll do it for you. Ted, you are our new handy-man. I'll send you a prioritized list tonight and tomorrow I'll show you where we keep our tools and supplies. Also," he held a long bony finger up to my face, "you are assistant cook. We always need more help in the kitchen. Breakfast is at 06:00 tomorrow so I expect you to be in the kitchen by 04:30 to start getting set up."

He knelt down next to Alice and hugged her. She put her arms around him and he said to her, "Alice, you don't know how I prayed for you to be here with us."

After a few moments whispering to her, he stood and walked to the door. "Rest well, both of you." The door closed behind him and then he opened it again, peering around the edge at us looking very stern. "I should warn you. The walls here are thin and my room is just down the hall. Don't be too loud, newlyweds."

The door closed again and we could hear him laughing as he walked away.

I sat on the floor next to the bed and took Alice's hand. "What's wrong, my love? Is it that we can't seem to get Mac to run away?"

She shook her head, then nodded, then shook it again. "Maybe, partly. It's mostly Father Ryczek."

"Really? I like him a lot already."

She sighed. "He messed up my plan. You were supposed to volunteer to be the handyman. It was supposed to be your idea."

"I was about to, if it makes you feel better. Is this the first time someone's gotten the jump on you?"

She rolled her eyes. "My dad does it to me all the time. Most people never even see it coming, like my two Lieutenants on the Margo Islands. Philip, and now you, seem to enjoy it and I'm OK with that. My dad and Father Ryczek see right through me. That I hate."

I climbed up onto the bed, pushing her backwards as I came until I was straddling her on all fours looking into her eyes. "Well, newlywed, how quietly do you think you can make love to your husband tonight?"

"Hmm, only one way to find out, I suppose. Although I like it better when it involves screaming as loud as I can."

"We'll do that again one day."

"Promise?"

"I promise."

CHAPTER 15

THE WARRENS

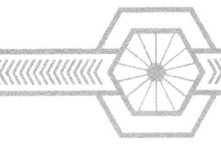

Alice threw up at 04:00 the next morning. The bathroom was too far away down the hall, so I held a trash can for her with one hand and pulled her hair back away from her face with the other. I kissed her gently on the forehead when she was done.

"I'm worried about you. You've been sore and achy and tired all the time. Now you're throwing up. I want the medic to check you later this morning."

Alice sighed. "Put your head here on my belly. Merrimac is close enough that you should be able to feel it even without him touching us."

I put my hands on her and she pushed my head down. "Feel for it. Listen."

After a moment, I could feel it and I looked up at her. "Little soul."

"Yes. Little soul."

"There's a small girl soul floating inside you, content, sleeping now, I think. How long have you known?"

Alice bit her lip. "Since the night you put her in me. Our first night."

"How is this possible?"

Alice raised her eyebrows.

"I mean..."

She smiled at me, putting her hand on my cheek. "I know what you mean. I had my fertility reversed when I married Philip because we wanted to wait. We were young and there was plenty of time, or so we thought." She shrugged. "No technology is perfect. This child, our child, was determined to get knit together."

I kissed Alice's belly. "My fertility was reversed too. It's a requirement for RuComm service. She's going to be stubborn and willful and hard to control, just like her mother."

"She's going to have you doing whatever she wants the moment she takes her first breath."

"Why didn't you tell me?"

"I wasn't sure at first. It seemed impossible. Later, I was afraid that you would leave me when we were rescued. In my mind, I kept seeing Hannah standing on the shuttle ramp waiting for you with that look in her eyes she gets when you're around. Mostly there just never seemed to be the right time to say to you 'I'm pregnant'. I was afraid; afraid you'd be mad at me, afraid you'd think it was just one more way I was trying to manipulate you."

I stood up. "So what am I feeling?"

She smiled up at me, pale and sleepy in the dim light coming in through the window. "Happy. I made you happy."

"You can go back to sleep, it's still very early. I'll clean this up for you and then I need to go help fix breakfast before Father Ryczek starts pounding on our door." I kissed her nose. "See you there later?"

She nodded and curled back up on the bed.

There were four of us in the kitchen. They showed me how to prepare the potatoes and load them into the machine that diced them. I added seasonings and made enough hash browns to feed a couple of hundred people. The crew sang as they worked; simple songs that were easy to learn and offered opportunity for improvised lyrics. Father Ryczek came to check our progress at 05:30. I was feeling pretty good about the day.

"How's our new recruit?" he asked the head cook.

"Well, he's slow and he's clumsy. I don't think he's very bright, but he's stronger than he looks and he has a decent voice so I suppose he'll do."

"High praise, indeed." Father Ryczek came over and leaned against the counter next to me. "You seem happy this morning, Ted. Alice finally told you her secret?"

"Not exactly. She almost threw up on me. She only told me after I was going to force her to see the medic this morning."

He shook his head. "Alice tries so hard to be brave, but she needs help sometimes. Did she tell you that she applied to come here over fifty times? I read every one of the applications. She kept rewording them, adding a new rationale or different justification. I rejected them of course. A Dulcinean on Bodens Gate, especially one like her? I was certain our gravity would crush the life out of her. But she was the one who wore *me* down."

"She doesn't like to take no for an answer. I suspect she tries to manipulate God the same way she does the rest of us."

"She'll need all that strength to carry a child to term here." He looked into my eyes as if he was trying to see into my soul. I was glad he didn't know that there was a creature under my bed that could help him do just that. "Are you still sure you want to go looking for your 'friend'?"

"Yes, sir. Even this doesn't change what I have to do. I need to find a way to contact the Bovita clan safely."

"Come to my office when you finish cleaning up after breakfast. I may know a man who can at least keep you alive while you try."

Father Ryczek introduced me to a man called Cuza, no last name. His body seemed as adapted to Bodens Gate as Alice's was to Dulcinea. He was fifteen centimeters shorter than me and at least that much wider. He was bald with the tattoo of a dragon on top of his head. The wings wrapped down his cheeks and across his mouth, making it look like the wings had talons when he smiled.

"Brother Cuza may be able to help you, Ted, if you can convince him that you're serious and won't get him killed."

Cuza's hands were huge, but his grip was gentle when he shook my hand. "Tell me why you want to contact the Bovita, Teddy. Don't leave nothing out."

"My friend, Hannah Weldon was brought here by the Bovita about three and a half months ago. RuComm ransomed her, but she went missing again a few days later. The CG says she was killed, but I think she was taken again by the Bovita."

"Was she a looker?"

"Yes. Twenty-six, no twenty-seven now, and pretty."

"Plenty of clans would pick that up in a heartbeat. What makes you think the Bovita snatched her?"

I glanced at Father Ryczek and Cuza said, "Come on. Spill it all if you want my help."

"I think she went with them willingly. I think she was the one who made it possible for them to steal my ship by subverting and crippling the AI. The damage that was done is consistent with a tool Hannah developed to keep the ship from seeing things she didn't want seen. I think she's still working with them. The strategy the Bovita are using to expand feels like something she would plan. She must be providing leadership to the clan in some way."

Father Ryczek looked at me, eyebrows raised. "So our little Alice isn't the only one carrying secrets."

"You gonna kill her? I hear you lost two shipmates when that happened."

"No. This is a rescue. RuComm had drugged her heavily during the days before it happened. It suppressed her emotions. While she was coming off them, she could only feel anger, almost uncontrollable. I'm sure it was the drugs. It must have been. It *has* to have been."

"Why'd they do that to her?"

I sighed. The conversation wasn't going where I wanted it to go, but there was no stopping now. "Hannah and I were lovers. RuComm doesn't allow that on board ship. We tried to hide it, control it ourselves, but…"

Cuza was nodding his head and looking at me, disgusted. "Rescue. That's what you're gonna call it? You already have a woman, Teddy, and one is all any man needs. Father Ryczek taught me that. So let's get a few things straight. First, no clan has ever let women take leadership roles. Women are for making babies, keeping the house clean, and sometimes trading or selling to seal deals. Second, if you're right, she don't want rescuing. Third, if she's the one behind what the Bovita are doing then I don't want you to stop her either. If they pull this off the Warrens will be a better place and we can tell the CG to go fuc–" He cut himself off. "Sorry Father."

Father Ryczek smiled at him.

"And last," he continued, grinning so the dragon had talons, "I know for a fact that the Bovita have not one, but two women leading them."

"Do you know who they are, what they look like?"

"Buna, second wife of the old Hetman is one of them. The other calls herself Ysabeau Romee. Nobody knows nothing about her other than that she's not Bovita. Not many have even seen her."

I took my display pad out of my pocket and unfolded the screen. "Hannah is a linguist. She loves words and names and the history behind them." I typed in the name and nodded. "Ysabeau Romee was Joan of Arc's mother."

Cuza was still confused, but Father Ryczek chuckled. "I think you may have found her."

I turned to Cuza, pleading with him. "I need to talk to her. Face to face. Can you help me?"

He looked at the ceiling. I think he was praying, probably for me to go away. After a couple of minutes, he looked back at me. "How much money you got?"

"Some. I have my RuComm pay for the full year. I may be able to get a little more."

"Will you give me all of it to meet with her?"

"Yes. I can do that right now if you want."

He grinned at me. "I don't need your money. I might ask you to pay me back for a bribe or two, but it won't be much. Mostly this is gonna take time. It needs to be done gentle like or the Bovita will spook and we start over. Or they kill me. I wouldn't like that."

"Thank you. How long do you think?"

He shrugged. "Six weeks if it's smooth. Maybe double that or more if it's not. Father Ryczek has other things for me to do too. And I'll have to find my way through parts of the Warrens where I don't normally go. It's easy and dangerous to get lost."

"I can get you high resolution imagery if that will help."

"Recent stuff?"

"Real time for optical. Delayed by an hour or less for infrared and radar."

He smiled at me again. Looking at that dragon was disturbing. "You know the CG don't allow that, right?"

"I have friends in high places. Friends that want Hannah to have the chance to come home."

Cuza looked at Father Ryczek. "I can do this. I'd like to meet her myself, see if she has any job openings. I'll bet she pays more than you do."

"What would you do with more money, Cuza?"

He stood and gripped my hand while he answered. "Just waste it, same as I do with what you give me now."

Father Ryczek frowned at me after Cuza left. "So this is who you want to rescue? She betrayed you and that betrayal resulted in the murder of your team leader and a boy Alice tells me was your best friend. Cuza's question is a good one. Do you plan to kill her? That I could understand. Not condone, but at least understand."

I shook my head slowly, my eyes closed.

"No, I suppose not," he continued. "I see the look in your eyes when you talk about her. If Hannah has become who you think she is then she is the most dangerous person in the Warrens. I need to pray about it before

I let Cuza begin. If he gets himself killed, his blood will be on my hands as much as yours."

"Thank you, Father."

"You and Alice need to sit down and talk. Three months alone with each other and you both have secrets like this? What did you do the whole time?"

I opened my mouth to answer and he held up his hand to stop me.

"No, don't tell me. Alice is carrying the evidence of what you were doing."

When I told Alice what I had told Father Ryczek she didn't seem surprised, just disappointed, which hurt more.

"You're getting really good at lying, Ted. When I first met you, I could read the truth on your face. Now I suspect you could lie to me about anything having to do with Hannah and I'd never doubt you. You know she was probably the one pulling the trigger when Angela was killed, pulling it over and over until there was almost not enough left to bury? I wondered what kind of monster could do that and now I know. She killed *Wandering Star* too and maybe Jake. She killed everyone she could reach who had caused her pain and she left you and me to die slowly and alone. If Cuza is successful, what do you think Hannah's going to do when she sees you? I had thought that what I saw in your mind was love for her and that scared me enough. But your obsession is worse than that. I think you want to see her again so badly that you don't care if she kills you. I think you *want* to die."

"That's not true."

"Do you remember Marcus asking you if you would ever *not* run toward the point of greatest danger? Please don't prove him right."

"I won't."

"Huh. At least I can still sometimes tell when you're lying."

I smiled at her and she put her hands on my face, talking softly. "The only lie I want you to tell me is saying how pretty I am. Tell it to me every day no matter how fat your baby makes me or how much I waddle when I walk."

"I don't have to lie about that. You are the prettiest woman God ever created."

She kissed me. "That was good. It sounded like you believed it."

The next month passed quickly. I cooked and cleaned and fixed as many things in the old Mission as I could. The front gate opened smoothly now despite the colder temperatures, but the light panel in our room still flickered. Alice was teaching the abandoned children that lived at the Mission basic math and how to read. She also taught them music and art, often coming home to our small room covered in paint or glitter. She was tired all the time, but happier than I'd ever seen her. The new curve between her hips was starting to show.

Merrimac refused to leave us. The kids loved him, but Alice never seemed to forget he wasn't a dog. To me it felt as though he was waiting for something, but I couldn't quite see what it was, even when I buried my face in his fur. Alice refused to touch him.

Captain von Muller had been delighted when I contacted him and we spent several hours a week talking about his effort to restore *Wandering Star*. He was more than happy to provide targeted imagery of the Warrens.

"Anything you need," he'd told me, "if it will help find the hero who risked her own life to save my XO."

I told him nothing about what I suspected Hannah was doing now or what she had done to his ship.

Cuza told me not to ask him for updates. He came to me when he needed information or imagery and he seemed to be making progress, but it was hard to tell. I'm sure he thought I was an idiot for trying to find her when Alice was already mine. He was probably right. But Cuza was looking for her for his own reasons. When the Bovita released their Articles of Confederation, I saw him studying it closely with Father Ryczek.

"It's not just clan against clan anymore," he'd told me. "This is about ideas bigger than the clans; it's about rights and freedom. We'd be the same as citizens." I think he really was planning to ask Hannah for a job.

The season's first snow fell when Alice was well into her fifth month. I was in Father Ryczek's office giving him a report on the condition of the Mission's heating units when it started, small white flakes falling fast and darkening the dirt in the courtyard where the ground was still too warm for it to stick.

"Do what you can, Ted. I don't see us being able to afford anything new this season and probably not the next. You've performed miracles for us the past three months. Just do what you can."

I sighed, looking back at my list of problems. "Yes, sir." I nodded and started to turn away.

"Ted, I talked to Cuza this morning."

I turned back toward him and took two halting steps closer to his desk, feeling my chest tighten. Cuza's progress had been very slow as the Bovita and the new Confederation became increasingly careful.

Father Ryczek sighed, looking at me. "Never play poker, Ted. And never let Alice see what I see in your eyes."

I blinked and looked away. "She's seen it. I can't help what I feel for Hannah, but I can control what I do about it."

"Brave words. I pray that you can live up to them because Cuza is close to being able to set up a meeting."

"How soon? Has he confirmed that Ysabeau Romee is Hannah?"

"Another week or two, maybe. He hasn't confirmed anything yet, but you and I both know that she is. The carrot he's dangling in front of her is an alliance with this Mission."

"Is that a ruse or are you serious?"

"Oh, I'm serious. The Confederation is nearing a tipping point. They represent almost twenty percent of the population of the Warrens now. None of the unaffiliated clans control even one percent and the leaders of those clans are going to join soon voluntarily or their own people will overthrow them.

"Ted, this Mission exists to preach the kingdom of God in the Warrens. I can't do that effectively while ignoring the political reality around us. The Central Government is finally getting worried, worried that the Warrens will declare independence and start a civil war. The church has asked me to mediate a settlement that will prevent bloodshed. I'm hoping that having you in the room with me will help reduce the tension."

"Just tell me when and where."

He frowned, not pleased with my enthusiasm. "Alice is back in your apartment and you should go to her now. She had to leave classes early today because the baby is starting to cause her problems in this gravity. It's getting harder for her."

I thanked him and went to find Alice. She was reading while she sat in the rocking chair by the window. The snow behind her was coming down harder now, starting to accumulate.

"I heard you were playing hooky this afternoon."

She put her pad down on the table, glanced at me, then out the window. "I can't seem to catch my breath, my back hurts, and I have to go to the bathroom every thirty minutes. Do I look as bad as I feel?"

I took the bait. "You look like the prettiest girl God ever created."

She smiled weakly and struggled to her feet. She held her arms straight out and slowly turned in a full circle. "Look at me. I'm huge." She was wearing a very oversized sweatshirt that hid any evidence of her growing belly.

I knelt in front of her and lifted the shirt up enough that I could kiss her stomach.

"Whoa. Your nose is cold," she complained.

I pulled the sweatshirt down over my head. "There's a lot of room in here. You can get much bigger, no problem."

Alice's hands pressed on my head through the fabric, holding me close. "How is the little soul today?"

I closed my eyes and could feel the little girl soul floating so close to me. "Happy and comfortable, unlike her mother."

I pulled my head from under her shirt and looked up at her. "Captain von Muller was worried about you when I talked to him this morning. If we need to, we can get you up onto *Wandering Star* and keep you at reduced gravity for the rest of your pregnancy."

"I can't imagine RuComm or the Union would approve of that, so I assume this is because he has a soft spot for you and what you're doing to rescue Hannah."

"Probably. But it's an option if you need it."

"After all this, you'd walk away from meeting her?"

I didn't answer.

"I see. You want me to go to the ship and you'd stay here. I don't think so."

"It's not how you're making it sound." I looked at Mac sleeping on the bed. "My heart is yours, Alice. If you can't feel it when you touch me, we can–"

"No, I'm not using the Tarakana to see inside your mind."

"Then you're going to have to trust me."

She ran her fingers through my hair. "I do. I'm just scared, like I always am, thinking about what might happen."

Four weeks passed and there was still no word from Cuza. I concentrated on doing repairs and keeping Alice as comfortable as possible.

Another month passed and I was up on the Mission's flat roof doing preventative maintenance on the communications array, checking and tightening connections and fine tuning alignments. The temperature had briefly hit fifteen or sixteen, a rare winter's day when the sky was clear and the sun felt warm on my skin. Father Ryczek joined me as I was finishing and we stood together looking out at the Warrens over the chest-high stucco wall that surrounded the roof.

"It's all changing so quickly out there, Ted. I'm from here. I grew up less than a mile from where we're standing. I thought I knew these people. I thought I was doing everything I could to help them. I saved a few of the children, protected some of the women that one clan or another might have otherwise killed or sold. When I redeem men like Cuza, I can feel God smiling on me. I never thought to try to change the way the clans related to each other and to the Central Government."

"You sound jealous."

"Maybe I am a little. The Confederation is giving these people something they never had. It's providing hope that their lives and the lives of their children will be better. It makes me want to be part of it. But it's still so fragile." He looked at me. "Is Hannah really the kind of person that can drive this all the way to completion?"

I thought a moment before answering. "I wrote a geology sim that was just words and symbols on the display until I put it in the right operating environment. Then it did magic. Hannah is beyond smart. She's insightful, fierce, and determined. She knows history and how freedom has been won—and lost. Hannah is doing magic."

"I would have talked about seeds needing the right soil to grow, but I get your point. You know the church asked me to meet with the leadership council of the Confederation, to head them off from challenging the status quo with the Central Government. Apparently, the CG doesn't think much of my efforts. Cuza tells me they've sent operatives into the Warrens to kill her and other leaders of the Confederation. It's put me in a position where I have to pick sides in a political fight, something I didn't want to do."

"What will you do?"

"Do you mean am I going to side with the men that oppress these people? No. I'm going to do what I've always done. I'll try to save as many as I can, starting with Hannah. This cannot be allowed to turn violent."

We stood silently for a few minutes watching the scattered plumes of smoke rising lazily into the air. I hardly noticed the smell anymore.

"Ted, I got a message from one of our churches in Eindhoven this morning. They have some donations for us, clothes mostly and some new toys for the children. Can you take the truck up to the north gate and pick them up at 15:00? They should be in the same place as last time."

"Sure."

I turned to leave and Father Ryczek said to me, "Ted, you need to watch out for Cuza."

"Oh?"

"I don't know if he's met her face to face, but I think he's in love with Hannah." He smiled at me.

"Yeah, I can understand how that might happen."

I went back to our apartment and Alice was there.

"Not teaching this afternoon? Are you feeling OK?"

"I'm fine. Little soul is riding comfortably today. With the weather so nice, Leticia decided to let the kids spend the afternoon on the playground. She sent me home."

"I'm headed to the north gate to pick up another load of donations. Want to ride along?"

"OK, I'd like that."

Merrimac looked up from where he had been sleeping on the bed.

"What about Mac?" I asked.

Alice sighed, looking at the hopeful expression on both our faces. "Fine. But he stays in the back with the boxes."

Father Ryczek was right about the changes in the Warrens. There were more people on the streets as we drove and more waved to us as we passed. It felt like a neighborhood.

I parked at the control building and got out, walked around, and opened Alice's door. "This shouldn't take too long, just the guards usual sorting through old clothes looking for contraband."

"I'm going to leave my sweatshirt in the backseat," Alice told me.

"Are you sure? It's getting cold out again."

"Yes, I'm sure. I'm going to leave my sweatshirt in the backseat with me in it taking a nap." She smiled, proud of herself for being clever.

I laughed. "OK." I helped her into the back and she made herself comfortable. I kissed her and said, "Back in a few. Mac, keep her safe." She closed her eyes and started humming to herself.

I walked toward the control building and there was a man leaning against the wall by the door, partially blocking it.

"Excuse me," I said reaching for the handle. He didn't move. I looked at his face and he wasn't smiling. Out of the corner of my eye, I had a quick glimpse of two others coming up on me from each side. I didn't have time to react or cry out or try to run. There was sharp sting on the back of my neck, a hot, burning, greasy feeling like the sting from a wasp. Whatever they were using was fast. I had one last glimpse of the truck as I collapsed. I knew Alice was probably still happily humming to herself in the backseat if she wasn't already asleep. Then there was a roaring in my ears and then there was nothing.

CHAPTER 16

FREEDOM

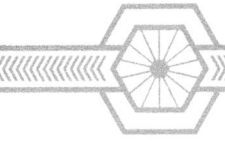

I heard the sound of children somewhere nearby. Light was shining on my face and my eyes were closed. I spent a few seconds trying to remember where I was and why I had been asleep.

I opened my eyes, squinting at the sunlight coming through the open window that looked out onto a courtyard where the children were playing. I was lying on a couch in a large room with bare wood floors. The pieces started coming back together. The Warrens. Driving in the truck with Alice. Attacked. Alice in the truck. Alice.

I tried to sit up and the room spun and grew darker for a moment. I closed my eyes and braced my hands on the cushions.

"Please be careful. I don't want to have to pick you up off the floor."

"Hannah." I couldn't open my eyes, but I knew her voice so well from my memories and my dreams.

"Sorry about the sting. There're too many people trying to find me just now."

"Alice. In the backseat of the truck."

She sighed, a quite sound that felt like a slap across my face.

"Alice has been taken care of. Your dog ran off, but he acted like he knew his way home."

I looked at her, not able to say anything. She was sitting on an old settee opposite me, legs stretched out with a display pad on her lap. She had tied her hair back and it was longer than I remembered. I couldn't look away from her face.

Finally, she laughed. "Ted, what are you doing here?"

"I had to make sure you were all right. I thought you might need to be rescued."

"You knew I was safe months ago and still you had Cuza looking for me until I had to either hire him or kill him. What are you *really* doing here, Ted?"

My head was starting to clear. I got to my feet and slowly walked toward her. She looked back at me, defiance in her eyes. She was wearing a holster under her left arm that I hadn't noticed before.

"I told myself that I came here to ask you the same question, to find out what you're doing in the Warrens. Then I was going to ask you to explain what happened on Cleavus while I was gone to the caves. I was going to demand that you tell me what happened to Angela."

Her eyes flicked away for a moment and then came back to mine, hard, cold.

I was directly in front of her and I knelt on the floor. "I was going to ask you why you couldn't save Jake and why you did save Velena. I told myself that I needed you to answer those questions. Those were the lies that I told myself."

She licked her lips and put her hand on my shoulder. Her fingers traced a line down my arm. "What is the truth, Ted?" she whispered.

I put my palm to her cheek. She closed her eyes and tipped her head slightly, inviting me to caress her ear and down the side of her neck. "The truth? You and I have unfinished business."

She opened her eyes and warmth had come back into them. She smiled gently. "Yes, I think we do." She took my hand and kissed it. "Before we get to that discussion, would you join me for dinner in a few minutes? There are some people I'd like you to meet. After all, that's why Father Ryczek sent you."

"Sent me?"

"Yes. Sit with me a moment."

I sat next to her and she shifted to face toward me.

"He sent you because I told him I wouldn't meet with him until I met with you. And then of course, you had to bring Alice with you. I guess that shouldn't have surprised me."

There was anger in her eyes, and I remembered how quickly her moods could change.

"What is she, seven months along now?"

"Yes."

"So it took you about six weeks after I left before you knocked her up."

"Do you mean six weeks after you left us there to die?"

"They told me you were dead!" She took a deep breath and wiped her eyes. "They said that they had killed you when you came back into town and I believed them. I attacked the man that told me. I hit him so hard that I broke his nose. His blood went everywhere, on my shirt, on my face, covering my hands. They had to carry me on to the shuttle and I was fighting the whole time, kicking and yelling. Charlotte held me down once we were on board *Wandering Star*, telling me how brave I was to have tried to fight back and that it was going to be OK. I couldn't tell her the truth, I couldn't tell her what I had done to all of you."

"The Central Government said that you had been killed too."

"That's what we wanted them to believe. You should have believed it too."

"Or that maybe you had been taken by one of the clans and sold."

"You understand that if that had been true, that you would never have found me? That it would have been merciful for you to never have found me?"

"I had to try."

"With Alice by your side." She crossed her arms, the fingers of her right hand tapping on the gun in her holster. "How many nights was it before she invited herself into your bed? Or was it the first night? Did she say that she was scared and didn't want to be alone? I imagine she was in your bed every night after that, wearing you down until she got what she wanted and made you believe it was your idea all along."

"What about you? Whose destiny are you sharing now?"

She looked away from me and her voice dropped. "My destiny is my own. I sleep by myself, when I can sleep."

"I'm sorry, Hannah. Coming here to fight with you was the last thing I wanted to do."

She tipped her head and looked at me. "Really? What was the first?"

"I had lost you and by a miracle found you again, not dead, not broken. All I want to do is take you in my arms and hold you close. But you know that."

She shook her head and sighed. "Do you realize that every moment of our relationship has needed to be secret? From the first time I took your hand and led you to my hotel room until right now, we haven't been able tell anyone how we feel about each other, let alone show it. When they brought you in here I waited until everyone left and then I sneaked over and kissed you before you could wake up." She wiped her eyes with the back of her hand. "I'm pathetic."

"Not pathetic. Human."

"Yeah, well, I can't afford to be either one."

There was a tap at the door and a woman entered. "Ysabeau? Apologies for interrupting. Dinner is ready."

"Thank you, we'll be right in."

Hannah stood, straightened her blouse and pushed her hair back away from her face. The transformation was remarkable. She was no longer the young woman struggling with lost love. She became the serious, sharp and decisive leader capable of remaking a world. She looked at me, her eyes clear and penetrating.

"Ted, I don't expect you to be able to speak for the church. Your role here is to take our concerns and proposals and pass them along to Father Ryczek, nothing more. We don't dare put anything in writing or send it electronically, so you need to remember everything word for word if you can. I'll set a time and date for a follow-up meeting when we're done. Do you understand?"

"Yes, ma'am."

"And please remember to call me Ysabeau Romee. It's a small thing, but it helps keep me alive."

We walked past several guards on our way up the stairs to dinner, including one I recognized.

"Ysabeau paying you enough, Cuza?" I asked as we walked past. He smiled, but didn't answer.

"That tattoo still bothers me," I commented to Hannah.

"Really? I find it charming."

A round table had been set up with eight chairs in the upper room.

"Mr. Holloman, would you please sit here?" She indicated a seat one away from hers. "It will give you an opportunity to talk to Hetman Bsilnik of the principal clan Bovita."

He nodded to me as we sat, but did not offer to shake my hand. "Are you clan or citizen?" he asked.

"Mr. Holloman is offworlder, like me," Hannah answered. "He will be our courier to Father Ryczek if his memory proves adequate." She leaned over and whispered loudly to the Hetman, "Cuza says he has trouble remembering people who should be important to him."

He looked at me. "Is that true?"

"A result of having been abandoned by all who I loved when I was younger."

The Hetman nodded sympathetically. "Yes, I had to fend for myself when I was little too. A hard life."

I smiled at Hannah and she soundlessly mouthed back to me, "I've missed you."

The conversation during dinner was surprisingly intelligent. Having met the old Hetman on Cleavus, I was expecting a group of ignorant, violent men interested in personal power. I found them to be better versed in the intricacies of freedom movements and rebellions throughout the history of the Union than I was. My knowledge was primarily of Earth history. It made me feel suddenly parochial.

Hannah called the meeting to order. She was still reviewing action items when one of the jammers placed around the room pinged a warning. Everyone fell silent.

I looked around the room and saw a brief shimmer in the shadows underneath a sideboard along the wall. I suppose I should have expected that Merrimac would be following me. I continued to stare at where he had concealed himself, thinking, 'Please, Mac, please don't mess with my emotions right now. They are brittle enough as it is.'

When the ping didn't repeat after a few minutes, Hannah said, "Automated scan most likely. Where were we?"

"Amnesty."

"Right. Most of the clans that are still unaffiliated fought against the Confederation with casualties on both sides. It has been proposed to grant a blanket amnesty to these clans to ease their transition."

Debate continued for nearly an hour before deciding that amnesty would be granted to all except those who had committed 'war crimes'. She assigned two members of the committee to draft a definition of what actions would fit that category.

The next topic was the proposal to work with Father Ryczek and the Warrens Mission as intermediary to the Central Government. Hannah allowed the debate to swirl until people started repeating themselves.

"Let me see if I have captured your concerns accurately."

Hannah scrolled through the list. Some members of the council were worried that an armed clash with the CG was inevitable and any contact could compromise their position or make the Confederation appear weak. Others worried about their own safety and wanted assurances that the church was not covertly supporting the Government. There were several other items detailing what concessions the Confederation wanted from the CG including self-rule, freedom for residents to travel, study, and work outside the Warrens, and for businesses to be able to sell their goods to citizens directly instead of through CG controlled monopolies.

I repeated each message back three or four times to make sure that I wasn't distorting their meaning. Hannah closed the meeting and the members of the council left individually by different exits, trying to avoid suspicion.

Hetman Bsilnik was one of the last to leave and he asked me, "What is your opinion of Father Ryczek? Will he support us?"

"At the service last Sunday the scripture he preached on was from Romans, if I remember correctly."

Hetman Bsilnik put his hand on my shoulder. "It's OK if you don't." Hannah put her hand over her mouth and turned away to hide her laughter.

"The scripture said, '*The hour has already come for you to wake up from your slumber, because our salvation is nearer now than when we first believed. The night is nearly over; the day is almost here. So let us put aside the deeds of darkness and put on the armor of light*.'"

"I like those words."

"So do I."

The Hetman left, and it was just Hannah and me and, somewhere hiding in a corner, a dog that was not a dog.

"I should leave too," I told her.

"You should stay."

"Why?"

"It's dark now and the Mission is too far. Did you notice the empty chair at the table? That was Buna's, the old Hetman's second wife and my friend. A CG assassin killed her last week. They shot her in the back while she was walking down the street trying to make it to a safe house."

"Will you be spending the night here?"

"No, we change locations every night. But it's not far."

"No guards?"

"They just attract unwanted attention."

"I'll walk with you. I want to make sure you're safe."

"Safe? That's something I don't think about much anymore."

We reached the front door and Merrimac was there waiting for us. I could feel the hum of the Tarakana inside him from three meters away.

"How did he get in here? Our security shouldn't let anything bigger than a grain of sand pass through." She looked at me. "And where did you even get a dog, Ted? There were no dogs on Cleavus."

"There are some things I need to tell you."

"Hold that thought. I need to clock in at the next safe house soon or they'll start looking for me."

She pushed the door open and a gust of wind tried to close it again, snow swirling in around us.

"When did this start?" I asked.

"That's the Warrens. Always changing."

I looked down and Mac was rubbing up against Hannah's legs, his nose nuzzling her hand. '*Oh, Mac*', I thought, '*Please don't.*'

I looked into her eyes and they were wild and free. She smiled at me, a challenge. Then she was gone, running fast. For a moment there was nothing but the wind and all I could hear was the sound of her laughter.

I ran after them as fast as I could, catching a glimpse of her legs or of Mac loping along next to her until she stopped in a doorway that looked like all the rest we had passed.

She smiled at me when I caught up, her hair full of snow. "Beat you."

"Not exactly fair when you knew where you were going and I didn't."

She pressed her palm to a hidden panel and the door opened. "I never race fair." We stepped into a small foyer with stairs leading up to the second floor and the door closed behind us. "I like your dog. He didn't have any trouble keeping up. Where did you find him?"

"Cleavus. He's not a dog."

She thought a moment while she ran her fingers through her hair knocking snow everywhere. "Tarakana? You taught one of the Tarakana how to look like a dog?"

"Taught? No. He reached into my mind and pulled out the memory of a dog I had when I was little." We looked down at Mac who was sitting at our feet, his tongue out, still panting from our run.

"You are looking at a representative of a space-faring civilization possessing technology far more advanced and sophisticated than our own. They live in massive colonies and communicate telepathically." Mac licked my hand, looking pleased. My heart started pounding as every emotion was amplified.

"That's insane. He's a dog."

"Pet him," I told her. "Bury your fingers into his fur."

She looked at me with a mixture of confusion and concern and then, as her fingers reached into him, her face went blank and she said, "Oh."

I let it go on for a few minutes and then reached to pull her away. Before I could touch her, she said, "He told me I should do this." She grabbed my hand hard and pulled it down into Mac's fur.

I saw Hannah. The darkness and the wounds and the scars were all there for me to touch and understand. She didn't try to hide and I could feel her moving through my mind, her touch gentle where she knew I was hurt.

Mac pulled away from us and we sat on the stairs afterward talking together.

Hannah took my hand. "He showed me every reason why I should let you go. I didn't know how much Alice means to you, how you love her, how she looks through your eyes. I have no right to, to..." Her words stumbled and stopped.

"And I saw every reason why I should stay. What you're doing here, it's magic. That's what I told Father Ryczek, but now I know how true it is. I've spent the past several months fixing bits of broken machines and cooking potatoes. You're remaking a world."

I kissed her cheek and it felt very soft against my lips. "It's crushing you. Those men on your council are intelligent and committed, but without you, it will all fall apart in a month, maybe less. Let me help."

"It's their world, not ours. They need to be able to carry it through, not me. We are so close." She leaned back on the steps, looking at the ceiling. "To them I am Ysabeau Romee. I never make mistakes and I never have doubts. I am infallible and our victory is assured."

"You can't live this way."

"No, but maybe I'm not supposed to. Maybe I'm supposed to die this way, like Buna."

I leaned back next to her and she tipped her head onto my shoulder.

"You can't," I told her. "You have a paper to coauthor with me on Tarakana language."

Her smile was wistful. "That seems like so long ago. Was that even me? Ted, tell me again why you're here."

"I came to make sure you're all right."

"I'm not."

"And I came to rescue you."

"I need to be rescued." She sighed. "I don't want to be Ysabeau Romee and I don't want to be infallible. I have doubts and I'd like to make mistakes. Just for one night, can the world not exist outside these walls? No Confederation, no men out there in the dark hunting me like an animal." She lowered her voice to a whisper. "No Alice."

"Just Hannah and Ted?"

"No, not even them. Just two secret lovers sharing a warm bed, wrapped in each other's arms while the storm rattles the windows and moans across their roof."

I picked her up and started carrying her up the stairs. We reached the top and I looked down at her smiling at me. "Well, which way?"

"Sorry. Left, first door."

I set her down gently on the bed and tried to turn on the lights, but they didn't work.

"We pulled all the wires out of the walls," Hannah explained. "The CG was using them as a passive antenna. There should be a candle on the night stand." I lit it and placed it on the floor a couple of meters away. Hannah looked at me questioningly.

"I don't want to hit it accidentally later," I explained.

"Oh."

"And heat?" I asked.

"No. There's a fireplace, but the heat signature would be too obvious. This part of the building is supposed to be abandoned."

"How am I supposed to keep you warm?"

"Come here and I'll show you." I sat down next to her.

Mac walked in and crawled under the bed and Hannah looked at me. "That should scare the hell out of me, but it doesn't. I don't know why."

"I understand. Do you think we brought him here voluntarily? There's some kind of symbiotic relationship between us, but every time I try to think about it my mind just gets all fuzzy."

Hannah moved the covers out from under her and started to get undressed. "I would prefer you to do this for me, slowly, piece by piece, but I don't think it's over ten degrees in here." She removed her gun from the holster and placed it where she could reach it easily. I helped with her blouse.

"I don't remember this scar across your back."

"Did you know that some of the clans still use swords? Neither did I."

When I laid down on top of her the feel of her skin against mine sent a shiver through me and I gasped.

Hannah wrapped her arms and legs around me. "Yes," she said. "Just like that. Hold me for a few minutes. I need to remember this."

When she was ready, I felt her thoughts move in me. I knew what she wanted and nothing else mattered but to touch her where she needed to be touched and to kiss what needed to be kissed, and to fulfill the desire of our bodies as urgently as possible.

We were soon panting for breath, my head on her shoulder. She kissed my hand where it was cradling her cheek, my fingers tangled in her hair. "Smart move, putting the candle that far away."

I kissed her in the hollow between her breasts, long and slow, tasting her sweat and then looked at her watching me, her eyes catching the candle light.

She smiled at me, the aggressive, arrogant smile I remembered and loved. "You better not think we're done, Ted."

In answer, I kissed her shoulder and then explored slowly across her chest, feeling her mind and her body responding to the touch of my hands and tongue. She moaned and I moved lower, down along her ribs and across her belly, pulling the covers over my head to keep her warm.

"There can't be... uh... much air... under... um... under there," she warned me.

I bit gently on the inside of her thigh. "There isn't, but what there is tastes sweet." I heard her start to laugh and made sure that it ended in a long groan.

Not long after, I was back resting my head between her breasts, kissing them gently and feeling her heart pounding under me. We slept that way for a time.

Sometime in the night, Hannah rolled over on top of me. The candle had burned out by then, but I could make out the curves of her body by the light leaking in past the curtains. We made love for the third time that night, Hannah's hands braced on my shoulders until she collapsed across my chest, her arms and legs shaking with exhaustion. I held her close to me and we listened to the storm beating against the house as it swept through the Warrens. She slept in my arms until dawn.

When I woke, Hannah was already dressed. She was sitting in the room's one chair working on something on her display pad with Mac sleeping across her feet. Another dog, lighter in color, was sleeping on the floor by the window.

She glanced over at me. "Yeah, there's more of him now. Whatever they are, they're doing a good job of suppressing the fear I should be feeling."

"I've been expecting that he would start to multiply, but I'm sort of glad I didn't see it happen."

"There were two others here when I woke up, but they disappeared when I opened the door to go down the hall to take a shower. We steal hot water from the apartments next door, so go easy on it."

"Thanks. I suppose I need to get cleaned up."

"Yeah. I know I certainly did. Go quickly and then we'll talk."

Showered and dressed, I sat on the bed and Hannah pulled her chair over close to me.

"Ted, you were right yesterday when you said we had unfinished business. There was a hole right here," she tapped her chest, "from the way we were separated from each other. After last night I think it might start to heal."

"That sounds like goodbye."

"You know it has to be. I can feel what's in your heart too. It's strange, but I think I know what you're feeling."

"You do." I pointed at Mac. "It's a gift."

"Maybe that explains the intensity of what happened."

"Maybe. Partially. He only amplified what we were already feeling."

"I stole something from Alice last night. I had no right, but I needed it so badly that I took it anyway."

"I won't pretend it was the right thing to do, but we both needed it. I think I can help you now with the Confederation without needing," I gestured toward the bed, "this again." I looked away from her. "At least for a time."

"No. I need you to promise me something. When you get back to the Mission give our messages to Father Ryczek, then take Alice and get out of the Warrens as soon as possible. Get off-planet if you can."

"What's happened?"

"Hetman Bsilnik was killed last night. A kinetic energy weapon, probably dropped from orbit took out the entire block. At least thirty killed, but we're still sorting through the rubble."

"How did they know where he was?"

"Maybe he lit a fire to keep warm." Her voice was bitter. "That's three of us in three weeks. Bsilnik and Buna were the ones I met on Cleavus. They were the ones with the original vision of remaking the

Warrens into a place just a little better for the people that live here. The one they killed before that was the man who published our news and distributed it to all the clans in fifty different languages. He was a poet when I first met him. When he gave me the first draft of the Articles of Confederation, he told me it was the most beautiful poem he had ever written.

"It's all coming apart, Ted. The CG doesn't want to negotiate. They want the chaos back. They'll kill us one by one and the Confederation will just be a cautionary tale for anyone that wants to challenge them."

"Hannah, I need to get back to the Mission. Father Ryczek may be able to get them to stop as a condition to begin talks. Come with me."

"Claim sanctuary in the church? No, that's not what Ysabeau Romee would do. You can try to get them to stop, but they won't. A couple more bombs and a handful of bullets and they'll have won."

"Last night you told me I needed to rescue you."

"And you did. My heart is freer now than it's been for a very long time. I know that yours is too." She sighed. "Go down the stairs and turn right when you leave the building. Turn left at the end of the block and Cuza and another man will meet you and see you safely to the Mission."

She walked down the stairs with me and we kissed goodbye. I opened the door a crack to peek out. The snow was melting quickly and a few people were walking by on the muddy streets.

Merrimac pushed past my legs, trotted across the street, and jumped up on a man that was standing in a doorway opposite ours. Mac grabbed the man by the throat with his mouth and threw him to the ground.

It all happened without drama and so quickly that it took me a moment to realize what had occurred. I ran to where Mac was crushing the man's trachea. His jacket had fallen open as he thrashed in the mud, revealing a silenced handgun. I took it.

I kicked the assassin hard in the ribs and then pointed the gun at his head while Mac held him down for me.

Cuza had reached us by then and pushed my arm down. "Easy now. Alive he can talk, dead, not so much."

Mac let go of the assassin's throat and the man with Cuza dragged him away, disappearing quickly down a side alley.

I was feeling a cold anger burning in me, anger at the CG for the killing they were doing, anger at the Warrens, anger at the assassin for trying to take Hannah's life.

I was angry with Cuza for not letting me kill the man lying unconscious with Mac's teeth in his throat.

Cuza and I walked back to where Hannah was still standing in the doorway, and I was angry with her for putting herself in a situation where she would probably die. I released the magazine from the gun and ejected the round that was in the chamber. I picked it up out of the dirt and handed it to her.

"This is the one that was supposed to have killed you."

She looked at it lying in her palm, feeling the weight of it. She slipped it into her pocket.

"Would you have shot him if Cuza hadn't stopped you?"

"Yes."

Mac came back and sat at her feet looking up at her. There was blood on his muzzle and I could feel the cold anger in him too.

"Tell Father Ryczek that I want to meet with him as soon as possible."

"Yes, Ysabeau. I will do that for you."

"Cuza, will you please make sure he arrives safely?"

"Yes, ma'am, although he seems like he might be OK without me. We need to get you out of the Mission more often, Teddy. You ain't half bad in a fight."

"Have him tell you about the Margo Islands sometime, Cuza."

"I'd rather not." I handed the gun to Hannah. "I still have nightmares."

Hannah handed the gun back to me. "Keep it, *Teddy*." Her eyes crinkled in a brief smile. "You may need to defend me again some time."

When Cuza and I started to walk away, Mac stayed with Hannah. I turned and looked at them standing in the doorway.

"Keep her safe, Mac."

She closed the door and the lock clicked shut.

CHAPTER 17

THE PLAN

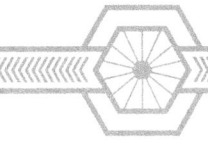

Cuza and I walked along in silence for several blocks before he asked me, "You spend the night with her?"

I thought about lying to him, or telling him that it was none of his damn business, but then decided that we had too many things in common for that. We were both willing to kill for her or die for her. And we both loved her.

"Yes, Cuza. I did."

He nodded. "I won't tell nobody. Unless you plan to make a habit out of it, make her a second wife."

I laughed. "Can you see her being a 'second' anything?"

He smiled, showing his teeth. "No, not her." He looked at me closely. "When you gave her that cartridge, I realized I knew something about you. I was bent down petting the dog and telling him that he was a good dog, and it just slammed into my brain."

"What was it?"

"Well, I seen the look in your eyes when you talked about her back at the Mission, and then, yesterday, there was that same look, but in her eyes when she looked at you. Putting you together is bad news. All the good inside the two of you gets stronger, but so does the bad, and both of you got plenty of bad. With Alice," he stopped and looked into my eyes. "With Alice the good gets stronger, but most all the bad is canceled out. If you have to choose just one woman, Alice ain't a bad choice."

He laughed and we started walking again. "That don't make no damn sense now that I say it out loud."

"Oh, it does. You're a wise man, Cuza, wiser than me."

I went to find Alice as soon as we reached the Mission. Cuza went back the way we had come to, as he put it, 'help a guy answer some questions'.

Alice was sitting in a chair reading a story to a semicircle of children on the floor in front of her. I lifted her to her feet without a word and held her close to me while the children giggled.

"Careful, Ted, or you'll squish your baby right out of me."

I leaned back and kissed her. "Your eyes are red. Have you been crying?"

She shook her head in denial. "Not me, it was little soul. She wanted to cry, but she doesn't know how yet so I had to do it for her."

"I need to deliver my messages to Father Ryczek then I'll be back. Can you get off early today?"

"There's an elephant that needs to find his way home first," she tapped the display pad she had been reading to the children, "but then I'm all yours."

Father Ryczek was in his office. I repeated my messages to him while he took notes and asked questions.

"I'll contact the church in Eindhoven and set up a meeting with the CG as quickly as we can."

"The assassinations have to stop, Father. More than thirty civilians were killed last night."

"The news media in the capital said it was a gas explosion."

"You know better. Those old buildings don't even have gas."

"And Ysabeau Romee? Where is she now?"

I paused a moment before answering. I almost told him about the assassin that had been waiting for her, but decided not to. "I have no idea where she is. She's not safe."

Father Ryczek turned his back to me, looking out into the courtyard. "Try to find out where she is, you or Cuza. We need to bring her under the protection of the church and stop these killings. Too many have died already."

"Yes, sir."

He dismissed me and I went back to our apartment where Alice was pacing the floor.

I embraced her and I could feel that she was angry with me, then relieved, then angry all over again. "I can still feel your emotions," I told her. I looked at her and smiled. "You're mad at me."

"That makes you happy? All I feel from you is like this stupid happy glow because you're with me." She frowned. "Stop it. It's making it hard for me to stay angry."

"Mac isn't here anymore. He stayed with Hannah, but I still know what you're feeling."

"Do you? I woke up in the back of the truck to the sound of the door opening. I thought it was you, but when I opened my eyes it was Cuza's face smiling down at me. Do you know what that's like?"

"I can imagine."

"Then he said to me, 'Ted has gone to be with Hannah.' Just like that, no other explanation."

"He didn't mean it that way."

"I think he did. He meant it exactly that way. I couldn't talk the entire way back to the Mission because my heart had been ripped out."

"I'm sorry."

She looked at me, biting at her lower lip. "I felt that just now, and more. Your heart is different." She stared at me, pale blue eyes cutting into mine and then she put her head against my shoulder and wrapped her arms around me. "Huh. Not as mad now."

She held me for a few minutes and then asked too calmly, "So, how's Hannah?"

"She's leading a rebellion from behind the scenes and watching the few friends she has die violently one by one. She knows she'll be next."

"You couldn't have just said, 'oh, she's fine'?"

Alice and I sat down on the bed together and I told her about the assassination attempt that morning. I put the gun on the bed between us and took out the magazine.

"I gave Hannah the round that was meant to end her life, but there are so many more out there."

Alice removed the next cartridge and tapped my forehead with it. "This one was yours." She looked at the expression on my face. "Or hadn't you realized that?"

"No, I didn't." I took it from her and put it back in the magazine. "Did you meet a man named Bsilnik when we were first on Cleavus?"

"I remember him."

"He died last night. At dinner, I had told him about the scripture Father Ryczek used last Sunday, about how our salvation is nearer now than when we first believed. The Confederation almost made the Warrens a better place for these people, but it's slipping away now."

"Father Ryczek used Romans thirteen last Sunday?"

"That's right. I had forgotten you weren't there. I was letting you sleep in that morning."

Alice was shaking. "You need to read all of the chapter. What you quoted is out of context. The theme of that passage is submission to the governing authorities. I don't think Father Ryczek is planning on supporting the Confederation."

"Damn it, he told me he was."

"Are you sure? Do you remember his exact words?"

"Not exactly, no." I closed my eyes. "He was upset about having to choose sides in a political fight, I think because it compromised the mission of the church. He said he wouldn't side with those oppressing the people in the Warrens. I asked him what he was going to do and he said, 'the same as I always do, try to save as many as I can, starting with Hannah'."

"He's going to betray them and turn the leaders of the Confederation over to the Central Government. Hannah is a citizen of both Earth and the Union. He probably made a deal for them to deport her. The rest?" she shrugged. "They won't live long. The Confederation will fail, but there won't be a civil war that would have killed thousands. Not a bad day's work."

"You admire that?"

"I admire the technique and the goal. And it will keep Hannah alive."

"Now you sound like Marcus. You're going to save her life, but she'll lose her soul."

"You have a better idea?"

"No, not yet. I need to talk to Hannah or at least get a message to her. I should find Cuza and go back out there."

"No." It was a simple word, but I could feel all of the terror that was behind it.

"Alice, what scenarios were playing through your head last night?" I could imagine her, curled into a ball on our bed, shaking as her fears overcame her and having no one to comfort her.

"You're alive, so the worst ones didn't come true." She kissed me, letting her lips slide against mine, her tongue briefly touching mine at the end. "Your heart is freer of her now than I have ever felt it. I don't know what it took for you to achieve that and I won't ask. You can't go back out there, not without me."

She took a step back and stared at nothing for a moment. Then she put her hands on my cheeks and her eyes sparkled. "You and I have some planning to do."

"What kind of planning?"

"My kind."

She sat down at her desk and opened her display pad. "I need to contact my father first."

"Messages will take almost five days round trip. We don't have that kind of time."

"I know! I'm going to have to assume that he's successful for this to work. We can't wait for a reply to confirm it." She continued to talk to me while she typed. "Then I need to talk to Father Ryczek. I need to stall him a few days. He knows I have cause to hate Hannah so he won't question my motives."

She paused and glanced up at me. "Then we need to find out where Cuza is and set up a meeting with Hannah. I wish I could trust you to go to her on your own." She returned her attention to the message she was typing to her father.

I opened my mouth to protest then closed it again. I saw her eyes narrow while she typed. "Do you know what I love about you, Ted?"

"Tell me."

"No matter how hard you try, or how much you want to, you are incapable of hiding the truth from me." I saw her hit the 'send' command and she looked at me, not smiling. "Even to save your own life."

I swallowed hard. "I thought you said I was getting better at it."

"No, that was lying to save *her* life. You're damn good at that. Which is why I need you to contact Captain von Muller. We can't do this without *Wandering Star*."

"OK. Are you going to tell me enough of the plan so I know what to say?"

She smiled and reached out for me. I moved closer and she rubbed her hand up and down my chest. "And do you know what else I love about you?"

I shook my head.

"I love that you still can't tell when I'm bluffing. Or that, no matter how hard I may want to at times, I am incapable of not loving you." Her hand slid down, she wrapped her fingers around the waistband of my pants, and she pulled me up close to her. "I'm going to win this war, preserve the Confederation, and save Hannah." She laughed. "My dad is going to be so proud of me."

She took my hand and guided it to her stomach. "Do you feel that? Little soul is excited too. I think that's her foot."

I kissed the bulge, feeling movement under Alice's skin. "We should give her a proper name at some point."

"I've been thinking about that. Leticia heard me calling her 'little soul' and said that in her clan's language that would be Mala Dusa." She looked at me hopefully.

"That would be fine. I like it."

"Good. Now go find Cuza for me. I have more letters to write." I turned to leave and she said, "Bring lunch back with you, please. Mala Dusa wants something with chocolate in it."

I smiled at her even though she wasn't looking at me. "I'm sure she does."

Cuza proved easier to find than I expected. He was sitting on a bench outside Father Ryczek's closed office door appearing to be studying his huge hands.

I sat down next to him. "Alice would like to see you if you have a moment." He nodded and continued looking at his hands. "What's wrong?" I asked.

"I was just in telling Father Ryczek about this morning, how we saved Ysabeau's life. He said you didn't tell him."

"No, I didn't."

"That was smart." He looked at me, confusion hidden somewhere under the dragon's wings. "He said maybe it would have been better to let her die. How can he say that?"

"Let's go talk to Alice." I took his arm and steered him back to the apartment while he wrestled with his conflicting loyalties to Ysabeau and Father Ryczek.

I apologized to Alice when we arrived for not having lunch for her yet, and explained the conversation between Cuza and Father Ryczek. Cuza was sitting on the corner of our bed looking uncomfortable, so Alice made it worse. She stood in front of him rubbing her belly to emphasize her current condition, then she knelt in front of him and placed her hands on his cheeks.

"Brave Cuza," she told him, "I need your help. Father Ryczek is a good man. He wants to stop the killing in the Warrens because of his love for every individual. But the only way he sees to do that is by betraying Ysabeau Romee. I need to talk to her before it's too late. I think I can save her, the Confederation, and keep there from being a war. Will you help me find her?"

Cuza looked at her, then glanced at me.

"It's OK, Cuza," she told him "There's nothing about the two of them that I don't already know. Love means understanding and forgiving."

He nodded, looking relieved. "I told him you was the right woman for him. I'm glad you forgive him. Teddy ain't such a bad guy and the two of you belong together."

It would have been perfect if he had stopped talking right then, but he didn't.

"And Ysabeau, well, there's something damn magical about her. There ain't a man alive that could resist her if she wanted him."

The gentle smile on Alice's face became a little forced. "Of course. Will you help me find her so I can save her life and keep the Confederation alive too? It would mean not telling Father Ryczek anything about it for a couple of weeks. You'll need to tell him that you don't know where she is."

"Yes, ma'am, I can do that for you. Would tonight be soon enough to go see her?"

"Yes, that would be fine." Alice kissed him gently on the lips and he blushed under his tattoos.

He told us, "We'll go walking sometime after dark."

After Cuza left, I went to find lunch while Alice continued writing letters, laying the groundwork for the Union to support an insurrection that they didn't even know was happening while making them think it was their idea all along.

Late in the afternoon, Alice woke me from a very nice nap with a well-aimed pillow to my head.

"There's no time for sleeping," She told me. "What time is it on *Wandering Star*?"

"She's synchronized with Eindhoven, so same time as here. Are you ready for me to talk to von Muller?"

"Yes. You need to convince him to have one of Wandering *Star's* shuttles on the ground in the Warrens in a week, contrary to Central Government regulations and the risk that they'll arrest or shoot him. And you need to make him think it's his idea. Can you do that?"

"Sure. I'll just think like I'm you."

She rolled her eyes. "I know you can't really do that, so I have some notes for you, some things to say and some you don't want to say no matter what. I want to rehearse with you a few times too."

She spent the next hour pretending to be a very obstinate, suspicious Captain while I did my best to deceive her. When she was satisfied that I could guide Captain von Muller where she wanted him to go, I asked her, "Why can't we just tell him what we're doing like you did with Cuza?"

She looked at me, surprised. "I didn't tell Cuza what we're doing. I told him enough so that he'd do what I need him to do. His role is to lie to Father Ryczek and take us to Hannah. I'll tell him more when I'm ready for his next task."

"And my role is to convince von Muller to drop a shuttle into the Warrens at a specific time and place."

"Exactly, and I'll tell you more when I'm ready for *your* next task." She smiled at me, very happy.

"You're really enjoying this, aren't you?"

"It's been a while since I've done a plan. I'd almost forgotten how much fun it is."

"How long? Like nine or ten months?"

She took my hand and placed it on her belly. Mala Dusa pushed against me. "That was a simple plan, but very pleasurable in its execution and with an incredible payoff." She kissed me. "Now set up a secure connection and talk to the Captain while I go visit with Father Ryczek."

I had come to regard Captain von Muller as a friend. He had supported my search for Hannah and I had commiserated with him during his struggles to save *Wandering Star*. He and his team had restored most of *Star's* command and control functions and there was no longer talk of scrapping her. But there was still more work to do repairing the damage Hannah had caused before RuComm would accept his ship back into service.

It was hard for me to lie to him, but I did it because it was necessary to give Hannah a chance to survive. I started by telling him that I had found where she was being held and that she was physically OK. I then outlined the perils that I would have to navigate to reach her in the heart of Bovita territory, set her free, and get her out of the Warrens to safety.

We talked about the current political situation and how the people of the Warrens were uniting to fight against generations of life under unjust laws and brutal treatment, and how the Union tacitly supported this oppression with their agreements with the CG for servicing and resupplying ships. In the end, he suggested that he might be able to get one of Star's shuttles down into the Warrens for me, but that it was risky.

"Perhaps the Central Government will believe that it is a malfunction of the automation that sends one of the shuttles back to where the Bovita had last flown her. The CG knows *Star* is still wounded." He shrugged, discounting that he was about to destroy his career. "The truth is that *Star* cannot control her shuttles yet so I will pilot one personally. Hannah is worth the risk and so are you."

I thanked him for coming up with such a bold solution and told him that I would let him know the exact time. I disconnected and felt terrible about what I had done, but elated that I would soon have Hannah and Alice safely on board a RuComm ship.

When Alice returned she asked, "Success?"

I nodded. "I hated lying to him. Or I should say lying to him more than I already have been. What about you?"

"Father Ryczek believes that I hate Hannah enough to betray her to the Government and destroy the Confederation along with her. Let's get some dinner and then we'll be ready to go with Cuza and mislead Hannah."

"Does it ever bother you, messing with people's lives like this?"

"It's like what I did with the undergraduates at the University. I maneuver people into doing what they should be doing and in the end, they'll be happier for it. Like with Father Ryczek. I could probably convince him to do what he's about to do, but it would take weeks or months. By then Hannah would be cold in her grave. I don't think you want that."

She stopped in the hall and looked at me closely, biting her lip and searching my emotions. She put her hand on my chest. "I need to lock down that part of your heart that was recently freed before it slips away again."

"It all belongs to you. When this is done Hannah will remain here working for the people of the Warrens, but on behalf of the Union. You and I will be on our way to Dulcinea to raise our daughter, go camping in the summers along the Dulcinean Heritage trail, and maybe work on building more babies."

She wiped her eyes. "I want that, Ted. Do you feel how badly I want that? It's been so hard. My life will finally be back where it was supposed to be."

I held her close for a few moments and then we went on to dinner.

Cuza arrived at our apartment a little after 21:00. "Dress warm," he told us. Then he looked at Alice and put his hand over his own stomach. "It's a dark trek on muddy roads, but only about a mile each way. Will you be OK?"

"I'll be fine, Cuza. Thank you for worrying over me." She kissed his cheek and I realized how thoroughly she had won him over.

"Does Hannah know we're coming?" I asked.

"Me with friends, that's all."

We left the Mission through a narrow tunnel that I didn't know existed and came up through an abandoned house a hundred meters outside the Mission's walls.

"Why was this built, Cuza?" I asked.

"Clans sometimes don't have no respect for the Mission. They come in and we got to get somebody out quick to keep them from dying. Clans killing clans goes back a lot of years."

"Is it better now with the Confederation?"

"Better, but not good yet. Killing folks you don't like is a hard habit to break."

We walked down narrow roads and narrower alleys, sometimes cutting through buildings by going in the front door and out the back. I quickly realized I'd never be able to find my way back to the Mission.

"Cuza," Alice asked after about fifteen minutes. "Is this the most direct route or are you making it complicated so we'll never find this safe house again without you?"

He smiled at her, looking guilty. "Some of both. Sorry, but I gotta protect her."

"You're doing the right thing. Don't trust anyone unless you have to."

Cuza stopped after a half hour and pointed to a building across from us. "There. Second floor, front room on the left. She'll be expecting you."

We opened the door to her room and I was not surprised to see a gun pointed at us.

"Alice." Hannah said, not lowering her weapon.

"Hannah." Alice replied.

Two of the Tarakana dogs in the room raised their heads, sensing emotions that were new to them.

"Do you plan to shoot us?" I asked her.

"I'm not sure yet. Why don't you tell me why you're here instead of on your way off planet like I told you to be?"

"Because Ted lied to me. He's very good at lying to me when he feels he needs to protect you. Unfortunately, he's right this time. Father Ryczek plans to betray you. If you or any members of your council accept his invitation, your lives will be forfeit. I have a plan to save you and your Confederation, but you'll need to trust me."

Hannah slid the gun back into her holster. "I don't trust you, Alice, but what choice do I have?"

Alice smiled. "Absolutely none."

We sat around a small table and the dogs put their heads down and appeared to go back to sleep.

"How many of them are there now?" I asked.

Hannah swept her hand around the room. "I... I don't know. I lost count after fifty. They keep eating and then one of them will sort of tear apart down the middle. Have you ever seen a dog tear itself in half down the middle? It's disturbing."

"They're eating?"

"Vegetables. They seem to really like potatoes."

"Have you tried not feeding them?" Alice asked.

Hannah looked confused for a moment. "I hadn't thought of that. It doesn't seem right not to feed them, you know?"

"We know just how that is," I answered.

Alice turned to look at them. "I wonder what set them off last night to start doing this."

I glanced at Hannah and I saw the slightest of smiles in the corner of her mouth. Her eyes sparkled and the memory of the passion we had shared the night before was clear in my mind. I pushed it away before Merrimac could grab on and amplify it, hoping Alice hadn't noticed.

Hannah was trying to focus on Alice, but I could still feel her emotions like a sharp taste on my tongue. She swallowed hard. "Tell me what you're planning for me."

Alice told her. "It's time for you to die. Ysabeau Romee has done all she can for the people of the Warrens. You will die a martyr's death next week and be reborn as Hannah Weldon once again. You will continue your fight as a member of the Union commission investigating the mistreatment of residents of the Warrens and corruption within the Bodens Gate government."

"I didn't know such a commission existed."

"It's new, but it's very real. The Central Government will fall and you can be part of determining what replaces it. Or you can choose not to trust me and die here as both Ysabeau Romee and Hannah Weldon sometime in the next few days. The end result for Bodens Gate will be the same, so I don't really care whether you trust me or not. I told Father Ryczek a lie this afternoon. I told him that you and Ted are planning a secret meeting for next week. I also told him that you are the key to stopping the coming civil war and that I want you eliminated. I even cried a little when I told him and he's convinced now that I hate you."

"You don't?"

"Every deception requires a little bit of truth. The point is that Ysabeau will die very publicly at the same time you can be leaving the Warrens."

"Who will be sacrificing their life for me this time?"

Alice pointed at one of the dogs. "He will be. Or she. Tarakana don't really have genders, but I'll pretend it's a female dog once we show it how to look like you."

Hannah laughed. "Damn, Alice, I wish I could like you. If you had been with me for the past nine months the Confederation would be running the capital by now."

"Thank you. You're almost as good at this game as I am, you know, you just use different techniques. Give it another six months and you *will* be running the capital. After I save you."

"I still don't trust you. There are things you're not telling me."

"Of course there are. I haven't talked the Tarakana into this yet, for one. They scare the crap out of me, and you and Ted just helped them create a new colony because you couldn't control yourselves. Now I have to talk to them. There's no choice."

Two of them had approached her while she was talking. "Ted, push them away from me if this goes on more than a few minutes. They really like Mala Dusa. I can hear them talking to her even before we touch." She closed her eyes as she reached out and wrapped her fingers into their fur.

"She's very brave." Hannah told me. "I don't remember her like this when we met on board *Wandering Star*."

"She changed a lot while we were alone together on Cleavus. She had been hurt pretty badly not long before we first met her. She is very brave."

"You're good for her, Ted. If the commission she talked about is real, I'd like to have her there with me. Would the two of you consider staying around Bodens Gate for a while?"

"I'll talk to her, but I don't think so. Maybe she can provide help to you from off-site." I paused, looking at Alice humming to herself. "We need to go back to Dulcinea. The truth is that it's difficult for me being this close to you."

"Really? I'm not even trying tonight. I'm too afraid."

"Of the CG?"

"Of Alice. She knows how I feel when you're around. She knows what we did."

"I didn't tell her, but you're right." I looked at Hannah, not wanting to, but unable to turn away. "Heart not healing?"

"Not like I'd hoped."

"I think it's time to bring Alice back." I pulled her away from the Tarakana and put my hand up against her cheek supporting her head as she swayed a little. "Did they agree?"

"Sure, they did right away. To them it was no more than asking for a single drop of blood. I stayed in there for a while because Mala Dusa was playing so nicely with them." Alice giggled, still not quite back in the world. "She is such an amazing little girl, but she thinks like you, all straight lines and distant horizons. I'm going to have to work on that."

We spent the next couple of hours going through the details, including where Ysabeau Romee was to die to give maximum exposure. Alice didn't tell her about the shuttle so I didn't either. We also worked with the Tarakana to make sure it could imitate Hannah's appearance while being fifteen kilograms lighter.

The first attempt, based on Hannah's image of herself was unconvincing. "How could you not know what you look like?" Alice demanded.

"I only see myself in pictures or flat mirrors, maybe a couple of times in a 3D mirror, but that made me look weird."

"I suppose it doesn't really matter. There aren't many who know what you look like up close."

"Cuza does," I replied. "And others. It needs to look like her. Let me try."

"No, Ted." Hannah tried to stop me, but I was already touching the Tarakana. I closed my eyes and let it see Hannah through my mind. When I opened them again, both Alice and Hannah had a hand up to their mouths.

"What?" I turned and there was a perfect Hannah standing beside me, just slightly smaller. She was also naked.

"Do you really have a scar on your...?" Alice asked.

"Uh huh," Hannah replied quietly from behind her hand. "You couldn't have imagined clothes for me too?"

"She'll need to be wearing real clothes when she dies. You can't just have them growing out of her like fur."

"I suppose."

The Tarakana reverted to dog form and rubbed up against my legs, happy.

"After the Tarakana looks like me, how do I get it to the marketplace where the CG is waiting to kill me?"

"I'll take it," I answered, knowing that Alice had left me no choice but to volunteer. I could see her satisfied smile out of the corner of my eye. "I'll walk Ysabeau to the market, get her looking at the stalls and then quietly and quickly run like hell to the rendezvous."

"And if they arrest you?" Hannah asked.

"Then Alice will have fun planning *my* rescue."

"And if they kill both of you?"

"When the Confederation wins and they erect a statue to us, I'd like to be standing on your left."

There was a knock on the door and Cuza stuck his head in. "We need to be getting back if you all are done with your talking."

"We're done," Alice answered. "Hannah, keep low and don't be late. Please trust me, for the sake of the Warrens."

"For the sake of the Warrens, I will."

CHAPTER 18

HOMO VIATOR

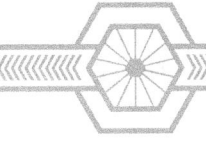

Alice was humming in her sleep, curled on her side with my arm wrapped around her. It was our last morning in the Mission and how she could sleep at all was a mystery to me. I could feel Mala Dusa moving under my hand and how Alice could sleep with a baby swimming around inside her was an even greater mystery. Yet whenever I tried to remove my hand she would mumble 'nope' and pull my arm back around her.

I was out of time so I kissed her ear and told her, "I need to go make breakfast."

She sighed and let me go. "Waffles," she murmured. "Want waffles this morning. You know how much I like them."

I'm not sure who she was talking to since I had never made waffles for her or anyone else. I kissed her gently again. "Waffles it is." She smiled and drifted deeper into sleep.

Two hours later, when she came through the line I put a scoop of hash browns on her plate and told her, "Sorry, no waffles."

"Waffles?"

"Yes, you asked for them for breakfast when I left this morning."

"Really?" She stopped, considering this for a moment. "Philip used to make them for Sunday brunch. Why would I be dreaming of that?"

I leaned forward and whispered to her, "Because we're starting for home today."

She leaned close and whispered back to me, "Yes. I want to go home."

"I like the shirt you're wearing this morning. It's blue like your eyes, but you'll need something a bit warmer when you go for your walk this afternoon."

"I'll be wearing my sweatshirt over it. And my coat. I wish we could take more with us."

"Think of it as a donation to the Mission."

"I love you, Ted."

"And I love you. Now move along. There're hungry people in line behind you."

At noon, Alice asked Cuza to go with me to the community market because she was craving some of the local fruit. Alice knew that Hannah had already sent Cuza a message that morning saying she was tired of spending all of her time confined in the safe house and requesting protection so she could go to the market.

Cuza shook his head. "Don't think I should. I already told Ysabeau that I would escort her and it ain't safe to have them out there together."

Alice reassured him. "You being there makes it safe. I know you'll bring him home to me." She smiled, kissed him, and her last deception was in play. I would guide the Tarakana Ysabeau and Cuza would be there to witness her death.

It was cold out, but the sky was clear and the smells of the Warrens seemed muted. As we walked, Cuza told me how lucky I was to have a woman like Alice in love with me.

"The baby coming soon?" he asked.

"Five weeks. The extra gravity might make her come sooner. It's been hard for her here."

"This ain't no place for her or her baby. You ought to take them back home when she can travel."

I nodded agreement and we stopped in the shadows across from a house with boarded up windows.

"You go fetch her," he told me. "I'll be waiting here watching." He smiled at me and rested one big hand on my shoulder. "You ain't back in three minutes and I'll come in there and toss you out in the mud, understand?"

"You're a good friend to both Alice and me," I answered. "I'm here to go to the market with you and Ysabeau, nothing more."

"Good."

There were two Hannahs waiting for me in the upper room. One of them looked scared so I hugged that one and gave her a quick kiss.

"Wait for us to be gone a couple of minutes and then start toward the field where the Bovita landed the stolen shuttles."

"Why are we meeting there? Dear, God. Please tell me you're not planning on stealing another shuttle."

"Is it really stealing if the Captain is the one doing it?"

"Von Muller? You talked him in to this? I don't want to see him again. I'm sure he wants me dead."

"No, you're his hero for saving Velena's life. I think I may have forgotten to tell him about what you did to *Star's* brain. I'd suggest you forget it too."

"You lied to him for me?" The wild look was coming into her eyes.

"Yes, several times. Now let me go. Cuza only gave me three minutes to fetch Ysabeau before he comes in here to pound me. I'll see you soon, Hannah Weldon. Don't be late."

Ysabeau walked with me down the stairs and out onto the street, her hand on my arm and her legs moving gracefully. I could feel the Tarakana hum within her, tied loosely into my mind. I knew that no one, including Cuza, would think to question anything about her slightly smaller stature and inability to talk. Cuza stayed several meters behind us as we strolled down the muddy street toward the market. He said it was so he could better watch for danger, but I think it was really because he wanted to make sure I was behaving myself.

The market was crowded with people, just as Alice had hoped it would be. I walked to a few of the stalls with Ysabeau, browsing, picking things up, putting them down again, and making sure she knew what I wanted her to do. I slowly increased my distance from her and watched Cuza watching her while he pretended to be interested in a display of used plates and cups.

I wanted to tell him what was about to happen, that the Ysabeau that he was about to watch die wasn't real. It seemed cruel to set him up this way, but when I had suggested to Alice that we find a way to let him know the truth she had been horrified. I stuck to her plan.

I waited until he wasn't looking and then drifted away, cutting around behind him and walking down the street that I knew led toward where a shuttle would soon be waiting. I walked slowly at first and then a little more quickly, thinking that by the time I reached the end of the block I could start to run.

I felt the push against my back first, as if strong hands had hit me between the shoulder blades. It tossed me several meters and dropped me hard into the middle of the street staring up at the sky. Then came the sound of the explosion. It roared around me mixed with human screams and black smoke. When that passed, there was the feeling of debris landing all around me. There was the taste of dust and the smell of things that had burned. Then there was nothing for a time.

I woke up tasting blood and with Cuza's face close to my own, the talons on the dragon's wings looking very sharp.

"I saw you trying to sneak away, but you didn't quite make it far enough, did you?"

He pushed on my shoulder and pain rolled through me.

"You killed her sure enough and about fifty others besides. You'll be joining them soon. First, I want you to tell me why. Revenge for your friend? Are you working for the CG? Was Alice behind this? Maybe Father Ryczek?"

He punched my shoulder, harder this time, and there was nothing in the world but pain.

"I'm having trouble hearing you."

"She's not dead," I managed to gasp. "Decoy, only a decoy." The pain was starting to subside enough for my brain to work and I knew that the truth was the only thing that could save me. "That wasn't Ysabeau. We thought the CG would shoot her, not destroy the whole damn market. Ysabeau is safe. We're taking her off world."

Cuza moved his hand as if he was going to hit me again, and then stopped. "You playing straight with me, Teddy? She's alive?"

"Yes. It became too dangerous for her here. She can continue to fight for you. Just not in the Warrens. We need to get to where the Bovita landed the shuttles last year. We have to hurry. I'm not sure I can walk very fast now."

Cuza looked down toward my legs. "You ain't walking at all for a while. This might hurt."

He lifted several chunks of what had been a building off my legs and stomach revealing the blood-soaked clothes underneath. I tried not to think about what was under the fabric.

"I can carry you slow and try not to hurt you, or we can go fast and it will hurt like hell." He looked at me, uncertain. "No. We gotta go to the Mission. You ain't gonna live long otherwise."

"Get me to the field. Twenty, thirty minutes after that and I'll be in *Wandering Star's* infirmary. Her medical AI can fix me."

"Twenty minutes to the field maybe." He looked at me again. "Stick with me, Teddy. I'll do my best."

I faded between periods of pain and nothingness, wanting to stay in the nothingness more and more as we went. Then the floor of the shuttle was under me instead of Cuza's shoulders. I opened my eyes and Alice was next to me, her face scrunched with worry as she opened my shirt enough to examine my shoulder and chest.

"Certified medical tech," I managed to whisper.

"Hush." She injected me with something that felt warm and the pain level dulled a little. "I'll be right back."

Hannah leaned over me. "Still on the ground?" I asked.

She nodded. "You were late. A CG patrol got here right after you arrived. Now they're outside demanding to search us before they'll let us leave. Von Muller is holding them off. He's claiming they don't have the right to search a RuComm ship. There's a Confederation militia gathering around the field, thanks to Cuza." She looked up toward the open shuttle door. "We need to go now or give up. You need more attention than a certified medical tech can provide. You need it soon."

"Can you close the door and get us in the air?"

"No. The shuttle is set on full manual and if von Muller tries to reach the cockpit we'll have a squad of angry CG soldiers following right behind him."

"Can you fix the AI?"

She kissed my forehead. "Maybe. If I can remember what I broke. I'll have to do this from the cockpit."

She left me and I listened to the argument taking place on the ramp, the Captain firm and obstinate, Alice calm and trying to manipulate the CG into walking away before the militia had them trapped. After a few minutes, I heard Hannah's sharp "Ha!" of triumph. The ship rocked slightly on its landing struts and the whine of servomotors spooling up to retract the ramp and seal the door filled my ears.

Hannah was back by my side. "She's on full auto now. This shuttle is on its way back to *Wandering Star* and nothing can stop her. I'm going to go drag Alice and von Muller up the ramp. They're moving too slowly."

As she stood, I heard a single rifle shot followed by automatic weapons fire. Alice and Hannah were both yelling and von Muller was swearing in a language I didn't recognize. The shuttle door sealed and there was complete silence. For a moment, I thought the shuttle had left everyone else behind and that I was the only one on board. Then Alice collapsed on the floor next to me with Hannah next to her.

Hannah was angry. "They pulled von Muller down the ramp before he could get inside. The way they were all running at least he should have been clear of the thrusters." She looked at Alice. "I guess you have another rescue to plan."

Alice was looking at her, but not seeing her. Her eyes had lost focus and she started to topple over. Hannah caught her and helped her down onto the floor next to me.

"Damn it, Alice, if you got yourself hurt protecting me..."

"You owe me, Hannah. I'll never let you forget."

Hannah struggled to pull Alice's coat off, swearing under her breath as her hands became wet with blood.

"How bad?" I asked.

"Bad enough," Hannah replied. "Upper left, through and through. I have to stop the bleeding. She'll be OK once we get her to the medical AI in the infirmary." She looked at her watch, frowning and then at me. "Same as you, you're both going to be fine. Twelve minutes now until we dock. Just hang on twelve more minutes."

Alice talked to me for the first five or six minutes. I listened to her voice while I drifted in and out. She was telling me about what our home would be like in Palma Sola, where she wanted to plant a garden, with what kinds of flowers, and how it would look in the summers. She talked about all of her favorite places on Dulcinea and all the things she wanted us to show Mala Dusa.

We docked with *Wandering Star* and the deck plates rumbled as the landing ramp deployed. Hannah yelled for help and there were a lot of people around me. I caught a glimpse of Alice looking very pale, her eyes closed.

We arrived in the infirmary and nothing happened.

"What do you mean?" Hannah asked, desperation in her voice.

"That part of *Star's* brain is still full of holes. The surgical AI was a lower priority. We can do first aid, but for anything more we need to go to Bodens Gate."

Hannah was breathing hard. "We just came from there. They won't survive long enough to go back, do you understand? We just barely made it here."

"Maybe we can get them stabilized and then–"

Hannah cut him off. "Start on that. Where's the damn terminal?"

A man's face appeared above me. "This might sting a little." Something sharp felt like it went into my shoulder and out through my back. I slept and I dreamed.

I was hiking in the Sonoran desert. At first, it was the real desert back on Earth and then it was the outer ring corridor on *Wandering Star*. Jake was there with me part of the time and then the path I was following changed to the Dulcinean Heritage Trail. Alice was twenty meters ahead of me wearing her blue t-shirt and shorts, leaving her thin legs bare and her feet clad in big brown hiking boots. I was trying to walk fast enough to catch up to her, but my legs hurt and she was starting to pull away. I called to her just as she was about to enter a dense stand of trees and she stopped and waited.

"I don't know what's wrong with my legs today," I told her, "I can't keep up."

She kissed me very gently. "That's OK. Why don't you rest here under the shade of the trees for a bit? I'm going to go on ahead to where we always set up camp. You can take your time and I'll be there waiting for you."

"Can we swim in the lake again?" I touched her shirt. "You could leave this on. At first."

"Of course, you know I'd like that. But there's no rush. Go slowly on the trail, OK?"

"I'll try, but knowing you're waiting for me makes me want to hurry along."

She kissed me again, hard this time with her arms wrapped around me and then I was alone. I sat on the ground, leaned back against a rock, and listened to the sound of birds singing and chirping around me. One of them was getting louder and more insistent until the chirping was no longer a bird, but an alarm.

I struggled to bring myself back to consciousness, remembering the countless drills Captain von Muller had put us through, afraid that I'd be the last one to the rally point again.

Someone yelled, "I'm losing her," and then there was the sound of the alarm again.

I heard Hannah yelling, "I'm almost there, ten minutes. I just need ten minutes."

The alarm cut off. "Make it five and we can save the baby and maybe him."

I tried to turn over, but the best I could do was to roll my head to the side. Alice was there next to me. They had cut her blue t-shirt in half and it was soaked in her blood. I tried to reach for her, but my arm wouldn't move right.

A woman's face came down in front of me blocking my view and she asked, "How are you even *awake*?" She adjusted something and I slept again, uncaring of the life and death around me.

When I next opened my eyes, Professor Vandermeer was sitting in a chair by my bed typing on a display pad. I wasn't sure if he was real or not so I asked him. "Are you real?"

He smiled. "Been dreaming again, have you?"

I looked at the wires and tubes still attached to me. "How long was I out?"

"Twelve days and a few hours. You were awake some of the time, but I doubt you remember it. You weren't making much sense."

"Days?" Reality started filling me back up again, pushing out the dreams that had comforted me. I looked at the empty bed beside me. "Where's Alice?"

He moved his chair over closer to me before answering. "She's gone, Ted. She didn't make it."

"Are you sure?" It was a stupid thing to ask, but the words just came out of me.

He took my hand. "There was too much damage. Everyone here did all that could to save her. It wasn't enough. When Captain von Muller got back on board he told me that Hannah was able to do more repairs to the medical systems in twenty minutes than the crew here had accomplished in nine months, but by the time the AI was back on line it was too late. They saved Mala Dusa. She wasn't quite ready to be born, but she's fine. And they saved you. Alice," he paused, getting control of his voice. "My Alice is gone."

"I didn't keep her safe. I'm so sorry." I cried, tears hot on my cheeks.

"Don't do that, Ted. It's not your fault, you can't blame yourself. Did you know that she sent me a letter every day you were on Bodens Gate?"

I shook my head.

"She was happier there with you than she had ever been in her life. It was being with you that made her happy. It was you that healed her."

I was still sobbing, unable to answer.

"I should let you rest now. I can get you something to help you sleep."

"No. I've been in this bed too long already from what you told me." I tried to move but wasn't very successful.

268

"Most of the bones in your legs have been either rebuilt or replaced and there's a block operating while your nerves are being regrown. You'll be able to move them in a day or two, but you'll need a lot of physical therapy before you can just roll out of bed and be ready for the day. Your insides were a mess, too, but the medical AI has put all that back together. We came very close to losing both of you."

I wiped my eyes on the pillow. "Tell me what Alice said in her letters."

"Much of that is between a father and his daughter, something you will have the privilege of understanding one day." He sighed. "Alice never told you about the time in her life after Philip died. She didn't want me to tell you either, but you deserve to know so you understand what you accomplished in her life.

"About two weeks after Philip was killed, Alice decided that there was no longer a reason for her to be alive either and she tried to kill herself. I stopped her, but being Alice her plots became increasingly complex and dangerous. She even tried to hire someone to kill her a couple of times. I was able to stay one step ahead of her, but only barely. I was nearing the point of having to institutionalize her when the University chaplain intervened and saved her.

"When you met her on the Margo Islands she was just barely Alice again. When I got the first letter from her after your rescue from Cleavus, it was as if she was finally back alive for the first time since Philip's death. You can't imagine what it's like to have someone you've lost be reborn that way. You gave her a year of life she would not have otherwise had, and you gave me a beautiful granddaughter so that Alice can live on through her." He bent over and kissed my forehead.

"Where is Mala Dusa? I'd like to meet her."

"With Hannah, probably. They've become inseparable. I have to fight with her for a chance to hold the baby."

"Is Hannah all right?"

"No, not really. She believes she's responsible for Alice's death, what happened to you, and the current chaos on Bodens Gate. I've found her in here several times in the middle of the night with Mala Dusa, talking to you and crying. I've spent quite a bit of time with her. She's more like Alice than she wants to admit. Hannah's a good choice for working with the Commission that Alice had me help set up, but she needs to stop trying to take personal responsibility for everything that's gone wrong. I find myself arguing with her and using the same words I used with Alice after she lost Philip. She's going to need you to get through this. And you're going to need her."

He looked at me as though reading my thoughts. "You don't have to look so uncomfortable, Ted. Alice told me about you and Hannah. I know that you were planning on returning to Dulcinea with Alice and leaving Hannah here working for the Commission. Alice knew she had won that battle."

"She had." I smiled. "She knew my heart was hers, but it didn't keep her from trying to manipulate me all the time."

"Of course not. She was Alice. Ted, you don't have to decide until you're feeling better, but I'd like you to stay here and work for the Commission too. We're going to make the bastards pay for what they've done and I want you and Hannah to be a part of that."

"I'll need to talk to her about it."

He nodded. "Let me ask her to come here now along with your daughter. *Star*? Where's Hannah?"

"Ms. Weldon is in the outer ring corridor near the starboard aft engine room on the Tech Team deck."

"Can you please tell her that Ted is awake and would like her to bring Mala Dusa to see him?" He paused a moment and then added, "And remind her not to run while she's carrying the baby."

"Ms. Weldon says she's not running, just walking very, very fast."

A few minutes later, I had a tiny baby lying on my chest. "Hello, there," I whispered to her. Little Soul didn't answer, but I could feel her smile.

Hannah stepped back from me and looked at Alice's father. "Now I'm going to have two of you trying to take her away from me."

"Someone will have to care for her when the Commission starts meeting next week," the Professor reminded her.

"I'm bringing little Dusa with me so people don't forget what it is we're fighting against and what we're fighting for. She's a child of the Warrens. There are hundreds more like her down there missing a parent or two, living on the street or in the Mission if they're lucky."

Dusa had a tight grip on one of my fingers and she was trying to focus on my face. It felt wonderful having her there with me. Alice's daughter. My daughter.

"She's beautiful," I said, "the most beautiful girl God ever created."

"I think she's going to have her mother's nose," the Professor commented.

"Like I said. Beautiful."

Hannah leaned over me and let Dusa take one of her fingers, which she tried to put in her mouth. "I think she's hungry again."

"Thanks for taking care of her. You'll have to show me how in a few days when I can get out of this bed."

"Sure. She's an easy baby."

The Professor reached over us and lifted Dusa up. "I think we best let you rest some more. When Hannah came in here with Mala Dusa, I saw your pulse on the monitor jump twenty percent. Now it's pushing over one hundred beats per minute. Ted, you need to rest and think, and start to decide what comes next for you. There's no hurry, but in the next few weeks you need to know what it is you want to do and where the Lord will lead you and my granddaughter."

"I don't think I *can* sleep, there's so much going through me right now."

He nodded to Hannah and I saw her reach for something behind me. "Of course you can sleep."

A month later, Mala Dusa and I were walking slowly through the Sonoran desert together. My legs hurt, but not as much as they had the first few times. My times were improving and *Star's* medical AI seemed pleased with my progress.

"Dusa, let's sit next to the ocotillo up there and rest for a minute." I sat down on the trail cross-legged, an achievement in itself, and lifted Mala Dusa out of her front pack and laid her across my knee. "Just two more kilometers and we'll go get some lunch. Would you like that?" Dusa didn't say anything so we sat and made faces at each other for a couple of minutes.

"Well, look at you. I can see you're exercising hard this morning." Hannah sat down in front of us causing Dusa to shake her arms in excitement. Hannah picked her up and leaned her against her shoulder rubbing Dusa's back. "You have it too cold in here for her."

"She was inside her pack until a minute ago." I reached over and touched her toes. "Her feet are still nice and warm."

Hannah had cut her hair short again, but it was still falling across her face requiring her to push it back impatiently whenever she leaned forward.

"Is the Commission on break again?" I asked her.

"Yes. Again. I wish I was down there instead of having to work through a holographic avatar."

"Professor Vandermeer wants to keep you up here because he knows you'd be running the whole show by now otherwise. And someone might recognize you even with your hair different. Are those blue and red highlights in it now?"

"Dusa likes the colors."

Mala Dusa was chewing on Hannah's hair, one lock clenched in her fist. "I like it too. It's pretty."

Hannah put her hand on my knee, tracing the scars that ran down my leg from there. "I don't know how you can stand to look at me or even be around me, but I'm grateful that you do."

I tried to lift her chin to look at me, but she jerked her head away and continued studying the scars on my legs.

"You're a hero down there in the Warrens, did you know that?" I told her. "Cuza is using your name as a rallying cry for all the clans. Even Father Ryczek has taken a stand now against the Central Government. A hundred years from now I think they'll make you a saint."

"It was Alice's death that pushed Ryczek off the fence, not Ysabeau Romee's. He's been in some of our meetings. He wanted me to die, and I should have. So many others did, why should I be allowed to sit here with you holding Alice's baby?" She kissed Mala Dusa's head and looked up at me. "Damn you, Ted, would you please hate me? It would be easier if you did that instead of staring at me the way you are right now."

"How am I staring at you?"

She put her cheek against Dusa's head and rocked gently with her. She said in a low voice, "Like you still love me."

"Oh, that. Cuza told me something after the night we were together, something that I think the Tarakana told him. He said that when you and I are together that all the good in us is magnified, but so is all the bad. I know the good is because I've experienced it and that's why I will always be in love with you.

"But right now I want to see what happens when the bad gets magnified. I've decided to stay here with you and together we are going to burn the Bodens Gate government to the ground and dance in the ashes."

Her eyes flicked back up to mine and there was that wildness in them. "I can do that, Ted. I want to do that with you."

"Alice wouldn't like me doing it, but I have to. She would want me to forgive them and she would be right, but I can't. It hurts too much, her being gone. Hannah, there was something else the Tarakana told me back while the abandoned city on Cleavus was burning and Angela and Jake were dying. They said that we use our appearance to hide the monsters we really are. At the time, I thought they meant the Bovita, but now I know they were including our entire species. I look at you, and you're so beautiful to me, especially when you hold Mala Dusa like you are now. I know you're a monster and I love you anyway because I know I'm one too. There will come a time when we need to cage our monsters again and step away from Bodens Gate. We'll need to forgive what the people there did to us and the ones we loved. Then I'll be ready to move on."

Hannah got to her feet balancing Dusa against her shoulder. She took my hand and helped me up. "But not yet. No forgiveness for them yet, Ted. We can tell ourselves that we're doing this for the Warrens, but you and I know it's more personal than that." She put her hand on my face and kissed me.

I looked up expecting a rebuke from *Star* since Hannah and I were both still officially RuComm personnel.

"She won't say anything. I came into the infirmary every night and kissed you. The first time she tried to tell me that it wasn't acceptable I told her that I'd put all those holes right back in her that I've been fixing. She's been remarkably quiet ever since."

"Monster."

"Damn right I am."

We walked together for the next two kilometers holding hands and enjoying the simulated smells of the desert.

"When this is over, here on Bodens Gate, what should we do next?" she asked.

I stopped and held her close to me, Mala Dusa balanced between us. I whispered in her ear and then leaned back and smiled at her.

"Oh. That's an excellent idea."

The End